ALIEN MORNING

A TOM DOHERTY
ASSOCIATES BOOK
NEW YORK

ALIEN MORNING

RICK WILBER

ALIEN MORNING

Copyright © 2016 by Rick Wilber

A Tor Book
Published by Tom Doherty Associates
175 Fifth Avenue
New York, NY 10010

www.tor-forge.com

Tor® is a registered trademark of Macmillan Publishing Group, LLC.

The Library of Congress Cataloging-in-Publication Data is available upon request.

ISBN 978-0-7653-3290-5 (hardcover)
ISBN 978-1-4299-6527-9 (e-book)

Our books may be purchased in bulk for promotional, educational, or business use. Please contact your local bookseller or the Macmillan Corporate and Premium Sales Department at 1-800-221-7945, extension 5442, or by e-mail at MacmillanSpecialMarkets@macmillan.com.

First Edition: November 2016

Printed in the United States of America

0 9 8 7 6 5 4 3 2 1

To Robin, who inspires me in so many ways;

and to Samantha and her bright future inspiring others to care for this world;

and to Richard Jr., who inspires us all to just be nice to one another

ACKNOWLEDGMENTS

As the first book of a trilogy, *Alien Morning* emerges from a series of stories I have been telling in shorter forms for more than twenty years. Thanks go to a number of editors, including Sheila Williams of *Asimov's Science Fiction* magazine and her predecessor at *Asimov's*, Gardner Dozois, both of whom found a number of S'hudonni Empire stories worth publishing.

Thanks also to noted editor Ellen Datlow, now at *Tor.com* and the editor of many highly regarded anthologies, who bought the nascent very first of these stories for her *Alien Sex* anthology, which is still in print many years later and has been republished all over this planet (and probably on S'hudon). Thanks also to editor Jim Frenkel, who was crucial in acquiring the story at novel length and seeing it as a trilogy.

And very special thanks to the late Tor Books senior editor David Hartwell, who took on the daunting task of bringing the story up to speed and into print and helped improve it immensely, and to his assistant editor, Jennifer Gunnels, who handled the production process with both skill and patience as I worked to complete the final details.

A sincere thanks to my agent, Bob Diforio, who has been instrumental in the success of several of my books and projects, not only on the negotiating end, but also as a deeply knowledgeable resource for the decision-making process in my busy life as a writer and teacher whose ambition sometimes exceeds his capabilities. And thanks, too, to several very trustworthy first readers, starting with my brilliant and well-read wife, Robin, and my close friend and sometimes writing collaborator, Nick DiChario. Writer Michael Bishop and my talented niece Kimberly Smith caught many a typo as they read it; and my writing colleagues at Walter Jon Williams' incredibly useful Rio Hondo writing workshop in Taos caught problems in plot and character.

The useful criticisms and supportive ideas from all these readers were most important. I also had a number of conversations about how to strengthen the book's appeal with writers Stephen R. Donaldson, Ellen Klages, and James Patrick Kelly, and with Dr. David Merkler, noted chemistry professor and researcher, and a cousin of famous writer Harry Harrison. I learned much about brain implants and the potential for a communication device like my sweep system from Dr. Daniel Bell of Central Neurology in St. Petersburg, Florida, and about running a medical practice and working with trauma victims from Dr. Joe Springle of St. Petersburg. Much of the Irish research was done under the tutelage of my favorite Kerryman, Michael O'Connor, and his wife, Kate, who have helped my wife and me lead student groups to Ireland for more than twenty-five years.

These helpful eyes and hands have encouraged and supported me in the writing of this novel and helped me get as close to the truth of things as I could while guessing at a future some years down the road. I have, of course, occasionally played loose with matters of society, geography, technology, and the location of people, places, and things for purposes of storytelling; but all these changes and any errors are completely my own and not reflective of the sound advice I received from others.

PART ONE

SWEEP IT UP

Life is a series of natural and spontaneous changes. Don't resist them; that only creates sorrow. Let reality be reality. Let things flow naturally forward in whatever way they like.

—Lao Tzu

1

The story begins with my seeming to make love to Chloe Cary, she working to revive her career, me looking to get mine started. The faux sex was good, and afterward we lay in bed, both on our backs, staring at the ceiling, wondering what we could do next to keep it entertaining. I thought it had all gone very well. It was, myBob promised, very editable.

Chloe was a nice young lady; too nice and too young at twenty-three, really, for the likes of me, an athlete worn out at thirty-two. She'd had a starring role two years before in a Comedy Box sitcom that had disappeared after eight episodes and now she was in the running for a recurring role in the very popular *The Family Mad-derz* sitcom. She needed it—she needed to get things back on the rails before she got too old at, say, twenty-four. She was on a media tour that included sweep interviews, so we'd met at Habana Café to eat and chat over *bistec de pollo* while I swept to my audience every tasty bite and every stirring look at those famous wet lips of hers as we sipped on mojitos and took our time with the meal. Sweeping was very new then and the audience was small, but the idea of it seemed good to me and I'd risked pretty much everything on its future. Chloe was a lucky break for me, the kind of audience-builder I needed.

The idea was that we'd have a faux relationship and help both our careers. Some dinner and alcohol, a walk on the beach, more drinks on my back deck with that splendid view of the Gulf of Mexico's setting sun, the green flash if we were lucky; and all the while those initial little touches—her hand brushing mine, my fingertips on the small of her back as she came through the door, her reaching over to put her hand on my arm as we talked about how the sun seemed to flatten at the base so it looked like an old bowler hat, albeit an orange one, or a classically styled UFO right before it disappeared.

And then that look, her eyes into mine, those lips opening as I leaned in toward her—toward them—and we finally kissed and it was as warm and wonderful and wet as it was scripted. Our standing there on the beach suited sweeping perfectly, with my sensory wash adding to the visuals and sound.

The numbers were good. myBob, my helpmate, had whispered them to me as we went through the motions. Eight thousand at dinner, nine thousand for the walk on the beach, over ten thousand for the sunset and those touches, and then up to twelve thousand for the edited lovemaking, give or take. There weren't more than five hundred thousand receivers in the country at that point (489,324, in fact, said the ever-exact myBob), so these were phenomenal numbers, thank you, Chloe.

And so now we lay there, enjoying the damp glow of the after-effects. Her numbers, no doubt, were ten times higher, but all she offered was old-media sight and sound. I offered touch, and taste, and smell, and, as soon as I could afford the surgery, the full limbic, scalable, turn it up to eleven. We had to remember to talk about that, Chloe and I, so her audience would come back to me when the upgrade went in.

I blinked with my eye to end the feed, knowing myBob would handle the fade-out and the stay-tuned-for-more, and then I yawned, shook my head in pleased amazement while I unclicked the contacts and pulled the bowl amp out of my ear, and looked over at Chloe. She was beautiful, no question: the straight black hair and those famous bangs, those breasts, the lips, smiling now as she listened to the fade-out in her own feed and said, "That was great, Peter, thank you. myBetty tells me your numbers were like super?"

Chloe had a disconcerting way of ending her sentences with a question mark, whether they deserved it or not.

"The numbers were great, Chloe, thanks," I said.

She sat up, holding on to the sheet to cover her breasts, and smiled at me. "I put a lot into that? I was like nervous about it? It's like weird, isn't it?"

"The sensory side, you mean?" Now I was doing it. Good grief. "You get used to it. You learn to make it part of the show."

"You know that's a first for me? Sweeping, I mean?"

I blinked. "And no one told me? Your agent didn't tell mine?"

Her smile was killer. She put her legs over the side of the bed and stood up, silhouetted by the thin light of the moon through the sliding glass door that led out to the deck.

"Don't worry about it," she said. "Kind of a virgin thing going on, right? First time? Probably just like made it better, right?"

"Sure," I said, "better."

It was clear that she wasn't the sharpest tool in the shed. But the lovemaking had been really good, and the conversation was fine when we were live, so she could act even if she couldn't hold an actual conversation. And, truth was, I liked her. Nice young lady. Heart of gold and all that. I bet she loved puppies.

She reached down to touch my lips and grinned. "I *did* enjoy that, Peter? It wasn't all acting, you know?"

"Me, too," I said.

She turned to look out toward the Gulf and that sliver of moon. "Why don't you put the bowl amp back in and click it live and we'll go for a romantic like walk on that beach of yours?"

"Great idea," I had to admit, thinking how the audience would love the romance.

"myBob," I said to my helpmate, "send a ping to the subscribers and let them know we'll be live in five minutes for a walk on the beach, all right?"

"Done," said myBob, and I put the bowl amp back into the right ear and clicked it in while Chloe slipped into shorts, a T-shirt, and flip-flops and then I did the same and we headed out for a walk on the beach.

My house sits behind a protective row of sand dunes that the state of Florida keeps replacing as the beach erodes and the water keeps rising. In twenty years, they say, high tide will wash right over our little barrier island and the last of the million-dollar stilt homes will be torn down as the island—or what's left of it—becomes a state park. I'll miss the place—it's my childhood home.

Beyond the dunes is the open Gulf, usually placid, but increasingly violent as the years go by, and once, when I was very young, horrific in its anger. To get through the dunes you stroll along a long, winding wooden boardwalk designed to keep you from doing harm to the sea oats that anchor the dunes. You can see the green blinks of the spyeyes atop poles anchored in the dune. Step off the boardwalk and you'll get a two-hundred-dollar Dunes Violation notice blinking in your Inbox.

myBob said "Live in five seconds" as we reached the three steps at the start of the boardwalk. The steps are worn and uneven, and Chloe stumbled in the dark. I grabbed her hand to help her and then didn't let go as we walked along the boardwalk toward the water. The moon offered enough light to make it easy to navigate once our eyes adjusted, but Chloe hung on to my hand as she chattered on about the offers she was supposedly considering: a hospital drama where she was a surgeon, a family sitcom set in Paris, a feature film set on a Martian colony. I didn't know if any of those offers were real but, of course, I was amazed and pleased for her officially, which meant squeezing her hand and stopping along the way to give her another kiss.

She kept talking as we reached the end of the boardwalk and stepped down onto the dry sand of the upper beach. Then we walked down toward the water. What plans did I have? Would I go back into sportscasting or stick with sweepcasts? Didn't know, I said. And was there any chance I'd make a comeback in basketball with the new league starting up? She'd heard I'd been offered a player-coach job with the Columbus Comets. Maybe I would be the live-sweep coach and player? Would I consider that? Maybe, I said. And on and on.

She knew her lines, for sure, and hit about every bullet point we'd mentioned in the contract, so that was fine. And then she got personal. Did I have any brothers or sisters? Yes, one of each, both of them younger. No, we weren't close these days. And my parents? Both were dead. I didn't go into how they died. My father, I told her, had been a nice enough guy but busy and distant. My mother was the one who'd really raised three rowdy beach kids and kept us in school.

Father'd had his secrets, but I didn't tell Chloe any of those.

The moon was behind us and the slight shore-break of the Gulf was in front. Magic stuff, and I took full advantage of it, taking in a deep breath of the salty air and noticing purposefully the feel of the sand beneath my feet, so fine and compact that it squeaked as I walked, a sound not all that different from basketball shoes on a parquet floor.

I stopped and watched as Chloe walked down toward the water, stepped out of her flip-flops and into the shore-break to stand there in the warm, shallow water. The sweep caught it all: the sand, the sea glinting in the moonlight, the rustle of the shore-break over the sand, the feeling of the sand beneath my feet, the smell of the salt water, and the faint tang of Chloe's perfume or skin lotion, something faintly citrus.

"Should I go for a swim?" she asked.

"Sure," I said, "it stays shallow until you get way out there. Just don't go out past the second sandbar." I laughed. "That's what our mother always told us, have fun but don't go out too far."

"Great!" she said, and turned around to face me, then started stripping off her T-shirt and shorts as I blinked twice to enhance for low light.

I watched her, knowing it was all more for the sake of the sweep than for me; but that was fine—the ratings would go through the roof with that body, that face. She finished the strip and then turned to wade into the inky water, up to those calves, then to the waist, then walking over the first sandbar and into the deeper water. And then she was swimming, heading out past the marker buoys and that second sandbar. I zoomed to keep track of her in the midnight blue of the Gulf, hoping this wouldn't turn into a shark sweep as she got out into the deeper water and then turned to face me and shout, "Come on out!"

But I didn't, couldn't, with my bowl amp in; a little salt water on the amp or corrosion on the contacts and I'd be out at least two hundred grand to replace them and I no longer had that kind of money. So I waved back and shouted no thanks and then walked along the beach, keeping pace with her as she swam parallel to the shore. She could really swim, little dolphin Chloe, and that made for a pretty good sweep, too, even in low light.

A few hundred meters down the beach, near the next boardwalk, she started splashing, yelled something, and I was about to yank out the bowl amp and go out to help her, corrosion be damned. A sand shark? Jellyfish? Sea turtle? There were a lot of possibilities out there past that second sandbar.

But then she calmed down, waved, and started swimming in, hard, for the beach. I waded out calf-deep to meet her as she got in to where it was shallow enough to stand up.

"Oh, my god!" She was shivering as she came to me and I hugged her and brought her back onto the beach. We didn't have towels and I'd stupidly left her T-shirt and shorts back up where she'd waded in.

"What happened?"

"Something was out there, Peter." No ending in questions now, no dropping in the "like" every third word. This was for the record and great drama and Chloe knew it.

"Wow," I said, playing to the moment. "What'd you see?"

I took off my T-shirt and started wiping her dry with it. She shivered. Great stuff. "I didn't get a good look, but it was something big. And smooth. It ran along my right leg and then when I stopped and yelled it went by so close I could feel the water move. It was huge. I mean, *really* huge."

Was she doing all this for the sweep? Maybe. But if she was, she was a much better actor than I'd thought.

She slipped my T-shirt on and then came into my arms. I hugged her hard. "You didn't actually *see* anything. No fins?"

She shook her head. "Something six or seven meters long, I think."

I smiled. There wasn't much that big in these waters, at least nothing that big that wouldn't have taken a nice bite out of Chloe as it passed by. Still, "I bet it was a porpoise, Chloe; there are a lot of them around here. They won't hurt you. Probably just wanted to play."

"Play!"

"Sure," I said.

"Oh, Peter," she said, and put her head on my shoulder. Her hair smelled wonderfully of salt and water. Her face, still wet from her swim, was damp and cool against my chest.

I wondered if it *had* been a porpoise. I hadn't heard of that kind of behavior from one of our beach porpoises, but it made a kind of sense to me. We had a lot them along these shores and they were used to swimmers and sometimes came right up to check people out. Maybe it *was* a porpoise. That made more sense than its being a shark, since she was standing here, alive, with all four limbs in place. Had it been a bull shark, for instance, that wouldn't be the case. We had a lot of those, too, along these beaches. I'd had a run-in with one myself, back in the day.

Chloe's shivers were gone. She pulled her head back from my shoulder. Looked at me, eye to eye, smiled, then leaned up to kiss me. "Let's go get my things and get back to your house, OK?"

"Sure. We'll get you into the shower and rinsed off and then you can stay the night or I'll have myBob call for your car. Whatever you like."

She stepped back, took a deep breath, threw her arms out wide, and put her face up to look at the stars and the moon. There were storms in the distance, out in the Gulf; you could see the distant lightning but couldn't hear the thunder. Most of the sky, though, was cloudless. "It's beautiful here, Peter."

"It is that," I said, and looked up myself, thinking if she stayed I could haul out the telescope and show her Saturn's rings.

And there, nearly directly overhead, something was moving. A satellite, maybe. No, two of them. No, five. More.

A group of satellites, moving across the sky in a slowly changing pattern? It made no damn sense at all. UFOs? There'd been a big scare the year before in Brazil, but, you know, get real.

I pointed at them and Chloe looked to see them. "What are they?" she wanted to know.

"No idea," I said, but I was sure sweeping them, full zoom, seeing it happen. They looked to me like the space stations. Both of those went overhead often enough and I had myBob tell me when the situation was right for me to see one or the other, bright in the night sky as they reflected the light of the sun, always zooming along until they fell into shadow and faded away.

These looked the same, but some of them were moving in random patterns while others sailed sedately along in a straight line. There were slight flares of light here and there among the lights. I counted ten of them just when the first of them faded into darkness as it moved into the Earth's shadow and then the rest and that was that. Interesting while it lasted, just a couple of minutes all told. There, and then gone.

"Did we get all that, myBob?" I asked my helpmate, and "We did," he said back, and asked, "I haven't posted it yet. Should I now?"

"Sure," I said. "Why the hell not?"

And he did that, and so that's how one's life changes: with a "Why the hell not?"

2

Sweeping had its critics; too explicit, too few filters on the content, too much celebrity and not enough real news, too much action, too little privacy, too little effort to establish context, too much tits and ass and not enough Shakespeare.

But the receiving sets were selling well and it was possible that within six months sweeping would really be The Next Big Thing and I'd gotten in early and so didn't mind all the carping. One thing I'd learned during my basketball career was to ignore the critics. I'd never read what the sportswriters had to say, didn't make friends with them, didn't try to win them over. I just played my game, got my rest, and stayed out of trouble.

And so it was with sweeping. It is, by its nature, a very public endeavor, inviting an audience into your head and your heart and asking them to come along for the ride. Crazy. Invasive. Foolish.

All of those things, yes, but after the insanity of the first few weeks, when I'd worn out myBob with instructions on keeping my first channel running twenty-four mostly boring hours a day, I'd learned to just play my game, pick my spots, and then shut it down every night at some point and, just like hoops, get my rest and stay out of trouble. Even as my numbers climbed as a sweeper I had my-Bob log off when I slid into theta waves. myBob read the interface and when I slid into sleep he uncoupled me from the clouds. In fact, I set myBob on manual and had to click in to recouple, so I could enjoy that half-awake state for a while in the morning as the sun came through the blinds and the smell of Blue Mountain coffee percolated upstairs from the kitchen below. I thought of all this as my daily visit to digital rehab.

The morning after Chloe's visit I stayed uncoupled as I came up from a good, deep sleep, my REMs fading away along with whatever I'd been dreaming about. I hardly ever remembered my dreams.

The spot next to me on the bed was empty, so Chloe was up and about. I sat up, said "Hey, Chloe, you here?" and got no response, so that meant she was downstairs. It occurred to me that some morning coffee and morning Chloe might make for some great sweep content, so I stood, as painfully as usual on my bad left knee, and hobbled on into the bathroom to piss and brush my teeth, in that order. Then downstairs, the knee working better, as it always did once I got it moving in the morning.

I stumbled down the stairs and headed toward the kitchen. I had the timer set to pour the beans, grind them, and brew starting at 7 A.M., and yet here the coffee was, brewed and ready, though the digital clock on the wall said it was just 6:39 and a pleasant 22 degrees Celsius on a nice November morning in Florida. Busy little Chloe, though she was nowhere to be seen: out walking on the beach, I guessed.

I poured myself a cup. It was stronger than usual, and good. I took a sip, thinking how there might be a lot of chatter once I brought myBob out of hibernation. What the hell had those lights been last night? Probably something military and provocative from the Chinese or the Indians. Or maybe some new ad campaign from Space-flight.com. Or, perhaps, it was aliens and the end of the world. I sipped. The coffee was really very good.

I heard the creak of the rusty gate that led out to the board-walk and then to the beach. That'd be Chloe coming in from her walk.

She was smiling, and drying her hair with a beach towel. She'd been for a morning swim in the warm embrace of the Gulf. Good for her. She wore a T-shirt over her swimsuit, and the shirt read "Sweep Me Off My Feet" across that very nice chest of hers, in two lines. I got the joke.

"Peter?" she asked, smiling. "You're not sweeping right now?"

"Correct," I said. "Left the bowl amp upstairs. You want me to go get it?" I couldn't remember what the contract called for, but what the hell.

"No, no. Just like checking?" she said. "I hope you don't mind that before I went out for my swim I had myBetty tell your coffee-maker to have a cup ready for you when you came down the stairs?"

"No, that's fine, Chloe, thanks. And the coffee is good."

"myBetty told me you take your coffee like dark, Peter? I hope that's OK?" She finished rubbing her hair with the towel. "You mind if I shower? myBetty has the car coming in a few minutes? I need to be at the airport by nine-thirty?"

I smiled, said "Sure," and took a sip of the coffee. Suddenly it tasted much too strong. I wondered if it was somehow because of all her question marks.

"By the way," she asked, "did you see like all the contacts you got from last night's sweep?"

"No, sorry? There were a lot of them?" There I was, doing it again myself, those damn question marks. "myBob uncouples when I go to sleep and I have to manually click in again the next morning."

"Really?" She greeted that with disbelief. I supposed she was al-ways connected, all the time. Like most of the country, most of the developed world. Everyone lived a double life, one of them in the real world, the other in the clouds; and most of the people I knew were living both those lives at once. Hence, my optimism about the new sweep technology. Live your life, sure; but live mine, too. And mine, I was betting, was a lot more interesting than most. I, for instance, knew Chloe Cary.

But I'd learned to pace myself, so "Really," I said. "I haven't gotten around to that yet." I held up the cup of coffee. "Taking my time with this great cup of coffee."

"You know," she said, "no one knows what those lights were all about? Everything I read and watched said that everyone is just guessing?"

"And are they still up there?" I asked, taking another sip of my coffee, and then blinking twice to wake up myBob.

"No, they like came and went?" she said. "They were there and then they like disappeared? We were like the only ones to get that great look at them? I don't know, I think it's just some promotional thing? Maybe they're—"

myBob, awake now, interrupted. "Yes," he said. "Chloe is correct. Ten objects were visible, but quickly disappeared. Very unusual."

"Thanks, myBob," I said.

"Would you like to see that information now? It condenses down, as Chloe says, to 'We don't know.'"

"No, messages first, please, myBob. After I look at those I'll read over your summaries." I took a final long sip of the coffee and then put it under the machine's spigot for a refill. It was starting to fill when Chloe came over and stood on her tiptoes to give me a kiss.

"Well, whatever they are I'm glad they came while we were on the beach, Peter?" she said. "My numbers are looking great and the celeb sites are all over us this morning?"

"Great," I said. "We'll follow up next week? I'll come out your way?" As per the contract, I didn't mention where. "Messages ready," said myBob. "And you'll be happy to know that your sweep of those satellites last night was the best footage in the country, perhaps in the world. There's a lot of interest in talking with you about the hows and whys of your capturing the imagery."

"They think I know something useful about those lights?"

"Not really, but they need to fill time, otherwise they don't have much to say. All questions and no answers," said myBob. "I'm deep into search, and it's all guesswork about what those were. Something is up there, doing something, and we don't know who it is or why or how it so easily avoided detection until last night."

"So I need to be presentable and get started with those interviews. Can you start setting them up for me, in order of importance, starting in ninety minutes—five minutes each, with a five-minute break in between. Got it?"

"Got it," said myBob. "There are messages from your brother and sister, too. You'll handle those on your own?"

"Absolutely," I said. "I'll do them first, on the smarty. The interviews—maybe they'll want those out on the beach, standing where we were when those things went by overhead?"

"Sounds good to me," said myBob. "I'll propose that when I'm setting things up."

A car horn beeped outside, two short taps, very polite. Chloe yelped in surprise. "Oh, that must be my limo?" She headed toward the stairs. "Peter, can you go out and say I'll be ready in five? I'll grab my things and then shower and change on the plane?"

"You're not going commercial?" That was a good sign for her.

"The studio diverted its plane that left JFK this morning after dropping off Tiffany Dust? Isn't that great?"

It was. "And that plane is landing in forty minutes and needs to be in LAX by eleven A.M. Pacific, I'm told," said myBob, audibly so Chloe could hear it.

"Wow?" asked Chloe, "myBetty's not that good. What version is your myBob?"

"I'm perfectly functional," said her myBetty, also now on audible and a little chippy, it sounded like to me. Great. "Quiet, my-

Bob," I said to mine, thinking he'd respond unless I shut him up. Good: not a peep.

I smiled at Chloe. "Sure, Chloe. We want to keep the studio happy, right?" And there, I'd done it again, ending with a question.

"Yeah, right?" she asked as she headed upstairs. I went outside to let the driver know. Nice limo, and the driver said he'd caught the ferry just right to get out to our island. If Chloe could hustle it up they'd catch it on the return crossing. She did. They did.

And then I settled down to handle the messages from my brother and sister. Do that, take a shower and shave, get tarted up a bit for the nets, and then do the interviews. A busy morning ahead. But the numbers! I was whistling to myself as I pulled out the smarty and swiped to the Family Inbox for the incoming from brother Tom and sister Kait.

Tom's was in written form, because he liked to read and write things. That was fine—I liked those things, too, much to the hilarity of many of my alliterate friends.

Tom wrote that he had a colleague at the university, a physicist, who *had* to talk to me, immediately. My brother and I had gone our separate ways since our parents died, and we didn't talk often. He was busy building his career in marine biology and I was busy sweeping my way into something vaguely successful. That was our excuse. But the truth of it was that the way our parents had died and the secret they thought they'd taken to their graves had pushed a wedge between me and my little brother. I knew things that Tom didn't know, about our father, especially, and I'd gone ahead and swallowed those realities.

Tom had adored the old man, and in turn he'd lived up to Father's expectations for him. He'd left high school with enough science credits to start as a sophomore at Vanderbilt; then he'd sailed right through his undergrad biology degree before turning to research in grad school as the way to find his truths in life. His doctorate, his tenure, his research at Rice and then the University of Florida, and now, home again, at St. Petersburg University: These accomplishments won him respect and love from Father. It wasn't surprising that Tom's response to my lack of enthusiasm over how we remembered dear old Dad had been to elevate Father to saint-hood: the perfect man, the perfect doctor, the perfect father, the perfect husband.

He was none of those things, and at some point, I supposed, Tom and I would have to deal with that. For now, though, it was easier to simply call him and set up a late lunch for one-thirty so I could meet with the colleague and see what was up. The call was brief and cordial.

The other family message was a voice-only from sister Kait, whom I hadn't heard from in a good six months: "IMPORTANT," it said in that neutral subject line auto-voice, and so I opened it and listened as Kait rattled off a semicoherent message about how she had a good friend who was a scientist and who *knew* the truth about those lights, and they were *UFOs,* from *another planet,* you know, *aliens,* and that the woman *had* to talk to me, immediately.

Kait's life had been a rough one: bad men, bad choices. She'd been a good student and a high-school athlete until her junior year, when things suddenly took a spin downward and out of control. I was on the baseball team in college then and so nearly two hun-dred miles away, but it got so bad between Mom and Kait that I kept driving home on my rare free days to play the referee role. Tom just avoided them both, having his own troubles as a high-school senior with great grades and no friends. Father, no surprise, wasn't about to get involved. Eventually, I found out why.

Kait, our little sweetie, was, at that time, becoming a wild enigma and hard to figure out. On the one hand, she did a lot of yelling and screaming at Mom, and even at me when I was home. "You don't understand" was mostly what she yelled at us. On the other hand, she would suddenly fall into sullen funks that could last for days. She quit the soccer team; her grades fell off the table. For a while, she plugged herself deep into the clouds, always with a screen open on her watch or her glasses, always with her music and her new, unknowable digitals. She left her circle of tangible friends—her teammates and her besties from middle school onward—and made no effort to find any tangible new ones. No one understood her, no one could reach her. In May of her junior year at St. Cath's, age seventeen, she ran away from home.

And then she pretty much unplugged in a kind of final step away from us. The first wearable helpmates were just out in those days, but Kait didn't want one. Too traceable; she wanted to disappear, she told me. She'd kept her old smarty, at least, and messaged me every couple of days with brief audios and the occasional short vid, just to prove she was all right. She'd found a job in Atlanta, she was living with a friend of a friend, she was doing OK. I was her only link to the old life.

It was horrible on Mom. She assumed the fault was hers and couldn't forgive herself. I thought there was some truth in that and included myself in the at-fault family members, and probably Tom, too. We hadn't helped when we might have. We hadn't listened to Kait. We hadn't reached out. Only Father seemed innocent. Distant Father, not culpable because, after all, he wasn't there most of the time. He was a doctor, a pediatric surgeon; he had young lives to save.

Kait came through it all right, eventually, but she put herself through hell to get there. In the snippets she sent me I got a feel for her struggles through the years. There was something about a guy named Patrick, a musician who'd had a drug problem but then had been clean for a whole month and really loved her. And then after that burst there was nothing for a time and then she smartied me about some grand plan to move out west and start over with a new guy, Paolo, who ran his own business and was doing great and she really loved him and it was going to be great in L.A.

But it wasn't, as it turned out, and so she moved back to Georgia and there was another guy, and then another and still another. Were drugs involved? Sure, and a lot of poorly selected lovers and a life where her wheels spun but she never got anywhere, and she never wanted to talk about it, and while I always put the best blush on things for Mom and Father and Tom, I'm sure they came to realize the truth of Kait's life just as well as I did.

Then Father died, and then Mom, and though Kait didn't make it to the funerals she did send me messages, telling me she'd finally gotten her GED and then gone to Gwinnett Community College and nabbed herself an associate's degree as a vet technician. It was the start of a better life for her, but it was too late for Mom and Father. For them, she'd been the child who'd never come home. For me and for Tom, she was the sister who didn't even come to the two funerals. For a time, that was a wound that looked like it might never heal. I hadn't heard from her in a year or so. She hadn't messaged me, and I hadn't tried to reach her in all those months and, frankly, it was a lot easier not hearing from her than dealing with the constant string of troubles. I hoped she was happier.

I thought of those days as I told myBob to contact her through the smarty since she probably still wasn't helpmated. She answered immediately, and it was a video call.

She looked all right. A little thin in the face, a little pale. But OK. "Petey? You there?" she asked.

I told myBob to put me on video, too. "I'm here, Kaity. How you doing? And how are things in Atlanta?"

"I moved back to California, Petey, a year back. I live in L.A. now; really in Pasadena. I should have told you. I should have told you a *lot*."

"That's OK, Kaity. Me, too, you know. We've been crummy about staying in touch, me and you. But I get out that way every month or two for interviews. Next time I'll call ahead and we'll meet for dinner and get all caught up, OK?"

She smiled. "Sure, Petey, sure." She gave me a nice grin. "That's great that you saw those UFOs, Petey. That must have been exciting. And I saw the segments with the young Hollywood type, too. Chloe? She seems really nice. Are you two serious?"

"No," I said, "really, it was business, Kait. But she's a very nice person, for sure."

"Business, huh?" Kait said, and grinned again. "Sure it was."

"I'll explain it some other time, Kaity. Right now I have to wade through a lot of videos and other crap today, so I can't talk long. What did you want to tell me? Something about UFOs?"

"You saw them!"

"I saw some satellites in orbit, Kait, and they were moving around in odd patterns. I'm guessing it's actually some government thing. Probably the Chinese. Probably a new weapon for us all to worry about."

"Petey, that's why I called. I have a friend—a client, really, a woman with a wonderful old border collie that we board sometimes—and she works for JPL. You know JPL?"

So she was still working at a vet's office? Sounded like it. "Sure, Kait. NASA, space robotics, all that."

"This woman saw your sweep and knew right away it wasn't anything of ours or the Chinese or Japanese or Euros or India or anyone else. So she and her friends started checking it out. And Petey, from something called the SST, a kind of telescope, they already have pictures of those things. Petey, it's aliens! Really! Real aliens!"

I thought they'd disappeared, those satellites? Maybe JPL had seen them, though, during the minute or two I'd seen them? Could be.

On the other hand, I'd seen Kait strung out on heroin twice in my life, years ago when I was up in Atlanta trying to help her. Both times she'd told me the day before that she was clean, that she'd never do that again, that she'd taken the new detox drugs and cleaned herself up and was facing life now and everything was fine and everything was great and then the next day she was sitting on her bed, smiling lazily, when I got there. She was so very, very sorry. It was the last time ever. Really. Ever.

So I'd heard too much make-believe too many times. Pie-in-the-sky dreams about rock 'n' roll and acting gigs in Hollywood and a lot more. All of it bullshit. But even as I had that thought I heard myBob in my ear saying, "Space Surveillance Telescope, a DARPA project, achieved first light in 2011 and put into operation in 2014. Now in its fifth iteration. Perfectly capable of doing what Kait says."

So it all hung together, at least a little bit. But, still, this was Kait. And what was a JPL person doing telling things like this to my sister, who worked at a vet's office?

But she was my sister, and I'd loved and cared for her through thick and thick. Maybe now this was some thin. "Kaity, that's amazing. Can you send me some of those pictures?"

"I'll ask her, Peter. But I haven't seen them myself. She says the things are disguised or something and most people can't see them. Super-secret stuff. She'd love to see your raw footage, she said."

"Sure, Kaity, I have the raw footage. Give her my number and tell her to contact me this afternoon, all right? Three o'clock my time, maybe? We'll talk, your friend and I. Look, Kaity, I have to go now, there's a lot of interviews I have to do. But I'll get back to you after I talk with your friend, all right? What's her name?"

"She's Abby; Abigail Parnell. Oh, Petey, thank you so much! I told her I could reach you in person and she got so excited. She's a fan of yours! She's a real sports nut, you know, so she loves all those interviews and things. She's been following you since I told her you were my brother. She's got a doctorate and all that stuff and she's just the greatest person."

And she grinned at me, did Kait, as she added, "Oh, and she's single."

I laughed. Good old Kaity, trying to set me up while the Martians invaded. Well, hell. Unless the conversation with this Abigail turned the whole thing into a joke, there probably was something here, maybe something big, maybe game-changing. It would be great to be in on that. So, "OK, Kaity, look, I need to come out your way soon anyway, OK? We'll have dinner, the three of us. Sound good?"

"There'll be four of us at that dinner, Petey, OK? I have someone else I want you to meet. So come on out here and spend a few days," she said, and then added, "I love you, Petey, thanks again." And then she hung up.

Someone else? Kait in love again? I didn't want to know, given her history; but now I was committed, so I got myBob busy talking to Chloe's people in the background and they loved it and wondered if I could show up the next day; they'd fly me out first class. Well, I'd been thinking in a week or two, not tomorrow, but what the hell, there was plenty I could do there to maximize my little hot streak, so I got myBob working on that and letting Kait know so she could arrange the face-to-face with her friend. In for a dime.

Then I got up and walked over to refill my coffee cup, thinking it through. I'd spent most of the past year as a celebrity journo and sweeper, sharing my life—both personal and work—with a group of a few hundred early adopters that had grown to a few thousand and would explode, I hoped, to tens of thousands, hundreds, millions, real soon now. I had three channels—Immersive, Noteworthy, and Social—and an audience for each, with a lot of overlap. They generally seemed to like what they got from me, which was interviews with athletes and celebrities in Noteworthy, and a lot of bars and nightclubs and B-list beautiful people in Social, like with Chloe. Immersive kept me busy with what sports my bad knee would let me handle, playing golf with Tomiso Banfi or hiking up a mountain with Sienna Pham or jumping out of an airplane with Jacob Weis. It was working for me, and the ads that got swept in paid me some decent coin, though not as much as I'd hoped for. I was still searching for the home run.

Maybe this was it, maybe following up on those satellites or asteroids or whatever they were, would be a way for me to break out of the women-and-jocks-and-celebrities business and into something more respectable, something more important, more worthy? One could hope.

And I laughed at myself for having that thought. "Worthy." Right. My father had always made it clear that he didn't think much of the turn my career had taken. A pediatrician and a local hero for all his flaws, Father had been proud of my brother Tom's science and dismayed by my life as a minor-league basketball player and part-time sports journo. I'd been an embarrassment to Father, but I'd dealt with it. It was decent money and I was an all-star at my level of the game, and one who enjoyed some minor-celebrity status in Ireland, playing off-guard for Dublin Rovers. Good times had by all, I used to think, in Dublin's fair city where the girls were so pretty.

And then my parents died and my career, such as it had been, ended about the same time with a blown-out knee. Things had been good, living in Dublin and playing in the second-best Euro circuit, and then, in a dizzy three months, it all came crashing down. I had some money, too much time, and not much future. So, in a sort of desperate move to find something to do with my life postsports, I spent the two hundred thousand euros I had in the bank and borrowed forty more and bought a sweep system, gambling that the new fad of social immersion media would really catch on.

And it did, sort of, and here I was making a living and building a reputation. Not much of one at first, to be sure, and one that my father would have found humiliating had he seen where it had taken me. But I liked it just fine. And the future looked pretty good.

I'd tried to convince Father of sweeping's potential that one day, a month or so after I'd returned from Europe. I wanted his blessing; despite what I knew about him, the dark side of his life and his soul, I wanted him to say he was all right with the life I was planning to carve out for myself.

But he wouldn't, or couldn't, and then, a few hours after the last terrible conversation we had about it, he was gone, dead, leaving us all in a shambles.

I shook my head: daydreaming there, pal. myBob was pinging me, the volume rising as he worked to get my divided attention.

"Yes?"

"A follow-up message from Chloe Cary. She's delighted that you're headed her way. It looks like you're chasing her, which is exactly what she needs. She said thank you and she'll meet you at LAX."

"Great, myBob. But I'll have to get to Kait's place tomorrow, too. Let Chloe know that, all right? Build it into the schedule."

"Of course. Two hours with Kait and her contact? Three?"

"Four, please; I don't want to hurry through that. And now I need to finally get that shower and shave, so hold all calls until we start the interviews out on the beach."

"Got it," said myBob. "But there is one more thing."

"Which is?"

"You'll want to step outside, maybe onto that deck."

"myBob, just tell me what it is." I was annoyed.

"A noise," he said. "High-pitched, at twenty kilohertz. Barely audible, but perhaps you'll be able to hear it."

I was walking up the stairs to the bedroom. "And what's causing it?"

"I don't know," said myBob. "Something out in the Gulf, perhaps?"

Nothing but questions, all day long.

I got to the bedroom, walked across to the far side of the room, opened the glass doors, and stepped out onto the deck. Eight-thirty in the morning on a perfect November day: blue sky, our protective dunes with sea oats and vines covering the sand, the white beach with its perfect sand in the morning glow of a rising sun. Beautiful. I loved it here.

And no sound. I heard nothing but the sound of waves hitting the shore a hundred meters to my west, rolling in and over the tiny hard-shelled coquina so that the water seemed to crackle as it withdrew back to the Gulf.

"myBob?" I asked my helpmate.

"It's down to eighteen megahertz, Peter. You'd be able to hear it if the waves weren't drowning it out."

I stood there, listening. Maybe something, a tiny and thin scream, barely audible.

"Seventeen megahertz, Peter. Sixteen."

And I did hear it. An unwavering line of sound, a mosquito whine from a very serious mosquito. Louder now. I looked around and saw nothing. Louder again, and still nothing to see, no indication of anything approaching.

And louder still, and then even louder, and then again. I turned to look into the bedroom, expecting the glass doors to shatter. I could see them vibrating, and backed away as I put my hands over my ears and turned again to look at the Gulf of Mexico as the whine, the scream, found a crescendo and held it, seemingly right out there, over the beach, and I watched as the shallow water rippled and then shook and then boiled in angry response to those sound waves. Behind me, I heard a polite crack that worked its way through the screaming, and turned back. The glass was gone from the doors, shards both large and small lying on the floor of the bedroom.

One more time the sound level seemed to ratchet, and I felt nauseous, my head spinning, and then, in an instant, it was done. Gone. Quiet. Nothing but the sound of the water rushing over the shells of the beach.

I looked around. Up the beach a hundred meters there were two beachcombers walking along, looking for shells. They strolled along calmly, must not have heard a thing. Straight out in front of me a lone dolphin swam by, rising and sinking a few times and then exhaling a mist from its blowhole before taking a sharp turn to the west, out toward the open water, and disappearing under the waves.

"myBob," I whispered quietly to my helpmate, "did you get all that?" myBob, I knew, would have the answer, myBob would be in the clouds, figuring it all out. myBob would tell me what the hell that had been.

But myBob wasn't answering.

3

No myBob. The presence that was with me constantly, available at a murmur, knew everything or could find it out, kept my appointments and organized my life, handled my communications, took care of all the details of my sweeps, sent birthday wishes to my friends and kept my life going . . . was gone.

I stood there on my back deck, stunned by what had happened, was happening. That horrible scream, glass-breaking and terrible, had apparently been aimed solely at me. And now this blankness, this hole in my reality. A nothingness. Since I was fifteen years old I'd had myBob. Six or seven different models, actually, and innumerable upgrades. But I'd thought of all of them as my-Bob and, learning my preferences, they'd all become myBob, to me the same myBob, over time. My pal. My helpmate. myBob.

I tugged on the back of the Adirondack chair and pulled it up so I could brush some glass shards from the seat, then set it back and sat down on it. "myBob?" I tried. Nothing. I listened. I could hear the wind rustling the sea oats in the dunes below me. I could hear the murmur of the shore-break of the Gulf onto the beach sixty or seventy meters west and the crackle of the water withdrawing over the coquina as each wavelet came and went. The sound of the neighbor's air-conditioning unit next door. The taste of coffee on my tongue. The feel of the pine planks on my bottom as I sat on the rough chair. "myBob?" again. No myBob.

No anything else, either, it occurred to me. I felt like I didn't know anything. Couldn't remember anything. Couldn't find my way from one place to another. I was alone: couldn't talk to my friends and acquaintances, couldn't call for help, couldn't sweep any of this to anyone.

"myBob?" Nothing.

There was a rising sense of panic. When was the last time I'd been alone? Isolated? Disconnected?

Childhood—and that was a long time ago. Growing up on this very beach, connected to nothing. Playing in the sand, snorkeling the shallow Gulf water with my brother and sister, Mom watching over us under her umbrella, book in hand. Good days. Excellent days; the four of us. Sometimes, rarely, Father along with us for an evening stroll on the beach, the whole thing instantly more formal, less fun. But worth it, very worth it, to have Father along. A long time ago, all of that, twenty years ago or more.

I stood up. There was a kind of faint, distant roar in my ears. I was listening too hard to nothing. "myBob?" I asked again, with that same whisper of breath that he always hears. "myBob? I asked, louder, audibly. Nothing.

I walked down the steps from the desk to the path, followed it to the narrow boardwalk, went out toward the beach. It was other-worldly, some other me, some disconnected me walking along as if I were all right, as if everything were fine. I viewed it as from out-side looking in, that funny Peter Holman fellow walking along, onto the soft sand now, walking down toward the wetter, firmer sand and then into the water, up to his ankles, his calves. Standing there. Looking west. A faint shimmer out there, a blurring. Something.

And then myBob asked "Are you OK, Peter?" in my ear.

"You're back!" I said.

"Peter, I never left. What *are* you talking about?"

"You've been gone, blank, for the past five or ten minutes."

"No, Peter, sorry, that's not so."

"How did I get onto the beach, myBob?" This was annoying. He needed to know what had happened, and he needed to fix himself so it didn't happen again.

"You walked out to the beach eight minutes ago, Peter. You watched several people walk by. An older couple, in swimsuits, stooped over, looking for shells. A young woman, early twenties, that you smiled at and she smiled back. An older woman who said hello and you said good morning to her. And then you waded into the water, calf-deep, and stared out to the west. You seemed lost in thought, so I didn't disturb you."

Jesus Christ. "You remember telling me about that sound?" I asked.

"Yes, Peter. You listened for it," he said, being patient with me, "but you never heard it, and after about a minute it faded away."

"And what do you think it was, myBob?"

There was a moment's hesitation. "No way to know, Peter. I've been analyzing it, and don't have an answer for you."

I nodded. "All right, then. Let's go back up onto the deck. I want you to see something, myBob."

"You have your first interview coming up in forty-seven minutes, Peter. Newschannel One, a reporter named Allie Palmer."

I was out of the water and walking across the fine-grain sand at the top of the beach, squeaking along step by step toward the boardwalk. "Fine," I said, "but first let's take a look at the deck and see if we can get someone in to clean up the mess and put in new sliding doors, all right?"

Again, a weird few seconds of hesitation on myBob's part. "I'm not sure what you're talking about, Peter. Damage to the deck?"

I stepped up onto the boardwalk, didn't say anything as I walked on it away from the beach until I reached the end. I stepped down onto the sandy path, walked along that for ten yards to get into my backyard, grabbed the handrail at the bottom of the outside

staircase that led up to the deck, and started climbing. Very master-
ful sense of drama, right? Setting up myBob this way. I was thinking that when he saw the damage it would force him to recalculate
things, find those archived memories or at least recognize that
they'd been wiped or lost somehow, and we'd go from there.

So I walked on up, steady on, and then stood there to look things
over.

"I don't understand, Peter," myBob said.

"You know what, myBob," I said back, quietly. Everything
looked fine. No damage, no shattered glass, nothing. "I don't understand it, either."

So I'd imagined the whole thing? I'd had some sort of hallucina-
tion and conjured up that terrible high whine that screamed at me
and shattered that glass? That wasn't possible. I knew what I knew,
and I'd heard that horrible sound and felt it vibrate right through
me and I'd heard that glass crack and turned to see it shattered on
the deck. I'd watched the water tremble. I'd trembled myself. There
was no question in my mind that it had all happened just as I'd
seen it and heard it and felt it.

And yet here I was, on the back deck, looking at unbroken glass
and a deck that showed no sign that any of it had happened. I didn't
know what to make of it, and sat down once again on the wooden
Adirondack chair to think it through a bit. There was no need to
brush off any broken glass.

"Are you all right?" myBob wanted to know.

"Sure," I said. "I'm dandy."

But I wasn't. Not at all. If I accepted that none of that had happened I had to accept that I'd lost my marbles. Perfectly possible,
that, and maybe I'd never had my marbles at all, ever. That's what
my father would have said to me.

But what should I do now? Go see some doctor? A neurologist?
A shrink?

As if reading my weary mind, myBob had the answer: I needed to stay busy.

"You have the first of four interview appointments in thirty-two minutes, Peter. Newschannel One. Allie Palmer. You should clean up and get ready for that. I've chatted with her helpmate and you're clear to sweep the interview through your own channel."

Ah, right. Interviews. Lights in the sky. Alien blobs or something. Sweeping. My career. Right, right, right.

Cautiously, only half-believing what my senses were telling me, I reached out to the handle for the sliding glass door. Solid. I pulled it to the left to open the door. Solid. I walked inside and headed toward the shower. All of this seemed real and good and solid to me, and every act made those lost minutes of sound and terror a little less real. All right, then, get it done. And so I did.

Three hours later, I had the sweep system recording as I walked along the seawall that bordered half the campus of the University of St. Petersburg. I was thinking Tom and his colleague might have some news that I could use, and so I had myBob recording it all for a sweep as I parked my car at one edge of the scenic campus and walked across to Tom's building, threading my way through students and a few obvious faculty, all of them enjoying the pleasant campus, which sat on its own harbor, complete with canoes and sailboats and kayaks: nothing with any engines. Set back from a small beach and a lot of seawall were the usual classroom buildings and dormitories and a nice two-story student center and a splashy athletic center for the basketball teams. All of this was so peaceful and laid-back that I wondered how the hell anybody got any work done.

I was planning to put this all together later as a package I had in mind for a sweep. I made it a point to see, smell, touch, and even taste the atmosphere; the warm sun on a fall day in Florida, the smell of the oranges and grapefruit and tangerines on the trees that lined the main campus walkway, the bitter cup of coffee from the student cafeteria, the slap of the occasional wave against the seawall that edged the path I walked stiffly along—my left knee aching with the change in weather as a cold front approached—from the parking lot to the largest building on campus, the Aran Marine Biology Center.

myBob was storing all this in the new five hundred terabytes I'd purchased in cloud five a few weeks before, which came mainly from servers that occupied the better part of four hectares in Iqaluit in northern Canada, where keeping things cool was not a problem. I'd thought my own ten terabytes of home storage would be plenty, but I'd been sweeping for six months or so and already I'd stored three terabytes. Sweeping was heavy business, and I knew I needed to do a better job of discarding sweeps that weren't ever going out to my audience. Either that or I'd have to pay for a serious upgrade for myBob so he could work with more of my raw sweeps to whip them into shape. Right now I was only sending out maybe a tenth or so of what I recorded. I had to do better if I wanted to make any real money. And I could see a petabyte of cloud being necessary someday soon.

I was musing over all this while I walked, looking around, ignoring the usual deep ache in my knee as I listened to the raucous squabble of a flock of parakeets in the bole of the palm tree I was walking by. I could smell the tang of damp salt in the air. I reached out to touch the pink and red flowers of the hibiscus on the other side of the walkway, and stopped to smell the flowers and look around at the water, the blue sky, the hard shade of the citrus trees in the bright sunshine.

There was an early snowstorm raging in the Great Lakes, dumping wet fall snow on Buffalo and Pittsburgh. It was aimed at Philly and Boston, so I was hoping that maybe all the pretty sights and smells and sounds from sunny Florida would get me some audience up there, despite the big news from orbit having swamped about everything else at the moment.

"Peter!" My brother banged open a side door on the Marine Bio building and shouted at me. "Come on in this way."

And so I did, walking over to shake his hand and say hi. In the middle of that handshake Tom reached over to put his arm around me and give me a hug. Very unTom, that was. And then, smiling broadly and talking to me all the while about the school's new benefactor, he walked me toward the meeting.

He was excited. Spy stuff going on, he said. Top secret. Your eyes only and all that. "She waltzes in two months ago with ten million in funding and puts half of that into the foundation account right off the bat. She wants no questions asked and there's nothing—zip—that can be found on her anywhere in the clouds. Total mystery."

I nodded and chuckled. "Why am I just hearing about this now? This might be a hell of a story, Tom."

He crossed his heart. "Sworn to secrecy, brother. The real thing. And now she wants to meet you. That sweep you made of those lights up there really got her going. She messaged me at two in the morning on this."

"Yeah, it got a lot of interest," I said. "I just finished a half-dozen interviews on it before I came here. Two of them, Newschannel One and INS, actually sent reporters to interview me, standing out on the beach, talking about how I got that sweep."

"I know," he said. "We were watching those here. Just the digital version on the screen, no sweep stuff on, so we weren't tuned into you."

"How'd I do on the screen?"

Tom didn't answer. While telling me all this he'd been walking me deeper into the building, down several long, narrow corridors with metal office doors on both sides, most of them closed, and then, after two turns, we came to the only wooden door I'd seen in the whole building. "Newsome Research Laboratory," the small sign said on the door. Tom knocked, grabbed the doorknob, pushed the door open, and walked in with me right behind him.

It was a paneled office, large enough to have a couch against one wall and two comfortable chairs against another. In the middle of the room sat a large desk, mahogany I was guessing, and behind it, rising to stand as we entered, was Heather Newsome.

The mystery woman had light brown hair; straight and then curled in at the neckline. She was thin, fit, and looked like an exercise freak. Strong chin, piercing eyes. Not unattractive if you like your diamonds hard and brilliant.

She came around the desk and reached out to shake my hand and said, "Hello, Peter, good to meet you."

"Hello, Ms. Newsome," I said. Did she have a doctorate? Was she married? I didn't know.

"I'm so glad you're here," she said as she waved me toward a seat. "But I'll have to ask you to turn off the sweep system for now. Nothing live, no recording. This is all off-the-record, all right?"

"Sure," I said, and told myBob to shut it down and then unsnapped the connections and pulled out the bowl amp, smiling as I did so. One of these days I'd get the new internal upgrades I'd been reading about and then I wouldn't need the bowl amp anymore.

Newsome took a seat on one of the large chairs and motioned for me to do the same. Tom walked over to sit on the couch.

"You know," she said, "the new implants for sweeping are going to be really excellent, they say. Thought-controlled, much wider bandwidth, extremely sharp sensory transmits. Have you signed up for that? I hear they'll be ready soon and there's a waiting list to get them."

So she was a mind reader, apparently. Or very, very smart and had set this up. "I've seen the data," I said, "but they're pricey: a million or more to get it done right."

"Well," she said, "we might be able to do something for you in that regard, Peter, if you were willing to work with us. For us."

I laughed. "A job offer, Ms. Newsome? That's *not* what I was expecting."

She smiled. "Call me Heather," she said. "And I'm quite serious, Peter. We can use someone with your skills, your audience."

I glanced over at my brother, who was smiling like he'd just eaten the canary. He'd known this was coming. The bastard.

"My audience is pretty small right now, Heather," I said. "And who, exactly, is '*we*'?"

Her smile was, I think, meant to be warm. "I won't be surprised if your audience doesn't grow very large very soon, Peter. And 'we' is a small group of people who have been in communication with the"—she hesitated—"the people, the beings, the travelers, who are in those ships you saw last night."

I sat back with a thump in the chair. I tried this: "Ships? UFOs? Aliens and all that stuff? You're sure? Really? From another planet?"

Her smile was fading. "Yes, Peter, that's our best explanation at the moment. Beings—very intelligent beings—from another world."

"Wow" was all I could manage for a moment. Then I leaned forward again. "And you're talking to them?"

"'Talking' to them would be a bit of a stretch, but 'communicating' with them works. Or at least gives you the right idea."

Tom was standing off to the side through this, listening intently. Now he spoke: "Peter, I've told Heather about your sweep success, and we've looked at your most recent numbers. They're good, but think of what this would mean for you. You'd get every sweep receiver on Earth tuned into your sweepcasts."

I looked at my brother. What was in this for him? A major boost to his career, I suppose, for putting it all together. Maybe something very splashy, an endowed chair or something else academic and respectable. Maybe something with this Heather Newsome, either business or personal? Or both?

But holy shit. Aliens! I tried to think of something else to ask, anything to keep this conversation going. "Heather," I said, "are you the only ones that are in on this conversation? Is this a kind of exclusive thing?"

She shook her head. "No, it's our understanding that at least five other groups like ours are in contact. Maybe more."

"And what would be my role in this?"

"Your role is to be part of it, Peter. Be there when we meet with them. Follow us; follow me, for instance, when that First Contact occurs. Be there, and be sending it out to millions, and soon billions, of people tuning in to your sweepcasts."

"Wow," I said. "Incredible."

"Chance of a lifetime," my brother said.

She nodded. "You're the right person at the right time with this technology, Peter. Have you seen the growth predictions for sweep receivers? Off the charts. We want to grab that audience before anyone else does, before the edited media can get any traction at all. We'd like to have you aboard to do that for us."

"What are my restrictions if I do this?" I asked her.

"You'll work closely with me and one or two others, Peter. We won't tell you what to say or how to say it. You can write that into the contract, if you like. No prior restraint. No editing. No censorship. Just you telling the story."

"And it's mine? Exclusively?"

Another one of those smiles from her. I was starting to worry about those. "All yours. The contact team and you, Peter. It will be your story."

"And this is all happening right away?"

She shook her head. "No, we think it might be months, so you can keep the day job for now and we'll put you on retainer." She smiled. "In fact, we rather like the idea of your continuing to build your audience. But if things go the way we expect them to we'll need you exclusively when it all really begins."

"I understand," I said, though I didn't, really. Aliens? Negotiations with aliens? The UN, maybe, doing the negotiations? The U.S. government? And me. Peter Holman. Minor-league athlete, second-string reporter on celebs and jocks, being the sweeper for all this?

Well, hell, what do you do when lightning strikes? If you're lucky, you survive it. This was my chance to give it a shot. To be on the inside of something world-changing. Actually, literally, world-changing. Deep inside, I didn't see how I could say no to that.

"All right," I said. "Count me in."

Heather rose from the chair, and I did the same. "That's wonderful, Peter. There'll be some details coming to your helpmate shortly. Read things over, give it some thought, and then we'll all sign the agreement."

"Sure," I said. And then I asked the question that had been bugging me for the entire conversation. I did sports and celebrity sweeps, and a fair amount of reality-dating sweeps with enough sex, implied or explicit, to keep the numbers up. I didn't do science. I didn't do politics. I most definitely didn't do aliens.

"Heather," I said. "Why me?" And, I wanted to ask, Why her? Why in a small Gulf Coast city? Why this big deal with the marine science research lab? Why my brother Tom?

I looked at Tom, who was grinning. He nodded. I was betting he had all the answers, did my scientist brother.

"You'll find out more about that a little later, Peter," she said, and reached down to open the middle drawer of that mahogany desk and pull out some sweep receptors. "For now, it's simple enough. Tom told me a few weeks ago about your sweeping and I thought I'd give it a try. It's great, and I love your work. All of it, from the interview with the Clippers coach to the date last night with that celeb."

"Chloe Cary," I offered.

Newsome smiled. "Yes, her. Very effective, that sweep."

I smiled. Interesting choice of words.

"Really," she added, "we think you'll be the perfect person for us, the spokesperson, the face, as it were, of our group when the time comes to make contact."

Part of me wondered when someone would bang open the door and yell "We got ya!" at me, laughing about this elaborate prank

I'd fallen for. But another part of me was thinking that I'd stumbled into something profound, something so huge I'd be remembered forever for being part of it. Walter Cronkite when Neil Armstrong stepped on the moon, Herb Morrison making the call when the Hindenburg caught fire before his very eyes, Russ Hodges calling Bobby Thomson's home run, Teresa Whytas describing to the world the assassination of Pope Francis as the knifing took place a meter away from her. That kind of impact. That kind of famous. I had to try it.

I nodded my head at them both and shrugged. "Okay, then. I'm your guy."

Tom clapped his hands together, beaming. "This will be perfect, Peter," he said. "You're just right for the job, and it will be a chance for us to work together on something important, right?"

"Right, Tom," I said, "absolutely right. Me and you, the two of us, together."

"And me," Newsome said, smiling again as she stood, walked around her desk, and reached out to shake my hand. I reached back, we shook, and there it was.

4

I flew to the West Coast early the next morning. Took a while, but the edited media and the celebnets had finally put two and two together and come up with the fact that Chloe Cary had seen those strange lights in the sky and it had happened during a date with her new boyfriend, an ex-jock who worked for the media! Now that's news!

So Chloe's people got the limo organized and got me to the airport, sat me in first class, and got me headed west by five a.m., where they'd arranged for a liveweb and sit-down presser with me and Chloe for eight A.M. at LAX. Afterward, we'd go on a very public date, the two of us, fulfilling contractual obligations all the while: holding hands, kissing in the backseat of the limo, having a quiet meal at Spago, and then heading to her place for the night.

I wondered, as I flew on through the evening sky, what would happen once the real news got out. That those lights in the sky were visitors from afar. Aliens. First Contact and all that. I supposed that Chloe and I would disappear from the news then, our faux fun overwhelmed by real news, earthshaking news.

Well, what the hell. I hoped they were friendly.

No studio planes for me, of course, but first class on a nonstop flight did fine, especially since my strained budget wouldn't have allowed for that, as myBob reminded me several times during the journey. We went over the books before we'd crossed the Mississippi, and until today we'd been bleeding money. Not enough ad support and too many expenses, starting with the half-million for the sweep system and then nickels and dimes after that, the premium sweep channels, all the usual standard alternate formats, all the travel money spent to spring-ski in the Rockies and parasail in St. Barts and all the rest, doing sweep interviews all the while, building the business as more people started to buy the receivers and a precious few of them worked past the free previews to actually pay for a subscription. It was hard going and I wasn't all that far from being out of money and out of collateral except for the family home and brother Tom would have to cosign that and there was, literally, no way.

And then those ten lights in the sky went sliding serenely by overhead and suddenly my numbers looked great and myBob was handling the ad details and taking the subscriptions and here I was, sitting in first class, heading to L.A. and an evening with Chloe Cary and maybe, I thought, this was all going to work out after all.

Except I knew—or thought I knew—that those were aliens up there.

The plan was to spend the night with Chloe and then the next day with sister Kait and her friend. I'd had myBob send Kait a message saying I'd be at her house by 10 A.M. on the morrow and hoped we could have lunch with her JPL friend and this mysterious other friend. I hoped he'd be a nice guy and not a recovering addict or, god forbid, a drummer in some hot new band.

And then I'd also had myBob schedule a couple of sports interviews while I was in Los Angeles, thinking I'd try to bring along the new celeb audience to the interview channel, and if that didn't work I'd at least be pleasing my five thousand or so sports fans. Mid-afternoon I was playing one-on-one with Antoine Skiddick, the recently retired Laker guard. His outside shot versus mine, all for fun and for Skiddick's charity, Lost Children. I wouldn't make any money on it, but it would build some audience and I knew Skiddick a bit and really liked him. Plus, hey, my outside shot had made me a decent living in Europe for more than five years. We'd see how I did versus an NBA all-star. Maybe we'd figure out whose knees were in worse shape.

And then the next morning I was scheduled to interview Marcelo Vera, the Galaxy goalie who'd won save-of-the-week a few times over the past season, though the team hadn't done all that well. We'd chat, we'd laugh, we'd talk soccer football, and then I'd risk some knee pain to take five penalty kicks on him and we'd see how that went, too. It was another charity case, but one does what one must, myBob told me. I'd bring in new audience with each one of these, and I needed that audience.

Of course, almost none of it worked out the way it was planned. Oh, the presser went well enough. Lots of celeb journos there, no surprise, but also most of the major edited news media: Newschannel, CNNBC, BNN, Disney, AP, Reuters, Al Jazeera. Most of them were live-streaming and so was I, with my new fans enjoying the sights and sounds of being on the receiving end of a major media event—the bright lights, the barely controlled chaos. And then, of course, the hug from Chloe and the quick kiss, and the careful touches on the hand and the knee that she gave me during the presser; electric little things, those touches.

She took the first three or four questions, answering them with that question-mark style that had made her a hit persona a couple of years ago and just might find success again.

"So is this a serious relationship?" the Associated Press asked us.

Chloe gave the answer. "We're enjoying being together? And we're just taking it step by step?"

I got a laugh by leaning forward to speak into the microphone and saying, "I agree with Chloe."

And, "What are your plans for the next few days?" Newschannel wanted to know.

Chloe leaned into the microphone, said, "Disneyland? Or maybe the La Brea Tar Pits? Or maybe we'll just go to the beach?"

And I got another laugh by leaning into my microphone and saying, "I agree with Chloe."

And then when the laughter died down I mentioned that I'd be doing some sweep interviews while I was in town, making sure to plug my sweeps with Marcelo Vera and Antoine Skiddick.

It says something about the news business that it wasn't until the sixth question of the evening that anyone got around to asking us about those ten lights in the sky that zoomed past us just the night before. It was the Al Jazeera reporter, a woman, who asked it.

"The lights you recorded last night, Mr. Holman," she said, "do you have any idea what those are? All we've heard all day from official sources is that no one's been able to find out anything about them. And whatever they were, they seem to be gone. So I have two questions, really. First, what do you think they were, Mr. Holman? Miss Cary? And second, why do you think they seemed to have appeared just seconds before you recorded them going overhead and then disappeared a minute or two later?"

The laughter died away and the room went quiet, nothing but the clicks of cameras and the rustle of a roomful of journos suddenly paying attention to what I had to say.

Marsh gas, I wanted to say, but instead, wisely, I listened to myBob in my ear, telling me that "JPL has put out a couple of ideas. One, that the lights were satellites, recently launched from China, and that they've been powered down in response to having been accidentally discovered by you and others. Two, that an old Russian satellite launched back in the 1990s burned up in the atmosphere and that's what you and others recorded."

I tried that out on the Al Jazeera reporter, starting with, "Look,

I'm just a reporter like you. I do interviews, I sometimes let people feel what it's like to play sports or jump out of airplanes or scuba-dive on Caribbean wrecks or spring-ski in Colorado or hang out with Chloe Cary. Stuff like that. I'm no scientist. But I know that JPL right here in L.A. thinks they're most likely recently launched satellites, maybe Chinese, and they were never meant to be seen. I was just lucky, I guess, the way the sunlight reflected off them up there for just a few minutes."

"And no one's been able to find them again?" she followed up.

I turned to Chloe, who just shrugged and smiled, happy to leave the response to me.

"Stealth?" I said. "Some sort of new technology that keeps them hidden?" And then I asked the reporter, "What do you think? You know more about them than I do, I'm sure."

That got a nice chuckle from the room and things went back to celeb questions again for a while and then, fifteen minutes later, Chloe and I were escorted from the room and to a limousine and got ourselves out of there.

The next morning I rented my own Tesla, and come back down to earth after a very heady day, indeed, with Chloe. I'd had myBob working overtime on editing the sweeps and getting them out in installments as Chloe and I had lunch at Spago and then the Tar Pits and then dinner to nightclubs to her place and a walk on her beach at Malibu before things got more intimate. Alas, no lights in the sky. Eventually, about 3 A.M., we managed to get some sleep. At 9 A.M. I used Chloe's limo service to get me from her garage to a car rental office five miles away and there, suddenly, I was anonymous again. No one recognized me, and I was both happy and disappointed about that.

By ten-thirty I was pulling into the driveway at sister Kait's house in Pasadena. I was impressed that the house looked nice and the grass was cut. Maybe Kait had come to the West and found stability at last? I could hope so.

Me, I'd always looked east when it came to travel and business, starting in college where the basketball and baseball teams played schools up and down the East Coast but never got farther west than St. Louis. After that the Eurocup League came calling for my skills as a shooting guard and I wound up playing those good years in Dublin and enjoying the road trips to Spain and Germany and England. I loved it there, so when the knee finally blew out for good and the surgeon botched the surgery not once, but twice, I'd hung them up by coming home to St. Petersburg on Florida's West Coast and never even gave California a thought.

Kait, though, had always seen things differently. For her, getting away—far away—from who she'd been seemed so important that she'd finally given up on life in Atlanta and gone west, and then farther west, finally landing in L.A. to try and become a new her. Kait 2.0.

I didn't know the details of how she'd come to L.A., but I'd had them on my mind during the drive over from Malibu. Given Kait's history, by the time I pulled into the driveway on McAllister Street I was ready for the worst. Instead, just looking at the neighborhood as I drove toward her house, I got the feeling she was reaching for peace and, maybe, finding it at last.

I pulled in and there was Kait, waving at me and arm-in-arm with her friend, a big bear of a woman with a huge smile on her face. I got out of the car to hugs all around, and I could feel the tension and worry oozing away. Kait, it turned out, was married, and her spouse, Sarah Chu, was so welcoming and kind that the whole vibe of peace and love washed away my worry.

I was pinged once by Heather Newsome right about then, but she really had nothing new to say. She knew I'd be talking to someone from JPL and asked me to keep her in the loop after that conversation took place. myBob told me the first check for my retainer had already cleared in my bank account, and I liked all the zeros. I told her I'd let her know what was said.

Still, it was very strange sitting in the living room with my sister and her spouse and drinking a beer over normal conversation when I knew something that very few people on Earth knew. Those strange disappearing satellites? They weren't as mysterious to me as they were to almost everyone else.

We were talking about my "relationship" with Chloe Cary, and Kait and Sarah were laughing at the truth of things when Kait's smarty chirped with a message from Abigail Parnell, her JPL friend. Could we meet—just the two of us—for lunch at one P.M.? She'd arranged a pass for me at the main entrance to the Jet Propulsion Laboratory campus, and we could meet in the 303 cafeteria. The front gate guard would explain how to get there.

Well, OK, sure. With any luck I'd get a tour of JPL and some good interviews out of the deal, and I could sweep those. The campus was only twenty minutes away on the far side of Pasadena, and it was just noon, so I finished my beer and chatted with Kait and Sarah some more, then got my quota of sister hugs in and headed across town.

Getting to the parking lot was easy, and the walk across to the 303 building in the mild sunshine was every bit as pleasant as the walk I'd had the day before in St. Pete. Better, in fact, with the San Gabriel Mountains off to the north, improving the view as I walked along the sidewalk. I put on my sunglasses and clicked in so my-Bob could have the sweep system record it all as I walked.

Abigail Parnell—a good patriotic Irish surname, I noted—met me at the main front door to the building and we walked in to the first-floor café, where the food wasn't too bad, with the usual salad bar and a grill.

Abigail, who looked more Caribbean than Irish, with mocha skin and black hair, was very definitely in charge of the conversation. I'd done my background on her, of course, and knew she was Canadian by birth, from a Barbadian mother who practiced law in

Toronto and a professorial Canadian-Irish father who taught engineering at Ryerson. She held a doctorate in physics and astronomy from Berkeley, and had done her postdoc work at JPL on assemblage packets for quantum comm units for starships. She was everything Kait had hinted at and then some. Plus, she was down-to-earth and friendly, despite all the credentials and the take-charge personality. I liked her.

We started with the usual hello and a handshake, and then some polite chitchat about Kait and her talent with border collies. Then we went through the cafeteria line and loaded up our trays with salads and, for me, what looked like a nice piece of apple pie, and then we found a quiet booth off in a corner of the large, open room and sat down to eat and talk.

I was happy to hear Abigail praise Kait for the great job the vet's office had done with the dog after the collie had lost a fight with a neighbor's dog. The collie's ear was going to heal just fine.

We talked about Kait and Sarah for a few more minutes and then, after we'd each made good progress on our salads, Abigail reached into her bag and pulled out her smarty.

"I enjoyed watching that news conference you and Chloe Cary had last night," she said. Then she laughed. "It's amazing, really, that everyone wanted to know about your relationship first, and then, Oh, by the way, what about those lights in the sky?"

I knew more than I could tell her, but I was sworn to secrecy with the agreement I'd made with Heather Newsome, so I just chuckled back and said, "Yes, it does make you wonder, eh?"

"Were you really surprised to find out that they'd winked into visibility right before you saw them, and then winked out a few minutes later?"

"I was," I admitted. "I kept recording for the minute or two they were passing overhead, and then when they moved farther away and disappeared I just assumed they were no longer reflecting the sun or something."

"So what do you think?" she asked me, tilting her head a bit and smiling. She had something she was dying to tell me. "Satellites? The Chinese or someone else? Aliens? Time travelers? Some expensive ad campaign?"

"Not much of an ad campaign if no one can find them," I said, and laughed. "Unless maybe it's meant to drum up interest by disappearing?"

"Could be," she said, "but I don't think so. And I don't think you think so either, right?"

"To be honest, I don't know what to make of it. I mean, 'aliens' sounds crazy. Really? *Aliens?* Come on."

She nodded and smiled. "Well, yes. I mean, I'm in the business, so to speak, and even to me it all seemed pretty far-fetched." She opened up her smarty and touched the screen a couple of times. "And then there's this," and she turned the smarty around so I could see the screen.

And there it was, a big thing, roughly in the shape of a rugby football, sort of an extra-fat American football, big in the middle and tapered at each end. Abigail zoomed it in and then we coasted along the surface skin of the thing, the ship, the robot, the alien-manned craft, the menace or maybe the friend. Hell, who could know?

She pulled back. "It's about two hundred meters long," she said, giving me some perspective. "You can see the surface is perfectly smooth—no openings or hatches or antennae or anything that we can see. And get this: Just to prove it can, maybe, every now and then it disappears. It winks out, and suddenly all our sensing equipment says there's nothing there."

"Maybe it goes somewhere else when it does that?"

"That's been said," she agreed, nodding. "We have no idea how it's being done, of course. That's way beyond any kind of technology that we have.

"And even when it's in view to us and a few others, most of the world can't sense this ship at all. The ship, or whatever it is, completely controls who can see it, and when. There are just a few of us who know it's there and who've been able to send craft to check it out. Interesting, right?"

"Right," I said. "Sounds to me like you've all been invited."

She smiled. "We hoped you might say that, actually."

She toggled the screen. "Along with us, the others who can 'see' the ship are ESTEC in Noordwijk, Beijing Aerospace Command, Shriharikota, Alcantara in Brazil, and the Russians."

And as she said that I could see the other ships, all but one of them a good distance away from the alien craft.

I was forgetting my real reason for being here. "Can I record this, Abigail? For future use?" I asked. I'd stopped recording when we sat down in the lunch booth.

She nodded, said yes. "That's why you're here. But not here in the café, all right? Let's finish up lunch—you have that piece of pie to get through—and then we'll head back to my office, where I'll be able to show you what we *really* have."

I laughed, pushed the pie away. "Ready when you are." And she stood, too. We bused our trays and headed out the door.

Her building was across Mariner Road and down a hundred meters or so. We reached it in five minutes. As we were walking she was speaking with her helpmate, getting things lined up for us. "Orbitals, mySally, but no sharing," I heard her say, and "full control while engaged, right?" And then a moment later, after that, "Good."

"What's she up to, myBob?" I said quietly to my own helpmate.

"She seems genuine to me, Peter," myBob said. "Let's see what happens."

And so, like I usually do, I followed myBob's advice as we walked into Building 302 and went down two flights of stairs into a basement. There we walked along for a few doors, and then in we went. Inside was a large, open space with a half-dozen people sitting at various terminals, keeping an eye on whatever they were keeping an eye on. The only screen I could see as we walked by was up on a beige wall, and all it was showing was that same craft, up there in orbit. Motionless. Still.

Abigail was talking as she sat down at a desk and pulled out some sweep reception hardware. "We've only seen this one ship, but we assume there are more. But maybe not all ten, you know? If they can stay hidden they could certainly make us believe there are more of them than there really are."

She handed me the hardware. "Put this on," she said. "I think you're going to find this really amazing."

I took the headgear from her and tried it on. Too small, so I started adjusting it while I asked, "Are they manned?"

"No way to know."

"Have they shown any movement? Did the ship move, or something on it move?"

"No," she said, "but we're not as willing as some of those other agencies seem to be to put lives at risk, so we have just the drone you're about to enter."

I tried the headset on again. Pretty good fit. I started fitting in the mouth and nasal tips. "Propulsion? Weapons?" I asked.

"No way to know."

I put on the glasses and the earphones and sat back in the chair.

"Ready?" she asked.

"Sure," I said, and heard myBob whisper in my ear that we were recording.

The truth was that I was worried. I'd never much liked being on the receiving end of a sweep. To me, getting lost in someone else's world, seeing it all through their eyes, hearing and smelling and touching the world through the senses of another person, was a frightening thing. I'd done it only a few times and felt, each time, like I'd lost myself inside the mind and body of someone else. The disorientation left me queasy, and I'd been happy when it was over. I didn't mind having thousands being part of my life; but I wanted nothing to do with being part of theirs.

But I wasn't about to tell that to Abigail. Instead I waited for the click of the connection and then, in an instant, I was in the drone. I *was* the drone. I swear I could taste cold metal, and hear a slight susurrus of mechanical humming, and see with impeccable clarity the alien ship, stubby, huge, silent. Above it a few hundred meters was what I guessed was Brazil's famous new *Viajante* two-man craft, very innovative, able to reach near-Earth orbit after hitch-hiking on the new Airbus jumbo up to fifty thousand feet. It was a beautiful thing: flat-bottomed, winged, windowless, with dozens of high-res cameras built into the hull for viewing by the pilots. The Brazilians were rightfully very proud of themselves for having built it. As far as I knew it wasn't armed.

I looked farther to the left and there were two ships, one from India and the other Russian, given their markings. Both of them stubby, squat, simple technologies built to get to orbit atop a rocket and return via a heat shield and a parachute. You couldn't tell by looking, but I had to think the Russian ship, by far the bigger of the two, was armed.

I looked even farther left and found myself looking up close at something that looked ceramic. Too close.

"I'll pull back for you," said Abigail, who was watching it on her screen. My view pulled back and then back again and then again and then the ship from China finally resolved itself, that red flag with the gold stars on the side making it pretty obvious where it was from. It was close, very close, to where the probe was that I was taking the sweep from. And too damn close to the alien ship.

Dimly, in the dark distance, I heard Abigail talking. "New de-sign," she was saying. "We don't even know what they're calling it. Has a sort of malevolent beauty to it, doesn't it?"

It did. The Chinese had built a flat-bottomed craft for reentry, stubby wings with weaponry attached. What looked like an open mouth at the front. It reminded me of an old MiG jetfighter.

"Yes," I heard her say, so I must have spoken that last bit out loud. "We monitored a Long March launch yesterday and this was inside the final stage. We had visuals on it as it docked with their space station and either picked up or dropped off some taikonauts. After undocking, those wings unfolded and that front irised open and they came to visit. Probably some sort of pulse weapon from the front and more traditional rockets under those wings."

"Do you like the view?" she asked me, and I nodded yes, the scene in front of me sliding along with my head motion. Amazing. "You're receiving all this input from an X-56ai. Launched from a new Boeing Aurora, then scramjet to hypersonic and over to rocket power once in orbit. It's about a half-meter long. Looks like something you'd fly radio-controlled from your backyard, except it's thought-controlled. You don't need me to zoom or wide angle or pan. Just think it. You should give that a try."

I practiced a bit with this amazing new toy. Hard to believe I was in Pasadena, California, and this drone was somewhere up above, as I watched mankind's future unfold before my very eyes. I *wanted* to pan right, and so it happened, giving me a great look at the alien whale of a ship that sat there, silent, unperturbed by these goings-on. I *wanted* left and there, in the distance, were the ships from India and Russia, and then, mouth open, malevolent, the Chinese ship. I *wanted* to see more of that Chinese ship, up close, and in a few seconds I could. No windows, all embedded microcams to tell the crew inside what was happening. Their visual technology was probably as good as mine, I thought, and probably made in the same German or Swiss optics factory.

I was feeling more in control now, less overwhelmed, more like perhaps this was me, Peter Holman, connected closely to this tiny drone, rather than being totally lost in the mechanical apparatus that seemed, at first, to have taken me over. I hoped I could keep control, could hang on to the knowledge of who I was, down on that planet below, connected somehow to this thing, this other-me.

I looked, and in that open maw at the front of the Chinese ship was a kind of screen. I zoomed in, hoping like hell that this was a lens-zoom and I wasn't actually moving closer. Surely they would detect me? Surely they already had?

It was a mesh in that open maw, finely woven, some sort of protective device. I zoomed closer, then closer again, and then it was as if I were falling into that open maw and getting close, closer, closer until I could see the openings in the mesh and look through them. A tube, three meters long, a meter in circumference. Humming. No lights. Vibrating. Increasing in pitch, ready to do whatever it was that it would do.

A niggling voice in my left ear. That damn human, Abigail.

"Peter. I'm still watching on my smarty. That's a nanotube mesh. Carbon-oriented nanotubes. That's technology we didn't think the Chinese had. It's very advanced."

I wandered back from my new reality to the old one. "What's it do?" I asked her.

"I don't know. Some sort of magnetic field emissions, taking the energy from that tube behind it and enhancing it? It might be some sort of sensory probe, sort of long-distance magnetic resonance? I have people checking on that now."

I drifted back into my second state, but held on to my own reality enough to murmur to her, "Whatever it is, I think they're about to let it loose."

"If they do . . ." she was saying when there was a vibration, silent in the vacuum but visible as a kind of trembling of the mesh, and then the mesh itself detached and shot out of the mouth of that ship toward the alien craft.

Somewhere in the background I could hear Abigail talking to me, but I was too busy hanging on to the ride to pay her any attention. In an instant I'd gone back to seeing the whole process from a distance and then zooming in again to watch the square meter of mesh travel quickly across the void to reach the alien ship, to which it attached itself and clung there.

And then, as I found myself looking closely at the site of the attached mesh, I saw a sort of glowing on the hull of the alien ship—a round, warm, cheery orange glow that was three or four times the size of the mesh—and then, with no warning, there was a bright flaring and I saw as that flaring light reached out to touch the Chinese ship and the ship began to disintegrate, melting and falling apart as the light moved up and to the right and then, quickly, effortlessly, lingered for a second on the other ships from Earth without destroying them and finally, while I watched in horror and amazement, found its way to me—or to the me that was connected to the micro-drone. That light touched me and there was an amazing, blazing whiteness and then a scream, that terrible scream I'd heard the day before, back here again, bringing pain, a searing pain that started at my eyes and grew to encompass me totally and then, blessedly, there was nothing.

Darkness.

But I existed. I knew I was me.

"Do you know why you are here?" a human voice was asking me. I knew that voice. I struggled with remembering who it was. Female.

No, it wouldn't come to me, but, still, "No," I said.

"Because I asked for you," the voice said.

5

I swam back up from some dark place and emerged from that noth-ingness, that deep gray of not-knowing, into a kind of pleasant memory: the start of Life as It Was for me.

I was making love to Tricia, a girl I'd just met a couple of hours before at Woody's Beach Bar, and I was recording it all on the brand-new sweep system that I'd bought in Barcelona two weeks before. It all seemed very cutting-edge, and I'd been trained on the equipment thoroughly, but I was still making plenty of mistakes. But, hey, as I'd learned so often in my athletic past, prac-tice makes perfect. So I practiced, starting with Tricia, who found it all very funny. I was clumsy with the headgear and so lots of giggles seemed to be involved along with some curse words now and again when I got something wrong. But I was enjoying the eve-ning, from the first flirtation to the walk back up the beach to my place to the introduction of Tricia to my equipment and then to the careful lovemaking and myBob's recording of the sweep into my new terabyte holding dock. I didn't even have any channels open yet, so I couldn't export.

The evening's festivities had really started six months earlier when my European basketball career came to an end. My Dublin

Rovers were on the road, playing in Barcelona. I drove the lane one time too many, me at 190 centimeters and 82 kilograms crashing in among the trees and paying the price, knowing it was foolish even as I did it and winding up tangled and torn in a heap on the floor. First to Hospital de Barcelona to stabilize things, then back to Dublin for the second surgery on that knee, even less successful than the first time. Anterior and medial ligaments both ruined now and needing vat-grown replacements. The doc got me walking again and I could even play a little pickup ball, wearing the brace. I could lead a normal life, she said, but there'd always be some pain and my professional basketball career was over. Time to hang them up.

While still in the hospital recuperating I was reading messages and seeing visitors when the mobile pinged me with a call from Barcelona. I answered and found myself with a new career as a sweeper, courtesy of tech entrepreneur Alvaro Colom, whose Todos Sentidos immersive-media startup was looking for people just like me to be early adoption sweepers. One month later I was back in Barcelona, within a kilometer of the arena where my career had ended. Only now I was hoping to get started doing this new thing Colom and his friends were offering to sell me. It was new, seemed like it would be fun and interesting, and might make me enough money to continue the lifestyle I'd enjoyed as a professional athlete.

I'd listened to my newly upgraded myBob tell me when and where to turn as I limped along on my postsurgery, postrehab, still-in-pain left knee to the second floor of a great old building and the offices of Todo Sentidos, LLC, at Numero Dos on Carrer de Santa Anna, near where La Rambla empties in Placa Catalunya. I'd then spent the better part of three weeks buying the system, powering it up, loading in the software, and then getting tutorials from Alvaro's team.

Todo Sentidos was convinced that BCI—Brain Computer Interface—was the future of home entertainment. Most of the technology had been around for a decade or more, but it was Alvaro and his friends who'd had the great insight that some people—journalists, entertainers, athletes—would want to use their Brain Computer Interface to record, edit, and send their sensory input out to the masses. Others, perhaps by the millions or billions, would be content to sit safely at home and receive those messages and enjoy the sense of being there: whether "there" was a lover's bed or a mile down in the Mariana Trench or aboard the Virgin space station or taking a lead off first base in the seventh game of the World Series or, more likely on a global scale, dribbling and darting past three defenders on the way to scoring a goal against Real Madrid or mighty Glasgow Celtic.

I was in it very early, Alvaro assured me. No one else had seen the BCI light yet and so Todo Sentidos was out in front with the technology for encoder and decoder. Just like the ancients in their early days—radio and television—the audience wasn't there yet. But when TS geared up in six months with the inexpensive receivers, the world would explode with interest. He was sure of it.

And what the hell, I believed him. Remember radio? It's nearly gone now, but in the first fifteen years of the twentieth century it was a very hot item indeed. Marconi had sent signals across the Atlantic from Ireland to Newfoundland, and the signal brought news from afar so fast that governments and their armies scrambled to control the new medium before it controlled them. One man, a young Russian immigrant in America named David Sarnoff, realized that radio didn't have to be point-to-point. All the generals and politicians were worried that radio signals were easy to intercept. Sarnoff realized that that was a good thing, and in a famous memo proposed to his bosses that one radio station could send out a signal that could be heard by simple receiver sets in hundreds, maybe even thousands, of homes.

He was right, of course, and by the 1920s radio was a huge success, with millions, not thousands, receiving the signals of the stations that cropped up in big cities and hamlets coast to coast and then throughout Europe and then all over the world.

David Sarnoff changed the world, and Alvaro Colom and his friends at Todos Sentidos wanted to do the same. I believed and I bought into it, literally. It cost me five hundred thousand euros before those two weeks were over, and so my savings from a modestly successful basketball career that had ended were about gone and instead I was deep in debt. But I believed.

Each night I had a late dinner and some drinks in the bar at the Hotel Ramblas, enjoying the atmosphere and enough sangria to dull the ache in the knee. I kept to myself, but the women of Barcelona are beautiful, with that black hair and those eyes and those smiles. And if my aching knee meant I couldn't do certain things as well as I had before, there were other areas where my expertise held up nicely. And so I enjoyed my evenings and in doing so I began to think this was another area where I could sweep. Interviews with celebrities and athletes and the occasional skydive and scuba adventure and all that—surely. But wouldn't dinners and nights out at the restaurant with interesting people and then the occasional liaison with someone beautiful draw an audience, too?

The social whirl with friends new and old? The new people you meet? The flirtation, the seduction, the yes and the no. Wouldn't that be of interest to an audience plugged into my sweep? And wouldn't people want to be part of my experiment in this new medium? Wouldn't the ambitious and the kind and the greedy and the passionate and those hungry for attention want to join me in this new thing? I thought so. I hoped so, since I'd spent my life savings to acquire the hardware and software.

I flew home to Dublin at the end of my tutorials and began to tinker there with my new sweep system to get to know it and let it get to know me. It wasn't easy. First, I had to turn off myBob's firewall. This wasn't easy, since myBob was my longtime helpmate, my wingman. He'd started as some simple software in my first car, and then he'd grown over the years of upgrades to the point where I forgot he wasn't alive. It was his job to be my personal secretary.

He lived, as it were, inside a small piece of hardware that fit into my left ear. I depended on him to be my memory, my tour guide, my answer man for a hundred questions a day.

But myBob's software read the sweep system installation as an attack and blocked it, so I had to disable his firewall, and that wasn't easy.

"myBob, firewall off for one hour, please" should get a "Sure, Peter," and a little jokey sound of battered bricks falling to the ground as he disengages the wall. But when I was installing the sweep software and putting on the hardware, myBob complained. "It's not just a firewall problem, Peter. The new system you are trying to install is not really compatible with me." myBob sounded worried.

I apologized and said, "I'm sorry, myBob, but this new sweep system is important to me. If I'm to enjoy any success as a free-lance journalist, I have to use this system."

"I understand," myBob replied, "but the new system *is* incompatible with my system. This means I won't be able to intervene if there are problems. In fact, it's possible I may not be able to return once you've installed this new system and then try to bring me back."

"I'll be careful," I told him, "and you're backed up, too. So if I can't retrieve you I'll get the patches or upgrades that I need and bring you back as the new and improved myBob, OK?"

"I normally get those and install them myself, Peter. I always enjoy that process."

"Great, myBob, and you can do that as soon as you're back. If for some reason you're not, I'll get the patches but not load them, then I'll reinstall you, and then you can install them when I bring you back, all right?"

Hard to believe I was arguing with my helpmate about all this, but myBob was like a favorite car that you've had a long time and grown fond of. He had a name. I liked him. I wanted to keep him around. But I also really needed to install the sweep system.

myBob seemed to sigh. "All right, Peter. I'll hope to see you soon then."

"Goodbye for now, myBob. Now. Please. myBob. Off for one hour."

And myBob was gone. No fake leak of air, just an abrupt sense of empty. You do get used to your helpmate.

And then I put on the hardware, clumsy stuff at that early stage of sweeping. I had to get the headset so that it was snug, shaving the patches for the receptor plugs and taping them in, fitting the earpads, getting the annoying tongue receptor into place. I left the penile pad alone for the moment and wondered if I'd have to use that to complete the software upload, but decided to face that problem when it arose, as it were. Then I placed all my fingertips into the launch pad, felt the slight sting at the end of each fingers and thumb that they'd warned me about. Piriform cortex: my sense of smell. The postcentral gyrus of the parietal lobe: my sense of touch. A pinprick. Connected.

It was all very weird business, but it worked, and myBob returned to me completely, upset but none the worse for the wear. I opened a single channel and interviewed the coach of Dublin Rovers, who was kind to me about how much I'd be missed. I was clumsy in my questions, and only his practiced responses got me through it. I had an audience of hundreds.

More followed, all of it as active and interesting as I could make it in old Eire: I walked the Gap of Dunloe, I stood on the Cliffs of Moher, I went to one of those castle banquets and enjoyed the food and the music and the silliness and the talent.

And then I went home to the States and my beach town, and there, on the second evening, was Tricia. I managed to please her in one good way or another for an hour or so. I wasn't perfect, and I felt guilty that she was pleasing me more than I could please her; but one does what one does in the interests of new media. And fun. And profit. Eventually, with timing that happily worked out to be

about right, we reached that welcome peak together and then collapsed onto the sheets.

Later, recovered from the exertion, I turned to put my legs over
the side of the bed and sat up, then took off the headset and bowl
amp, feeling the tug of the tape as the contacts came free. I set them
on the bedside table and stood.

"Did it work?" Tricia wanted to know. "You'll show me the
recording, right?"

I laughed. "Sure, but first let me see if it came through all right,
OK? If it worked I'll let you see it, and if I decide to save it, you can
tell me which parts you want me to edit out and I'll make sure those
are completely deleted. Fair enough?"

"Fair enough," she said, on her knees on the bed and bouncing
a little bit up and down in anticipation as I walked over to the dresser
that occupied nearly half of the bedroom's far wall. I opened up
the wide, top middle drawer, and reached over to the memory and
wireless unit that sat atop the dresser. It was the size and shape of
an old-style print book. A terabyte of memory, the top transmission
rate, full stream. I touched my bowl amp to turn on the receiver
and hit the start button on the desk unit and everything went dark
and deathly quiet, and I heard a woman's voice telling me that I
was all right, that I'd be fine, that she'd see me soon, that all I had
to do was wake up, just go ahead and wake up as a number flashed
before my eyes, a bright red ten, then a nine, then an eight, and then
came an annoying bright light and a voice talking to me, a woman,
her hand on my shoulder asking me something. "Peter? Are you
all right? Peter, can you wake up? Wake up!"

So I did.

Abigail's face was peering down at mine. "You're awake now?
Really?"

"Oh, god yes." My head was pounding with a deep ache that

seemed centered behind and above both eyeballs, thumpingly, rhythmically painful. I was sitting in the same comfortable chair I'd been in at the start of this wrongheaded adventure. I reached up to rub my forehead.

"Headache?"

"Yes," I told her, "a bad one. Maybe it's easing off, though."

"Not surprising, I guess," said Abigail, and I turned to look at her as she added, "You were doing fine with the drone up there, controlling it, moving your head around and even reaching out to touch things, and then—Wham!—everything went dark and you slumped in that chair like you were dead. We were really worried."

I sat up, put my legs over the side of the infirmary bed. The headache was fading away. I was thinking I might survive.

"In fact, we're *still* worried," said Abigail. "The nurse will be back in a minute. Someone's been watching you the whole time."

I sat up straighter, then tried to stand. Made it, but not steady. Abigail stepped over and grabbed my elbow to steady me. .

"How long was I out? And what the hell happened? I was watching the Chinese probe on that alien ship and then it all went white."

"Down here, it went black. And then blank for a few seconds, and then back to normal," said Abigail. "And you've been out for about twenty minutes."

"Normal?" I remembered it differently. The Chinese sending out that mesh, the alien ship responding. Destruction. Death, no question. "Really? Normal?

"Sure," she said. "Look here." And she opened up her smarty, whispered a command, and turned it around so I could see the screen.

Serene. Calm. Cue the waltz in the background. The ships floated there, the various Earth ships around it. One of them, the Chinese ship, pulling away, leaving, little pulses of light from the steering jets, turning as it pulled back. The view was from that same drone I'd become part of, had gotten lost in.

I didn't believe what I was seeing. "That's not what happened,

Abigail. I saw the Chinese ship do a kind of attack on the alien ship. It sent out some kind of mesh net that attached itself to the other ship and there was a reaction. Lights, some kind of laser or energy weapon or something and then the Chinese ship exploded and the alien seemed to be turning its attention to me and then that bright light and then I lost it. I thought it was the moment of my death."

She smiled, patted my arm. "It wasn't. You're here. I think you're fine."

"But how in hell?"

"I have no idea," she said, "and I'd guess there's no way of knowing which is real: what you saw or what we're seeing here."

I looked at her, puzzled.

"My thinking is that this ship—these ships, if there are more—has control of all our electronics. I think that ship could make that drone—and you, at the receiving end of its sweep—see anything at all it wanted you to see and sense."

"And the other way, too, right?"

"Exactly. What you saw might be what actually happened, and this scene we're seeing here right now? This might be the fabrication."

I sat back down. "Damn," I managed to say. "But at least it means that maybe I'm not crazy."

"You're not crazy," Abigail said, putting her hand on my shoulder. "In fact, I'm not all that surprised that this went the way it went. I figured something was up."

I looked up at her. "Not surprised?"

She nodded. "Haven't you wondered why I contacted you and brought you right into the heart of the action?"

"Kait," I said. "The vet's office. Your border collie."

She smiled. "Well, yes, that's all true."

I looked at her.

"Thing is, we've been in communication with that ship for a week now. In English. Very clear and very specific English."

"And?"

"And we were told to bring you here, Peter, and hire you to sweep for us as this whole wonderment progresses."

"This 'wonderment'?"

"That's my phrase," she said, "but you'd use it, too, if you'd heard what I've heard. I've heard them speak. I think they're good and true and we'll benefit, Peter, as they change the world."

In the end, I can say from where I sit now, writing all this down, it might have all gone so much better if at least some of that had turned out to be true.

6

Two days later I was knock, knock, knocking on my brother's door at his home on the bay in St. Pete. On the third rap he opened the door and there he was, smiling. Next to him was Heather Newsome.

"Thanks for coming over, Peter," Tom was saying as I looked at Heather. She'd changed, softened somehow. Short, straight blond hair now framed the firm jaw of that face, with its dark eyebrows, brown eyes, no lipstick, thin lips but a nice smile. I liked her. Tom stood proudly next to her, put his arm around her. She leaned toward him a bit. So they were, after all, an item.

After another long night with Chloe and an equally long next day shooting penalty kicks and three-pointers for charity, I'd changed my ticket and taken the red-eye home from LAX, arriving back in town at nine in the morning. It was noon and all I'd had time, or interest, in doing was getting home, drinking a few cups of coffee that didn't seem as good as Chloe's, taking a shower, going out to the back deck to stare thoughtfully at the placid Gulf of Mexico for a few minutes, and then stumbling over to my brother's house. I'd sent him a note that I wanted a meeting with Heather Newsome, and I wanted it soon. I let myBob do the driving.

I hadn't been able to sleep on the red-eye, or really anywhere else. I'd managed a couple of exhausted hours in Chloe's bed just before dawn and we'd argued—our first disagreement—over something I forgot by the time the argument had ended in a simmer. Then I got up and got going to do the interviews and kick and shoot the balls that paid the freight. I was glad to have something that would take my mind off my confusion.

Thing was, for the first time in my life I didn't trust myself. Twice now in three days I'd seen and heard and felt things that everyone else—including trusty myBob—said hadn't happened. The scream at the beach that shattered glass or didn't, the attack up in orbit that wiped out that Chinese ship or didn't.

Abigail thought I was being manipulated, but I believed her when she said she didn't know how or why. This craziness was happening to me for a reason, presumably. All right, what the hell was that reason? Heather, it had finally come to me, might have the answer.

Until then, until I knew what was going on, everything seemed doubtful and unreal. I expected my plane to crash and then have it not be real. I expected the aliens to come swooping down out of the sky and attack us and have that not be real. I expected that all the good things—the new sweep success, the relationship with Chloe that felt more real each time I saw her, the weird respect I was getting from the edited media and even from people like Abigail Parnell at JPL—couldn't possibly be real. It was all a balloon. It would burst.

"You must be exhausted, Peter," Heather said. "I'm sorry you've been through so much these last few days."

I thought, at first, that she was talking about the red-eye, and all the travel. "No problem," I said. I wondered, as I shook her hand and gave Tom a hug, how long they'd been a couple. They were acting like they'd been together for a while. As we headed through the living room and out to the deck and that nice view of the Sunshine Skyway Bridge in the distance, she made her way to the kitchen for coffee, acting at home, comfortable, like she knew her way around.

"Black?" she asked me. I nodded yes, and then opened the sliding door to the porch and looked for a comfortable chair. Tom was right behind me as we walked onto the wooden decking that edged out from the screened porch. He lit a Camel, blew out a cloud of contentment. "We've been seeing each other socially for a week, Petey. Can you believe it?"

"No," I answered truthfully.

He laughed. "It's like I've known her all my life. I didn't know it could be like this."

"True love, you mean?"

"Hell, I guess so." He shrugged his shoulders, took another pull on the cigarette. "What else would you call it? It's like we're perfectly made for each other. Fate, I guess."

"Am I hearing you right, Mr. Scientist? 'Fate'? You're meant for each other?"

He laughed. "It's really something, huh? Office down the hall for a couple of months and no hint of anything beyond the collegial, and then, wham."

"Yeah," I said, "wham."

Heather came through the door with my cup of coffee. I took a sip, and it was strong. Good. I needed that.

She sat, all business. "Peter, I won't beat around the bush. Things have changed since we talked last week."

"No kidding."

She looked over at my brother. "Tom, can you step inside for a few minutes while I chat with Peter about this?"

Tom nodded. "Of course. " And he opened the sliding glass door and walked into the living room, closing it firmly behind with a click.

Heather smiled at me. "Tom knows there are certain things he can't be made aware of yet. He's OK with that."

"Great," I said. "But you're about to make me aware of these things? Do I really want to know this?"

"You do," she said firmly. "But first, you'll have to ask myBob to hibernate for about ten minutes. This needs to be very private."

"Sure," I said. "myBob?"

"Done," he said, and I felt him close down.

She stood up, came over to where I sat, opened up her smarty and set it on the coffee table in front of me, turned it around so I could watch the screen, then stood next to me, her hand on my shoulder. "Play video," she said, and together we watched.

It seemed like a simple flat-screen version of the view I'd had when I'd been swept up by the micro-drone from JPL. No sound, no senses except sight, as we saw what the drone had seen: the alien ship, the Brazilian *Viajante* two-man craft, the spacecraft from Russia and from India. And then the Chinese ship, the one that looked ready for a fight. As I watched, it was slowly creeping closer to the alien craft.

There were no close-ups, none of the zooming in and out that I'd done—or thought I'd done—when I'd been in control of the drone, when I'd *been* the drone. Instead, the video panned back and forth again and then took a good, long look at the alien spacecraft: bulbous, but thinner than I'd seen it, almost the shape of an American football, no protrusions on it anywhere, no windows, no visible hatches or antennae, the color a dull gray.

"Now watch," Heather said, as the Chinese ship moved closer still, and, finally, the alien ship reacted. A slight glow emerged from the bulbous middle, then grew bright and widened, expanding in all directions, moving right past our view through the drone with no effect before it reached the Chinese ship and began pushing it backward, then reached the other Earth ships and pushed them as well. Away. Then farther away, then farther away still until only the alien ship was visible.

Then came a brightness, a distant flaring of white light. Then the screen went blank.

I could feel Heather's hand on my left shoulder. It seemed too intimate a touch for the time and the place where we were, but I can't say I didn't like it. "What do you think?" she asked, leaving that hand in place.

"That's not how it happened," I said. "The Chinese ship sent out a probe, a kind of mesh, and that got to the alien ship and—"

"We know, Peter," she said, finally removing that hand. She came around in front of me, sat in the open chair next to me. "We were sent a recording of that sweep you received through the drone. The Chinese effort to probe our friend's ship. The response from the friends. The destruction. All of that."

"Our friends?"

"Yes, Peter, our friends. Most definitely our friends."

"I don't suppose we'd want them to be our enemies is what you're saying, right?"

She smiled. "Well, yes, there's that."

"So what did I just see, then?"

"You saw the truth."

"No. I didn't, and we both know that."

"Peter, how do you know that what you sensed from the drone was what actually happened? How do you know which version is true?"

I managed a smile. "I heard that theory yesterday."

It was Heather's turn to smile. "And Abigail might just be right, you know."

So she and Abigail were talking. Hell, they were probably working for the same people, had the same goals, were using me in the same way. "Or both were true," I added. "I get it. Who knows what the truth is?"

She smiled. "Exactly." Then she reached out to touch my shoulder again. I found that flirtatious, and I was glad that Tom wasn't on the porch with us to see it happen.

"Peter, you stood on your deck about an hour ago, before you came over here. You looked out to the Gulf for quite a while. What did you see out there?"

"You have cameras on me? At my own home?" I was shocked.

"No," Heather said, smiling. "There's no need for that, Peter. We have help from those friends up there. We see just about anything we want to, and we don't install cameras to do it."

"Drones," I said. "Minidrones. Hell, nanodrones."

"Something like that, if you like. But tell me, what did you see out there in the Gulf?"

"Nothing. Calm water, more green than blue. Distant thunderstorms. Blue sky. Contrails."

"And?"

Time to admit this, since I was sure she already knew. From that moment when I'd first heard that shattering scream, I'd thought there was a shimmer out there in the Gulf. "There's something there, something big, hiding somehow," I said. "But myBob can't see it or sense it, so maybe it's not there?"

She nodded. "Very good." Then she smiled. "We need you to sign your agreement with us now, Peter."

I wasn't surprised. "There *is* something out there. I thought so. Am I still the one to get to break the story?"

She leaned over, said softly, "You are, Peter, when the time is right. And it will be a global exclusive." She smiled. "But we need you to remain quiet about all this for now. No sweeps of the night skies, no discussion with experts on what's going on. Just keep it to the routine sweeps you were doing before all this started. All right?"

I nodded.

She held up her smarty to me, said, "Retinal signature. Left eye open, stare at the target, please, Peter, and then it's done."

I leaned over, looked at the target with my left eye as I heard the sliding glass door open and knew Tom had come back out on the porch. I heard the ping of acceptance, sat back, and looked up to him. "Signed and sealed, brother."

He was carrying a bottle of wine. He held it and smiled. "Me, too, Peter, a week ago. It's just a research contract for me, so I'll remain in my regular faculty slot at the college. Still, the Holman

brothers are in business together at last, eh? Let's drink a toast
to that."

"Sure," I said, "a toast," and then watched as he poured the
wine, a deep red, and handed me and then Heather a glass. Hell, I
thought, at least this would get me out of the soft-porn business for
a while.

We raised our glasses. "To the Holman boys," Heather said, and
we all clinked and took a sip. Merlot.

"To our friends," I said, and raised mine again. Heather smiled.
Tom grinned, and we clinked them again. Right, I thought. Me and
my loving brother, Tom. The Holman boys.

I spent my life playing games. My father was disappointed in this.
Father was loved and respected by the families of the hundreds of
children he'd served. The funeral cortege on the day that we buried him in Wooded Glen Memory Gardens was a half-mile long and
made the local television news. He had been more than a pediatrician; he'd been a community activist, raising funds for his favorite
charities, vocal in his backing for the politicians he liked and admired. He had a reputation as a good, strong, intelligent, caring
human being; and he expected his children to be the same.

Only Tom lived up to his expectations. I was too busy wasting
my time throwing balls into baskets and dribbling with both hands.
Kait was too busy being moody and unreachable and making bad
friends. But Tom, his second son, had the porridge just right. Tom's
academic accomplishments won him respect and love from Father,
and there was no question who Father favored. When we were
young, Kait and I used to laugh about it, and even Mom seemed to
be in on the joke, shaking her head as we all watched Father and
Tom play chess together or head off to the museum or, more likely,
to the office, where Tom often tagged along.

My father smoked cigarettes most of his life: Camels—good,
strong stuff that he'd started in on while an undergraduate at

Princeton. You might be surprised to hear how many smokers there are in the health field: nurses, doctors, EMTs, even some oncologists here and there. Stress, they will explain, is why they smoke. And, of course, their certain knowledge that as medical people they are immune to the diseases of more common men and women.

Father found out on his fifty-seventh birthday that the cough he feared was lung cancer was, indeed, small-cell, stage 3B, revised after the first surgery to stage 4. The radiation, the surgery, the chemo: They were all palliative and he knew it and we knew it.

Strange, isn't it, that we couldn't cure lung cancer that was that far along? My guess is that as fewer and fewer people smoked and the incidence of that cancer dropped the medical establishment lost interest. No profit in a cure anymore. Everyone quit caring.

Except for Tom, the great research scientist, the Great Mind, the Boy Wonder who'd had research published while he was still an undergrad, the man who always had The Answer.

Tom kept insisting that Father should try one new trial or another, look for that wonder drug, keep up his hope, stay positive, beat this thing. Tom, I thought, seemed increasingly angry with Father for accepting the cancer, embracing it, allowing it entry into his life and death. As the months went by, Tom's calm urgings to Father turned into strident hectoring about battles and struggles and never giving up.

About a year after he got the news, on the last day of his life, my father walked over to me after yet another angry outburst from Tom and said this to me: "Son, I do wish you'd done more with that fine mind of yours, but at least you've always been happy."

Then he shook his head. "Now, your brother, for all his brains and all his publications and all his money and all his awards: That's about the unhappiest guy I know."

Then he coughed, almost politely, and turned away from me.

We were all gathered at Tom's house that day to share a Sunday meal and celebrate Tom's being short-listed for the Carr Prize for Marine Biology.

An hour or so after dinner Mom and I sat in folding chairs on Tom's back deck and watched a distant line of thunderstorms boil and grow with deep rumbles and long, bright streamers of lightning.

I'd flown home from Dublin for this little gathering. Mom had messaged me and we'd videoed back and forth a few times and I knew I had to be there. It was during my third season with the Rovers and I was an established starter and would miss a couple of important games, but Coach was a human being and understood when I told him. I told the sportswriters the truth, that my father was dying, but for his sake I wanted to call it "family leave" and they, too, acted like real people for a change and honored the request. So here I was.

"How long does Father have?" I asked Mom, holding tight to my beer, some unpronounceable Belgian brand that Tom liked. Me, I stuck with Corona when I was home.

"A month or two," she said.

"He looks better than that," I offered. "And he seems happy enough. I thought maybe things were a little better."

A slight shake of her head, a thin smile: "No, they're not. He accepted it a long time ago, Peter, that's all. The inevitability of it." She chuckled a bit. "I caught him in the backyard a couple of days ago smoking one of those Camels. I couldn't believe it, but he just said it didn't really matter anymore, so what the hell."

I didn't say anything, but looked out toward the distant storm clouds as they lit up the evening sky.

An hour later I walked over to Father to say goodbye as he and Mom got ready for the drive home. He got up off the couch and wouldn't let me stop him from standing. I gave him a firm handshake and his grip was just firm enough in return to be a reminder of whom he'd been. I looked at him, gave him a quick, clumsy hug, and told him I loved him.

"Thank you," he said. He seemed at peace.

As I got to my car in the driveway that line of thunderstorms was almost to us, drifting west in the land breeze, but I beat the worst of the rain back to my hotel. Just as I was pulling into the parking lot, my parents were getting into their car for their longer drive home across the Sunshine Skyway and out to the beach. Father, despite his health, always insisted on driving, a control freak right to the end. It was pouring by then, blinding rain obscuring the road across that high bridge. Rain, cancer, control and its lack: These are the things that ended my father's life and put my mother's into ruin.

The police gave me details on how Father died. I reconstruct it this way: A driving rain on the Sunshine Skyway, the big bridge over Tampa Bay. The pickup truck to their left going much too fast for conditions and trying to change into their lane. The driver—a young guy running his own pool-cleaning business and hurrying home—lost control and started fishtailing. He clipped Father's Lexus and sent it spinning just after the crest of the bridge where everyone starts heading downhill. The Lexus hit the right-side rail and flipped over while climbing the rail and then tumbling as it fell 130 meters into the water below. Air bags and belts kept Mom and Father alive through all that, but sinking twenty feet to the bottom of the bay cost Father his life.

Mom lived through it. She was on her mobile—voice only—with Tom when this all happened. They were talking about me, Tom told me later; talking about how odd it was to be able to make a living playing basketball. And then he heard her crying out and heard Father's angry curse and then nothing more for a few seconds and then an "Oh, sweet Jesus" from Mom as the car started to sink into the warm embrace of Tampa Bay. Mom managed to unclip her belt and the power windows still worked as she hit the button. She'd been a competitive swimmer at Harvard when she'd met Father, and that background saved her as she got through the window and up to the surface. Only there did she have the time to think about Father. So she went back down, the car nose-first in the sandy bottom. She got back inside, got to her husband, who sat there quietly, eyes open. She got to the belt latch, unsnapped it, tried to maneuver her way back out the window she'd come in, tugging and pulling on Father all the while. Twenty seconds. Thirty. Fifty. Down there with Father, trying to get him out. Trying very, very hard to get him out until, finally, she had to give up on him and surface.

Several weeks after signing that agreement with Heather I woke up in my own bed in my own house in my own beach town and, in turn, told myBob to wake up and check for incoming. There wasn't much.

I was in a strange lull. All the hubbub of the original sighting, all of the craziness of what was real and what wasn't—all of that had died away as the world kept turning, the friends up there stayed quiet, the news was taken over by super-typhoon Sarita's ruination of Manila and then the damn Yankees winning another World Series and the October we'd just sweltered through was the hottest since the Pleistocene and the world's oceans were rising ever more and life went on.

"You have a two P.M. sweep with Stephen Arce," myBob was telling me as I walked out onto the deck to enjoy a slightly cooler November morning. Arce was the closer for the Pelicans, and had a 100-mile-an hour fastball. "He'll throw you some batting practice and you'll hit them all out of the park, I'm sure."

"Sarcasm, myBob? First thing in the morning?"

myBob chuckled, a new thing he'd picked up along with the sarcastic attitude in some recent upgrade. He seemed smarter than ever, more alive than ever. Amazing, really, what they could do. "His helpmate says he'll make sure you can hit him," myBob added. "Nothing faster than ninety."

Like I said, sarcasm.

"But first," myBob added, "there's the usual lunch with Heather Newsome."

"Café Pont?" I asked him.

"Of course," myBob said. "At your usual table. At your usual time."

Heather. She was the only thing that held my interest, really, as the days passed with nothing new happening. Heather, who seemed to be warping and changing right before my eyes as we met for lunch several times a week at Café Pont.

I'd found her formal, even severe, the first time we met, with a kind of forced friendliness, a falseness about her, that was off-putting. So I'd been surprised to see how much looser and friendlier, and more honest, she'd been a few days later at Tom's house. There she'd seemed much more genuine, even though we'd talked business.

She'd even changed physically, I thought. Her eyes, her lips, those long fingers that so often reached out to touch my arm at lunch, those athletic legs, the cascade of hair that had gone from nearly blond to dark black, that deepening voice, the casual comfort of her leaning forward over the table to chat with me about nothing important or, sometimes, things very important indeed. So close I could smell her; not her perfume—I didn't think she wore any. Just the human smell of her seemed to pull me in. I was falling hard and I knew it.

Change is everything, isn't it? Change is constant, sometimes good and sometimes not but always happening, for all of us, all the time. I thought of the different versions of me there'd been at different times in my life: the high-school pitcher; the undergrad English Lit student reading Elizabeth Barrett Browning and Robert Heinlein; the basketball player who finally got his chance in college and found some success; the dutiful son and caring brother; the sweeper hoping to find success and do something worthwhile; and on and on and on. Changes, all. Changes I'd embraced, without really giving it any thought. Changes I'd welcomed, without thinking through at all how they'd come my way and where they might lead me. Thoughtless, but there I was, changing.

And, to be honest, that's what I wanted with Heather. I wanted to embrace the change, physically and emotionally. I wanted to admit to her how I felt. I wanted, I hoped, that she felt something for me as well. I wanted.

But she was, of course, my brother's girlfriend. He was serious about her. He said he loved her. And that was that.

I took a sip of the cheap white wine I'd poured over ice to help me put up with the heat on the back deck. I looked out to the Gulf and thought maybe I could see that shimmer again. It was ephemeral, but now that I knew it was something real and I was in on the secret, there was some satisfaction in noticing it.

The afternoon sweep had gone fine. I'd managed to get the bat on the ball a few times and even stroked some obvious base hits off the Cy Young winner Stephen Arce, much to the amusement of the few people standing around the batting cage. Then he'd upped the velocity a notch or two and I was lucky after that to foul off a few. Then he'd turned it up another notch and I was terrified as a fastball in the mid-nineties smoked its way by me while I trembled in fear. An interview, those pitches, a few swings. It was good and myBob was cleaning it up and would send it out for me soon. It would do fine in the ratings. It might even go viral. I took another sip of that cheap wine and stared toward the west.

myBob pinged me: incoming video call. It was from Heather, and she wanted to see me. My place, she said, in twenty minutes. Things were going to happen. We needed to talk. She looked serious.

So maybe this was it? Some action at last? The Big Arrival? All right, then. "Sure," I said, "I'll be here. Will I be sweeping?"

"No, but that's coming soon, Peter. That's one of the things we have to talk about."

"And the other things?"

"You'll see," and she laughed and then added, "Oh, and you should call your brother right away. Today is the third-year anniversary of your father's death."

"What?"

"Tom mentioned it to me the other day. He doesn't expect you to remember. Why not surprise him?"

"All right, I *will* surprise him."

"Good. You're both in for a lot of surprises, Peter," she said, "so being nice to your brother will be a good start to all that." And I saw her smile and offer a faint shrug.

"What the hell does that mean?"

"See you soon," she said, and clicked off.

Only when Heather knocked did it occur to me I hadn't gotten around to messaging Tom. No problem, I'd do that later.

She stood at my front door wearing blue jeans and a short-sleeved black T-shirt that showed the Milky Way galaxy and a line that said "You Are Here" and pointed to a spot out near a spiral edge. Her hair seemed longer, somehow, and so black it drew me in. It fell free over her shoulders. She was beautiful, and effortlessly so.

I smiled and said hello. Blue jeans, T-shirt, hair down, no makeup, running shoes. And truly beautiful. Tom was one lucky guy.

"Hello, Peter," she said. "How are things?"

"Boring," I said. "But maybe you're here to fix that?"

She turned to walk away from me, out through the living room and up the staircase that led to the bedrooms and the wooden deck. I followed her up the stairs, my bad left knee complaining about every step, as it always did. Then I walked through the bedroom and out through the glass doors to the deck, where Heather was pouring herself a glass of wine. She finished that, took a sip, then turned away from me to stand at the rail, looking out toward the Gulf and the looming sunset.

I walked over to join her. "How's Tom?" I asked her. She turned to look at me, her face wondrous in the long light of the setting sun. She was Tom's girl. She'd been spending some nights at his place, he'd told me. There'd been rumblings from Tom about asking her to marry him. I'd told him I thought it was a great idea. I'd told him she was smart and nice-looking and seemed in love with him and what more could you possibly ask than that?

She shook her head slightly, almost smiling. "He's fine, Peter."

I couldn't think of anything else to say. She smelled like the energy in the air right before a summer downpour. I looked at her and she looked back, not saying anything. She smiled, leaned up a bit, and kissed me on the neck. My brother's girl, the one he was talking about marrying.

"No sweeping now, Peter, all right?"

"Sure," I said, and myBob said "Done" before I could ask him.

"Thank you, Peter," she said, and then kissed me again on the neck, the left cheek, the nose, the lips. Softly. Barely.

We went very slowly. She didn't say a thing at first, stepping back so I could reach down to the bottom of that T-shirt and slowly pull it up and over her head.

She reached back with both hands to unclasp her bra and then set it down on the deck chair behind her. I hadn't seen her bare breasts before, though god knows I'd fantasized about them. They were round and firm and perfect, the areolas a thin dark band around the deep red of the nipples. I stared at them.

"They're yours, Peter. I've wanted you to see them for a long time. Kiss them for me, please."

I did. Later, after, in bed, I did again. It was three in the morning by then and I was trying very hard to not think about Tom as I kissed those breasts, kissed her on the lips, and then again. Entered her one more time while she brought me to her, the electricity crackling.

We fit together. It was perfection. I didn't want it to be, but there it was. Making love to her, making love with her, was the best thing I'd ever done, the only true story I'd ever read, the best truth I'd ever discovered, a weird and welcome transcendence from what I'd thought, with so many women, was sex. Or love.

But there was Tom to think of. Jesus, there'd be hell to pay. Here we'd been getting along again after years of cold disagreements, and now I was making love to his girlfriend. Hell, I was in love with his girlfriend.

Was I? Was I in love? I'd been close just once before and this had that same desperate need that I'd felt then. One of the things I'd learned is that great sex and true love aren't usually in the same neighborhood. And yet here, with Heather, the sex was great, and I was also feeling some surprising, wonderful, frightening emotion. I had to think it was something real. Like love.

She left about dawn, waking me after she'd slipped back into her jeans and T-shirt. She leaned over the bed to kiss me and say, "I'll see you soon, Peter. There's a lot going on and I'll be gone for a bit and then we'll be together again, all right? Be patient." And then she walked away.

I couldn't fall back asleep, so I told myBob to come back to life and then I lay there, waiting for a ping from him saying that Tom was calling. Or worse, waiting to hear a sharp banging at the door of Tom's hurt and angry fists. The minutes crept by.

Finally, around 7 A.M., myBob pinged. I answered the call live. It was audio only.

"Hello."

"Petey." He sounded terribly hurt.

"Yeah, Tom."

"Pete. She's gone. Heather's gone."

"Gone?"

"There's a note here. She loves me, but she has to leave. She's gone."

"She doesn't say where she's going? Or why?"

"No, none of that." He was crying. Poor Tom. We talked it

through for a while, me feeling his heartache and my guilt at the same time. But eventually he calmed down, and then he clicked off and slowly, over the next day or two, he got over it. He said her campus office was closed with a note on the door saying she was away on indefinite leave. No one seemed to know anything beyond that.

And so it went. As the next few weeks passed, Tom seemed to get used to it. His turtle research helped him with that. He was close to finishing a major bit of research on sea turtles that he'd spent years working on. It was important. It mattered.

Me? I couldn't believe. Be patient, she'd said, but the days turned to weeks and I had to wonder. Maybe, I thought, she'd left for good, breaking it to me softly. Maybe she'd done the right thing for us both. With her gone, I didn't have to tell Tom what had happened.

More secrets from my brother. Just what I needed.

7

I put the spout of the water jug to my lips and took a sip. It was getting hot. I squirmed around some on the canvas chair that I'd placed behind the low dunes, so I could see the water without disturbing the beach. I tried to get comfortable, but it wasn't easy. I asked myBob if there was anything new from Chloe or Abigail. Chloe and I were "dating" again, and we were both beginning to think our little arranged relationship wasn't really all that mercenary an idea. I liked her. I hadn't heard from Heather, and that whole thing I'd thought we had now felt cheap. I was thinking I'd been used and didn't know why.

And since the ten ships had reappeared the week before, I'd been talking to Abigail at least once a day. They were visible, there were ten of them, and that was that. No one could get close, no one could find out anything about them. The Ten, the edited media were calling them, and the headlines had screamed for days about what was next. But now eight days had gone by and nothing had happened, so the edited-media stories were slowly becoming a little more reasonable. Interviews with astronomers and the military and political leaders. Lots of pictures. Lots of guessing. Lots of looking up at night to watch them go by overhead in various places at various times.

But no Heather. And Tom had spent ten long years on preparing for this little clutch of sea turtles to arrive, so here I was, the dutiful brother, sweeping what we hoped was Tom's success, the return of some Kemp's ridleys to an island in the mouth of Tampa Bay.

"There's nothing to report on the so-called Ten," myBob was saying to me as I sipped from a bottle of water and adjusted my sunglasses. I looked out at the Gulf of Mexico, a brisk sea breeze stirring up a foot or two of shore-break. That looked very promising, Tom had told me; the Kemp's ridleys were the only sea turtles to nest during the day and they liked windy weather for it.

But the turtles? They weren't in sight.

I looked over at Tom. He looked back and smiled, gave me a thumbs-up. He'd already forgotten to worry about The Ten. Today was the day, he'd told me a couple of hours ago, before we'd settled in to be quiet. Everything was just right for the turtles: the weather, the tides, the timing. I smiled back, returned the thumbs-up, asked Bob for an update, and got the same response. I squirmed some more. Looked toward the water. Sighed. I should have been working to cover the story of The Ten; but no, always the devoted brother, here I was in the sun with genius Tom, watching the wavelets roll in. I squirmed again, thinking of excuses to leave, wondering if I was kidding myself, if The Ten's return was a false alarm and all I was doing was looking for an excuse to get up off my folding chair and head home.

This little gathering of turtles would be big news, if and when they arrived. Until this day, all the Kemp's ridleys in the world had laid their eggs on a single stretch of beach in Mexico—a place called Rancho Nuevo. In the old days, thousands of females would arrive nearly at once; an *arribada,* they called it in Spanish. In the 1940s, one local with an eight-millimeter film camera caught footage of some forty thousand of the turtles crawling ashore on the same day, pushing and shoving and climbing over each other to find a spot where they could dig, lay, bury, and scoot.

That one little home movie damned the Kemp's ridleys to likely extinction. There had always been a smattering of local fishermen and some raccoons and bobcats along that beach to grab and eat a few of the turtles and their eggs. But once that film got out, people from all over that coast and then from all over the Caribbean came to harvest the eggs and the turtle meat and feed their families or make their profit.

For a while, they did; all those earnest egg-laying mamas were awfully easy pickings. But it couldn't last with all that pressure on one site: Best guess was that by the turn of the millennium there were maybe two hundred of the turtles left. Sixty years turned out to be plenty of time to wipe out a species.

Over the years, there'd been any number of efforts to get the turtles to change that nesting behavior and spread things out to other, safer beaches, but the Kemp's ridleys were having none of it. One group of scientists on the Texas Gulf Coast had spent millions on a site at Padre Island and managed to coax a total of eight turtles into nesting there. None of their eggs hatched. By the time Tom was in college and got started on his project, the experts thought the Kemp's ridleys were gone in the wild and everyone had given up on them.

But not my little brother Tom. He'd succeeded, he hoped, where no one else had. A decade ago, Tom Holman, doctoral student in wildlife ecology, offered fishermen in the Bay of Campeche a reward if they found any Kemp's ridleys. The fishermen, over the course of six months, found five.

Two of them were females. Tom opened them up, took somatic cells from the ovaries of both turtles and fused them with enucle-ated eggs—eggs with the DNA removed—from leatherback turtles, then grew those eggs in the lab, where he had all the substrates and environmental parameters required. Tom's mitochondrial DNA analysis said it ought to work; but it was out there, very edgy, doing something like that for turtles. Kemp's ridleys aren't sheep, and the cloning didn't come easy.

But it *did* work, and the process resulted in nearly one hundred viable eggs from the greens. Tom and his team had buried them—no mean feat there, getting that done just right, he told me—into nests here on Egmont, and then watched with joy as ninety-four of those genetically clean Kemp's ridley hatchlings boiled out of the nests sixty days later and headed for the water.

Question was, how many would survive and would those survivors return? Had they imprinted on this beach or were they lost forever, artificial creations that would never find their way home? They weren't real, it seemed to me; they were creations, conjured up in a lab. But if some returned to lay eggs and those eggs hatched and the species was saved, wasn't that worth the fakery? I thought so. I hoped so.

Tom tracked as many of the turtles as he could, attaching the latest in transponders just inside the lateral scutes, up near the head. The batteries were good for five years. Problem was, it takes ten for the turtles to mature, mate, and return. That meant Tom had a year or so at the midway point to try and capture as many of them as he could, put in new transponders, and start the tracking all over again.

It had kept him busy, catching them, one by one, from all around the Gulf of Mexico and even on up the East Coast as far as Cape Cod. Two turtles, in fact, drifted with the Gulf Stream all the way to the coast of Ireland. He'd gone to them, put in new transponders, and wished them well as he released them.

It was a hugely ambitious, and expensive, effort: all the lab work, all the tracking and retagging. It became his life's work. It defined him, made him who he was. Sitting here in the sand dunes waiting for the payoff, I figured he'd sure as hell earned the headlines I could already picture in my mind: "Dr. Thomas Holman, Savior of the Kemp's Ridleys"; or better still, "Dr. Thomas Holman, the

Architect of Change for a Doomed Species." I would sweep the hell out of this. I'd make him famous.

If it worked. Now, sometime this month and maybe even today, we'd find out how worthwhile all that work had been. The survival rate for hatchlings is never more than 25 percent of those who make it to the sea, and often a lot lower. Tom hoped a dozen or more mothers might show and start laying their eggs.

And then, right on cue, I saw something. A shape at the edge of the water? Something coming in through the tidal pool? Just a big ray, probably; this was their time of year to lay eggs, too, and they did it right up at the edge, in inches of water.

I put the binoculars to my eyes and there she was, a turtle the size of a meat platter—bad comparison, I thought right away, since the sweet taste of their meat was one reason there weren't many left. But there she was, coming clean out of the water in her frenzy as she headed toward shore. I told myBob to start a live sweep with the usual intro, and then turned to let Tom know. But he'd already seen her and had his wearable strapcam, the one with that great telephoto lens, going. I turned back and hit the zoom on my sweep bowl amp and got a close-up of the turtle. I wanted to follow this girl all the way up the beach as she came ashore. Then I saw, on both sides of her, more of them. I zoomed back. More still, a couple of dozen maybe, all at once, a tiny *arribada*.

I grinned like a son-of-a-bitch. Good for Tom. He'd earned this moment's satisfaction, my baby brother. It'd been a long, hard trail for him getting to this, and it was the damnedest thing I'd ever seen, a regular D-day of turtles invading this one beach. I kept my eyes on them as more emerged, sixty or seventy of them. I tried to count but couldn't keep up, so I watched the moms come ashore and marveled. This was big-time, all right. At that moment, I couldn't imagine anything bigger.

I turned to sweep Tom and saw that he had a worried look on his face. As the turtles kept coming ashore by the dozens, he and I got up from behind the dunes and walked out into them, not worried anymore about disturbing a few hesitant females

"There can't be this many, Petey," he said. "There were just ninety-four hatchlings. I can't figure this out."

"Some sort of herd instinct? Others turtles joined your group?" I asked, and then added, "Hell, Tom, enjoy the moment and figure out the details later. You're the genius who saved a whole species." And I patted him on the shoulder as we walked. He just shook his head, overwhelmed by his success.

The turtles were blind to us, so focused on nature's imperatives that we didn't exist for them. Invisible, we walked into the warm surge of the shore-break, and out to the sandbar, moving through them as we went, shoving them aside every now and then when we couldn't avoid it. Tom wanted to get out there and look back so he could tape them moving into the beach and see the beach as they saw it during their approach.

We got past the shallow water over the bar and waded into the deeper, far side of it. In a few steps it was thigh-deep. I made sure I went live with my sweep and kept my eye on Tom. My sweep bowl amp was touchy about salt water and way too expensive to risk, so I was working hard to keep it dry. Was the risk worth it? You bet.

We took another couple of steps and it was hip-deep; then, still on a downward slope off the sandbar, it was waist-deep and I got really worried about my bowl amp. We stopped there.

Tom turned around to film. I stood next to him, and before I made the turn I saw, out there in the darker blue of the deeper water, something headed our way.

"Tom. There's something out there behind us. It's big."

"Barracuda," he said, not taking his eye away from the eyecup. "They won't bother you, Petey, don't sweat it." He paused. "Damn, Petey, look at these turtles. God, there must be a hundred of them."

I trusted him on the barracuda. Tom had always been the smart one growing up, the one who knew the real facts about things while

I was the hazy dreamer who wanted to do nothing but play sports, read books, and daydream. I was into religion and was going to be a priest. He was into science. We were altar boys together for one year when I was twelve and he was ten.

There's a moment in the Catholic Mass when the priest holds the host—a little wafer of bread not much bigger than a quarter—up high with both hands and says, "This is my body," and then, a bit later, holding up a chalice of wine, "This is my blood." At that moment, Catholic belief says, the host becomes the body and blood of Christ. Not *like* the body and blood, but the actual, real thing. It's called transubstantiation and I'd believed it, firmly, until that year when Tom became an altar boy.

The first time Tom served at Mass—this was during the Latin Revival, when we both were kids—he was kneeling on the cold marble of the altar in St. Thomas Aquinas Church as the priest, Father Mullan, raised that host up high. Tom watched, and shook his head. I was there with Mom and Father, in the front pew, watching him. They didn't notice that disbelieving shake, but I did. After Mass, he showed me the host he'd sneaked home and then he put it under the microscope so we both could peer at it. Just bread, he concluded. Then he took snippets of it and ran it through his chemistry set to see what it really was. It was a grievous sin, stealing a consecrated host and bringing it home for analysis, but Tom thought he needed to do that, and so he did. It was bread, that was all, and even then I knew better than to argue with him.

Now I needed to get far enough away from my scientist brother that I could be looking at the turtles in the foreground and have him in the background and then I could play with the depth of field to focus on turtle or Tom, back and forth. I headed away from him, fifty or sixty meters up the beach, where the water was a little shallower.

I got out to the spot I wanted and turned to look at Tom. I felt a bump against the back of my leg and panicked, jumping away from it. But when I turned around to look it was a turtle, that was all, coming up from the darkness to find the sandbar, climb over it, get to the beach, and lay her eggs. Just another turtle.

And then, beyond it, deeper, a large shape hurtled by. A barracuda? God, I hoped so; I didn't want it to be a bull shark. I'd been snorkeling all over the Caribbean, from Grand Cayman to the Turks and Caicos; that's how I used to spend my vacations, with someone I liked, on an island with a good reef and a good bar or two. In those places I'd learned not to worry about barracuda; they were curious, but for all their sleekly vicious appearance they never seemed to bother anybody, just like Tom said. Not like bull sharks—those'd come and get you when they could. People survived it when a bull shark hit them if they could get away after the first attack. Usually it was just a chunk of calf that was gone, or a long slash on the arm where the shark grabbed and then let go, a little exploratory nibble before coming around for a second strike, the serious attack. You didn't want to still be there for that second go-round.

There was another shape out there. Two of them now, moving fast, back and forth, feeding, maybe, in the deeper water. One shot off in a hurry and disappeared. The other slowed, then just drifted there, a gray shadow in the water, just deep enough to be hidden from view.

"Tom, you about done?" I shouted out, turning to look at him. He was returning to the beach, filming it all as he went, the shallows filled with scrambling turtles. He turned back once to wave at me. I could see the grin on his face as he shrugged, full of wonder and triumph at the same time. He'd done it, damn it,

As he reached the shore, a good hundred meters away from me, I saw something move by to my left. There, in the trench just this side of the sandbar, surrounded by the *arribada* of Kemp's ridleys swimming to shore, something was rising up from the water, a blur in the bright splatters, shimmery then clearing as it stood, looked toward us, and raised a hand in greeting. My god, I thought, the aliens—our visitors, the great unknown—had arrived. Here. Now.

What was I supposed to do? Run? I turned to look at Tom. He

was filming a mother scratching out a hole in the sand to bury her eggs in. I turned back and stood there as the still-arriving sea turtles shoved their way past me.

It was, though I didn't quite realize it then, the end of things as I'd known them to be. The alien, the visitor, the thing from The Ten, was no more than ten meters from me, standing in the shallows. Near him there was another shape in the water, something as large as him, scuttling as I approached, a quick flick of a tail and then gone.

His skin was dark and slick, and from ten meters away I could smell him, a sort of low-tide salt tang: familiar, not unpleasant. His fat, porpoise-shaped body was short of two meters tall and he had on what looked for all the world like comical soaking-wet Bermuda shorts that ended at the knees of short, thick legs. Halfway up the torso there were thin, tiny arms coming out from the side.

"Hello," he said, in passable English, a bit of a lisp but with that mid-Atlantic flat dialect the edited-media anchors use. "I am very pleassed to introduce myself."

"myBob, go live with the sweep," I said to my helpmate as I started to raise my right hand in greeting to this emissary from another world. In an hour or two the whole world would know him. For now, for this moment, it was me, and now I was sweeping it live to the lucky few thousand or so fans—hell, probably a half or a third of that during the daytime, and with me sweeping sea turtles— who were watching. I figured those numbers must be rising fast, and the edited media would know in minutes. But, right here and right now, the moment, this meeting, First Contact, was all mine.

"You are Peter Holman, yess," he said in that sibilant whistle of a voice I would soon get used to.

I nodded, said, "Yes."

"Good. You may call me Twoclicks." He waved at that high blue sky. "We are from Imperial S'hudon."

I looked up to see what he was pointing at. No clouds, a solitary frigate bird circling over us, hoping to spot a handout.

And then I felt, more than heard, a distant rumble. It vibrated through me, subtle at first and then stronger, a steady background timpani that grew in intensity until I could hear it, too: a low distant rumble that grew louder and louder—a plane doing some low-level thing right over us? Some big boat rumbling past just out of sight?

I looked back at Tom and he was looking my way, shaking his head. He touched his ears, shouted something I couldn't hear.

There was a scream: a metallic tear in the sky above us. I grabbed the side of my head, covering my ears as it screeched, fingernails against the ultimate blackboard. That same sound I'd heard before, that same pain. Awful.

And then it was gone. Ten seconds, it couldn't have been longer, and then gone.

I stood perfectly still, afraid to move. I looked at my brother in the distance as he, too, stood quietly in the shallow water. I glanced around, and there, out in the Gulf, I saw that shimmering I'd seen so often, only now getting brighter, more obvious. I am in the business of description, but it's hard to say how it looked as it firmed up, brightened, took on a shape. For all its size, it was delicate, its spidery legs connecting at their top to that round main body as it appeared, standing on those legs in the shallows of the Gulf of Mexico.

The only sounds I could hear were the slight slap of the six-inch shore-break against the packed, wet sand of the beach and, even at this distance, the scrinch of sand being dug out by the turtles back on the beach.

"Hah!" Twoclicks said from behind me, and as I finally moved, turning to see him he held those delicate arms of his out wide. "Iss very impressive, right? We come and go all the time and you never knew until now, right?"

He seemed very pleased with himself. I was speechless, and terrified. But I nodded in agreement and turned once more to look at Tom. He was videoing, and I knew he'd be zooming in tight on us. I told myBob to keep the sweep going live, and then I zoomed onto Tom and then back out to pan: the warmth of the water on my legs, the bumps now and again from a turtle hurrying by, the blue sky, that egg shape upright in the distant background, this strange Twoclicks with that odd frozen smile on his face, the smell of salt and sunblock, the taste of fear in my mouth. I felt like I had when that one ship of The Ten had struck back at the taikonauts and the other probes. I'd been there and I knew what these things, these aliens, could do. I wasn't at all sure that I wanted to be part of this story.

Not that I had any choice. I watched as Twoclicks let his arms drop to his sides, then lowered himself into the water until only the top of his head, and those strange eyes, were visible. He stayed there for a second, then rose again.

"Ahh, your water iss very nice here. Warm. Safe." He seemed to take a deep breath and went into a little prepared speech. "S'hudon hass arrived, Peter Holman, and we seek your friend-ship."

"What?" I couldn't think of much else to say. Why the hell was he seeking my friendship? Where the hell was the President and where were the Joint Chiefs of Staff and the UN Secretary-General and all that crowd when you needed them?

Twoclicks was staring at me, waiting for my response. "Sure. Our friendship," I managed to say, wondering how in the hell it had happened that I was in charge of intergalactic peace and diplomacy. "But I don't think I'm the one you should be talking to. In a few minutes, I'm sure, there'll be some people arriving here. . . ."

"We have brought giftss for you," he said. He held out his hands, nothing in them.

"I don't understand," I said. "Gifts?"

"Yess. Gifts. All these turtless," and he waved one stubby arm toward the beach, where mother turtles by the dozens were digging into the sand, laying eggs, renewing a species that the experts had predicted was doomed.

"You had something to do with this? The Kemp's ridleys? The *arribada*?"

"Yess. We have"—he paused, seemed to think it through for a moment—"duplicated them, the turtles, and added to their numbers. We have been working on this on that ship," and he pointed toward the craft visible in the distance. "These turtles, they will return here, alwayss." He smiled, a strange, artificial, lipless grin that he must have taught himself for our sake. "Their species is saved now, yess?"

These aliens had saved them? I had to wonder what Tom would think of that. Yes, it was great that the disappearing Kemp's ridleys were saved. But Tom had spent a decade building a career based on midwifing today's rebirth of this disappearing species and now, in a few minutes, he would know it was all a falsehood; his success was a lie, a fabrication. In fact, as I thought about it for a second, my brother Tom was about to realize that his level of science was as far behind what these aliens brought as the discovery that two sticks rubbed just right could start a fire. I supposed I'd have be the one to tell him.

I wanted to disbelieve it all, wanted to blink hard once and wake up back in Kansas, back in reality. I thought of myself as a professional skeptic. But here this thing was, right in front of me.

"How did you do this? And why?" I asked him.

"Oh," he laughed, a jovial belly-rolling laugh that I came to know well in the following months. "Oh, that. You have the highest recommendations. Very highest." He pointed out toward the ship again. "We have creations, creaturess. These creations are capable of great changes. They have been here for ssome time. Working. Searching. They found you."

Found me? What the hell? Then, as if to prove how much he knew, he said to me, "You make sweeps, yess? Entertainments?"

"News, too," I said crazily, trying to score some kind of point. I did do news, damn it, and a lot of it. Interviews. Sweeps of approaching aliens in the night sky, conversations with portly alien emissaries in the shallow water of the Gulf of Mexico.

"Ssure," he said, and then, I swear, he winked at me, a thin membrane sliding down over one eye as he squinched it closed for a second. "And," he said, sliding into that belly laugh again, "you are excellent at communicating with others, yess? Meeting people. Mating rituals, yes?"

I stared at him. "What the hell are you talking about?"

He held out his arms in a practiced move, palms up, faking innocence. "Iss what I have seen on your ssweeps." He chuckled a bit more, a deep rumbling from inside that fat, sleek body. "We have sstudied you. We know you."

"I'm confused," I admitted. "I'm not sure what you mean."

I glanced to see what Tom was doing. He was standing there, thigh-deep in the water, and watching through his video lens. He was probably catching this whole conversation, could see it all. Good, I'd want that for verification that I hadn't made all this up with myBob's help and my editing software. I kept my feed live.

"We'll show you, yess?" he said, and waved to his right, where there was something headed our way in the water, something dark and fast. It swept in below the surface, neared us, then veered away, turned, swept back by one more time, then veered away again.

Then it slowed, finally, and drifted in toward us until I could see it, another of these porpoise-shaped things; no, this one more like a shark, sleeker, longer, leaner. There'd be nothing Tom could catch with his camera, though, unless the thing stopped and stood up.

While I watched, it started to shimmer and blur, vibrating under the water. I couldn't quite see exactly how it was happening, but the water trembled with the change, wavelets of energy obscuring what we could see.

Then it calmed down, and things cleared up. It had changed,

lost its shark shape, grown thinner, longer, with limbs. Nice limbs, in fact. Beautiful.

There, rising from the sea, was Heather.

She started wading toward me, moving through the water with a liquid perfection that now made sense to me. I shook my head and laughed at myself, at how stupid I'd been, as she came near us.

"Hello, Peter."

I just stared at her. Jesus, Tom was wrong all those years ago at Mass. Here it was: transubstantiation. The real thing, body and blood. I turned to see what Tom was doing. Had he been able to see her change? Did he know she was changeable? Of course he didn't, couldn't. I could see he still wore the strapcam and had another vidcam in his hand and probably had it zoomed; but even that wouldn't have shown him what she was in the water. To Tom, she was somehow just emerging from the Gulf.

I waved at him to come toward us, join us, bring the camera in and get close to all this. He might as well know, and the sooner the better. But he stayed where he was.

Heather smiled, reached up to push the hair from her eyes. "So here it is, Peter. The Big Story, the Biggest News of Them All."

"Yeah," I said, and just kept staring at her. Her skin was rippling, like she was fighting to keep it under control: like there was something about being in the water that made it difficult for her.

"It's yours, Peter," she said, the smile fading. "This is your story to tell. All about us. All about your new future—*everyone's* new future."

"It's a hell of a story, that's for sure." I looked at her, standing there, beautiful and perfect, the woman, the thing, I'd made love to. To her left, Twoclicks was reaching down with those fragile arms to scoop water into his hands. He splashed it on what passed for a face, then smiled at me, wet and dripping.

"We need you, Peter," Heather said, "as the project here begins."

"The project?"

"Twoclicks is my employer, Peter. He has some changes planned for you, for here. You'll all be better for it, eventually; many of you will benefit greatly, in fact. But it will take some time and not everyone will be happy about the changes. Governments, politics, the *way* you live here, *how* you live . . ." She smiled again. "All that's going to change."

"And you want me to help you do that?"

She smiled that perfect smile, stable now, under control. "No, not in making the changes. But in communicating those changes to Earth, yes, we want your help. Tom will help you, we hope. Someone has to explain it to everyone, someone people here can trust. The two of you, working together, you can do that."

I shook my head. It was all too crazy to even think about.

"Someone will speak for us, Peter. Why not let it be you?"

"And why bring Tom into this?"

"He's brilliant, more so than you know. He can understand some small parts of what we are, of why we're here for you. When we tell him what we've done with the turtles, how we've saved them, he'll understand. Not many of you here could." She chuckled. "You, for instance, couldn't. But the two of you, together, will be perfect, Pete. You can explain for us, can communicate. If it goes well, your work, a lot of people will be better for it."

"And if it doesn't go well? If we don't sign on?"

She shrugged. "It *is* going to happen here, Peter, there's no stopping that." She waved her hands toward the ship out there, settled and quiet in the shallow Gulf of Mexico. "We *need* to be here, or this wouldn't be happening."

I turned away from her, looked again at Tom, tried again to wave him toward us. He stood there among the Kemp's ridleys and watched us through that zoom. Around him, the turtles dug their holes, dropped their eggs.

He took his eye from the lens. Lowered the camera. Shook his head slowly, staring at me across the water. He was my brother. I thought of the price he'd pay for all this. I thought about what I owed him, how I could possibly, ever, make it right.

Heather's face was rippling a bit as I turned back to look at her, those perfect cheekbones widening for an instant, then settling down. My god. Then she smiled again, that face stable for a moment. "Tom's science will matter. He'll be famous."

She reached out to touch my cheek, let her fingertip trail down to my lips, pressed there lightly. "And you, Peter. It was very, very good between us, wasn't it?"

I nodded. myBob was beeping at me. Tom messaging? No. my-Bob whispered in my ear, "Your sweep system is down. It went dark and off-line thirty-one seconds ago."

"You'll be the most famous journo on the planet," she was saying. "Every sweep you send. The whole world will watch, will sense what you're sending. The whole world will listen to you."

"Keep it recording, if you can, myBob," I said to my helpmate. Then I looked past Heather, out to where that ship stood. I hoped like hell my sweep was capturing this. I shook my head at the thought of it. "Good between us"? This incredible, beautiful thing and I? Yes, it had been. It sure had been.

The whole world would watch, listen, touch, taste? Yeah, well, that was surely a lock.

Heather and Twoclicks were silent. I turned back to look at Tom. He had started wading slowly through the water toward us, still using the vidcam as he approached, watching me, watching us, through the lens as he came closer.

"Your sweep is recording," myBob whispered in my ear. "You may have lost a few minutes of feed, though."

"Thanks," I whispered back, and then heard a small splash behind me. I turned and Twoclicks was gone.

Heather was smiling. "We have to go now, Peter, but I'll see you and Tom soon and we'll begin making arrangements, all right? For now, it's best, by the way, if you keep me out of things in terms of your media. As far as you know I'm a human, an Earthie, who's working with the S'hudonni. All right? You're good with that? "

"Sure," I said, "but wait!" It was too late. I watched as she turned and dived into the waist-deep water. I kept my eyes on her as she swam a strong stroke, then another, then things began to blur and there were no more arms making strokes but, instead, a shape, perhaps a small bull shark, streaking fast toward deeper water, toward that ship out there. And then it was gone. Sure, keep that quiet, that she can change shapes. No problem.

"Peter," I heard from behind me, and turned. Tom was staring at me. "Peter," he said, "I don't understand. The turtles, that thing, that alien thing, the ship out there, and where the hell is our military? And Heather? What the hell? I mean, Jesus, what the fucking hell, Peter!"

He seemed angry. Furious, in fact.

Couldn't say as I blamed him. "Sweep off," I whispered to my-Bob, who whispered back in my ear, "Done."

"I've turned off the sweep, Tom. If you'll turn off that viddy, we can walk back to the beach and get back to work watching those turtles, all right?"

He just stared at me. "Peter," he finally said, slowly, with a dark anger. "Peter. What the fucking hell is going on?"

And so, as we walked back in and went back to work, not knowing what else to do as we heard helicopters in the distance and heard, more than saw, the sound of Air Force ghostships from MacDill Air Force Base over in Tampa, I told him what the fucking hell was going on as best I could.

It wasn't an easy conversation.

8

To the great relief of some nine billion inhabitants of Earth, the First Contact with our new friends was surprisingly peaceful. After all those many weeks of worry and speculation about lights in the skies and rumors of alien ships or time travelers or tricks by the Chinese, it was with some relief that my sweep of this Twoclicks character seemed to show a being more interested in communication than conquering. Good thing, given the technology that had allowed them to engage in those weeks of hide-and-seek and false images, topped off by the incredible ability to enter Earth's atmosphere undetected until the ships appeared in varous shallow-water sites around the globe. They didn't destroy us. No attacks, no death rays, none of the fictional horrors that we'd read about or seen since H. G. Wells and early Hollywood came to pass.

And for reasons I couldn't fathom, it had been arranged that I'd be the first to not only transmit live images of the ships in orbit, but now their landing and, most incredibly, the emergence of the short, dumpy, porpoise-like alien who wore a smile and spoke with a sibilant lisp.

Within an hour the rest of the world had caught up, as some of the few other sweepers and hundreds of edited-media reporters got to meet their own S'hudonni in the Mediterranean near Cassis on the Cote d'Azur, Hong Kong's Repulse Bay, Jakarta Bay, Arcadia Bay in the Black Sea, and other places. But I got a lot of play for having been first—again!—and my sweep numbers jumped to nearly a million. Sweeping was growing fast but still new, so probably every receiving set on the planet was tuned in to me there at some point.

This was great, and some advertising revenue kicked in from the aggregators and IICAP, and that was nice to see. But the truth was, since not many people had sweep reception sets, what most of the world saw and heard was the replay of my live encounter, without all the sensory contacts. It was just sight and sound, but at least it was mine. I hoped that meant more people were ponying up the money for an introductory sweep reception kit. Soon, soon, soon, I hoped, I'd be the first real star to come from sweeping. One could dream.

Fifteen long hours after that first encounter I'd been allowed to go home, with the local police and some hired guards surrounding my house to keep the craziness away long enough for me to sleep. But, no surprise, sleep was hard to find. Instead I kept the house dark and quietly snuck onto my deck, looking into the darkness of the Gulf of Mexico on a moonless night. Somewhere out there, west and a little south, was the ship that been shimmering at me for weeks. And on that ship, surely, was this Twoclicks character and Heather. What else did I know about the ship, our visitors from wherever, their motivations for coming to the Gulf Coast of Florida, their height and weight and aspirations to conquer us or to welcome us to some great galactic federation or to subjugate us and make slaves of us or to hunt us for sport or to serve man by preparing us as food?

I didn't know much of anything, and that's what I'd been saying in response to all the questions for hours, ever since our new friends had gone back to their ship and I'd left Egmont Key and come home, leaving Tom to his newfound fame as the scientist who'd been there when that first alien had risen from the shallow waters of the Gulf of Mexico.

The media had talked to me and to Tom out at the Egmont Key site, and when we finally left the key, hours later, they wanted to talk to us more. We decided to split up and each head home to hope for some quiet, but I knew he was as barraged as I was by messages and interview requests once he got home.

I did my best, even coming out to the beach in front of my house three different times to talk to actual live newsies and a great gaggle of cloud bloggers and, lo and behold, a dozen sweep competitors. And then it finally petered out around 1 A.M. and the hired guards and the local island police promised to keep everyone away for a bit. I'd even told myBob to shut down and shut up, please, and he'd understood and closed himself with an audible click to let me know he was quiet.

So there was finally some peace and quiet for me, and I hoped that Tom had found some, too. I sat in a folding chair at the back of the deck, listening to the polite murmur of the shore-break a hundred meters to my west as the Gulf rolled in. You can hear the new spyeyes the edited media use—their rotors whir like angry mosquitoes to float them around—but I couldn't hear a single one for the first time in all those long hours. It was quiet, the sea breeze schussing through the palm trees, the wavelets against the sand, and the crinkle of the retreating water over the shells of a thousand tiny, dead coquina.

I had a glass of cheap wine in my hand: pinot grigio with ice cubes in it for this hot night. It was my fourth tall glass in the last half hour or so as I tried to sort things out and get some idea of what to do next.

There was a rustling in the hyacinths and azaleas that lined the boardwalk that led from my back deck, over the protective sand dunes, and then down onto the beach. The boardwalk was overgrown and I liked it that way, shady and cool on even the hottest days as I walked to the beach.

More rustling and then I could hear the pad of bare feet on the wood of the boardwalk and then, just below me on the path, smiling up at me, was Heather. Fresh from a little swim in from that ship, she was beautiful in that thin moonlight with the hyacinths wreathing her. No, more than beautiful—stunning. Slim hips, muscular legs and arms, those breasts, that face, those eyebrows, that wet hair framing that wonderful face. Damn.

"Hello, Peter," she said, and smiled. "Can I come up?"

I laughed. "I think you can pretty much do whatever you like." And I meant that in every way you could imagine.

She walked over to the steps, grabbing a beach towel from the line as she walked by it, then wrapping herself in the towel as she climbed the stairs, tucking it tightly between her breasts to make it tight. She sat down in the chair opposite mine. She smiled.

"So you're one of them," I said.

"I am. But I'm still me, Peter. You know what I mean?"

"I know what you're saying, Heather—that can't be your real name, can it?—but that's not true. You're not you. Not the you I thought I knew. Not the you I made love with."

"Sure I am. I'm all of those things. I'm all of those things and more."

"It's the 'more' that's the problem, Heather. I saw a shark in the water near me and then I saw you, standing there." I remembered something that Twoclicks character had said. "And your boss, your colleague, your whatever-it-is, said something about your being a creation, a sort of machine, something capable, he said, of 'great changes.'"

"Aren't we all capable of great changes, Peter? Haven't you made great changes in your life?"

"I'm not a shark, damn it, Heather. And I'm not some visitor from another planet."

She stood up, used her towel to dry her hair, and then came over to stand next to me. "Peter, we made love. We found something in each other, didn't we? Wasn't that real for you? Wasn't it wonderful?" She reached down to take my hand. "It was for me. I've changed because of what we found in each other, Peter."

Sure, I thought. Right.

And then she tugged me up and out of the chair to stand next to her. And then we walked inside and shut the glass doors, stood there in the darkness, looking out toward the Gulf.

She closed the curtains and stood there by my bed, still holding my hand. "Peter," she said, "I want to see if that was real, what we found."

My god, what a day. My head was spinning. I'd seen what I'd seen, hadn't I? But here she was, Heather Newsome. I'd fallen hard for her, though she'd been my brother's lover. And now it was even more complicated, yes, but . . .

She leaned over and kissed me on the cheek, then the lips. And I responded. That simple, really: I responded. I wanted to make love to her. I wanted to be with her. Despite everything. Despite the dangers and the worries. Despite Tom. Despite it all.

The kiss ended. She reached up to run her finger down my cheek, from below the eye to the jawbone, over toward my lips, touching the lips, pushing the lower lip down a bit, reaching up to kiss me again. Incredible. I was bursting, dizzy, barely able to stand, and so, I swear, I needed her help as she turned us away from the doors and led us through the master bedroom to the far side of the room and the bed and then, slowly, slowly, onto that bed and from there to places so pleasurable I lost myself in them.

There would be a price to pay for this, I thought, dreamily. God, it might be awful. Was it worth that risk? Yes, oh yes.

I knocked on Tom's door. myBob had warned me that he couldn't reach Tom's helpmate, and that Tom, in fact, seemed to have turned off all his electronics. It was eleven in the morning and the house was shuttered tight, the blinds drawn shut, the place still.

It hadn't been easy getting here without any of the media—citizen journos and the edited-media types, both—catching on that I'd left my own place and come across Boca Pass to my brother's. Now I wanted in before someone figured out that the man in the county police uniform knocking on Tom's door was actually me using a trick I'd just learned from my brother. I knocked a second time, a sharper rap, longer. "Tom," I yelled. "C'mon, man, answer the door."

I could hear spyeyes whirring behind me. They were expensive—at least the ones with enough power for extended flight were expensive—so that meant the edited media. I needed to get inside and get the windows shut and then talk to my brother, privately.

It had been a rough morning. myBob had pinged me awake at 5 A.M., insistent that I get out of bed. "You have messages," he said.

Heather was gone, back out to the ship before daylight, I guessed, and totally undetectable by the media keeping an eye on me, I was sure. She'd left a handwritten note on the nightstand.

I picked it up and started to unfold and read it. "I thought I turned you off last night," I said to myBob. "Why are you waking me?"

"The home alarm pinged me out of hibernation, and once I'd taken care of that I had a conversation with Heather, who left a message with me for you."

"Along with this handwritten note?"

"Yes, in addition to that note," myBob said.

I got the note open and read it: "Dearest Peter," it read in a very nice hand. "You were wonderful. See you later today." And she signed it "H."

"What's going on, myBob?" I asked. "Why leave a message with you, too?"

"Your brother was here last night, Peter."

"What? How?"

"He had help from the police guarding his house. He was dressed as a police officer. He arrived here at two forty-seven A.M. and knew the entry code."

"Oh, my god."

"There was nothing I could do, Peter."

"He saw Heather here?"

"She was awake. She took him downstairs and they talked."

"Why didn't you wake me, myBob? I should have been the one doing the talking."

"Heather said it was important that you sleep. That it was dangerous to wake you."

"What the hell?"

"Tom left a message with me for you. Should I play it?"

I walked over to my desk, touched open the smarty, said "Sure," and watched.

Tom was sitting in a tall chair at my kitchen counter, looking into the cam on his smarty.

"You're a fucking monster," he said. "I can't believe. Cannot. Believe. It. My big brother."

He ran his fingers through his hair. "I thought we were in this together, Peter. Jesus."

He reached down and turned the smarty so I could see Heather. Turned it back. "You. Her. Jesus, I don't know what to say."

"Tom," I heard Heather say.

"No!" he said, angry. "Just no!"

"Tom. You need to listen to me for a minute," Heather said, off camera.

"No!" he said. "I don't want to talk to you about this, Heather. And you, Peter. Fuck you. I don't want to see you ever again. I don't want to fucking know you. I'm going home. Don't call me. Don't come over. I don't want to see you again. Ever. You got that? Ever."

He slumped in the chair and started to sob, his chest heaving and the pain of the all of it, of everything, bubbling out of him in gasps and anger and sorrow and fury.

Then he gathered himself. Sat up. Stared at the cam. "All right," he said. "All right. All right." And he began to rise from the chair and said "Off!" to his helpmate and the screen went blank.

I tried knocking a third time, more fist than knuckles this time, the door rattling a bit with my pounding. Nothing. I needed to see my brother.

Then a voice, tired, from inside. "Pete?"

"Yeah, Tom, it's me. I'm here. Let me in, all right, it's already getting hot out here."

The door opened. I was expecting the worst and got it. He was in his underwear, a plain white T-shirt on over boxer shorts. He smelled of vomit and alcohol. He looked like hell.

"Oh, Tom," I said.

He waved at me. "Don't give me that shit, Peter. You're not sweeping, right? No recording, nothing. No fucking electronics at all, right?"

"Right," I said. "myBob?"

"Off," said myBob, and I felt the click.

"All right, then," said Tom. "Come the fuck in. Find a seat. I felt pretty good a half hour ago and now I feel like shit again. I need some water and some more ibu."

I headed for the couch in the living room, which looked clean. I think he'd saved his debacle for the media room, back beyond the kitchen. I sat.

He had walked into the kitchen, came back drinking from a tall glass of water. He tossed a couple of ibuprofen down his throat, took more water, and then sat across from me, on the wing chair. The thing hardly got any use and he looked so frail and worn that I thought he might slide right off the cushion and onto the floor. "Tom," I said. "I'm sorry."

He waved again. "I'm sure, I'm sure. Jesus, Peter, how did you arrange that with her? Have you been in on this thing the whole time? That's how it looks from here. You, Heather, that fucking porpoise character: everyone setting up Earth for the big fall, and little Tom Holman is collateral damage."

"No, no, Tom. That's not how it's gone. I didn't know anything about what happened yesterday until it happened."

"Right, and me and the fucking Easter Bunny saved the Kemp's ridleys from extinction. Jesus." He sat back in the chair. "I'm a little better again. Man, my head is fucking pounding. I didn't know I could feel this shitty without really being sick."

"You're hung over, Tom."

He leaned forward, stared at me, managed a chuckle. "You know I'm an adult, right? That I'm twenty-eight years old, right? That I have a great education and a good job and used to have a bright future? That I don't need you helping me and defending me from your bully high-school friends anymore, right?"

"Yeah, Tom."

"I hated you then. Did you know that?"

"No."

"You and your fucking jock friends and all those pretty girls who teased me about being Pete's little brother and my being 'the brain' and all that? Until I got to college, school for me was one long, unadulterated humiliation. You and your fucking sports. Sports! Worthless crap! And they loved you. Everybody loved you."

"I didn't know it was that bad, Tom. Honest. I was trying to help. I wanted you to feel like you fit in. I wanted to make sure no one bullied you."

"Sure. Trying to help."

Tom reached over to an end table, grabbed a pack of Camels, pulled one out, lit it, took a long drag. "I miss Father," he said.

"Sure, Tom. Me, too."

"He was the glue that held us all together. You know that, right? He was like, like . . ." He rubbed his forehead with his left hand, took another long drag on the Camel with the right. "He was the only one I could trust. Not you. Not poor, fucked-up Kait, not Mom.

It was Father—he was the one person that I believed when he said something to me."

I thought of what I knew, but didn't voice it.

"You know he talked with me a lot toward the end, right?"

"I'm sure he did, Tom."

"He told me stuff. About Mom. About Kait."

I smiled. "And me?"

"I am feeling a little better, but this headache's a motherfucker." And he rubbed his forehead again, added "And here's the best part, Peter. He didn't say shit about you. You and all your fucking sports, all your free shots . . ."

"Free throws." I set the school record in those in college. Hit 96 percent of my free throws, thank you very much.

"Free throws," Tom said, and gave me a bitter little laugh. "Fucking free throws. Stand at a line and throw a ball through a hoop with a net at the bottom. And go to college for fucking free, and then go live in Europe and get paid a lot of money to just stand there and throw that ball toward that hoop with the net. Dumb as hell. Dumb as a brick."

"Sure, Tom."

"You were entirely off his scope. He'd given up. You know what he said to me, Peter?"

"No, Tom. No, I don't."

"He said he was proud of me. That was the night he died, that fucking bridge, that pickup truck, the rain. Just before they left my place to head home he put his arm on my shoulder and said, 'Thomas, son, I'm proud of you.'"

"That's great, Tom. That's really great."

Tom took one final drag on the Camel and crushed it out in the ashtray. He stood up, and so I stood up with him. He shook his head, trying to clear the cobwebs, maybe.

Then he stared at me. "He was honest, Peter, that's the thing. He told the fucking truth. You know what that is? The truth?"

I did, but said nothing.

"Fuck you!" he said, hard. Then again, "Fuck you."

He walked over to the door, opened it. "Get the fuck out of my house, asshole. This is goodbye, Peter. This is it. We're done. We're through, me and you. Get the fuck out and don't try to talk to me again. Ever."

"Tom," I said. "Tom, you don't need—"

"Fuck you, telling me what I do or don't need. Fuck. You."

"Tom," I tried one last time.

"Just go." He shook his head, pointed out the door. "Go, you lying fuck. You son-of-a-bitch. Asshole. Fucker. You fucked her, you fucker."

I didn't say anything. About Heather, or Father, or Kait, or Mom, or what I knew and what I couldn't say. None of that. I just walked out the door and Tom slammed it behind me and I heard one good last "Fuck you" through the closed door and that was that for me, and for Tom.

PART TWO

THE GRAND TOUR

Seek Truth and Report It.

—Guiding Principle, Society of Professional
Journalists Code of Ethics

9

I recall all of this as if it happened yesterday.

I woke from my nap with Heather on top of me, staring into my eyes with that strange, reflective half-smile that was such a puzzle to me then. Everything was supposed to be back to how it bad been before my surgery—my "installation," as the surgeon had called it with a smile—before I'd seen what I'd seen in the shallow waters of the Gulf of Mexico, before I'd spent that day in Palo Alto with Chloe.

She was beautiful, was Heather. Perfection. Her face above me, her body pressing into mine. I'd been here before. I'd fallen so hard I'd hurt myself, and my brother. But now, knowing what I knew, there were changes.

"I'm not getting a rise out of you?" Heather asked, and reached down to touch me and confirm that. Ironic, I thought, that she'd ended her sentence with a question mark.

"I don't know," I said. "Maybe I'm still jet-lagged?" and laughed at myself, thinking of question marks and Chloe. I'd arrived earlier that morning in Dublin after the long, long overnight flight from Palo Alto, and I *was* jet-lagged, the feeling made all the worse by the long limo drive from the airport to our quiet retreat in the middle of County Tipperary.

"It's all right, Peter," she said, leaning down to kiss me. "I know this is all very strange for you. Don't worry about it." And she moved off to the side of the bed, put her feet down, and stood. "You'll be fine in a day or two, I'll bet."

"Sure," I said, and added, "I'm sorry."

"It's fine. I can tell you're still getting used to the implants. I followed your recovery closely, you know."

"The doctors gave you updates?"

"Something like that," she said. "I know it's been hard, but it had to be done, and now, as you recover from that, we really need you up and running as soon as possible."

"The docs said I was ready. I mean, I think I am. Watch." And I gave thought to the light switch on the wall in our hotel. I pictured it, I reached out to it, I gave it that mental nudge and—voila!—the light in the room came on.

Heather laughed. "That's what we get for all that money?"

I smiled back at her. "That's it. That's all I got."

She reached down to take my hand, that strong grip grabbing me firmly, and pulled me to my feet. "OK, Peter. Let's get to work today, starting now, so we can get you past those Palo Alto doldrums."

In Palo Alto a couple of weeks before, I had, in fact, been in the doldrums—lonely and isolated and worried—as I'd been getting prepped the day before the scheduled implants. Only Kait and her spouse Sarah had been there for support. Or worry. I was the object of their concern. Did I really want to do this? This wasn't a new tattoo or an imbedded wristpod or a new kind of digital lens for my right eye; this was brain surgery. There were risks. Was I sure? Really sure?

I was. You don't look a million dollars' worth of gift horse in the mouth. Heather had offered the surgery to me a month ago as we came in from a very disturbing morning swim in the Gulf of Mexico. In the water there'd been some kind of test that I hadn't known I was taking, and I'd passed it. She held my hand. She offered me a most interesting future. I said yes.

She'd wanted a swim. There were media spyeyes buzzing around but she'd said not to worry, that what they were seeing wasn't us. I didn't bother asking how that was done. Those questions never got answers.

So we'd stripped, the two of us, left it all on the deck, including myBob and all my sweep equipment, and I grabbed my goggles from the nail on the stairs as we walked down and then took the boardwalk out to the beach and into the water, warm even in November.

I'd spent a lifetime swimming in the Gulf in this very spot, running from the house out over the wooden boardwalk and down onto the hard-packed sand and then running and diving into an oncoming wave. I belonged here. This was my place. I was as comfortable in this water as a human could get.

And then there was Heather, who looked so wonderfully like one thing but was most definitely another. Or both.

She dove in right behind me. Beautiful and very human. We swam alongside each other for a few moments and then . . . well, it was not a pretty picture, watching her change from the one thing to the other. I'd seen it happen just a few days before, when she and Twoclicks arrived along with those sea turtles. But that had been in the middle of chaos—turtles everywhere, Tom shouting at me, me trying to capture him and the turtles on video. Then, the sharklike thing I'd seen in the water, blurring and morphing while the water rippled and tiny wavelets hid from my sight what was happening. And then suddenly Heather, my Heather, standing there.

That was stunning. Here, seeing it happen with no distractions, watching it, hearing it, being in the water next to it, was another thing entirely. Underwater at first, I could hear crackling noises, a kind of tearing. What the hell? So I surfaced and there was something terrible rolling and writhing just below the surface, not two meters from me. Heather. Changing. Snapping and rippling going on—terrible sounds of bones breaking and skin tearing apart and re-forming, the soft pops of tendons and cartilage letting go—and then, finally, settling into something sleek and blue-gray and utterly at home as it nosed into the next wave and then turned and came back and an eye, her eye, peered at me as it, as she, approached and a small fragile hand extended and I took it and off we went, hand in hand, into the deeper water.

The swimming was surreal. Even now I can hold my breath for two minutes or more; then, in much better shape, I could manage three. We went deep, down fifteen meters or more, and circled around a large rock mound, pockmarked and covered with seaweed and a few struggling corals. Fish were gathered around it, small pinfish and some sheepshead and trout and one large redfish watching over some mullet. Suddenly the creature whose hand I was holding let go of me and swept in. Eating. Pinfish in a panic; sheepshead, though quick and sly, engulfed; a mullet gone into that hungry maw. Only the big redfish escaped.

I watched in amazement, and some fear. The whole process was thirty seconds, no more, and then she, it, was back with me and again we held hands and we rose to the surface so I could breathe, and wonder, and worry.

A few minutes later, when we came back in, the creature, the alien, Heather, was beside me and then, once the water was knee-deep, came again that crackling and tearing and things I couldn't really watch and then it was her, in all her human beauty, walking hand in hand with me back through the shallow water and up onto the beach, where we turned around to sit down on the sand and I took off my goggles as we looked out to the Gulf and there, in the distance, nearly more than a kilometer away, that great ship of hers and Twoclicks', standing there, serene on its spindly legs. The size of a five-story building, perched on those stilts, quiet, absolutely unapproachable, we'd learned. Waiting.

We sat there until I finally spoke. "I didn't know. I suppose it hadn't really occurred to me." I paused, wondering if I should even ask, but then did. "I suppose that's the real you. The one out there? This one here, the one sitting next to me, is the fake?"

She squeezed my hand. "I'm real. This me is real, Peter. But you had to know that other one is real, too. And others. I'm changeable, Peter. I am who I need to be. What I need to be. It's important that you know that."

"Does Twoclicks do that, too? Does he change forms? Is that him walking our way right now?" I nodded toward a beach walker headed our way, splashing in the shore-break.

"No. He is what he is. He doesn't change. He can't change. He hasn't, in hundreds of your years."

Hundreds of my years. I nodded. I got it. This was all a reminder of who was in charge.

Heather reached over to take my hand in hers. "We have something we'd like you to do, Peter. So you won't have to worry about things like going for a swim with your sweep gear on." And she stood, helped me up to my feet, held my hand as we walked back to the boardwalk and up the wooden stairs and into the bedroom, media spyeyes buzzing by all the time but none of them interested in us.

There we spent the rest of the day doing what we did. Somewhere along the line she explained what would be happening to me, for me, over the next few weeks, while she and Twoclicks went on a diplomatic tour, meeting with world leaders—building bridges, as she put it. Right. And then came the long, delicious night as I forgave her and forgave myself and wondered if I was doing the right thing.

The next morning the limo arrived and took me to the little-used St. Petersburg airport and a private jet and a long flight in comfort and worry, headed toward Palo Alto, California, the beating heart of the tech industry and the center of the universe for BCI. Brain Computer Interface. My brain. My hardware in my brain. My software in my hardware in my brain.

There was, a couple of days later, a five-hour surgery that turned into eight, but no sweat, no big deal, there were some complications, some additional hardware and a lot of software to load; but everything went fine and I'd stay in the hospital for a night or two to make sure there was no infection, no reaction, no problems, you know? Oh, and then there'd be another couple of weeks or more to practice using these new wonders. Mr. Sweep all the way, that was me. A million-dollar surgery. Mr. Radio Wave. Think it and it obeys. Think my thoughts to myBob, who hears and then obeys. Think the room lights on and they are. Think the smarty on and it is. Think. Think. Think of the possibilities!

I was lost in all of this as I lay in my hospital bed the long, boring day after the surgery. For one thing, there was no myBob for now. He'd be returned when the docs thought I was ready for that. His hardware was sitting in there somewhere, tiny, harmless. His software, his self, wasn't yet loaded. So I was lonely. I thought about contacting Chloe but I didn't know how to do that except through myBob. Call her publicity agent on some ancient mobile phone? I didn't see how I could do that without word getting out about what I was having done. Second, we'd have to keep it very private if Chloe came to visit and I wasn't sure if Chloe—or me, for that matter—was ready for that next step, even if we could keep it out of the newsfeeds. And there was Heather, in her various guises, to think of, too. Was Chloe any kind of good idea? Surely not.

So thank god Kait and her spouse Sarah had come to visit with me and get me through the crises of faith and morals and headaches and heartaches and worry and fear as I learned in the next few weeks how to get to know the new me.

I got better. A few days with Kait and Sarah and I had it under some control. I checked out of the neurology institute and went to the apartment they had ready for my convalescence. Two large bed-rooms, a kitchen and a sitting room and a very welcome balcony, looking out over University Avenue and the strolling techs of Palo Alto. Sunshine and cool breezes in mid-November.

On the first day in that apartment I sat with strong coffee and Kait on the balcony while Sarah went grocery shopping. I'd begged for comfort food for lunch and dinner, sandwiches from the Peninsula Grill for the noon meal and pasta primavera for dinner. Sarah, thank god, loved to cook. Me, I sat with Kait out on the balcony, my face to the sun after the days of hospital gloom, and we talked.

"I've been meaning to ask," Kait finally got around to saying after a lot of nothing about the weather and the hospital's food and how much we both liked Palo Alto, "can you feel anything in there?" And she reached over to gently tap me on the skull. My head was shaved and there were marks all over the skull: small purple arrows and circles and five dots, the sites of the entry points, where the probes had gone in. Afterward, they'd stared at their screens and asked me questions. Feel any wetness? How about fear? What about heat? What about cold? What about anger? How about lust? Does this feel good? Feel bad? Let's try this: Is it love?

That, for hours, until they found the right spots to insert the hardware. Then hours more for that insertion. Kait had watched it all on the special flatscreen in the smaller waiting room.

"No," I said. "It's nothing. Like it never happened, except that I can remember every second of it."

Kait sipped on her coffee. "I don't know how you could do it, Petey. I mean, I know they paid you a lot for this, and you'll be famous—*more* famous—now with this, this stuff, in your head. But it just seems crazy to me. Like you're taking this huge risk. And you were always the one who was levelheaded, you know? The straight arrow? Star jock and college scholarships and A grades and then off to Europe. I mean, god, I was so proud of you for keeping your life sane when mine was so, so, crazy."

We had been on a different set of train tracks in those years, for sure. I'd decided I wanted to be a sportswriter and broadcaster if playing basketball professionally didn't work out, and the only way to do that at my small college was to be an English major, so I found myself reading John Donne and Jane Austen and Stephen Crane and Robert Louis Stevenson and Thoreau and Emerson and Melville and Karen Joy Fowler and Walter M. Miller and many more, classics all. I had to wade through them before they'd let me touch the camera equipment and the editing room, and it turned out I enjoyed Mary Shelley and Conrad and Dickens and Cooper and Defoe and the Brontës and on and on.

I was happy, reading and writing papers and then short stories and playing basketball. I wound up in the lit sequence instead of the media sequence. It was four years of heaven, really. Easy and fun. And then six more of fun and pleasure after that, playing basketball and living in Dublin. Hard work, sure, staying in shape and grinding through a seventy-game season. But it paid the bills and, really, I had a blast.

As opposed to what Kait went through in those years. A hellish decade for her. Whatever had driven her to be so self-destructive had almost ruined her; but she'd found her way through it and now here she was, sitting with me and perfectly normal with her coffee and her spouse and her worry over her big brother's crazy idea about putting all that technology right inside his head. "How stupid was that?" she said she was thinking while she watched the surgery. I couldn't blame her.

Then as she was taking a sip of her coffee Kait's smarty dinged and she read the message, old-school. Her face brightened into a happy grin. "Hey, big brother, I have some news for you. Chloe and I have been in touch about you, and she's decided to come up here this coming weekend on the bullet. She says hi, and asks if she can stay a couple of nights and then go back on Monday." Kait laughed. "And she says it's all very private. No one except the few of us will know. She says you won't even know who she is when she gets off the train."

Well, that brightened my day, or confused it. But, "Great!" I said, "tell her I'll meet the train and I'll bet her a lunch in town that I notice her right away." I rubbed my bald and marked-up head. "Tell her she'll have no trouble at all recognizing me."

Kait was old-schooling, typing that message. She sent it, then laughed when the ding came back in seconds. "You're on for that bet. She'll be here for lunch on Saturday. But now she's back to work—they're shooting an episode of the new show."

Well, how great was that? Chloe Cary coming up my way on the bullet train. A couple of days with Chloe, with no sweeping and no contracts. I decided that sounded wonderful.

And it was, starting with my standing behind the barrier on the platform at the station when the BSC Bullet came right on time into Palo Alto, braking down from 250 kph to a dead stop in just over a mile.

I'd walked to the station from my condo, and that experience had been surreal. And ironic. Here I was with more hardware installed inside my head than probably anyone else on Earth and yet I was totally disconnected from the clouds while everything healed. my-Bob was stored elsewhere; my Todos Sentidos hardware was sitting on my countertop in the condo's kitchen, useless since the install; my access to the clouds was blocked until I could safely handle the internals on my own; and I was spending my time learning to take mental baby steps all day long. In my morning session they'd told me I might be close to ready. They'd been teaching me how to call up the visual screen, a sort of window, that floated in front of me, showing me whatever the hell I wanted it to if only I could get a grip on my mental aim. It was a case of how to think and how to not-think and I wasn't very good at that yet, though the docs and the rehab people swore I was doing fine. Sure. Fine. What screen?

So I bumbled along on the long walk from the condo on Fulton Street west along Lytton to Alma and then over a few blocks to Embarcadero and then through the tunnel to El Camino Real and the bullet station. Sounds simple enough, but without that constant reassuring whisper from myBob to say when to turn left and when to go straight and when to cross the road and when not to, it all felt strange and lonely. Like back home at the beach when he'd flaked out on me, I found I could barely function without him.

I also found it interesting that I was about the only person walking the streets whose eyes and ears and vocal cords weren't otherwise occupied. Everyone was listening or talking with someone else through the clouds as they walked, alone or even with others. Some of them were gesturing as they swiped their floats to the next screen so they could get caught up on the latest news or, more likely in Palo Alto, see what app or conn the competition had just come up with. No one was alone with their thoughts as they walked, except me. It must always be like this, I realized, and I'd simply never noticed.

I got lost twice, but finally made it to the station and then fumbled my way through the float sign that promised the train was on time and would be there in fifteen minutes, and then sat down and did nothing—nothing—for those fifteen minutes while I waited.

Finally it was there, and the doors whooshed open and out came a quiet crowd of tech types, a few overdressed businesspeople in those retro gray suits that were all the rage with that crowd, and then one small, quiet woman wearing an LA Galaxy ball cap, cheap sunglasses, a plain Dodger-blue hoodie, and blue jeans. She took off the glasses when she saw me and I smiled to see those eyes and that smile as she ran over to give me a hug. I hugged her back. It was good to see her.

Chloe Cary. Here she was, the star of *The Family Madderz*, sneaking away from her Hollywood handlers to spend a little honesty time with me. No spyeyes, no attention, just the two of us with Kait and Sarah.

She had a small bag slung over her shoulder and I took that from her and we started out of the station and down the street.

"We're walking, Peter?"

"No tech, right? So no one can find us. So no cars unless we can find one old enough."

She put her ball cap back on, and the sunglasses, and put her arm through mine, said, "I like it," and smiled at me. "myBetty wasn't too happy, though, I have to tell you. I shut her down a couple of hours ago at home and left her on the kitchen table. You know, lots of pissing and moaning about how dangerous this was."

Not a question mark in sight in what she said. This was the real Chloe. I laughed at the irony of that as I tried to steer us past the station parking lot and down a ramp to the tunnel underneath the tracks. Part of me was talking and happy. The other part didn't want to mess up this nice walk by getting us lost. "This tunnel, then across to Alma, then left and a long walk to Lytton and then right to Fulton and we'll be home safe and sound," I said, holding her hand. "But I'm navigating without any help here, all right? So don't be surprised if we get lost."

She smiled at me, took off the ball cap, shook out her hair, then pulled it back into a ponytail as we walked, wrapping it with a hair tie pulled from her pocket. Everyday. Normal. Girl walking with boy.

We turned too early and wound up on University Avenue, the streets packed on a warm November Saturday. No one noticed that I was holding hands with Chloe Cary, television star and the girl on the cover of *The Hollywood Reporter*. Party girl, wild child, star-gazer with that lucky sweepcast jock who couldn't possibly last as her boyfriend.

We stopped at Joya and sat down for a drink and some tapas on the outdoor patio. Still just the two of us, unnoticed. Chloe wasn't wearing any makeup, and had her hair tied back in that ponytail, and was wearing those sunglasses; and the cumulative effect of that was that no one noticed her.

But I did. "Chloe," I said, "you look great."

She laughed. "You don't mind me walking around town without the makeup and the wild hair?"

Not mind? "You're terrific," I said. "I feel like I'm finally meet-ing the real you."

She took a sip of her water. "I've been thinking about you a lot, Peter. I wanted to come up here and say that to you privately, face-to-face."

Privately? "What a concept!" I said, and smiled back at her. "I know it was crazy, that last night in L.A.; but it was great get-ting to know you better. Know the real you, I mean."

"Exactly," she said. And she reached over to take my hand. "Look, we live crazy lives, you and me. Two lives, really: the one for the public and then, over in the corner, the real one."

"The one that matters," I said.

She blushed. "Yes, the one that matters."

Well, all right, then. I liked Chloe; I liked her a whole lot. But we were teetering on the edge of a precipice here, young Chloe and I. "So we're serious about this, you and me? You could be serious about someone as old as me? I have to be ten or twelve years up the road from you, Chloe."

Another sip of water. Another smile. "Look close, Peter. Look around my eyes." And she leaned forward. Beautiful.

"I don't get it. What am I looking for, Chloe?"

"Wrinkles, Peter. Signs of aging. Can't you see them?"

"No," and I was telling the truth.

"Well, I'm older than you think I am. A good seven years older. Classic Hollywood bio, right?"

I shook my head. "I don't think that's possible in this day and age, Chloe. Anyone can find out anything. All the facts in the world are out there. Just ask your helpmate."

She sat back. "People believe what they want to believe—like that I'm twenty-three years old. Or that we're fighting, you and I, and about to break up."

"I saw that in the *Reporter*," I laughed. "Good ink for you, anyway."

She was waving at the server to get the check. We were leaving,

I realized. This was a good thing. "Yep, good ink. So let's break up in public, you and me, and make up in private, all right?"

"Right now?" I asked.

She laughed. I laughed. She tapped her phone on the check from the server to pay and we got out of there, holding hands and walking toward the condo. I wanted to know more of Chloe's truths. I wanted her to know mine.

A week later I stood in the small terminal at Hayward Executive Airport with Kait and Sarah to say my goodbyes. myBob was back and in full operation, so I could multitask like everyone else and watch the NBA highlights while I waited to board. Instead, I'd asked myBob to go dark for a few minutes while I talked with my sister and her spouse. They'd been wonderful, and I told them so. I needed them and they were there for me and I told them thanks. I hugged them both and thought maybe sister Kait and I were at the start of a new, good, long relationship that would carry us through the years. She was all better, I was convinced, and Sarah, charming and stern somehow at the same time, was a major part of that. "I love you, Sis," I said to Kait, and "Thanks so much, take care of her, and of yourself," I said to Sarah.

"Will you be talking with Tom?" Kait wanted to know.

I shook my head. "Not likely. He made it all very clear last time we talked. I made some mistakes and he's not going to forget that anytime soon."

She nodded. "I know. He can be bullheaded and angry, for sure."

"For sure," I said, and meant it.

"I haven't talked to him in years, Peter. I'll send him a message. See if I can break through. It'd be good for the three of us to get along, at least a little."

"You can try," I said. "But I'm not optimistic. Really, Tom and I are miles apart, Kait. I don't see how it can heal."

"We'll see. It couldn't hurt to try."

"OK, then," I said, and hugged her again, and hugged Sarah, and turned to walk through the double doors and out toward my plane, headed to Dublin. On that long flight I had myBob tell me all about the surgery that, it turned out, had changed us both. I asked him and then, as he was in my head explaining, I tuned him out, thinking instead about that last chat with my sister. There were as many lies as there were miles between my brother and me. I felt honest, and better, now with Kait. But it wasn't just Heather that lay between me and Tom; it was our father, that image looming. Dear old Dad. Tom adored his memory. I had other ideas about the old guy.

So here I was, the man with the million-dollar brain, standing at the window with a glass of the Dew of Kenmare in my hand and looking out to see all the various shades of green now that the rain had eased again and you could see the countryside through the ripples of the ancient glass on the tall, narrow window. There was someone out there, short and stocky, standing in the mist. The Irish, I said. Amazing how they'd learned over the thousands of years to just ignore the rain and get on with it, whatever it was.

Heather came up behind me, put her arms around me to give me a hug. Looked out the window herself. She laughed. "Thank you for this. It's Twoclicks out there, singing in the rain, I suppose. He's a child, really, isn't he? Playing in puddles?" She shook her head. "The great leader for a new Earth." And she turned to smile at me.

"A note of sarcasm, there?" I asked, and she reached up to touch my cheek, still smiling. "I like it, actually," she said. "He needs a break. I was surprised he admitted it, but I'm glad he did. And I'm glad you knew the right people in the right place to get away for a day or two."

I hadn't done much, really. One call, live comm, to Sean O'Reilly at Ballina House, a place I'd stayed before, and things had happened. Yes, just like that. Twoclicks had been unhappy and now he was happy and the hell with the rain, life was sunnier.

"Nothing but meetings and dinners and always he has to be gracious," Heather was saying. "Coming here and seeing reality for a few days, letting Two see how you really live and play. What you do. How you do it. What your lives are like. It's wonderful, Peter." And she looked up and I looked down and we kissed, briefly.

She pulled back. "We need to do this everywhere we go. Get away for a day or two. Thank you for setting this up. The real thing." She looked out the window and there was that bulbous body, arms outstretched to the rain, standing on the front lawn, enjoying himself.

"It's just rain," I said, thinking of how much of that I'd seen in my five years of life in Ireland. Plenty. "I'm sorry I wasn't along for all of that. It must have been interesting, all those heads of state bowing and scraping and worrying about Twoclicks, and about you."

"I'm nothing to them," she said, "and I'll keep it that way. They think I'm a staffer and nothing more."

I looked out the window. Twoclicks stood there, alone in the mist. As I watched, the arms finally came down and he turned around to walk back toward the manor.

"myBob searched you and found a whole history for you," I said. "High school in New Jersey, Dartmouth for college, some public relations work back in New York. How do you do that? No one's caught on? No one's dug in to it to see if that history is real?"

"No one cares, Peter. There's a whole gaggle of us, standing around, bringing water to the front table, setting up the technology, opening doors. Plus," she shrugged, "I'm very boring, right?"

"Twoclicks would like to meet with you both," myBob interrupted. "He's drying off and will meet you in the library."

Heather was walking toward the armoire, where she'd hung up her clothes. She'd received the message, too. "Five minutes?" she asked me, giving me a glance. "He says it's important."

"Sure," I said, and headed toward the bathroom to splash some water on my face and clean up a bit. Important? What might Twoclicks think was important? A private meeting with the Irish Taoiseach or the British prime minister, or, as was the case just yesterday, Heather had told me, an exciting new kind of ice cream that he hadn't tasted before. Still, when the boss calls, you get moving.

The day had started with my being met by a limousine at Dublin Airport and then driving across half of Ireland to a small village in County Tipperary and joining Heather and Twoclicks at Ballina House, three centuries old and stately. We were the only guests. I'd arranged it midair, somewhere over Canada, when I'd gotten the request from Heather for someplace quiet and I'd told her I knew just the spot.

All of this was done quite privately, the spyeyes buzzing around but seeing nothing, Heather's technology altering their view so that the edited media didn't even know that Heather and Twoclicks had left the Shelbourne Hotel and headed west. The digital news solos were just as clueless. The edited media and the solos both trusted their technology to keep them tuned in. Bad idea. By the time they all got up for breakfast the three of us had met at Ballina House and were settling into our rooms, ignoring the light rain to go for a walk on the spacious grounds and look for some rumored red deer, and then coming in when the rain hardened.

Inside, later, we sat in chairs in the library room, drank whiskey, and admired the manor's stunning collection of books, including several signed Yeats first editions and the same for Synge and for Shaw and for Lady Gregory. There was even a signed *Dubliners* from Joyce. Incredible stuff, really, and perfect for us to admire with the turf fire going in the fireplace, the tea and the coffee, and the whiskey with an "e." Very aristocratic, we were.

I used my new hardware to record it all, sweeping it up, from the moment the limo met me at the airport, to walking in the damp woods with their brooding and damp sessile oaks, to looking closely at the centuries-old wainscoting and other details of the old library in the manor, to talking to Heather all the while and, once or twice, chatting briefly with Twoclicks. Most of it wasn't for public consumption yet; that was part of the contract. But myBob would pick out some highlights, get the OK from Heather to share those, and then store the rest in the clouds and back it all up on the hard drives I'd brought along with me. In a few months it would make for one terrific documentary.

It wasn't easy. Learning how to use the new implanted hardware and its software was heavy lifting, despite the weeks of training I'd had in Palo Alto. I thought I knew what did what, but half the time I got it wrong. Happily, it was all on my end. When I thought the right thing, the new hardware worked like a charm. The implants were working, myBob had quit complaining about them, and, he promised, those who bought the new receiving hardware would really be immersed in me, in what I was doing and what I was feeling. Everything, really, except my thoughts, and like the surgeon had told me, that wasn't far off. So I had to learn to control them. Funny how when the surgeon warned me of that I flashed back immediately to my Catholic youth. Pure thoughts, that's what this altar boy needed, good pure thoughts.

Of course, I still had some control issues. Until the thought control worked better—and that might take a month or two, they'd told me—my contact window in my right eye had to read my right hand waving around in front of it and put that together with the floater screen that seemed to drift along in front of me.

And now we were here, Heather and I, walking down the wide staircase from our room to the first-floor library. On the landing, halfway down, there was a large window that looked out toward the front of the property. Rain spattered against the old glass of Ballina

House. The view out this window was, I'd been told, a good one: the Bonechill Woods to the left, the River Shannon straight ahead as it curved past the manor. Tountinna, the tallest of the Arra Mountains, was in the distance behind, smaller hills to the right. All very nice, I supposed, on a day when you could see them. But that wasn't today here in County Tipperary.

I sipped on the drink I'd brought with me from the room as Heather led the way down the next flight, to the left, and along a long hallway to the library. Inside, there stood Twoclicks, wearing sandals, black shorts that ended halfway down those spindly legs, and a hooded rain slicker over his top half, the entire outfit glistening with moisture. He'd just come in from the rain and was pouring himself a glass of whiskey, the same stuff that had been up in my room: the Dew of Kenmare.

He sipped, then drank down half the glass. "Iss very tasty," he said.

Great. Just what I needed, a drunken alien to take care of. I looked at Heather, and she smiled and shook her head. "No," she said quietly, "the alcohol has no effect on him, Peter. He metabolizes most of it in minutes, and will eliminate the rest. Not to worry." And then she took the tumbler from my hand, still almost full, and sipped a bit of the Dew of Kenmare herself. A long sip. Another. She smiled. "Me, too," she said, and added, "It's very good, isn't it?"

I didn't know if she was making a statement or asking a question, but "It is," I said, and turned to see Twoclicks carefully sitting down on a large high-back chair, a small tote bag next to it. Good: If Twoclicks sat that meant I could, too, and I needed to—my left knee was aching in the rainy weather. There was another chair over by the window and as I headed that way, I looked out to see the gray falling onto the green. Pure Ireland: my knee aching in the rain. Just like that last painful year, when basketball had stopped being fun and started being painful. I'd walked away from the game, limping all the way.

There was a kind of jovial bark and laughter from behind me, and I turned to sit down even as Twoclicks sat stiffly upright. "Peter!" he said, holding up a bottle of the Dew. "Thiss iss what we have needed!" He lisped, though I wasn't convinced it was anything more than an affectation, something he did to seem less intimidating, more genial. Cute, even.

Heather took the bottle from his hands. "You like the whiskey, Two?" she asked.

"Yess!!" he cried. "Iss wonderful! Iss our answer!!"

I looked at Heather. "What was the question?"

She shook her head. "It's about profit, I'm sure. That's all he talks about lately with me, how to turn a profit from his territories."

She was wearing one of my T-shirts—"Dublin Rovers," it said in Celtic script across the front. I didn't recall actually giving that to her, but it was amazing how well it fit her once she'd slipped it on. She came over to stand next to me, putting a hand on my left shoulder, looking at me and smiling and then looking at Twoclicks, who was beaming. "This is what Two loves best, Peter: finding things that are special, unique to planets, to cultures. Those are the things that can be marketed to the other planets in The Six." She smiled, said, "Sorry, The Seven, probably, right?"

"Sure," I said, "The Seven," and wondered if I'd just committed Earth to being part of this empire or whatever it was. Laughable, that. "So it's all about sales?" After just a few hours of this diplomacy thing I was catching on fast to what really mattered.

"Yess!" the exuberant Twoclicks said. "Iss it exactly! Made by Earthiess, only in one small place. Aged in wood barrels. Local grains. Everything! Iss perfect!" And then he moved back to his chair and sank, slowly and heavily, into the padded cushion.

Heather walked to a sideboard behind the chairs and pulled out a clean tumbler. She came over to the small table and poured the tumbler full to the brim. Handed that to Twoclicks. He drank it down, straight and thirstily.

"Like I said," Heather murmured to me as Twoclicks held out the empty tumbler and she poured it full again. Rinse. Repeat.

Sitting wasn't helping the ache in my left knee. I stood up, walked over to the window, and slowly flexed the knee while I stared out at the rain. It was easing off. In the distance, to my right, I could finally see, dimly, the promised view of the mountain; and there was a hint of the River Shannon straight ahead. To the left were the woods and, there, a kind of glimmer over the wide expanse of lawn, and behind that, at the edge of the woods, some movement. A deer?

"See that?" I asked myBob. "Something there, in the air over the lawn where I'm looking now, and then in the woods. Something?"

"Let's look, Peter. Zoom in and I'll analyze."

"Zoom in?"

"Yep," myBob said. "It's a digital zoom, installed as part of our upgrade. The quality should be good, and I'll be able to tweak it for clarity. Let's give it a try, all right?" And before I could reply myBob did one of those things that myBob always seemed somehow able to do and zooming in I was, the woods coming close and blurring as they did and then, a second or so later, sharpening. Incredible.

And there was a deer, just inside the deep shadows of the woods, starting out toward the open grass. Nice set of antlers.

"Yes, a young male, roaming on his own, perhaps," myBob said, reading my thoughts; no surprise there. "So not really of interest, but it is good to know the zoom works so well, right? I'll pull back to normal."

"Right," I said, and watched, dizzy with it, as the zoom backed out and then "Stop!" I thought at him. "See that? That shimmer, wavy, likes heat waves rising off hot pavement." But there was nothing out there to cause that heat.

A touch on my shoulder: Heather's hand. "Twoclicks wants us to come with him into the town, Peter. The limo is waiting out front to take us to a local pub that the hotel owner says is very—how'd he phrase it?—authentic."

The shimmer was gone and myBob was silent. Heather was tugging me gently away from the window. I looked back. Nothing. And we headed toward the pub.

10

I loved my father. Really. A famous pediatrician, he was a man worth admiring, someone held in the highest regard by generations of families.

He was a serious guy, even taciturn. And he worked so hard at being the best possible doctor he could be that he wasn't home for most of my childhood. Tom and Kait and I were raised by Mom, who somehow found the time for us despite her own teaching career. But we knew, I knew, that Father was doing important things, saving young lives, keeping us and our friends healthy, wealthy, and wise.

I was proud to be his son. The money he made never really occurred to me. It wasn't about the money, it was about the work, the job, the service. I understood that he couldn't be at my high-school basketball and baseball games; he was far too busy. I recall moments from my personal sports history when I missed him: the buzzer beater against Central Catholic in the Sectionals, when I slipped past the screen to get open and drained a twenty-footer from deep in the corner as the clock wound down; the final strikeout that finished off a no-hitter against Boca Ciega.

Mom was there; Mom was always there. But Father had a job to do, in his office or at the hospitals or at the free clinic he ran. He was working hard and it was important and I knew it, even as I scanned the stands for him and smiled at, at least, seeing Mom there clapping for me.

In the spring of my senior year at Jesuit I was proud to be the ace of the pitching staff. I'd worked hard to get there. Pitching is the throwing of baseballs at certain speeds to certain spots to get particular results. I wasn't wise enough to realize it in those days, but the pitching of a baseball toward the plate is a wonderful physical act, a joyous expression of mind and body working as one, self-belief guiding the ball, self-confidence leading to physical control leading to success. I am many years and vast distances from my little beach town now, but I still enjoy grabbing my glove and a ball and walking outside into the cool mist of this time and this place to warm up and then pitch, throwing the ball against a wall that is 60 feet, 6 inches away, a strike zone painted on it. To the left of that strike zone, ten meters away, is a basketball rim and net and backboard, exactly 3.048 meters high. Ten feet. I shoot free throws and jump shots for an hour at a time when I feel the need. I have an endless supply of baseballs and basketballs, and these are the things that keep me sane.

I am very good at both things, and they are similar in that they require a unity of mind and body, a belief that the ball will go to the right place. I could shoot, that was my gift; and I could hit the catcher's mitt, could paint the corners, time after time.

On a warm early February high-school day in Florida I started my first home game of the season and threw a no-hitter as we beat Boca Ciega, 2–0. It was a Saturday-afternoon, seven-inning high-school game that didn't take even two hours to play. I'd walked one hitter when the ump blew a call, and my infielders had bobbled a couple of routine grounders over the course of the game, and so Boca Ciega had put some men on base. But they hadn't scored and

I'd pitched really well when it mattered the most so I was feeling good about myself, the team, the weather, and the hard slider I seemed to have mastered at last. Everything glowed.

Mom had watched, with Kait beside her in the rickety stands. Kait was in the early stages of her downward spiral then, suddenly mopey and angry and belligerent all at once; but she mustered a smile and a hug for me as I stood behind the dugout after the game. Mom was more expressive. She even commented that the hard work on the breaking ball was paying off. And then she and Kait headed to the mall, where Mom had some shopping to do and Kait planned to meet her friends. Tom was at the high school, in rehearsals for the spring play. He'd surprised us all by auditioning for and getting the role of Brutus in *Julius Caesar*.

So I decided to stop by and tell Father how I'd done. He was working, as ever. Saturday afternoon was his weekly visit to the free clinic he ran down on the Southside. It was a no-questions-asked clinic, where you could bring in your sick child without involving the national health system or putting your name into a database; so it was often busy.

I'd never been to the clinic before. I visited Father's main office on Gulf Boulevard every few weeks and so I knew the staff there and they knew me. Some of them would be at the clinic and I liked them all and they were, no surprise, nice to me and my siblings, so that was another reason to visit. Father, too, seemed to like it when his children dropped by, and since we didn't get to see him much otherwise we liked the chance to say hello. For a long time, we'd gone together, the three kids, being cute, no doubt. Then, as we'd gotten older and our schedules diverged, we came less often as a trio and came instead by ones or twos to get a free soft drink from the machine in the break room and to bask in the importance of being the children of Dr. Allan Holman, pediatrician extraordinaire. Kait, in recent months, had quit visiting entirely.

But I'd never been to the free clinic on a Saturday. There was no particularly good reason for this, other than the fact that Saturdays were mine for sports or the beach or reading or just hanging out with Tom, kayaking in the mangrove swamps near our house or snorkeling with the manatees or the porpoises. It never occurred to me to ask Mom to take me to the clinic to see Father. And in the couple of years since I'd acquired my driver's license I'd been busy constructing a life that now included girls and a growing circle of friends but didn't include driving to a rough part of town to visit Father as he dealt with the health issues that come to the children of poverty and violence.

So I'd never been to the clinic and didn't know what to expect, beyond the certainty that I'd see my father at work and get another chance to see Tracy, his receptionist.

Ah, Tracy Lowell. I was seventeen, you must remember as I admit these things. I had arrived at that point in time when a young man's fancy turns toward romance. I seemed to have erections all the time, and I fantasized about every attractive girl who smiled my way. Jesuit was an all-boys high school, but that hardly slowed down my interest in the opposite sex. I was the top scorer on the basketball team and the quarterback on the football team and the pitching ace on the baseball squad. All of that carried an attractive scent. I had dates every weekend with girls from the local public high schools or the Catholic all-girls school, Holy Innocents. The irony of that name, I should add, never occurred to me, as I met, liked, and fell in love with one girl after another. But I was one of those high-school boys who seemed to always wind up the friend of the prettiest girls, not the boyfriend. There wasn't much romance involved in my relationships, and I told myself that was fine.

And then there was Tracy, beautiful Tracy—the most beautiful, delightful, charming, sexy woman I'd ever seen. And she worked for my father.

Tracy had short, blond hair that framed the sides of her face. There were lighter streaks through the darker blond and it was, to the seventeen-year-old me, incredibly alluring. She was medium height and build, and I guessed that the breasts beneath that light blue smock she wore as the receptionist were perfect, as I pictured them in my hands. Her face was perfection, too: dark eyebrows over blue eyes and a small nose and a mouth that I was usually sure was saying something but couldn't hear the words for losing myself in those lips as they moved, opening and closing, over those perfect teeth and that tongue. I had wet dreams over that tongue.

And for all that, it was her smile, and her touching, that *really* did me in, starting with the first time I saw her, on a rainy day in August just before I started my junior year of high school. It was at Father's main office. With my new driver's license in my wallet it was my first time to drive to the ferry, take it across the pass and onto the mainland and to the Beach Medical Building, where, on the second floor, there was a nice big sign that said "Allan Holman, M.D., Pediatric Medicine," and a door to walk through so that, if one was the doctor's son, he could meet his father for lunch.

It was the week before school and I was going to meet Father, dash across the street in the rain to Woody's, on the water, where I'd order a grouper sandwich and hope I'd get enough cash or permission to use his credit app on my phone so I could do a little shopping, from the simplicity of Downboy jeans to the complexity of the preloaded touch text that Jesuit required all incoming juniors to buy (and to read *Middlemarch* on, for starters) before school began.

I opened the door and walked in and there, behind the receptionist window with the sign-in tab in front, was Tracy. Wow.

She smiled at me and the day was suddenly bright somehow as she said, "Hello, you must be Peter," and reached across the counter to shake my hand.

Her hand was cool to the touch, her grip firm, my imagination running wild as she hung on, I was sure, for a second too long before she said, "I'll let your father know you're here, Peter," and then smiled that smile and added, "It's great to meet you."

And then she got up to walk back toward the examination rooms and Father's office and I watched as she moved. Incredible. I was smitten, totally. I could feel the pressure in my blue jeans. It took considerable self-control to get that quieted down as Tracy came back and then ushered me into the back offices, where I sat in Father's office for ten minutes or so and tried very hard to think about baseball or basketball or school or anything-other-than-Tracy.

I didn't fool Father for a second. When the office door opened and he came in, he could see my flushed face and was kind enough not to notice how oddly I was sitting. I was embarrassed, but relieved. Incredibly, it seemed to me, he must have once been my age and wrestled with these same demons.

We took the back door out of the office and went down some steps, then through the side door of the building. Father, always prepared, opened his umbrella and we both stayed under it in the steady rain as we walked across the street to Woody's and got inside and out of the rain. There'd be no outside deck for lunch today. The deck sat over a seawall and Shark Pass and the open Gulf was beyond; but today we stayed inside and ordered lunch. A grouper sandwich for me and a shrimp Caesar salad for Father. Two iced teas, please, too.

While we waited for the food, Father cleared his throat. He had something to say.

"Son, you're old enough now for a little father-son chat about women, don't you think?"

"Is this Mom's idea, Father? She's been asking how I'm doing a lot lately."

He smiled, and I didn't get to see him smile often. "No, no. This is my idea. Father and son. Just to chat a bit about women, and sex, and love."

"OK, Father, sure. That sounds good," I said, though, in fact, it sounded horrible. The last thing I wanted to hear from my father was advice about women; it was humiliating and infantile and I was seventeen and pretty much knew everything already. But there was no kidding around with Father, who was a very serious man, so, "What would you like to talk about?"

"Well," he said, "we could start with Tracy."

"Your new receptionist?"

He smiled, for the second time in one day. "Yes, my new receptionist. She's very attractive, Peter, and I couldn't help but see that you noticed that."

"Yes."

"She has a bachelor's degree in English from the University of Florida, son. And she's starting in on an MFA this fall."

"Yes."

"So, she's highly qualified, overqualified, really, for the job. Understand?"

"Of course, Father." Why was he telling me this?

"Women aren't as mysterious as you've heard, Peter. I know that at your age they seem to be glorious and strange and alluring. And I see how all these beautiful young women are attracted to you and you to them. But you'll find, soon enough, that the better you get to know someone the more the veneer wears off and you see the real person beneath. Not the beauty, not the sex appeal, not the makeup and the perfume and the clothes: the real person, the one who's someone you could like. Or love."

Ah, I began to see where he was going. "Like Mom?"

The third smile of that unusual day. "Yes, like your mother. Beautiful all the way through, from outside to her very core."

I'd never really thought of Mom that way, as a kind of *person*, someone one could like or not-like, someone seen as attractive or not. She wasn't like that. She was Mom. But I got his point and told him so.

"It's just makeup and hairstyle and perfume, son. You need to rise above that, all right?"

"Sure, Father," I said, and then sat there as he rose, briefly put his hand on my shoulder, and then walked outside to the covered patio to smoke a Camel before the food came. Obviously, the discussion hadn't been an easy one for him.

And so now, here I was, eight months later, still fixated on beautiful Tracy but smart enough to make sure Father didn't notice my lust, driving to the free clinic to just stop in and say hello and let him know my pitching had gone well that day.

My new AI's name was Bob. He was the simple version of what would become, four years later and a lot more expensively, my-Bob. I'd switched it recently from a husky female I called Nikki to a male voice called Bob after one of my dates had complained about the competition. I told Bob that I wanted to do the driving myself, enjoying it the way you do when you're new to it. So, set on Advice, Bob's voice was dry and mechanical as he told me where to turn while we drove deeper into Little Rio, where the Brazilian refugees had settled after civil war tore their nation apart and the dirty bomb made Brasília uninhabitable. Brazil had gotten over that struggle and again was booming, but most of those who'd fled to St. Pete remained there. They'd been on the losing side.

I was expecting desolate poverty, but what I saw as I drove was a series of neighborhoods with small Florida-style shotgun shack homes sprinkled through a lot of huge Southern oaks and kids, lots of kids, on the street. The houses looked OK, the yards were clean, and there were people on the streets, most of them Brazilian, with soccer balls in every yard and homemade goals getting filled with great shots. Where was the gunplay, the danger, the addicts? I didn't see any of that. I wanted to stop and scrimmage with these kids, in fact, after having spent my childhood playing youth soccer. But then we reached the clinic and Bob told me, with a firm dispassion, "We have arrived at your destination."

I pulled into the almost-empty parking lot and slid into a spot. I'd thought the place would be packed; instead, all I saw was a young mom and her toddler leaving as I opened the door of my snappy used Ohm with the faded paint job and stood up, slammed the door shut, and started walking toward the clinic.

Why so empty? I got to the clinic door and saw the sign that showed the Saturday hours—7 A.M. to 3 P.M. Which explained a lot: It was nearly 3:30. But that was OK—it meant I'd get a chance to talk to Tracy in an uncrowded office. I tugged the door to pull it open and discovered it was locked. Of course.

I knocked. No response. I hit the buzzer but couldn't hear it ringing inside, so I guessed it was broken. All right, no problem, there was always a back door to a medical office, so I started walking around the side of the building to find it. On the far side, away from the parking lot and along an alley with large azalea bushes separating the alley from the building, I found the door. Locked.

No doubt it would only open from the inside, so I could pound on the door or walk back to the front and pound on that door. Both choices seemed silly for a doctor's son who was ostensibly stopping by just to say hi—though he was really there, of course, to cast his gaze one more time upon the lovely Tracy.

So I walked idly on over to the window a few meters farther along on that hidden side of the building. The window was closed and there were blinds shut on the inside. But the blinds were bent and twisted and I could see through them. Father's office, maybe? I could tap on the window if it was him.

There was motion. A man, standing with his back to me. I looked closer, rubbed the grime off the window a bit with my hand, carefully, quietly. It was a man, and he was speaking to someone, or reaching out. I couldn't hear anything over the whine of the outside unit of the building's creaky old air conditioner.

The man was my father. There was no mistaking that perfect hair, that posture. Examining someone? But in some kind of office room, not an examination room? I could see new Dellmac computers, a pair of them with the old double screens, to the left.

Father moved to his left and the other person came into view. Tracy. Beautiful Tracy. And while I watched, Father was unbuttoning her blouse, slowly, already halfway down. Tracy was looking up at him, her hands back against the desk she was half-sitting on as the buttons came undone, one by one by one until her blouse was open.

I was transfixed. Between the grime on the window and the two- or three-centimeter opening in the bent blinds Tracy couldn't see me even if she looked. Even if she wanted to look, to look anywhere but at my father's face, her mouth open, those lips. Father reached out to touch her right breast. Tracy sat back, brought her hands up to unclasp the front catch of the bra, let it open, and Father held her breasts as she undid the buttons on his white shirt. I couldn't quite see that but I could tell, watching her reach up to work with both hands.

She stood, let her blouse drop back behind her on the desk, pushing his shirt back off him so it fell behind him as he worked his arms out, the shirt still tucked into the back of his pants.

Not for long. She undid his belt buckle, undid the front button on his slacks, pushed open the pants, and then, from there, I watched them make love, unhurried, patient, something they'd obviously done many times before, kissing and touching and holding and then Tracy back against the desk as Father entered her, kissing her neck, moving, in and out, slowly. I thought, for a second, that Tracy had somehow seen me through the window, that she smiled and half-nodded, staring at me as her head, her body, that beautiful face and body moved back and forth and back rhythmically, slowly, slowly.

In ten minutes or so it was over and shirts and pants and underwear were all back in place and buttons were being buttoned and I was walking, stunned by what I'd seen, back around to the front of the building, the parking lot, my car, and getting in and pulling away before they could find out I was there, that I'd seen what I'd seen, that I knew what I knew as I told Bob to drive me back home, to Mom, to Tom and troubled Kait and real life. I listened to Bob the whole way as he told me where he was turning to get us home. Thank god for Bob.

11

I sat at a small, round table with Heather and a glass of Jameson in Hussey's Pub in the village of Ballina in County Tipperary in Ireland. We'd been here for a couple of hours already and I could see more hours in the offing. I tried to pace myself. We sat off in the corner of the large room, but over there, in the center of things, was the jovial Twoclicks, an alien visitor from a distant planet who'd come all this way to chat with the locals in the village pub. It was, I had to admit, pretty damn amazing. Late afternoon and the place was busy, and getting busier fast as the word spread locally. I looked at Heather and asked her if the whole world now knew where we were. She smiled and said no, she had that under control. I believed her.

I couldn't make anything out of the babble of voices from the bar and asked myBob, "Can you pick up what they're saying?"

"No problem," he said. "It's the locals telling Twoclicks what a fine representative he is of the newest tourists to come to Ireland. That woman with the expansive gray hair just said, 'Sure, and it's grand that you've come to visit with us, so.'"

"myBob, are you mocking our Irish hosts?" Unbelievable.

myBob had been very odd, indeed, since he'd come awake from the deep hibernation of my implant surgery.

"Jaysus," he said. "Sure and I thought you'd be laughing at that, so."

I did laugh, and Heather, sitting across from me, smiled to see it. My first laugh in a while, I suppose. "All right, myBob. It's good to know you can pick out the conversations."

"Ah, well, sure," he said.

"Grand" was my response, and then I took another cautious sip of the Jameson, which the locals seemed to be intent on pouring down our throats with funnels here in Hussey's Pub. They seemed to like me and Heather just fine, but to them we were just hangers-on and they devoted most of their attention to their new portly friend wearing the odd trousers and the loud floral shirt and calling himself that funny name with that lisp when he spoke.

"Ireland iss wonderful country!" in fact is what Twoclicks was saying, so loudly the whole room could hear him, holding up his whiskey high for a toast. "Ssslàinte!" Which had a bit too many "sses," but otherwise got the job done. He sure did like that whiskey. A rowdy "Sláinte!" came right back.

So Twoclicks was firmly convinced he'd found the key to his kingdom in craft alcohol, and you could credit me for that, thank you very much. In St. Pete, on my back deck, somehow invisible to all the surveillance on just the fourth or fifth night since our friends had arrived, the three of us had looked out toward that ship of theirs in the Gulf and talked about their future on Earth, and mine. Ours. I had some Paddy's, a few extra years added onto it through sitting in my kitchen cabinet since the day I'd brought myself, and the Paddy's, home from Dublin. I found the bottle and we sipped the whiskey, on the rocks and then neat, and history was made.

That was maybe four weeks ago, a couple of weeks after the initial craziness of the Arrival, and already headlines and interests had moved on and things on the alien front were calm. The S'hudonni seemed all right, not only to me but to most of the world at large. It was early innings, but they were winning us over. They were physically nonthreatening: a little shorter than us, portly, vaguely porpoise-shaped, with persistent smiles and calm, friendly voices that spoke to us in English, or French, or Farsi, or Portuguese, or Mandarin: whatever was needed.

The landings—one in the shallow water of the Gulf of Mexico and six more in other estuaries and deltas around the Earth: all of them shallow, all of them warm-water—told us something, not that the information did us any good. They liked warm, shallow water and glistening beaches. Great. So did we.

But we were easily impressed and they seemed willing to please. There were a couple of dozen of them touring around, some of them clearly more important than others. Twoclicks and another we called Whistle seemed to share the top of the ladder and got the most attention from governments and businesses. And Twoclicks, it seemed to me, was way ahead of all the others on the charm front. Whistle, from what I was seeing on television and online, was more formal, more careful about who he was with and what he was saying. Somehow he seemed a lot more threatening.

Twoclicks, on the other hand, loved to hang out with the locals. He'd done that in Beijing and Brazil, in Argentina and then in Italy and again in Sweden and Spain. I hadn't been on any of those trips but I'd watched the news from my hospital room and then, later, from my hotel suite while recuperating. Now I was finally on one of these jaunts, and I could see why they were so popular. Twoclicks spoke the language like a local—the S'hudonni translator software was a lot better than ours—and like a stand-up comic on tour, he knew the local jokes and was willing to crack them; so he'd commented in Portuguese about gauchos in Argentina and in Mandarin about how in Hong Kong they take your money very politely and in Dublin about the Kerryman who sat up all night with his new bride waiting for the sexual relations to arrive.

As the days went by Twoclicks, at least, seemed harmless, even silly—a high-tech buffoon with great technology and a sense of humor to go with it.

We liked, too, that he shared details about where he was from. The homeworld was a water planet with a name that sounded, in their language, like the front half of the trill of a songbird. For us, it translated as S'hudon, pronounced with a liquid "s" and no "h" and then followed with the emphasis on a long "u" sound and the "don," for water. So "Soodon": World of Water. And the inhabitants of World of Water: S'hudonni.

He came in friendship and all he had in mind was making some business deals. Whistle, it seemed to me, was saying about the same thing in Canada, India, South Africa, Malaysia and Japan, and elsewhere. No good hints in public on what those deals might be, but think about what might happen! The secrets of the universe? Unlimited power supplies, longer lives, cures for everything, and on and on. All we had to do was join the crowd.

And, it was noted, we could be part of an empire that already included the homeworld and five others, all peaceful members of a prosperous trading group. Twoclicks thought there were things we could export and knew there were things we'd like to import and so all we had to do was get ourselves organized. A few small improvements; that was all that would be required. Simple.

So I sat patiently with Heather and wondered if this was what she meant when she said "We have plans for you, Peter" in the shallow water off Egmont Key on the day those turtles made their unlikely arrival.

Sure, I was along for the ride, with all my new implants and that bright future up ahead. I was going to sweep everything, even though I was forbidden to broadcast live, using a very carefully edited fifteen minutes or so every night and saving the rest for what would be, I could hope, a documentary that would make me famous forever. Even with those brief edited segments my sweepcast numbers would rise as fast as receivers could be produced and sold. Alvaro and friends at Todos Sentidos had to be overjoyed. I wasn't wearing their equipment anymore, but all those on the receiving end were. The money had to be pouring in.

"Message from Kait," myBob broke into my thoughts. "Read it or hear it?"

"Hear it, myBob, please."

There was an audible click and then the message: "Peter, it's Kait. I hope you're doing great." There was a moment's hesitation as she took a deep breath. "I managed to talk to Tom for a few minutes." Another pause. "It didn't go all that well. Jeez, Peter, he really hates you."

I waited as I heard her take another breath. "He could barely talk to me about you. Whatever you did, he thinks it's so awful that it can't be forgiven. Peter, he sounded crazy. So angry! I tried to talk to him about forgiveness—and god knows that's something I've wrestled with personally—but he wouldn't listen, Peter."

Another long pause. "I'm so sorry, Peter. I know you'd like to patch things up, but Tommy isn't listening right now. I think we'll have to be patient with him. You know, like you've been patient with me? It took me a while to get over some things, too. Call me some-time. Maybe it's time you heard about that. The truth of it.

"So, sorry I don't have better news about our brother, but I love you, Peter. Thank you for all that you've done for me and thanks for being so great with me and with Sarah. She loves you! And I do, too, brother. I love you. Talk to you soon. Bye." And came another click.

"Return message, Peter?" asked myBob.

"Nothing personal right now, myBob, but acknowledge that I got it and tell her I'll call her tomorrow when the time zones match up better, OK?"

"Done," said myBob, and "I heard that, Peter," said Heather. She didn't explain how. "This is pretty rough. I'm so sorry. I know the fault is mine."

"No," I said, "that's not true." There was a lot to say but I didn't have it in me at the moment. I took a nice long sip of the Jameson. "You know what he did, Heather? He kicked me out."

"Kicked you out?"

"Of his house, of his life. Said he didn't want to ever see me again. End of story."

She stood. "Perhaps he'll calm down later, Peter," she said. "He's been through a lot, but he's your brother and the two of you have a history, right? Mostly a good history?"

"Sure," I said, and I finally sat back in my chair, took another sip to finish off the Jameson, and took a deep breath. "But, you know, the history I thought we had, me and Tom? Turns out it doesn't exist. Turns out that the way I remembered things, the way I thought I was helping and doing what a big brother should do . . . turns out I was all wrong about that. Turns out I just pissed him off and embarrassed and humiliated him. For years."

Heather came over to me, reached down toward me, and I responded by reaching up myself to take her hand—that firm hand—and let her pull me up to my feet. She was worrisomely strong, I thought, taking a deep breath and marveling at the smell of her—subtle, earthy, musky—as she pulled me closer and we embraced. Maybe that strength of hers was great and wonderful? Yes, it was, I thought, as she looked up and smiled and then kissed me on the cheek. Wonderful. Everything was fine.

I sat back, tried to relax, and watched Twoclicks work the crowd. "He's a heck of a salesman," I leaned over and said to Heather, and he was. The musicians over in the corner had quit playing and had, instead, joined the conversation. I could see a lonely fiddle and bodhran and some uilleann pipes set up against the back wall. No more "Come Out Ye Black and Tans" or "The Old Orange Flute" or "Four Green Fields" for a while. That was fine with me. In my career playing basketball for Dublin Rovers I'd spent a lot of time making appearances and playing friendlies all over Ireland. I loved the country and its people and I'd learned to appreciate the tortured history that had forged them as Irish and still had its remnants in the Northern Ireland Republic. I understood the backstory of the angry lyrics I heard so often in Ireland, but I liked "Trip to Cashel" and "Micho Russell's" a lot better. Let the fiddlers fiddle and the tin whistles play and let's forget about the singing, that was my philosophy. Too much of it did nothing but conjure up troubles that were hundreds of years old.

"Iss *delighted* to be here," Twoclicks was saying again as he poured down another whiskey. The locals, I thought, had to be amazed at his capacity. "And rain iss no bother. On S'hudon iss alwayss wet. Like Ireland!"

There was a round of applause and a lot of cheering and laughter. One of the aliens was *here*, in their tiny village, in their pub, with the rain beating down outside as darkness fell, early here in November. Yet, right before them, warm and jovial, stood a short, chubby being from another world who spoke English with a slight lisp and whose skin glistened as if it were always a bit wet, and who seemed happy to be with them, in Ballina, on this gray, damp evening.

It went on for another hour or more, Twoclicks switching from whiskey to Guinness to no apparent effect while he regaled the locals with his thoughts on all those places he'd already been: London, Paris, Edinburgh, Munich, Rome, Venice. He especially enjoyed Venice, he told them, because he could spend time in the water, though the new Venetian dike system made that a bit tricky as Venice struggled to keep its collective head above the rising climate tides.

"'O Sole Mio' comes next," I said to Heather, and smiled. She laughed. "He likes the Guinness almost as much as the whiskey. And he's really enjoying himself."

He sure was. It was hard not to like Twoclicks, who seemed genuine, honest, and open. And he was that way in private as well as in public. In the days after the landing he'd come by with Heather twice, in the middle of the night, appearing at my door without anyone able to tell, all the spyeyes useless against that technology. We talked, that was all, getting to know each other. He always struck that same chord: the genial visitor.

He usually sat next to Heather when we all chatted, and the two of them often reached out to touch each other on what there was of a shoulder in those bodies. That looked intimate and familiar to me, though I knew I could be wrong. Truth was, I didn't know what to make of Heather's relationship with Twoclicks. I thought that probably she and Twoclicks made a pair, but how did that work with these new alien benefactors of ours? Was it a kind of marriage? Had Heather been cheating on Twoclicks too while she'd cheated on Tom by making love to me? Whew. Sooner or later, I figured, I'd find out.

So it was all very genial now, traveling with Twoclicks and Heather. We were developing a kind of friendship, though I always knew my place. Ask the wrong question and I'd get a strange stare from Twoclicks; nothing too worrisome, I supposed, but how could I know? On the one hand, he chatted with me as an equal. On the other hand, I knew what he and his people were capable of, should the mood strike them.

At our table in Hussey's, I'd had one or two whiskeys too many and had started talking about my torn family and, mostly, how it had gone for Kait.

Heather took a sip of her whiskey and asked, "This all happened suddenly for your sister?"

I nodded. "Seemed like overnight. One day she's my happy sister, the next day the mopey and antisocial head case. That's how it seemed to me."

"Did you ever get her some help? A doctor? A therapist?"

"I think Mom did that for her. There was a whole series of times Mom drove Kait to 'the doctor's office' and they'd be gone for a couple of hours and then they'd be back. They didn't say what it was about and I didn't ask. I was too busy with my own life, girls and sports mainly."

Heather smiled at that, rolled her eyes, shook her head. "The lady-killer. The high-school hero. The quarterback and basketball player and the baseball thrower." And she laughed. "That must seem like a long time ago."

"'Pitcher,'" I said. "And it *was* a long time ago, nearly fifteen years now."

She smiled. Fifteen years wasn't much to her, I think. "And Kait never did those things? Played sports, joined clubs?"

"Drugs," I said, as if that answered anything, as if that were the reason, as if there'd been nothing deeper than that, something that had prompted the turn to drugs.

"But you said she's better now, doing better, making a life."

"I think so. I hope so. She's in a stable relationship, she has a decent job, she has some friends. And all of it, as far as I can tell, is clean."

"We should have her visit with us when we get to California," she said. "Would she like that?"

"We're going to California? That would be great. Her and her spouse both, right?"

"Absolutely, all the way around," said Heather, and leaned over to clink her glass with mine. And so here we were, in a small pub in a small village in a small country, drinking the local product (had Twoclicks tried the poitin, that Irish moonshine? I wondered) and enjoying the evening. Behind the bar there was an old thinscreen television. It was on and had been showing, with the sound down low, the replay of that afternoon's hurling match between Kerry and Cork. Funny sport, hurling, something like lacrosse with a heavy measure of baseball hitting tossed in. Hit the ball—the slither— with the bat—the hurley—and get it over the goalpost for a point. Get it under the goalpost and into the net for three points. Run up and down the field, swing those hurleys at the ball and at each other, score more goals than the other team, and have a whole country anoint you. Lots of action, a good mix of violence, enough scoring to keep me happy. I liked the sport. So I'd been keeping an eye on the match until Heather touched my arm. "Something's up," she said.

"Watch the news, Peter," said myBob suddenly, out of nowhere. "There's been an attack of some kind."

And there it was, a somber reporter breaking into the match and talking as something burned behind her.

The bartender saw it, too, and grabbed the remote to turn up the volume and we watched as the world watched, worried, and thought about what a war with our new friends from S'hudon would be like. "Short" seemed the best word.

Later, I found out that it went down like this: A S'hudonni ship, one that looked just like the ones I'd seen through my spyeye lens from JPL, had come to visit the Dryden Flight Research Center at Edwards Air Force Base in California. There is a football field–sized concrete slab at the western end of the Dryden runway and on that concrete slab sat a hypersonic ghostship that represented the latest, and best, in Sino-American technology. The spot is within easy sight of the traffic on Lancaster Boulevard, and the SA tech team was very proud of the fact that their ship sat there for a full week while the traffic zipped by and no one noticed their plane. The ghostship was the size and general shape of the classic UFO of your great-grandfather's 1950s wet dreams, and it sat there, shimmering and alive, powered up and ready for action but utterly undetectable not only with human senses but with the best technology we had.

The SAs had more than one hundred of the ghostships, fifty of them held by the United States and a few of its allies, the other fifty by China. They were armed with weapons meant for near-orbit space as well as atmosphere, since the ghostships were our first design to exit and enter the atmosphere easily, anytime, at hypersonic speeds: Los Angeles to Beijing in fifty-five minutes, wheels up to wheels down. Incredible, really. The apex of military success. Unmanned, of course, and flown by AIs.

And then, on a calm Southern California Saturday morning, there came a high-pitched, keening whine that grew in intensity to a scream that hurt the eardrums and frazzled the mind and then suddenly went silent as the first S'hudonni screamship—a warship, not one of their big spidery-legged transports—that anyone had ever seen appeared over that ghostship and, in something under five seconds, torched it. A bright light, a general collapse of integrity so that the ghostship seemed to melt, falling apart and then puddling into a liquid that sat there on that concrete pad, a liquid representation of what we'd thought and what we now knew about exactly who was the boss.

Then the screamship hovered there for a few seconds more, seemingly posing for all the vidcams and spyeyes and other equipment capturing every moment of this display. Then, quite silently save for the whoosh of wind filling the space where the ship had been seconds before, it departed. Straight up, smaller and then a dot and then gone.

The same thing happened to a ghostship on the tarmac at Feidong Air Base in Nanjing. Wu ahn, here's a little message for you. And Brize Norton in England, Spangdahlmen in Germany, Alfonsos in Brazil—where the tourists on the Rio beaches got to see the screamship fly over—and more. It was quite a display.

It was a message that everyone got—that was your best and it was nothing. The Warning War, some people started to call it.

Watching the start of all that in a pub in an isolated village in Ireland was a good way, it turned out, to see how the man on the street, or in the pub, reacted to getting the news that our technology was every bit as helpless as we'd been guessing—at least, it turned out, when it came to matters of defense against the ships from S'hudon. So much for joviality.

I was getting priority-pinged and I told myBob to answer it and take the message. It was Abigail, of course, and I told myBob to tell her I'd call her back soon. Another ping and it was Chloe, bless her heart. myBob handled it.

Twoclicks waddled over to us and whistled and clicked at
Heather, who answered him the same way. I knew I'd have to learn
to speak their tongue if I wanted to follow this whole story the way
it deserved to be followed.

Heather looked at me. "We need to get out to the limousine for
some privacy, Peter. Immediately."

All eyes were on the thinscreen for the moment, but that wouldn't
last. The door was right behind us. Quietly, quickly, we made an
exit. Our limousine was waiting for us outside, idling to keep the
heater on, its flywheel running to feed the battery that ran the motor.

We walked toward it, Heather and me helping Twoclicks along
the thirty meters or so between the pub's door and the limo. Happily, the driver saw us and hit the button to open the back door on
our side. The rain was soft and slight, maybe coming to an end.

We helped Twoclicks in and then Heather went in behind him
and I entered last. With Twoclick's girth, he and Heather fully
occupied the backseat, so I pulled down the jump seat and sat, as
I'd done on the way over. You wouldn't want to go too many miles
on that jump seat, but it was fine for the ten minutes to the manor
house.

I hit the button to lower the privacy glass. "Take us back to the
manor, Sean," I said to the driver—I was glad we didn't have an
AI driving the vehicle—who mumbled yessir and pulled away from
Hussey's. I pushed the button to raise the privacy glass again, so
we could talk in the back. I could see out the window as we pulled
away, and the door to Hussey's was open and those inside were
streaming out, looking for us. No one waved. Minutes ago, Hussey's
had been a convivial place. Now, instead, everyone was pouring
out to take a good, hard second look at the visitor from S'hudon.
I couldn't blame them.

But Heather was watching me as I watched those people. "This
is not our doing, Peter," she said. "Twoclicks says it must be his
brother's work. Twoclicks wonders if there was some threat from
those human ghostships."

Twoclicks whistled some more. Heather translated: "He wonders if you could ask your Abigail at the Jet Propulsion Lab if these attacks from our screamships are in response to some provocation."

I nodded and told myBob to contact Abigail immediately and he said, "Will do," and then, seconds later, "Done. Abigail is available, voice and video."

"Abigail?" I opened my smarty and she was on the screen. "We're all here, in a limousine. We've been watching the news."

"Hello, Peter. We're watching it, too, of course. This is not something we expected."

"I know," I said, and then added, "Abigail, I have someone here who wants to talk with you about it. His name, in English, is Twoclicks."

"The S'hudonni prince? The brother to Whistle? There, with you now?"

Well, hell, everyone knew everything except me. Not a good feeling. "Yes, Abigail, that's the one. He's here with me now. We're in a limousine headed to our hotel. The privacy glass is up behind the driver, so this is probably as private as we can get. I'll turn you over to him."

But Twoclicks whistled and Heather translated. "He'd like you to speak with her, Peter. He'll tell you what to say, through me. It seems clumsy, but he prefers S'hu for this and trusts my translation skills and your relationship with Abigail."

"Relationship" was overstating it, but it wasn't as if I had a choice. "Sure," I said, then to Abigail, "They want me talking to you. Translations going back and forth, all right?"

"Yes, sure," she said. "And I have others listening in. Is that all right?"

Heather whistled and clicked to Twoclicks, who clicked back.

"Yes," Heather said, "the more the better."

"All right, then," I said. "Let's get started."

There was some whistling back and forth between Heather and Twoclicks, and then she spoke. "Begin with this: Twoclicks expresses his surprise at these actions and wishes to assure Abigail and the people she is in contact with that this is not his doing."

I said exactly that to Abigail. I could see her in my smarty, sitting in some office, looking a little stressed, drinking coffee, so maybe it was morning in Los Angeles. I'd lost track of the time difference.

She nodded her head. "We thought that might be the case. We accept that statement as fact."

We could all hear her, of course, so I didn't have to relay that. Instead, Heather whistled and clicked at Twoclicks, paused, then added what sounded like a brief trill and a click. I figured it must be a clarification. "Twoclicks expresses his regret and offers to meet with your representatives to discuss an appropriate . . ." Heather hesitated, spoke directly to me. "We wonder if he should use the word 'response' in this case."

"You're asking *me* that question?" How in hell had this happened? It occurred to me that I was better suited to playing basketball and sweeping soft porn than I was to making decisions about diplomatic language. But here I was, and there was the question, and I needed to answer. So, "No," I said.

"Because?"

"Because," I guessed, "it makes it seem that Twoclicks has chosen a side, and is joining Abigail and her people and working against his own people." But who *were* Abigail's "people"? The military? The White House? Some shadow group that held the real power? I had no idea.

Heather smiled, and turned her head slightly to whistle at Twoclicks. "Iss good," he said to me in English, then whistled back to Heather.

"All right, then, Peter," she said, "he says you're quite right, and it's too early to take such a stand. Please simply tell Abigail that Twoclicks expresses his regret and offers to meet with her and her representatives to discuss the situation." She reached over to pat my hand. Small comfort.

I looked into the smarty display of Abigail's worried face. "Did you get that, Abigail?"

"I did, Peter, thank you. So let's pick a place and time for that meeting. And make it very soon. Tomorrow?"

I looked at Heather and Twoclicks. They offered no hints about their response until, long seconds later, Twoclicks said, "Yess, Peter. Tomorrow."

"We'll fly on human transportation tomorrow, Peter," Heather added. "So it will take some time to get there. Perhaps you and Abigail can arrange for tomorrow evening, at some mutually agreeable place?"

"Agreed," Abigail said through the smarty.

"And this is very private. No announcement, no media. Agreed?"

Abigail agreed, and so we closed the conversation and I had myBob turn off the smarty. I needed some time to stop and think. Or maybe that was a bad idea, since what was happening didn't bear too much thinking about. How had I gotten into the middle of this? Me? It didn't make any sense, but there it was.

"Relax," said Heather, smiling as she read my thoughts. "You're doing fine."

And you know, for a few minutes there I thought that, perhaps, what she said was true.

12

We were quiet in the backseat of that limousine after the conversation with Abigail ended. Twoclicks closed his eyes and might have been dozing for all I could tell. Heather looked at me, smiled, and then stared out the window.

In five minutes or so we reached the entrance drive to Ballina House, so there was a kilometer or more of winding road to go, leading from the elaborate wrought-iron front gate back to the one-time manor house that was now a small, five-star hotel. That long road in its original state had isolated the manor house from the riffraff in the village. And the manor house itself, three stories tall and extravagant in its historic grandeur, reminded me that the Irish were a handy society to study if I wanted to see how life might be like in the New Earth, as some of the edited media were already starting to refer to it. From the early 1100s until 1921 the Irish had labored feudally under the enlightened leadership of England's ruling classes, the very ones who built manor houses like this one while the locals worked the fields as indentured farmers. It was a great system if you were English; and enlightened; and very, very wealthy.

Finally, in 1921 the Irish managed to throw the bums out, though it was another twenty-five years before the shackles were completely removed. And now, here in this tiny village more than a century later, I was putting two and two together and worrying over it. I was beginning to realize I was a pawn in some huge game that, mostly, involved the hows and whys of S'hudon's use of its power over Earth. Until now they'd been playing nice, and Twoclicks seemed genuine enough, and he and Heather seemed fair-minded. But now, with our best military technology so easily destroyed, could I still believe in Twoclicks and Heather and the peaceful future they'd been promising? Did it matter whether I believed or not? Whether the S'hudonni were generous and kind or cruel and dictatorial, I didn't see how we'd ever be able to throw them out. They were our new British Empire, and they were unstoppable.

As if to punctuate what I'd been thinking, Heather started changing as we drove slowly up that long drive to the front entrance. I studiously looked out the window, but I could hear the uncomfortable snapping and tearing noises. It took only a minute or so and then, when I looked back, there were two S'hudonni in the limo with me, one of them looking out the window, the other looking at me and smiling. Why did she do that? I had no idea. Perhaps she needed to revert to her natural form every now and again? Perhaps she liked that form better? Perhaps it was all a mystery I'd never solve? I decided to not think about it; god knows there was plenty of other material to fret over.

We rode along in silence, the seconds dragging by slowly, until I noticed Heather putting her small, delicate hand to the side of that bulbous face and, I think, listening.

"Something is about to happen, I think, and we need to take precautions." She shook her head. "I have a screen up around us, full blocks, so we're undetectable. No one could know we're here. No one can call out. This isn't possible."

"What isn't possible?" I wanted to know.

Her hand touched a button and she spoke to the driver. "Stop immediately, please."

"Yes, ma'am," came the response from Sean up front, on the other side of the dark security glass, and the limo came to a stop. We weren't traveling more than fifteen or twenty kilometers per hour on that narrow, raised driveway, so the stop wasn't too sudden.

Heather touched her window down. "Listen," she ordered, and so we listened. Nothing: dead quiet, a slight hiss from the wind through the trees that lined the road. I lowered my window, stuck my head out to look around. The darkness was complete, and cool, and dank. The rain had stopped but the clearing clouds still blocked the full moon and only a few stars poked through here and there. There was no breeze.

And then, in the distance, a whisper of sound, high-pitched, eerie. "An animal?" I asked.

"No," said Heather. Twoclicks was rising from his seat to move toward the door that he and I shared, and Heather suddenly was speaking with a firmness I hadn't heard from her before. "Out. Now. Quickly." She hit the speaker button to the driver's seat. "Sean, leave immediately," she said to him. "Now! We are under attack."

Attack? From whatever was producing that distant scream, like a cat, maybe? A very big cat? Heather was talking to someone, asking for assistance, calling it an emergency as the scream grew louder. Not an animal sound now—more mechanical, engines whining or wind over wings or something artificial, maybe, and meant purposely to frighten, to terrify. Stuka theory at work.

I was out the door right behind Twoclicks and the driver was coming out his door right behind me as we headed for the side of the road, away from the limousine. I didn't know where Heather was but guessed she was on the other side of the car, moving fast, away from whatever trouble this was.

The road was elevated a meter or so over the boggy terrain in this part of the drive leading up to Ballina House, so we ran to the shoulder and then slipped down the side and away, I hoped, from danger. The scream had become deafening. The darkness was nearly complete but I knew Twoclicks and limo driver Sean were with me—I could sense their bulk and hear their breathing, one on each side of me—but while they couldn't be more than a meter away I couldn't see them. There was no sign of Heather.

The scream seemed to find a peak in volume and pitch for a second, and then surpassed even that. I had my hands over my ears and was screaming myself to try and survive the aural onslaught. And then, in an instant, the sound stopped. I realized I was whimpering.

I slowly took my hands away from my ears, not trusting the silence, and then, cautiously, started to rise up to look around. A thin hand reached out to touch my shoulder. "Stay," Twoclicks said. "Do not move. Stay down. Very important." There was no lisp, no faux bonhomie; he was deadly serious. I was surprised my hearing worked well enough to understand what he was whispering.

Five long seconds, maybe ten, went by, and then, from the silence, came a crackling noise, bacon in a fry pan, bubbling and snapping grease; and then a bright light clicked on just over the berm, searching for us perhaps? I stayed down and the crackling grew louder and the light brightened until I closed my eyes to avoid the glare and then, with a huge whoomph, there was an explosion that lifted me from my knees where I was cowering in the darkness, shook me, a rag doll in the concussion, and then slammed me to the soft, boggy ground.

I couldn't breathe after that and, for a moment, I panicked. Then, recognizing what had happened—I'd had the wind knocked out of me like this in high-school football—I tried to relax and that helped and then, a few seconds later, the lungs caught air again and I began to think I'd survive, at least for the moment.

That had hurt like hell, but I was alive, and when I heard a moan and some mumbles I knew Sean had survived as well. And then came a quick triple click and a low whistle and then, in English, quietly, "Friend Peter, you are all right, yes?"

"Yes," I whispered. "What happened?"

"A screamship did this, Peter," he said.

A screamship. Those ten satellites in the evening sky? The power, the might of S'hudon? The weapons that destroyed those Chinese taikonauts in orbit while I watched? The technology that had wiped out the ghostships an hour ago? Screamships, a kind of technology that was, to us, magic; so far ahead of what we could understand that we knew we were throwing spears at the colonizing culture. Slingshots. Sticks and cudgels. Stones.

All this passed through my mind in moments as I lay there on the wet, damp bog of County Tipperary. "Is it gone?" I asked Twoclicks. "And where the hell is Heather?"

"I do not know, friend Peter." And I knew he meant that as the answer to both questions. All right, then: The driver was moaning, terrified, Twoclicks was an heir to the throne, and I'd signed on to sweep stories about him. Sweeping! I'd forgotten completely.

"myBob, are you all right?" I thought to my helpmate.

"Yes," he answered. "And I assumed you'd want to be sweeping this, so it's been recording since you all left the pub in town."

"Great, myBob, thanks," I thought back to him.

So where the hell was Heather? I hoped to hell she was still alive. There was only one way to find out.

You must remember, I was an athlete and a sweeper but definitely no hero. Shooting basketballs through hoops requires some talent but very little courage. Interviewing celebrities and faux-dating beautiful women doesn't even require much in the way of talent, and no courage at all.

The clouds were moving on and that bright, full moon emerging. It was startling to suddenly have enough light that it cast shadows. I heard the distant scream of a banshee, another screamship coming or, more likely, the same one coming back for another pass. That meant, I hoped, it wasn't here right now, ready to fry me when I showed myself, stupid Earthie. OK, then, consider this: Wait and surely die. Or try.

I turned in the sudden clarity of a full moon's shine toward

Twoclicks. "Wait here, all right?" I said. "I'll get help. I'll do what I can."

And then I stood, and finding I was still alive, I walked; and then, still alive, I ran, across the narrow macadam of the road, toward whatever was next. To my left, the limousine was in flames, yellow flames bright through roiling black smoke.

The scream was getting louder again, and another scream, fainter, behind it. The soil was drier on the far side of the road, and greener. I could see a white crushed-rock footpath that ran briefly alongside the pavement of the driveway before angling away from it and leading straight for the small stand of woods. Heather must be in there. I ran on the path, fifty or sixty meters of it in the open before it reached the first of the trees. I headed for them, and was nearly there when the first scream became unbearable again and I staggered under the sonic onslaught, coming to a stop, hands over ears, and then fell down onto my knees.

And then, as before, suddenly it ended, and that second, more distant scream started to grow.

I stood. I looked up. There it was, five hundred or more meters above me, an enormous whale of a thing, several soccer fields long and at least that wide, smooth with a shimmering near-white color. Dead quiet, eerie in its hovering there with no sound of engines, no hum, no scream, nothing but the sight of it in the now bright moonlight.

"Peter?"

I looked toward the sound of that question and there was Heather, coming out from the woods. Returned to her Earthie form. Beautiful, so beautiful. I knew too much about the falsehood of that beauty, or about the temporary nature of it, perhaps. And I didn't want to admit to myself what I'd done and how much it had meant to me. Despite it all. Despite the falsehood, despite the manipulation. I wanted to protect her. I wanted to save her from that great device above us. It was crackling, bacon in the fry pan, the sound intensifying, the discharge, the power, about to let loose.

And she was walking toward me, arms out, palms toward me. "Stay clear, Peter. Stay very clear. Help is coming."

"Run!" I yelled at her.

She kept walking. She smiled. "Too late, Peter. This is a very old rivalry, and this time he wins. It's me that this is all about, not you, not Twoclicks. Me, and Earth, and all that's about to transpire."

"No!"

"Oh, yes," she said. "Stay clear. Help will be here in a minute. But now . . ." and she raised those outstretched arms, palms up, a supplicant. A crackling narrow, bright light fell upon her and there, as I watched, Heather fell apart into a million tiny particles within that terrible cone of light and those particles faded and were swept away in the light breeze and then it was as if they'd never been there, as if she'd never been there. Her face, that beautiful face, was the last thing to go, and I thought, perhaps, that I saw, in that final moment, her left eye watching me, knowing me, comforting me with some knowledge I did not have. And then it, too, was gone and I stood there, alone.

The light winked out. The screaming, surely a second ship, our rescuer, was growing louder, seconds away. But late. Too late.

The screamship above me rose and then disappeared, there one instant and gone the next, and behind me I heard footsteps. It was Twoclicks, and he was helping the still-stunned driver along as best he could.

"It's over for now, friend Peter," Twoclicks said. He whistled and clicked quietly to some internal communicator and the scream of the second ship quieted. I looked up and there was nothing there. Too damn late, and so staying out of sight.

We were at the edge of the woods where I'd seen that deer and that strange shimmer in the air. No deer now, but if I stopped and gave myself a few seconds to relax and sense the edges of my vision, I thought, I might find that the shimmer was still there. But there was nothing.

Twoclicks spoke quietly to me. "Come, into the manor. We are protected now. We will be safe." He took a good look at me, assessing me, I think. "We have to talk, friend Peter."

And I nodded at that. I wanted, I needed someone, something, to tell me what to do, give me my marching orders. We walked slowly, Twoclicks and me and terrified Sean, up the long and narrow drive the last few hundred meters to Ballina House. To our right lay the woods and no indication, anywhere, of the spot where Heather had been consumed. Heather, gone. It was difficult to process, difficult to believe. It was all I could do to stumble along with Twoclicks and Sean as we headed toward the wide front doors of the manor. To our left, the smoldering, crackling, cooling heap of metal and leather and oh-so-high-tech laminates that had been the limousine. Ahead? Only Twoclicks could say.

I sat at the antique writing desk in my room at Ballina House in County Tipperary and wrote some notes in longhand with the pen and ink that were ready for me at the desk. All our electronics were dead. Fried, Twoclicks told me with a sad sigh after we'd entered the manor. EMP? I wondered. Twoclicks wouldn't say but it didn't matter. No myBob, no smarty, none of the new internals for sweeping, no nothing. All that fancy new hardware and its occupying software in my head and I thought, now that it wasn't at work but just sat there, occupying space, that I could feel it somehow. Within. Waiting. All of it quiet. A dark hole.

A plaque on the door of the room said William Butler Yeats had stayed in this very room for a week in 1906, back when the home was still owned by the Herbert family. It was here, the plaque said, perhaps at this very desk, that Yeats edited the proofs for *The Tower* and worked on creating Red Hanrahan, his drunken and brawling character who stumbled, tumbled, fumbled to and fro and had but broken knees for hire and horrible splendor of desire. And for that he was a schoolteacher.

There was a copy of *The Tower* behind glass in the library of the manor. I'd seen it there just a while ago, after being interviewed in the manor library by the local garda about what had happened. Standing there, numb with grief, I'd looked at the shelved books and there it was. I'd asked the manager if I might hold it in my hands. He'd unlocked the bookcase and pulled it free and handed it to me and then left the room so I could read it in peace for a few minutes. It wasn't a first edition, but close. And there on the second page it was signed by Yeats to "My great friend and benefactor Henry Herbert" on the first line and "W. B. Yeats, October, 1906," on the next.

What was it worth? Hard to say, but hundreds of euros; perhaps a thousand or more? One of the great ironies of the Cloud Age was the leap in worth of increasingly rare printed books, tangible things, truly owned and not borrowed from those great collectives in the Canadian North.

Heather was dead. Consumed in flame. Every minute or two that thought had come back to me, overwhelmed me. Heather, the woman, the being, the thing that I'd fallen so hard for, been enraptured by. Gone.

Jesus wept. I'd been carefully turning pages in the Yeats book without even looking at them, lost in grief, when Twoclicks came into the library and stood next to me, saying nothing as I'd looked up from *The Tower* and glanced outside through the tall, narrow window to see that it was raining again, drops rolling down the glass. Rain. Cold. Wet.

Twoclicks had come up to stand next to me. He'd taken my hand in his. "Friend Peter," he'd said.

I didn't want to hear it, something supportive about Heather and all that. I didn't want to even think it. "Look at this," I said, and pointed to the books. "These are important Earth artifacts. Early books, very precious."

He looked at the spines through the glass. "Yeatss? You like him?" he asked, and I smiled and said yes.

"Yeatss wass very good, I'm told," he said. "I sshall read ssome."

He looked at me. "Friend Peter, I am very ssorry about what happened to . . ." and he whistled and clicked some S'hudonni name.

"Heather?"

"Yes," he said, "Heather. She saved our lives; you know this, yess?"

"I thought as much," I said, and could see her again in my memory, her arms raised, palms up, as that light disassembled her, breaking her down into minute parts that glowed and then died and then blew away in the breeze, gone.

"Very painful," Twoclicks said, and managed to shake his head sadly, a good imitation of an Earthie gesture. "But not so terrible as you think, friend Peter. And now all iss calm again."

What did that mean? "Not so terrible?" I asked.

"Yess. Be patient, friend Peter. More cannot be said. But be patient, yes?"

"Sure," I'd said, "patient."

And now I sat at this antique desk and thought about how things *were* calm, and I didn't trust it. There'd been a flurry of activity for several hours after the attack by the screamship. First had come the Garda Síochána—the Irish police—coming into the estate with lights flashing and sirens blaring, no more than ten minutes after the screamship departed. They'd quickly secured the scene with yellow tape and sawhorses and various vehicles and bright lights and then started asking questions about what the hell had gone down at Ballina House. We told them an edited version. Sean, the limo driver, had his head buried the whole time and hadn't seen anything to dispute the story we told, Twoclicks and I. No more than a quarter hour after that two garda detectives showed up to ask all the same questions and take the same recordings. They and the uniformed garda started looking at the evidence, starting with a melted limousine and several patches of burned grass and then began investigating for more subtle things.

And then they left us alone. Diplomatic immunity, the detectives told us. They'd been instructed to make sure we stayed inside the manor but to otherwise not bother us. We went inside and an hour or so later the commandant for the local wing of the Cúltaca an Airm, the Irish RDF, Reserve Defence Forces, came around to see us. He'd been assigned to cordon off the area and let no one in or out until everything was secure, and he told us that we'd be leaving in the morning in an armored limousine with a full RDF escort that would take us over to Shannon Airport, where our plane would be waiting. The Irish wanted us gone, and I couldn't blame them. So much for craft alcohol sales from Ireland.

That was it, and we were free to go to our rooms or the hotel bar. Instead I'd gone into the library to sit and grieve and look through the old books, and there Twoclicks had joined me for a chat about Yeats that wound up about Heather until, finally, I begged off and said I wanted to try for some sleep one more time and returned to my room and sat at the old desk.

myBob was still gone, but the old, small thinscreen in the room offered a few channels, and what I saw there reminded me that in the middle of my own troubles I'd forgotten about the world's. After the destruction of the ghostships, China had declared war but now was backing away from that, the United States had demanded an explanation, the Brits were in an emergency session of Commons, the Brazilians were outraged, India was on highest alert with its missiles armed and ready, as if that could achieve anything. And on and on and on.

But our little encounter with a screamship in rural Ireland hadn't made the news, so another impossibility was taking place, another example of precise control of the clouds. Not one among the locals had posted a video or sent a message or simply called someone to spread the news? All the coverage our visit was getting on Irish television, and there was no word of this destruction in Ballina? If there had been, what had stopped the viral spread? If there hadn't, why hadn't there? Had something crashed the systems? If that had happened, how was I seeing what I was seeing on the thinscreen?

I sat there at the desk, staring at nothing for a few minutes. I'd watched Heather die today and now I was trapped in this old manor house with my memories of her and my worries for tomorrow for Twoclicks and for myself and for the whole damn world. I'd gotten so caught up in the day-to-day of this tour with Twoclicks and Heather that I'd quit wondering about the amazement and worry and fear and anger of it all. I was outside of it, or inside of it in some protective bubble, or lost in it, or . . .

Hell. I picked up the old pen and ink and started writing a few scribbles on the hotel stationery. Maybe the ghostly remnant of Yeats would inspire me? Hell, anything seemed possible.

There was a polite knock on my door. Twoclicks?

But it was, instead, the hotel manager, Devon Casey, dressed in his suit, as always, and carrying a tray with a small pot of tea and a cup. "Mr. Holman, I thought you might like some tea."

Not a bad idea at all. I opened the door wider and asked him in. He walked over to the chest of drawers at the back side of the room and set the tea down. Then he turned to face me, reached into an inside pocket on his suit coat, and brought out the copy of *The Tower* that I'd held in my hands downstairs. "I would be honored," he said, "if you would accept this, Mr. Holman, as a small token of our appreciation for your staying with us here at Ballina House."

It was quite an offer, but I told him no, it was worth too much and it had been on the shelves there for more than a century. I'd feel like a thief taking it.

"It's true it's been on the shelves a good long time, Mr. Holman," he said, "but so have a thousand other books in that library, and, yes, people do read one or another from time to time. But to be honest, all the wondrous people who have lived or visited Ballina House since it was built in 1692 have been, you know, people. And Mr. Twoclicks is so clearly, wonderfully alien, and we are so saddened by the loss of his assistant, that when I heard you'd admired this Yeats, well, I knew you had to have it. Please do accept this small gift from us here at Ballina House. You will, won't you?"

I gave in, smiled, reached out to accept the gift, and then shook his hand. "It's wonderful, Mr. Casey, truly. I'll mention it most glowingly in my sweepcasts." And so there I was falling into the rhythms of the speech of this place myself, don't you know! "And I'll tell all those many millions of people, of course, of your wonderful hospitality."

"You will then? You'll tell them of our manor, so?"

"I will, indeed." And I smiled as Casey backed out of the room, smiled and waved, and then shut the door with a nice, solid click.

So the Yeats had become mine.

I loved reading, had a bachelor's in English Lit, knew the difference between a short story and a novel, had read the usual smattering of nineteenth- and twentieth-century American and English and Irish literary lions, and had, in my undergrad days, found a number of those lions whom I really liked for their prose or poetry: Dickens, Crane, Whitman, Austen, Papa, the Brontë sisters, F. Scott, George Eliot, Wells, Henry James, Conrad and his pal Ford Madox Ford, Oscar Wilde, Synge, Joyce, Lady Gregory, and on and on. It's a long list, no doubt because I was never a particularly good, or selective, reader.

In college, taking creative writing and working with storytelling in all its forms, old and new, I'd fancied myself a poet and a prizewinner, though I wrote mostly about sports. Now I was sitting at Yeats' desk and putting ink to paper, writing hopelessly bad verse and knowing that whenever myBob came back online I'd be recording a long personal note about Twoclicks and Heather and how it had gone when we came under attack. I wouldn't be able to sweep it all to the public until god knew when, and if things really fell apart there might well be no public anyway. But if there was a public, and if we still had a civilization and sweep technology, then the story would get, I was sure, a huge global audience. For now, with myBob silent, some bad poetry would have to do.

I missed Heather terribly. She was a construct, a creation. She'd shown me what was done, if not how it was done. I knew the truth

of her. But if what there had been between us was no longer opera-
tive, it didn't mean I didn't continue to like her, admire her. Was
she just myBob taken to the nth degree or did she have feelings? I
didn't know, but what I did know of her I'd liked and it was shattering to know this creation was gone now. I wondered, were there
others of her? How could I not have asked that? How could I not
have asked a hundred questions like that?

All these things and a dozen more at once ran through my mind.
What it all boiled down to, I thought, was that I'd been the lover
and become the friend of a strange and wonderful creation. And
that I missed her.

There was a knock at the door. Twoclicks, no doubt, perhaps
with some more information on Heather, maybe some reminis-
cences he felt he owed me.

"Just a second," I said, loudly, and I rose from my chair to turn
around and answer the knock. But as I did the door opened and
there, looking at me, was a face from the past. Marina, wonderful
Marina, long-lost Marina.

I felt dizzy. I staggered and looked away to grab my chair for support. Marina? How? And then I looked back and it was Heather
who stood there, confused and in pain. Heather, alive.

13

Playing a professional sport requires you to be selfish.

I didn't really learn that until I got to Dublin. For me, high-school and college basketball had been a breeze. I'd played and loved the game as a child, wearing out a series of nets that hung from the rim attached to the front of the garage. Father was too busy to put the rim up, but Mom hired a local handyman and he let me help by holding the ladder. I thought that was important work for a ten-year-old, and I felt some sense of ownership with that backboard and rim and the net. From there, playing the game was, mostly, a solo effort. Tom had no interest at all, though he did his best to humor me with one-on-one games from time to time, the same way he took part in throwing the football or playing catch with a baseball.

Kait enjoyed shooting the ball and running around chasing it, but she was too young and too small for me to really play against. Father was too busy saving young lives and keeping kids healthy, and I understood that and didn't mind. Mom did her best, but it worked out better when she sat on the beach chair in the shade of the oak tree and read her books while I took shot after shot after shot. I tried to make one hundred shots a day from all around the arc and added twenty made free throws for good measure. Eventually I got to be pretty good.

So, while I hadn't played any youth basketball—baseball and soccer were my games when I was a preteen—I went ahead and tried out for the varsity basketball squad in ninth grade and, to my surprise and my mother's delight, I made the team. I didn't have a clue about dribbling or passing or defense and didn't even really know the terms, so Coach Galley found it amusing that when he yelled at me to go backdoor I looked around to see which door he was talking about.

But I could shoot, and I was eager to learn, and I had boundless energy. By mid-season I was starting to get some playing time, and in a game against Northside Lutheran I scored my first two points. That was a very long time ago and worlds away from here, but I can still remember the dizziness and confusion that came from being lost in the excitement when the ball came my way and I was open and I took that fifteen-foot jumper from the baseline and the muscle memory from those thousands of shots in practice took over and the ball went in. It was glorious.

As a sophomore I earned a starting role, though my defense was poor and my dribbling dubious. I was the off-guard, the shooting guard, and I made the most of my limited skill set, averaging fourteen points a game and one memorable night in January scoring thirty-two, twenty-one of them coming from beyond the three-point line.

By my senior year of high school I was all-state and making a name for myself. I'd even acquired some ball handling and defensive skills and become something of an actual basketball player instead of just a shooter. But I was just barely tall enough at six-foot-four and my grades were mediocre and I spent time playing baseball, too, and so perhaps I didn't seem devoted enough to hoops. These things conspired against me, and so not many college offers came my way.

But Coach Galley (and yes, we called ourselves the Galley Slaves when the practices got long and the wind sprints and suicide drills got exhausting) spoke up for me with a friend of his who was an assistant coach at Florida Central, a good, small, liberal-arts college in a suburb of Orlando, and off to school I went, planning on having a good time and playing a lot of basketball for four years.

Florida Central, unfortunately, had a good academic reputation to uphold and demanded that even the jocks go to class and do some work. It took me a lost semester of ineligibility to catch on to this reality, but once I did I began to prosper as a student. Incredibly, I even found some classes I enjoyed and discovered a major in which I could keep my feeble head above water: English Literature.

When I was young I loved to read, mostly adventure books for boys that I downloaded onto my smarty. It took me a while, as I recall, to get to the point where I didn't need a lot of 3-D videos embedded in the copy to entertain me. During the summer after eighth grade I read my first book old-school, nothing but words making sentences and paragraphs and chapters and a novel on the smarty. I liked it. I liked getting lost in the story, getting to know the characters, exploring the cosmos or the Caribbean (science-fiction and pirate novels being my two favorites) and doing it without having to watch and listen, just building it all up in my head.

I was excited when I finished that book, and Mom was proud of me. Father, when I was home one weekend and told him, smiled tightly and said it was nice. Tom was unimpressed. He read constantly, but nothing so frivolous as fiction. And Kait was happily immersed in her smarty, not all that good at reading but not really caring. The videos, she said, were a lot of fun.

No surprise, I'd then done fine in English classes in high school. I thought it was great that I could read a book on the smarty and write a little paper about it and actually get an easy A. Those English grades helped keep me afloat in terms of eligibility in high school, balanced out my barely passing marks in the sciences, which I found confusing.

But in college it was all science all the time my freshman year, the college responding to the worries of our political leadership that we weren't keeping up with the Chinese. So I labored through chem and bio one and two and struggled mightily with calculus, which I'd dodged completely in high school. Ugh.

The tide turned when I was able to declare a major and ran as fast as I could toward the English Department and all those books and all that writing. Hallelujah, brother, and I was having so much fun in those courses that by November I was eligible again and back on the basketball team and, to my surprise, prospering on the court and in the classroom.

I felt like I was growing up, what with good grades and all that. And then the next year, as if to sign off on this new maturity, I met Stephanie, who was as important to my growth as any of the professors or coaches. She taught me to enjoy life and walk away. Play nice, play fair, bring pleasure, and walk away. Easy really.

I was good, if not great, as a small-college basketball player. Second-team all-conference as a junior and senior, led the team in scoring my senior year, and, the thing that made me happiest, led the league in assists that year, too. I'd learned how to play the game.

And so when I got a formal message offering me a tryout with Dublin Rovers of the European Cup League—a league that had once been important but had, in recent years, fallen on hard times—I jumped at the chance, got on a flight to Dublin and gave it my best shot, or shots. My outside-shooting skills were on display the week of the tryouts and I played most of the minutes of two summer-league tryout games, scoring eighteen and then twenty, dishing out twelve assists both times, playing adequate defense, and getting a contract offer of seventy thousand euros for the season, which was pretty good money in Ireland as it slowly recovered from the malaise of the 2020s.

I had an agent by then, a nice guy in Barcelona, and he nailed down the details and took his 15 percent and I was happy with that.

I was a professional basketball player at age twenty-two, living and working and playing in a city so different from anything in Florida that it was dizzying and wonderful. Plus, I discovered that Ireland is chock-full of attractive women, and as we got the season under way and made our trips for the away games I found out that the women in Madrid and Barcelona, in Prague, in Manchester, in Edinburgh and Glasgow, in Torino and Milano were beautiful, too.

The first time around to all those places I tried to steal an hour or two to walk the streets and get to know the cities a bit. In Second Division European basketball we didn't stay in luxury hotels but we never sank below three-star either and the locations were always in the city.

On my very first road trip I learned how it worked. We arrived in Madrid at ten in the morning, and were checked into our hotel—the Hotel Madrid Reina Victoria on La Plaza de Santa Ana—before eleven in the morning. Team lunch wasn't until two, so that gave me plenty of time to walk down the street to the Prado and spend a stunned hour in one of the world's great art museums. There was another American rookie on that team, Jacoby Williams from Niagara University. Jacoby was a tough guy from a tough town, a power forward with a lot of talent but the wrong size. Six-foot-seven had worked fine at Niagara, but he needed at least three more inches to survive in the NBA or First Division in Europe. That or a good outside shot, which he needed to work on.

Me? I needed to work on my defense and ballhandling skills, so we bonded for all the reasons you'd expect: two needy Americans trying to make our way into some playing time in a tough, second-division European league.

I dragged Jacoby with me to El Prado. He said I would owe him one, since he had no interest in paintings by Velázquez, Goya, Titian, or Bosch; but once we started to wander through the rooms he discovered that some of the paintings were interesting and, more important, the place was packed with beautiful young women. We didn't speak Spanish then, but as it turned out that didn't matter.

We had our Dublin Rovers jackets on and the women caught on fast, and in English.

Jacoby and I got a few rooms ahead or behind of each other as we walked through the museum and I found myself alone, standing in front of a famous Velázquez painting, *Las Meninas*. The painting shows a painter at work in the seventeenth century, with a young princess to his left and some courtiers around her. There's a dog, there's an odd character in a background doorway, there are a couple of people visible in a mirror behind the painter. It's a busy, complicated painting, and I decided to puzzle through it. Was the painter working on a portrait of the figures in the mirror or was he painting the little princess? Who was the mystery figure in the back? Who were those people in the mirror? I could have asked myBob for the answers, but instead I decided to try and puzzle it out for myself.

"You like the painting?" a voice, husky but female, said from behind me.

I turned to see her—young, very attractive, black hair and blue eyes, sturdy and athletic, very little makeup, wearing low heels, dressed in a short blue skirt and long-sleeved white blouse in the fashion, if not the color combination, of the day. I was suddenly especially happy that I hadn't asked myBob to explain the painting.

"Yes," I said. "I'm embarrassed to say I don't know anything about it. But it's wonderful—there's all sorts of business going on."

"Yes, that's it exactly. It's business going on."

She reached out to shake my hand. "I'm Marina. I am a docent here." She didn't release my hand. "Can I tell you something about this magnificent painting?"

"Can you tell me over a cup of coffee in the café?" I asked. "I could use a good cup of coffee."

She laughed, and finally let go of my hand. "Yes and no. Yes, I can tell you over a good cup of coffee, but no, there is no such thing as a good cup of coffee in our café. *Lo siento.*"

"So . . . ?" I asked.

"I have my lunch break in thirty minutes? Perhaps we can talk then, over tapas?"

"*Oui*," I said. "Or *sí*. Whatever."

"Close enough," she said. "I'll see you at the museum entrance in thirty minutes, all right?"

"Absolutely," I said, and a half hour later we met. But there were no tapas, there was no café, there was just a walk in the park while she talked all the while about *Las Meninas*, about Velázquez and the Golden Age of Spanish painting, about King Philip IV and his family, about the young Infanta Margarita, who's the one the painting seems, at first, to be about.

"When you saw the painting, what was it that drew you in?" she asked me as we walked along Paseo del Prado and then took a right down Calle de Felipe IV and walked through Parque del Retiro, through all the jugglers and street artists and flamenco guitarists, all of this a pleasant stroll of maybe half an hour. She was even more beautiful in the sunshine, somehow, than she'd been in the museum, and she managed to wear her docent uniform like it was high fashion, her heels clicking on the stone and concrete of the sidewalk.

I tried to keep up my end of the conversation, though god knows I was mainly interested in enjoying watching her walk and fantasizing about what might come next. Still, I gave it a shot: "I like the complexity of the painting, for sure. I could see the painter, and the little girl that he was painting, or maybe it was the two adults he was painting? And there's a dwarf that I'm guessing was there for the amusement of the princess, and in back the proud parents."

"That's good. That's very good," she said. "The little girl is the Infanta Margarita and you're right, she's surrounded by courtiers, a pair of maids of honor, a dwarf, another child, the dog, a nun and a priest—or perhaps he's a bodyguard—hidden in the shadows behind them, a man leaving the room and then, in the mirror in the back, the king and queen, who we think have just entered the room as we are looking and so several of these people are looking at them, while others haven't noticed them yet."

We were in the park by then, and we stopped to admire a chalk painting on the wide sidewalk. From thirty meters away it had looked for all the world like a subway entrance, with steps heading down and railings. Then, as we approached, we could see that it was all a matter of perspective, and the reality we thought we'd seen turned out to be nothing but a distorted picture of something, barely definable as steps at all, by the time we got up next to it. We tossed a few coins into the artist's hat that lay next to his masterpiece, which would be gone, washed away by street cleaners, by the next morning.

"Amazing," I said as we walked away. "I used to see that on television when I was a kid, those ads on the edge of the pitch during football matches. They looked upright and then when a player walked over them they turned out to be flat distortions."

"Yes," she said, and laughed, "life is full of flat distortions, no?"

I was working on a snappy retort to that when she added, "Thing is, Peter, that it's important to find the real truth of things, right?"

I nodded.

"But it's also very important to know the story around that truth. You know, how that truth came to be, the whole context of that truth. You see, yes?"

I nodded again.

"*Las Meninas* is perhaps the most studied painting of all time. The composition, the placement of people and things in the painting, makes one wonder what is real and what is illusion, you know? And what is the relationship between the painter and his patrons? And between the painter and you, the viewer?"

I hadn't really gone that far in my thinking, but her passion for the painting was infectious and I was listening intensely as we left the park behind and walked down a residential neighborhood.

"And the most important thing?" she asked.

"Yes? What?"

"The most important thing is that we have reached my home. Here." And she went into her handbag and pulled out an electronic key. She pressed it and the door opened. "Will you join me for lunch?"

And, of course, I did, though we never quite got around to lunch. Instead, carpe diem, I discovered something new about myself with Marina, something urgent, hurried, passionate. I wanted to stay and forget the world once we were done, pleased, exhausted.

But I had a basketball game to play, and a pregame shoot-around to get to, and soon. So we walked the kilometer or so to my hotel and I asked her if I could see her again. "Oh, yes," she said, smiling. She leaned up to kiss me, gave me a hug, said, *"Hasta pronto, Pedro. Es la verdad."* Which was just about my level of Spanish at the time. I got the message.

I gave her another quick hug and then hustled into the hotel. In ten minutes I'd been to my room, grabbed what I needed, and made it back to the lobby to join my teammates as we walked out to the team bus and headed for our shoot-around. I wondered, as I sat on the bus, if I was in love or something. So fast? So sudden? Could that be?

Sure it could. I left a couple of tickets for Marina at the box office and sent her a message to tell her I'd done that. I was looking forward to showing off for her, and had a pretty good game, with sixteen points and a half-dozen assists, but I didn't see her at the game that night, and afterward we took the bus up to Barcelona and the next game on our road trip, back-to-back nights of basketball, which is how it's done in Second Division.

She'd given me a contact point and I sent messages but didn't hear back. I'd left tickets for her again in Barcelona, just in case, but there was no one in those seats when I looked. Too bad, since I played pretty well again, scoring my points, making my assists, even working hard on defense.

So, I figured, it had all meant more to me than to her. For me, it was an emotional whirlwind. For her, I guessed, it was just some fun. The tables had been turned on me, and I was a big boy and could handle that, I told myself. Grow up.

And then the next day we had the morning off, with a 1 P.M. checkout and a four o'clock flight back to Dublin, so with my new respect for the art world, and especially for *Las Meninas,* I thought I'd see that Picasso museum Marina had talked about, which turned out to be maybe a twenty-minute walk from our hotel.

I thought about her the whole walk, of course, wondering why she hadn't responded. Maybe she was married? Had a steady partner? Didn't really like me all that much after all? Had thought better of her afternoon fling with the American athlete and knew enough to walk away? Maybe, I thought, she'd been checking me out. Was I who she was looking for? Did she want an American? A basketball player? I'd tried to hold up my end of the conversation intellectually, but I'd gotten the feeling I hadn't done a very good job of it. She'd looked me over, hadn't liked what she'd seen all that much, and that was that. Yes, I figured, that was probably it.

The museum entrance was down a tiny side street, Carrer de Montcada, and in just two days in Barcelona I'd realized that the best part of the city—happily, the part where our hotel was—was filled with these narrow streets, some of them crossed by stone bridges on the second story, linking buildings that were only a couple of dozen meters apart. In Barcelona, you're either walking down a broad boulevard or making your way through a narrow passage that in some cities would be an alleyway.

I had in mind the *Las Meninas* rooms Marina had told me about, but to get to them I had to walk through six rooms first—mind-boggling rooms, from early realist to cubism. All of this new and amazing, really, and a long, long way from worrying about setting that pick correctly and then spinning to roll toward the basket to take the pass from Eduardo. I'd done that move four or five times the night before and I was beginning to think that Eduardo and I were going to find some real success with it. I was happy because it meant I was traveling into the land of the giants instead of staying outside and shooting my threes. Growth, growth.

Growth, indeed, looking at Picasso's work, thinking of who I was and what he'd done and then I left one room and there, on the far wall, was a visual display—a large thinscreen—that showed Velazquez's *Las Meninas* and offered clickable links to the explorations that Picasso had made of that painting. Fifty-eight times he'd painted *Las Meninas* or some study from it. He was already famous when he'd done that, but he wanted to get better. Picasso wanted to get better! So he studied *Las Meninas*.

There was a tap on my shoulder, and I turned and Marina was hugging me, and kissing me quickly, and laughing, and saying, "I hoped I'd find you here."

She was wearing the same clothes, the uniform, as a couple of days before: the navy-blue short skirt, the white blouse. The same smile, the same eyes, those cheekbones, that slight body with that surprising strength.

"Well, hello," I said.

"That is all you have for me? Hello?"

"I tried to reach you. I thought—"

She put her fingers to my lips to shush me. "Don't ask. Let's just enjoy the museum. I can tell you so much here."

"Can you tell me that in"—I looked at my watch—"the next forty-five minutes? I have a team bus to catch at our hotel and then we're off to the airport and home to Dublin."

"Yes, I suppose I could, Peter. But I didn't know you were leaving Barcelona so soon. Perhaps there is something more important we could take care of for that forty-five minutes?"

"I'm checked out already."

"Ah, yes. But I have a room at Hotel Picasso. It's five minutes from here, on Passeig de Picasso." And she reached into her handbag and pulled out a room key, held it up for me to see and appreciate.

Which I did. And which we did. The lovemaking was impossibly good, like we were perfectly matched, perfectly in tune with one another, perfect in our timing and lost in those long, long minutes of love that both zipped by in an instant and yet stretched on into infinity while we were in the middle of things.

I made it, just barely, to the team bus an hour later, walking with Marina across Las Ramblas to reach the hotel, where we kissed, and kissed again.

I had to go, but in those last few seconds she tilted her head and smiled, giving me a look that gave me chills. "You'll do," she said, and reached up with her finger to touch my lips. I was falling hard.

We parted. I walked to the bus and boarded, my teammates looking at me and either smiling, or grinning, or nodding their heads. Coach looked at me as I walked by, shook his head, and looked away. I had scored eighteen and had ten assists for a double-double the night before, after all.

A few hours later I was back in Dublin and in that odd kind of reality bubble that professional athletes live in during the season. Yes, it was Second Division pro ball and a long way from the NBA, but we were treated well and the top clubs were always looking at us and some of my teammates ascended to heaven at FCB Regal or Olympiacos or Maccabi or Chelsea. Me? I was happy in Dublin. We drew a few thousand fans a game and I was starting and playing well and despite the rain I loved the city. I was learning to be selfish, learning that my focus had to be on myself and the level of my game. I had to stay focused. Everything else is everything else, Coach told us. Keep your head in it. Right here. And I did, and, really, life was good.

But I messaged Marina and didn't hear back. No problem—that's the way she was. I messaged a day later, and after that, and again. But I never heard back. That last look she'd given me? That tilted head and that smile? That promise that she'd see me soon? I would have sworn there was as much love as there was lust in that. I would have sworn it. But I never saw her again.

14

I sat back in my chair at Yeats' desk and tried to process what my eyes were seeing. It was, in fact, Heather standing there. She looked exhausted and confused, but there she was.

"May I come in?" she asked, and that broke me out of my reverie and I scrambled to rise from the chair and go over to her to put my arms around her and help her to the sitting chair in the corner. She sank into it, let her head fall back against the cushioned headboard, took a deep breath, looked at me, and said, "Hello, Peter."

There was movement in her flesh, slight ripples of changing. I got the feeling that she was struggling to maintain control of herself, of this version of herself.

"How?" was all I could manage to say as I pulled my desk chair over and sat down next to her.

She waved the question off. "Later, Peter. Everything later. For now, just shut the door, please, and let me rest."

I stood, walked over to shut the door, came back, and sat. "I saw you die, Heather. I saw you"—I struggled for the word—"decompose in that beam. Turn into dust and then blow away."

"Yes, Peter. But here I am." She waved at me, gave me a slight smile. "Right now no one, not even Twoclicks, must know I'm here. I'm very weak and vulnerable. I've set up firewalls everywhere. I don't think Whistle or his people have the scanning equipment to detect me here. You understand?"

"Yes," I said, "of course."

She managed a slight smile, shook her head the slightest bit, then whispered. "I need to recover, Peter, build up my strength." I nodded.

"All right, then. Please help me to that bed, and then I need you to stand guard for me. I need this tonight. If Whistle has locals working with him, working *for* him, they will be looking for me. They may look here. You'll have to keep them out of this room, do you understand?"

"Sure. Keep them out. For how long? Hours? Days?"

She didn't answer, but started to rise from the chair, pushing up with her tired arms. I jumped to help and, together, we made it to the bed, pulled back the blankets, and got her in.

"Should I help you take off your clothes?"

"No, no. I need them right now," she said, her eyes closing. "Keep watch, Peter, all right?" And she was asleep, or in a state something like sleep. I could see she was alive, and breathing; but those slight ripples in her flesh were still going on, though quieter now, as she fell into that deep sleep, or hibernation, or whatever it was.

So I was her bodyguard. Well, fair enough. Probably nothing would happen, probably I'd sit in the chair and read my Yeats and then the sun would rise and Heather with it, all revived and feeling better, and I'd get some answers about how she was here, how she was alive. Probably.

She didn't seem bothered by the light from the lamp stand, so I left it on and walked over to the Yeats desk and picked up that signed copy of *The Tower*, walked back over to the two chairs, side by side now, sat in the more comfortable one, and opened up the book, and read the first lines of the first poem: "What shall I do with this absurdity—O heart, O troubled heart."

Well, that sounded about right.

And then I saw out the window that faced the front lawn the lights from some approaching vehicle: some more military or police, I figured. I reached up, turned off the lamp, and, as the room went dark, walked over to the window and looked out. There, approaching, was a small truck. It was nearly to the circular drive in front of Ballina House before someone, a garda, I was guessing, came up waving a light to make it stop.

As I watched, the garda, then another and then two more, came up to the truck. The doors opened and several men got out, dressed like locals: two of them farmers, maybe, and one in a suit. The garda put them together in a line, searched them, were talking to them, and then I could see some laughter—ah, they all knew each other— and the men piled back into the truck and I watched as it wended its way along the circular drive and headed out, down the long road, past the smoldering remains of the limo we'd been in, and back toward the main road.

I pulled the chair over to the window, cracked it open a tiny bit so sound might drift in and the cool breeze might help me stay awake, and I sat. A good four hours to dawn, I thought. Well, I could handle that. And so I got comfortable in the chair, kept my eyes on what was going on outside, and had my thoughts to myself. From the bed, from Heather, there was nothing, her breathing so slight I could only barely hear it, the ripples in her flesh undetectable in the dark.

There would be some answers, perhaps, in the morning.

Heather woke me up around 9 A.M. She stood over me, smiling. She looked better, if still weak. I, on the other hand, felt terrible after a few hours of light sleep in the chair. The events of the night before had done me more damage than I'd realized. The ache in my left knee, that background pain that was nearly always there since those lousy final moments of my basketball career, had grown to something a lot sharper, more intense. I'd done damage last night to what cartilage was left in there. Scrambling around to get away from danger had strained, maybe torn, the meniscus. Damn.

But Heather, at least, had that smile. "Good morning, Peter," she said, and leaned down to kiss me.

She'd showered and was dressed now in some of my clothes, a Rovers T-shirt that was much too large and some sports shorts that I had with me in case there'd be a chance to cycle, the only exercise my knee could stand. Somehow she'd managed to gather together the extra material in the shirt and the shorts and tie it off. It should have looked funny; instead, it looked wonderful. She was here. She was alive, somehow.

I was waking up. I wanted some answers, and told her.

"First," Heather said, "let's get you cleaned up. Shower, brush your teeth, call downstairs and get some coffee and breakfast sent up—and don't mention that I'm here, all right?"

I let her take me by the hand—she was alive! It was still pretty much incomprehensible. I'd seen her die, right in front of me, dissolved into sparkling, awful, melting fairy dust that flared, then died down to nothing and blew away in the Irish breeze—and we walked to the bathroom. As we did I checked one more time for myBob, thinking there'd be no one home. I could still feel the hollowness, the emptiness, the lack of presence. There'd be no myBob, and there wasn't, so I pulled away from Heather for a moment, walked over to the small nightstand next to the bed, and called down on the old antique room telephone for breakfast and coffee to be sent to our room. Heather smiled and nodded. Then she took me by the hand again and walked me over to the bathroom, pushed me in, and shut the door behind me. When I got out of the shower

I felt a lot more human, and then I laughed at myself for having such a thought. Sure, human. After what I'd seen the past few months, and especially what I'd witnessed last night, feeling human didn't seem like such a big deal now, really.

Heather had changed by the time I came back into the main room. Boots, blue jeans, a T-shirt with a leather jacket over that. We were, apparently, headed outside. I started looking through my bags for something similar to wear when there was a polite tap on the door. Still in my bathrobe, I opened the door and breakfast was served, delivered by Devon Casey, the same hotel manager who'd made of gift of *The Tower* to me. "Full Irish it is, Mr. Holman," he said as he started to bring it into the room.

I reached out to take the tray from him. "Thanks so much, Mr. Casey. I'll take it from here." And I smiled at him.

"You're very welcome, Mr. Holman. Are you enjoying *The Tower*, then?"

"I am, indeed, Mr. Casey," I said, falling into those old familiar— and welcome—Irish rhythms. "You know, I could feel the connection between myself and Yeats from a century ago. I felt like I could hear the great man's voice speaking it to me."

Casey gave a slight shake of the head. "You're meant to be a storyteller, Mr. Holman. I know you've been in sport, and I hadn't mentioned this before but I saw you play basketball in Dublin a couple of years ago. The famous Yank with all those wild outside shots. It was glorious. And now you're here, back with us again. Ah, the stories you'll be able to tell from all this, eh?"

"Indeed, Mr. Casey," I said, "and thank you so much for bringing the breakfast. I'll have at it now, if you don't mind."

He smiled. "Of course, of course. Enjoy. Oh, and Mr. Twoclicks asked if you could meet him downstairs in a bit. He has plans for you all to leave us, I'm afraid, at some point this morning."

I smiled back at him. "No problem. You let him know I'll be there within the hour, all right?"

Casey nodded, said yes, and I finally had the door closed, the breakfast tray in my hands, and a chance for a badly needed cup of coffee for myself and Heather, who was walking out from the bathroom, where she'd hidden herself.

I set the tray on the Yeats desk, which seemed both blasphemous and somehow proper, and then walked over to the chest of drawers to get the empty teacup from last night. Then I poured two cups of coffee from the silver pot, black for myself and with a bit of cream for Heather. I turned back with one cup in each hand and saw she'd arranged the chairs to be side by side with a small table between. She sat in one chair, patted the other, and said, "Bring that breakfast and coffee over her, Peter. We'll eat and then go downstairs and there, with Twoclicks with us, we'll talk. All right?" And then she reached out to take her cup of coffee and sipped it. I sat down next to her and shook my head. "You people are incredible," I said. "I mean. Really."

She looked at the breakfast, said, "The eggs are getting cold," and got serious about eating. Me? I didn't have much appetite, but the coffee, black and strong, was good. Bewley's, I was guessing. I sipped it, then sipped again, and then packed my bag and got ready to leave.

Once, when I was in the good fourth year of professional basketball in Dublin, starting and playing well, making good money, enjoying life and working hard, I received a video call from sister Kait. It was just after noon Dublin time and I had a game that night. Some lunch and then the shoot-around and then the warm-ups and then the game. Slash or pull up or pick and roll and hard, hard on the D against Sheffield United, a good team, middle of the ladder, capable of beating the Rovers.

Noon in Dublin Fair City meant four in the morning in L.A., or five in Santa Fe, or three in Atlanta, wherever the hell she was now. She looked thin and pale, but she was smiling and excited as "Peter!" she said. "Have you ever heard this song? Listen, OK?" And she held out some ancient headphones for me to wear.

"Kait, Kaity," I said. "I'm in Dublin. I can't wear those, you know?"

"Oh, yeah," smiling at me. She looked tired and exhilarated at the same time. I'd seen it before. Tragic. Loaded up on smack. She unplugged the headphones and it was old classic Hendrix I could hear now, the wind whispering "Mary."

"I hear it now, Kait. Jimi Hendrix. Good stuff, but you're high again, aren't you? I thought you said you were in rehab, you were dumping the stuff."

"I did! I did twice!" she said, sitting back down on the bed. "And this is the last time. Right now, this is it, OK?"

"Kait," I said.

"No, listen," she said," "It's coming up. You have to hear it!"

And I listened as Jimi said the jacks were all in their boxes and the clowns had all gone to bed and somewhere a king didn't have a wife. And it whispers, no, this will be the last.

"Did you hear that?"

"I did, Kait. How long have you been this high? Should I call the EMTs for you?"

"No!" she said. "Didn't you hear that? 'This will be the last'? It's a message, Peter. This. Will. Be. The. Last. OK? OK?"

"OK, Kait. Sure, this will be the last. Where are you staying right now?"

She smiled, the energy fading. "Santa Fe," she said dreamily. And then "'Staying,'" she added, and tossed her smarty onto the bed and lay back herself. And just like that, she faded out.

I called the EMTs in Santa Fe and gave them her smarty number so they could GPS it and get to her. Then I left for lunch, and that shoot-around, and the game. When I checked, after lunch, she was in the ER and she'd be fine. Again.

Poor Kait. Good, good Kait. Happiness staggering on down the street. The wind whispers "Kaity."

15

I walked down the broad stone steps at the front of Ballina House, heading toward an armored limousine that sat in the middle of a little military motorcade of six vehicles, five of them armored cars, well-armed; and one of them our limo, in the middle of the line. Ahead of me, already getting into the limo, was Twoclicks. Behind him, getting in next, was an armed bodyguard, in a dark suit. I was next, ten steps behind, and I'd promised Twoclicks I would take a last look around from the top of the stairs to see if anything looked worrisome. I took that look, saw nothing threatening, and followed Twoclicks and the bodyguard into the relative safety of the armored limo, dark glass windows keeping the interior private as well as safe. Off we went.

Twoclicks sat opposite me, facing to the rear. To his left, going through some uncomfortable changes from a husky male bodyguard to the woman I knew, was Heather. I'd seen her change the other way ten or fifteen minutes before and found it just as fascinating as it was repulsive. It was interesting to know that she could change into something other than the two bodies I'd seen. Were there limits to that ability? I asked but she wouldn't say. Twoclicks sat silently as she changed. He hadn't been at all surprised to see her, though he'd been with me when she'd been decomposed, torn apart, by that terrible beam.

The Irish Defence Forces, the regular army in Ireland, had arranged transportation for us in a fortified limousine driven over from Dublin, and we were part of a motorcade the likes of which Ireland hadn't seen in the century since the fight for independence, including five British-made M-ATV armored vehicles, three in front of us and two behind. Our limo looked almost normal except for the bulky exterior, which the driver told us was the latest in buckypaper technology, built of long strands of carbon nanotubes that would hold up against "almost anything," as she put it. I was going to bring up the terror of a screamship from the night before but held off. Buckypaper wasn't going to be much better than an old pulp paperback against that sort of weaponry; but if the driver was happy believing otherwise who was I to dissuade her?

To her, this was a motorcade designed to get one alien and his friends out of town after those attacks around Earth the night before: the ghostships in ruin, the might of S'hudon on display, the fear that this was the start of what everyone had feared all along. She was following orders, and if that meant driving an alien to Shannon Airport, of all things, then that's what she intended to do. And no AIs driving anything in this motorcade, of course.

Our particular trouble from last night was not in evidence, the torched limo covered by a large tent with a huge "BH" emblem on it. She'd think, no doubt, that the tent and all the military and garda types walking around were there for security. She probably found some comfort in that. And to her, I supposed, the wheeled armored vehicles in front and behind us were little more than a wise precaution. For all she knew, the entire tour had been handled this way, with a high level of security and heavy weapons. Instead— incredibly, now that I thought on it—Twoclicks had been in the local pub last night with no one but Heather and me to guard him. I might have done OK in a fistfight with a drunken local, but I was surely helpless beyond that. And Heather was terrific in a number of ways, but I'd never seen her carry a weapon or display any kind of combat skills. She could, and did, change shapes between human and S'hudonni; but in neither shape did she seem likely to be a threat to an attacker.

And, I thought as I sat there, look what this lack of protection had cost us: an international—hell, an interstellar—incident.

An incident that, amazingly, only a few humans even seemed to know about. As we pulled away from the manor house I tried my helpmate yet again: "myBob, are you there?" But there was nothing but quiet. And if there were no spyeyes around—I certainly couldn't see any—and no edited-media types banging on our limo windows asking for details, then the world didn't know what we'd been through. Lots of attention paid elsewhere, sure; but we'd had an attack by one S'hudonni oligarch on another. Wasn't that news?

We pulled away from the manor house, following the big ATV right in front of us, just as it followed the one in front of it and that one followed the lead vehicle. There were two more of the armored vehicles behind us. It all felt pretty safe.

We made the left onto the two-lane main road that ran through Ballina and on toward the west, and we hadn't proceeded more than a half-kilometer when I heard, at last, from myBob.

"Hello, Peter. I'm back."

"myBob!" I said aloud, and Heather smiled at me. Twoclicks' eyes were closed as he dozed. I found that comforting. If he was dozing the danger couldn't be too bad, could it?

"Yes, it's me," myBob whispered internally. "But I'm not well."

"Damage?" I thought to him. "Were you awake the whole time and not able to communicate or were you blanked out?"

"Nothing," he said. "Worse."

"I'm sorry, myBob. What can I do?"

"Attacked. Gaps. Dark. Nothing."

Heather had heard it all, though it was all internal. This did not surprise me. She leaned forward from her seat. "Ask him if I can help."

"myBob, Heather wants to help."

"Reboot. Restore," he whispered internally. I knew Heather could hear it. Twoclicks seemed sound asleep, ignoring everything.

Heather reached over to touch me on the knee. "Can you do that, Peter? With your new hardware you might have that capability."

I had no idea if I could or not; certainly no one had explained how I might during the weeks of instruction I'd had in Palo Alto. There was nothing external that I could do: no switches, no touch-pads, no nothing. Maybe inside?

I gave it a try, closing my eyes and trying to picture that window I'd found just the once during my tutorials in Palo Alto.

Dark, with rectangles floating by, a diagonal line crossing them, a horizontal line appearing and then rising. The inside of something alive, spidery lines coming out from a central glowing core, yellow, filaments. Nothing, nothing really, nothing like that window I'd seen for a few seconds in Palo Alto. I opened my eyes. Looked at Heather. Shook my head.

She took my hand, said "Again," and so I gave it the old Florida Central College try, thinking wildly of basketballs rolling across a parquet floor. Foolishness. My hand in Heather's. Calm, se-rene, that touch. Comfort. Comfort. And a window opening, starting from a small spot of light in the middle of that mass of filaments and then growing larger, firming up, becoming more real, becoming something I could reach with my hand, touch up there in front of my closed eyes, extending my index finger and swiping, moving through, seeing the ratchet wheel for the toolbox, touching, touching again on the Restore that floated there; and then, in an instant, it was all gone.

I opened my eyes. "Maybe?" I asked Heather.

She nodded, and I knew that she'd been in there with me. She'd seen it. No surprise anymore on what she knew and saw. No sur-prises at all.

I'd reacquired that morning headache. I fell back against the seat, suddenly exhausted as I took one last look at her as she smiled and nodded again, and then I closed my eyes and was, in seconds, asleep.

myBob was buzzing me awake. I swatted at an imaginary mosquito for a second, then came awake enough to know where I was and who I was with. Heather was smiling, and Twoclicks, too, was awake, and wearing a kind of benevolent grin. We were moving at a steady fifty or sixty kph along a two-lane road with no other traffic on it. Heading straight west if I was reading the sun right.

I pulled myself up from the slouch I'd been in while napping. "myBob? You're back?"

"I've lost a lot of memory, but the operating systems are fine, Peter. I'm reacquiring the memories from the clouds now and getting things organized. It will take a few more minutes. At the moment I'm receiving quite a backlog of messages for you."

He seemed too official. What had happened to my old pal my-Bob? Where were the smart-ass jokes? Perhaps that myBob would be back, too, sometime soon. Meanwhile, I had to deal with things as they were.

"From?"

"The edited media—dozens of requests each from dozens of media. Two hundred requests, and they're still coming in. I've sifted through them and none of them have to do with what happened to us last night. It's all about the ghostship attacks and wondering if this means war. And wondering why Twoclicks hasn't spoken about it."

Heather was staring at me. "I'm allowing incoming but not outgoing, Peter. We could be located if you do that, so nothing yet, all right?"

As if I had a choice. "Yes, sure," I said. And then I thought to myBob, "Anything from my brother or sister? Or from Chloe?"

"Two from Chloe, three from your sister," myBob said. "Two of Kait's marked 'Urgent.' Nothing from your brother."

That sounded about right. "Can I hear the messages from Kait and Chloe, please?"

Heather was nodding. "Yes," said myBob, "in order of reception, starting at ten fifty-one last night our time."

"Peter." It was Chloe's voice. "I'm worried about you. Please answer on my private line, all right? People are asking me about you, and for the record I'm saying that I'm sure you're fine." And then again, another message a minute or two later, "Peter, it's me again. I hope you get this; I have it on maximum encrypt but I don't think that matters a bit to the people you're with. There's a lot of panic here. I'm watching video right now of the attack on the ghostship. Oh, my god, I drive by there a few times a week on my way to location! Peter! Be careful, love. Please. Send me a message. Please. Love you."

"Next, please, myBob," I said, and I heard from Kait: "Peter! How horrible! What's going on? I know you're working with the S'hudonni, but you're a friend with them, too, right? My god, I hope you're all right. Can you contact me? Please? We just want to know if you're OK."

And then essentially the same message again an hour later, and then something more chilling from Kait in a third message. "Peter, I hope you get this. I got a strange message from Tommy. He was rambling and sounded incoherent, crazy, talking about our humanity and something about this had to be done and he knew I'd been seeing you and he hated what was going to happen but it just had to. Peter! What's gone wrong with him?"

She took a deep breath—I could hear it happening—and then she added this: "Peter, I know I've had my own troubles with reality, you know. I've been horrible. I was lost, Peter, really. There were reasons, but put it all together and I was lost, that's all." Another pause, another breath. "And now I listen to Tommy and it sounds like that old me, that lost me, you know? Peter, we have to help him.

I'll try, I'll do everything I can from here. Travel's not even allowed right now, but I'll do what I can, OK? Please, god, you're OK, Peter. And contact me when you can." One more breath and another pause, then, "OK, OK, that's it, Peter. I just wanted you to know what's happening at this end. I hope you're all right. I hope you can contact me soon. Love you, brother."

And that was that.

I looked over to Heather, who smiled tiredly. I knew she had heard it all, every bit of it. "Sorry, Peter," she said, "but until we get ourselves safely home we're going to keep the lid on all this, so you won't be able to send."

"Understood," I said, "but I do have a few questions. Can I ask them?"

Twoclicks smiled, said, "Of course, friend Peter. Ask away!"

The motorcade slowed to a stop, and there was a moment of worry. Heather was listening intently to something internal, concerned; then she relaxed. "We're turning here to head south for a few miles, that's all," she said. And turn we did.

Then she turned back to me. "Peter, you know there are certain things we can't talk about yet, right? But we'll tell you what we can."

"Can myBob record this?"

"Are you with us, myBob?" Heather asked.

"Mostly," he said. "But even if I'm not really all here yet, I can certainly record it as a sweep."

I felt a kind of awakening internally, a certain sense of presence, or an expansion of presence. "Should I be able to feel that, myBob, to kind of sense it?"

"No idea," myBob said, with the first glimmer of personality I'd heard from him since he'd come back to life. And then, "Yes, I think so," said Heather.

Fair enough. "How is it you're alive, Heather? For the record, I saw you torn apart, scattered into what looked like shimmering dust. And now you're here. How's that possible?"

Heather looked at Twoclicks, who nodded his head. She answered:

"There is a device we use very sparingly. It's a kind of transmitter that copies you and sends you to a receiving unit. We had some hints of trouble and I installed the device away from the manor, in those nearby woods."

"I thought I saw a something there yesterday, a slight, I don't know, disturbance, a shimmer."

She smiled. "Yes, that was it."

"When you ran to the woods you used that?"

"That was my intent. But then the screamship came so soon, and you were there." She shrugged. "Plans change."

"Then you died."

"I did," she said. "But I've used that transmitter before, Peter, several times."

I put two and two together. "So you're a copy, some kind of previous copy, and you were sent here from somewhere else."

That explained the memory loss, it occurred to me. The copy—that other Heather, that other thing—would only know what it knew before it was copied and sent. Jesus Christ, I thought. "How many copies of you are there?"

Twoclicks interrupted. "Not many, friend Peter. Process iss very expensive. Heather's not worth that much!" And he broke into a deep chuckle, appreciating his joke.

A lot of things were starting to fall into place for me. I wondered if I had them right.

"That was Whistle's ship that did the attack, right?"

"Of course!" Twoclicks said happily, and then clapped his hands. "He iss alwayss so much trouble!"

Oh, my. So this was the usual thing? And they all had copies of themselves?

"I get it," I said. "It's all a game. No one dies, everyone pulls themselves together when the game is over and starts over again. It's all a lot of fun." Except for Earth, I thought, where all this frivolity would be taking place. Because we Earthies? We die permanently.

"Oh, friend Peter," Twoclicks said, reading my mind. "I ssee your problem. No, no, iss very serious. We know so. And we will not take unfair advantage. We have plans for that, for you." He stopped, sat back, closed his eyes, the strain of this conversation with his Earthie apparently all too much to take. He whistled to Heather and then was silent.

"One more question?" I asked.

Heather looked at Twoclicks, who seemed to be asleep in an instant. "Last one for now, Peter, all right?"

"Sure. There was a second ship up there last night. Twoclicks' ship, I think. Why hasn't it just picked us up and taken us out of here?"

She looked at Twoclicks, who whistled a bit without bothering to open his eyes. "Two wants to use this whole thing to his advantage, show everyone that it wasn't us, that we're the good guys; that we want to get along with the locals."

She could see I wasn't buying that one, and added, "And we're trying to travel incognito, remember? No electronics? No signature?"

"But aren't all Earthie flights grounded?"

She smiled, paused to get some information for a second, said, "There are, at the moment, about eight thousand Earthie military aircraft of one sort or another in the air globally. Two thousand in Europe alone, one thousand over the North Atlantic. Everyone is trying to keep everything in the air."

"So that's how we're getting home?"

She nodded, and then added, "Plus, as you've seen, he's something of a collector. There's a particular item that he wants to obtain before we leave Ireland. He's willing to go to some lengths to get this."

More games. More playtime for our alien friends.

"Some ancient artifact? A chalice out of the bogs, maybe? Or some illuminated manuscript? Something like that?"

"Yes, something like that," and she reached across to put her hand on my knee. "And that's enough for now, all right? Be a little patient and you'll see soon what he has in mind."

She sat back, took her hand off my knee. And so that was that.

I turned to watch Twoclicks. His eyes were closed. Was he asleep, that fast? Did he sleep? Ever? I didn't know. Hell, I didn't know anything. I thought I'd loved this beautiful lie sitting opposite me, but now I was beginning to feel differently. It was all a game.

"All right," I said, as if I were agreeing, as if I had a choice in the matter. And then I sat back and watched out the window as the Irish countryside slipped by in the now bright sunshine. Quiet. Calm. Strangely calm.

I confirmed with myBob that we had a sweepcast recorded of that conversation, and then asked him to check the clouds for any news of what we'd been through in the past day. Still nothing about us, he said, though there was plenty of the usual craziness from the bloggers and social sites, and some admirable restraint from the edited media, which seemed to be holding its collective breath.

I told myBob thanks and sat back in my seat, closed my eyes, trying to nap. That wouldn't be possible, surely, under these circumstances; but then I slipped into idle thoughts about Chloe and how someday soon I'd like to bring her to Ireland, which led me to Marina, long-lost Marina, and that led to basketball and how I'd felt playing the game, the joy I'd found in that, before the ruined knee, the career-ender, the pain.

I drifted along for a while, half asleep, until we rounded a tight curve and the movement brought me back awake. I looked around. Twoclicks was still asleep (though one never knew for sure), and Heather, still in the form of my Earthie Heather, was reading her smarty. She glanced at me and smiled and went back to her reading, tapping a few times here and there, and murmuring under her breath. Something about being "secure."

I assumed we were headed to Shannon Airport, which wasn't more than one hundred or so kilometers to the west from our hotel.

If I'd been napping for nearly an hour or so, I figured we should be getting close, which meant somewhere in the area of Limerick.

Which meant we should be on the N24, a major road, not on this tiny rural road. We passed a road stone post, two centuries old, that read "Limerick 5 Miles" and had a tiny arrow pointing in the direction we were heading, and then we passed an intersection that said "Sandylane."

"myBob, we're near Limerick?" I asked my helpmate.

No answer. I looked at Heather. She smiled, said, "There's been some trouble, Peter, that cropped up while you were napping. It's happening not far from here, near Shannon Airport, so I've closed down some more selected electronics in the region so that Twoclicks' safety won't be compromised. So no myBob right at the moment. Sorry."

"What kind of trouble?"

"Improvised explosives on the major road leading toward the airport. We would have been ambushed there, I suppose, once we were forced to stop."

"Can't we bypass the trouble spots?"

"Look around you, Peter. That's what we're doing right now. We'd already planned one extra stop on the way, and now that will take a little longer to accomplish, that's all."

"Ah" was all I could manage. And I recalled in wonder that when Heather had first offered me the job I'd thought the whole thing would be an interesting sort of press junket. See some interesting places, meet some interesting people, and get famous. And not in that order.

"An extra stop?"

"Yess, friend Peter," said Twoclicks, his eyes opening. "Iss something I must obtain. Very important."

"Ah," I said. Again. Which tells you how fast I was, or wasn't, thinking. "So where are we going?"

"Foynes," said Heather, clicking on the comm button to the

driver and saying, "Driver, I've programmed your screen with directions to a new destination. Please follow those closely. I've informed our escort of this route as well."

And as she said that the caravan reached an intersection and took a sharp left turn, toward Foynes, a village I was only dimly aware of. It was on the River Shannon and had something to do with seaplanes.

"The West of Ireland has an interesting aviation history," said Heather, smiling at me as she prompted Twoclicks.

"Oh, yess," said Twoclicks. "Most interesting. Famous flights, famouss people. Famouss aircraft. Iss full of history."

"And Foynes is part of that?" I said, calmly. Unbelievable. This was insanity. We were going out of our way to sightsee while the world waited to erupt? "Do we really have to go see this now? Don't we need to get home, back to your ship?"

"Oh, yess, friend Peter, mosst important. Heather will explain." And Twoclicks closed both membranes over his eyes and sat back, napping again, calm as he could be.

"Heather," I said. "What the hell?"

She was looking at her smarty. "It's important, Peter. A bargaining chip, a kind of contest between two sons. Twoclicks has to have it, and we're right here, just an hour away now, maybe less. This has been part of the plan all along."

"You'll risk your and Twoclicks' and all of our safety? For this thing, whatever it is?"

She smiled. "Absolutely. But it's not that risky, truly. Whistle won't try to use S'hudonni technology against us again, we're prepared for that now. That means it's just the locals to worry about, and they shouldn't be a problem. Trust me, as you always do, Peter. With the electronics closed down, even if someone sees us and tries to call for help, the call won't get through. And there seem to be only five or six people—all Earthies—involved in this. By going to Foynes by back roads we're avoiding conflict with them."

She looked at me. "We have our screamship nearby, Peter.

Minutes away if we need it. We don't want to use it; that would spoil some important plans and provoke Whistle. But we will if we must, and then those Earthies would all die, Peter, no matter what kinds of weapons they may think they have, no matter how inventive their bombs, no matter how courageous or smart or determined they are: They would all die. You understand this, right? You've seen what a ship can do?"

I did. I had. And this most definitely wasn't what I'd thought I was getting into. "I thought this was a diplomatic mission we were on, Heather. I didn't really sign up for all this shoot-'em-up, you know."

"You were courageous last night, Peter. You came to try and save me." And she smiled at me. Yes, yes I had done that. I'd tried.

She sat back, eyes staring into the distance, communicating with someone. "Yes," she said aloud so I could hear it. "Yes. Foynes."

She disconnected. I could see it in her eyes. "And so," she said, "let's go visit Foynes and save some lives, all right?"

Human lives, I thought. Somebody heeding that call to arms, somebody remembering glory days of past battles against colonial oppression. Most of those hadn't worked out too well for the Irish, and this, should the battle happen, would be a slaughter.

"Sure," I said, "absolutely. Foynes it is."

16

Foynes it was, not long after. As we drove along, Heather kept checking for trouble and saying we looked fine as we circled around what she'd named the "group of dissidents."

Twoclicks woke up from yet another nap and was suddenly quite chatty, lecturing me on the aviation history of the West of Ireland, with Heather offering elaboration where she felt it was needed.

"Friend Peter," Twoclicks said, "Foynes is where first transatlantic flightss landed. Seaplanes, flying from New York. Landed here to refuel and then on to Europe."

"The flights began in 1937, Peter," said Heather. "A Pan Am Sikorsky S-42 flying from Newfoundland. And right after that the British started, too, with BOAC flights from Newfoundland. As the equipment improved the flights got longer, and by 1942 it was Foynes nonstop to New York City."

"During World War II?"

"Yess, friend Peter!" said Twoclicks. "War made Foynes important! Very important!"

"Neutral Ireland, right?"

"Exactly, Peter," said Heather. "Your world was at war, but

Ireland was neutral and, to the south, Portugal and Spain, too, were neutral. So there was plenty of interest in civilian flights between North America and Europe, and about the only way for people to make them was to fly through Foynes."

"Yess," said Twoclicks. "In those years the way in, way out, for all ssorts of interesting people wass through Foynes."

"People fleeing Hitler, I suppose." And then it hit me. "In *Casablanca,* those letters of transit that Bogie and his buddies were all concerned about. Those letters got Ingrid Bergman and her husband to Lisbon. They caught a flight from there on the seaplane and flew through Foynes to get to America, right?"

Twoclicks clapped and nodded. "Just so, friend Peter, just so. And on a plane exactly like the one you will see in Foynes."

So, I thought, Twoclicks wanted to see some interesting Earth history firsthand. There must be a museum, maybe the original piers or an old plane or two, some old radios, some other memorabilia from those days. Lord knows Twoclicks had an interest in Earthie artifacts. Heather said he'd been collecting things all along the way, paintings from the Louvre and the Tate, small antique steam engines made by Scottish engineering students in the 1850s from the National Museum of Scotland, paintings from Venice's Ca' Rezzonico, a soccer ball from England's World Cup win with a signature from Bobby Charlton scrawled across it, and even a small silver chalice from the time of St. Patrick from the National Museum of Ireland.

I'd stood, awestruck, to look at that chalice during my playing days with the Rovers. Now it was, I was guessing, inside one of the military vehicles in our convoy with the rest of the loot—no, not that; gifts, that's what they were; gifts—from Twoclick's little excursion through Europe.

"And the days of flying aren't even the best of the history, Peter," Heather was saying while Twoclicks sat back, looking smug. We were rounding a corner and were now finally on a more major road, the N69. The sign read "Glin 4," and Glin, I thought, was near Foynes, so we'd be there in a few minutes. "Your Americans don't seem to realize it, but your Charles Lindbergh was the *third* human to cross the Atlantic from Newfoundland to Europe."

"Alcock and Brown," I said, smug myself there for a minute.

Twoclicks clapped his small hands, not an easy task given the body shape and the short, frail arms. He had to be very exuberant to bother with clapping. "Yes! Yess!" he said, and Heather added, with some surprise, "Well done, Peter."

"I lived here for years, Heather. I know all the stories: the June 1919 flight, the two of them in that converted Vickers Vimy bomber, the landing in the bog near Clifden. In fact, I spent a great weekend in Clifden once, with a woman I was dating. We visited the bog site with that marker on it." Showing off, I added, "And that's Marconi there, too, in Clifden."

More exuberant clapping. "Yess again, friend Peter. Sso ssmart!"

It was foolish of me to act that way, and even more foolish to be proud of my knowledge, but there it was. I probably should have been wagging my tail.

"Marconi's towers were there in about the same place, in the same bog, I think, sending and receiving wireless from Nova Scotia. They'd been up for more than ten years by then, but Alcock and Brown almost crashed into them. Now that," I said with some satisfaction, "would really have been a historic collision."

Heather smiled. I think she almost laughed. Almost. Twoclicks, on the other hand, had a loud, explosive chortle of glee. I thought for a second he was going to reach over and pat me on the head: his smart, little Earthie.

I allowed myself a smile and looked away to glance outside. To our right, just through my window, the River Shannon was widening to its estuary, where it emptied into the Atlantic. Wide and getting deeper here, in a tidal area, the Shannon was flat as glass, protected by hills on three sides as it curved gently to the south before it curved again to the west and north later. It *did* make for a perfect area to land a flying boat.

"You know it was our Charles Lindbergh who came to survey the Shannon for the best place to land flying boats, right?" I asked the two of them.

Heather nodded. Twoclicks had fallen back asleep in the few seconds I'd taken to look outside the window. "Lindbergh admired Hitler, Peter, did you know that? Lindbergh didn't want your country to go to war with Germany."

I nodded, though in fact, that was something I'd learned only after moving to Ireland. Lindbergh's admiration for Herr Hitler didn't come up often in American high-school or college history books. Of course, the Irish had their own problems in that regard: Éamon de Valera, their beloved "Dev," was also, perhaps, an admirer of Hitler, and it was Dev who'd kept Ireland neutral during the war. Dev, in fact, had gone to the German embassy in Dublin and signed the condolence book after Hitler's death at the end of the war, that pathetic suicide in the deep Berlin bunker. Not many people were interested in signing that condolence book by war's end, and no one seemed real sure why Dev did it. Something Irish, something to do with thumbing your nose at England one more time?

The road curved sharply to the right and then, a half-kilometer farther along, we were in Foynes. It's a small village with no traffic, so we moved cleanly through it, and there, at the far end, was the Foynes Flying Boat Museum. We drove past it. I looked at Twoclicks and he raised that small right hand of his, signaling me to be patient. Another hundred meters and there, on the water's edge of the wide Shannon estuary, was Malone's Pub.

Heather was listening again. "I think we're clear," she said. "Actually, there's no sign of them at all now. One bomb blew up a chunk of road outside Limerick and another was found near Bunratty, on the N18; but that seems to be it. I've opened up their comm abilities so they can talk to each other. If they do, I'll be able to hear it and trace it. For now, I'm sure we're perfectly fine."

And so the caravan came to a stop, three of the M-ATVs ahead of us, two behind. Our armored limo parked right outside the door to the pub.

"Really?" I asked. "A pub? Shouldn't we be getting where we're going?"

Twoclicks raised that right hand again, and then waited for Heather and me to get out and help him emerge from the limo. We did that, with a dozen or more security people around us, several in uniform and several in suits, but all well-armed, I was sure.

I shook my head. All this for a pint? But the sooner we got that done the sooner we'd be on our way, and away from this trouble and in some safer, saner place.

Heather was smiling. "You'll see what he has in mind in a minute, Peter. Let's just walk him into Malone's." Which we did.

Malone's was, at first glance, an ordinary pub in an ordinary village: a long bar with taps and a mirror behind and rows of bottles. A snug in the far corner, held over from decades before when women were improper if they didn't stay in their own small side room with a window into the bar. There was a smattering of small round tables with chairs, a wooden floor, tired wallpaper, and a lot of great old photographs of Foynes' glory days.

"Look, friend Peter," said Twoclicks, and pointed up to the high ceiling. There, rotating slowly, gracefully, was a large old airplane propeller serving as a ceiling fan, the four blades slowly circling its hub.

"That's one of the propellers from the Alcock and Brown Vickers Vimy IV, Peter," said Heather, coming to stand next to me and, putting her arm over my shoulder, looking up at the propeller. "Amazing, isn't it?"

I marveled. "What the hell is it doing in this pub and not in the museum down the street?"

"It's a long story," Heather said, and then the proprietor came out from a back door and did a double and then a triple take at seeing who his visitor was. The proprietor was a woman, in her sixties, and beside her was her husband. She held his hand as they entered.

He'd apparently had a stroke, or suffered from some kind of dementia that couldn't be treated. Before the vaccine, Alzheimer's
had claimed people like him by the millions. This man . . . well, it
had to be something difficult to treat, late-stage Parkinson's perhaps, or a recent stroke.

He shuffled as he walked, and he had a vacant smile on his
face as he reached out to shake Heather's hand and then did
the same with Twoclicks. The woman reached up to him, smiling,
and with a small towel wiped the drool from his mouth. I was
guessing the two of them had run this place together for years
and then whatever happened to him happened and now she kept
him involved as best she could. Heather walked over to her, and
Twoclicks waddled over himself, and together the three of them
started chatting. What could they offer him for that old propeller? Enough money for private, in-home care for her husband, for
starters.

I walked outside for some fresh air and a few minutes by myself
and hadn't gotten more than thirty meters before one of the security detail sauntered over to tell me to stay within the perimeter. I
was just about to ask why when, in the distance, I heard a loud
whoomph and a cloud of smoke rose from up the road, on the far
side of a wooded hill. It took a few seconds for me to realize that it
had to be a bomb, and that we were under attack.

I turned to run back into the pub, but didn't get there. Heather
had Twoclicks by the elbow and was guiding him toward the
armored limo. "Help me. Quickly. Get him into the limo," she ordered, and I took the other elbow and helped him waddle along
as quickly as he could.

Bursts of gunfire came from outside the perimeter, and it sure
sounded closer to us than the bomb had. I looked toward the hill
and saw the spark of gunfire. If we could see that, the shooter could
see us.

"Quickly," Heather was saying. "Come on Peter, quickly now."
In ten more steps we got Twoclicks into the relative safety of the

armored limo. I heard something whir by and heard a chip of pavement shatter behind me. Damn it. Close.

I wanted to get into that limo, but Heather had other ideas. She'd turned to run back toward the pub's entrance. What the hell, I ran, too, following her, fear driving me to perform the fastest sprint of my life into the pub.

The proprietor and three other men were on one tall and three short stepladders, disassembling the propeller from its housing, two of them reaching up to support it while the other was snipping wires and unscrewing attachments. As I watched, the propeller sagged and the two let it come into their arms. It looked heavy. Very heavy and cumbersome, with the blades nearly a meter and a half long.

Outside, it sounded like a battle was raging, a steady rat-a-tat of gunfire, the incoming indistinguishable from the outgoing, but a whole hell of a lot of it, damn it, going back and forth. Inside, Heather took one side of the propeller from one of the men, shoving him out of the way to do it. I, more politely, took the other side. It was heavy, and I wondered how Heather could possibly handle that weight. I was at my limit just to keep it from falling.

"Come on, Peter, we have to get it out to the ATV."

Sure, I thought, and in a second she was moving and so was I, at first with a little help from my friend the guy who'd had the propeller before I did; but then, when we were approaching the door and a stray bullet hit the door frame and sent splinters flying, he let go and fled, and I couldn't blame him.

We paused. Heather tilted her head, listening to something only she could hear. She smiled, said "A few seconds now," and then came a great screaming from outside, so loud it rattled the brain and overwhelmed me. A screamship. Twoclick's screamship. I saw, through the doorway, a series of bright lights and that crackling I knew from the day before. And then it was quiet. Deathly quiet, and Heather said calmly, "That's it, Peter. Let's carry it out there now and get moving."

I had help—two of the men who'd been working to get the propeller down from the ceiling emerged from behind the bar and came over to lend a hand. So the four of us tilted it up on one end. For a second I thought we were going to try and roll it through the doorway, but no, Heather had another idea. She held it by one of the four blades and the three of us held it by two blades on the opposite side and we lifted the damn thing to carry it through the doorway. The three men struggled mightily with our end as we tried to angle the blades to get them through. Heather handled her side with ease. Superwoman. Superthing.

We were outside with it, and there was no gunfire, just some smoke and distant crackling. Nothing in the sky; no great screamship.

And no guards. They were all out on the road, looking up, shaking their heads. One turned and saw us and yelled to his mates and five or six of them came over to help us move the propeller into the back of the M-ATV. Easy as pie with those guards doing the heavy lifting.

I took a glance into the large hold of that ATV. It was meant for a dozen soldiers or more to ride in, so there was plenty of room for things like Celtic jewelry and old propellers and famous chalices and more: just a few little trinkets from Ireland. Whatever was in there was covered with blankets, but I could imagine what it had to be. I shook my head but said nothing. The guard who was closing up the hold had a blank expression on his face as he swung the door shut and locked it. Then he turned, stared at me. I shrugged and I thought, perhaps, I saw the slightest shake of his head. And off I went, over to the limo.

Heather was waiting for me, standing by the door. "Fight's over," she said. "I don't know yet how they knew where we were and how they avoided my scans, but we had the screamship ready."

"Good thing."

"Yes, good thing, indeed. But we don't want that, Peter. We want this all to be peaceful and progressive for Earth. We don't want to fight. You know that, right? You believe in us?"

I wasn't really in the right position to answer that, having seen the looted treasures in the back of that ATV, but I tried. "Did you pay the woman for the propeller?"

"Of course. She's a millionaire now. She'll retire with her husband to some nice place in Spain or Italy. They'll be happy."

I shook my head. "You saw him, Heather. Dementia. A stroke, I'm guessing, maybe something worse. She'll spend the money on care for him."

"No," I heard from the limo, as Twoclicks joined the conversation, "we have helped him, friend Peter. He is better already but does not know. In a few weeks, good as new."

"Or back to normal, anyway," Heather said with a smile. "We can do these things, Peter. We can and we will—we simply need the time to put all this together. We need to persuade Earth, or at least our parts of Earth, that we mean well. That we can help."

"Oh, I get it," I said. " 'Persuade.' That's my job, right?"

"Yes," she said, "that's your job. You were sweeping and recording the entire time, yes?"

"Of course," I said, hoping that myBob had had the good sense to do so, since I'd forgotten to tell him.

"Good." And she pointed up the hill behind Malone's Pub. "Keep recording now as we go take a look up there, all right?"

Where she pointed I saw two upright stones. A cairn, maybe? "Sure," I said, and told myBob to keep it running as Heather and I and a couple of the security people went for a little stroll up a steep hill.

The summer after my rookie year with the Rovers I lived up to my agreement with Mom and came home for a planned six weeks. After having been something of a minor celebrity in Dublin, it was a shock to come home to St. Petersburg and realize that no one cared. Euro basketball wasn't high on the list of appreciated things in St. Pete, where beach sports and baseball and the local soccer franchise pretty much got all the attention.

Worse, all my friends were gone, some to jobs in other cities, some to grad school, some—the lucky and skilled ones—to summer-league pro ball and the hope of catching on with the NBA. Dreams are nice, but I realized I'd moved on from the person I'd been and now was the person I had become. So I told Mom and Father good-bye and got back to Dublin, and working out with the Rovers, and enjoying my celebrity status as a local—if minor—sports hero.

That was the summer and fall of Niamh, a Galway woman who was working on preparing for the defense of her doctorate at Trinity College on "Empires, Colonisation, and Revolution." That might sound to you like something the Irish would be especially interested in, given their history, and you'd be right to think that. Her doctoral dissertation had to do with Ireland's place in the European experience with imperialism and colonialism, and when I met her I didn't know much about that. Six months later I knew a lot.

Eventually Niamh was awarded the doctorate and got herself a teaching post in Canada, at Ryerson. I liked her, a lot, and gave fleeting thought to following her across the water to the New World. But by then I was firmly entrenched as a starter with the Rovers and there was rumbling now and again that I might get a chance to move up to a bigger club. More important, I'd learned to be selfish to succeed, and so she left and I stayed and that was that.

That was how it went for the next few years. Calm enough. A series of half-serious relationships that never worked out. A basketball career that kept me busy and mildly successful and allowed me to play a kid's game, throwing balls into hoops while getting paid pretty good coin for it.

I talked to Mom a lot by video calls and every now and again talked to Dad and Tom, too, when they happened to be walking by as Mom was sitting at her work desk chatting with me. Father was polite, though I knew he was thinking I'd grow out of it one of these days and go back to school and get a medical degree or at least some kind of graduate degree so my life wouldn't be quite so frivolous.

And Tom? While I was traveling around Europe playing basketball he was getting that master's and that doctorate and that first teaching post and then the second one and then tenure and then and then and then . . . The Road to Success. He did that progression in about half the time most people take to do it. Heck, I was proud of him—baby brother made good. "Dr. Tom" is what I called him, and I think he actually liked it. After a while I forgot I'd meant it as a joke. In my mind he was still the nerdy kid with braces whom I'd spent my childhood protecting from bullies and introducing to girls.

In real life, though, he was doing fine. Father, I'm sure, thought the world of him. It was during these years, in fact, that Tom became more and more like Father: sharing the same intellectual pursuits, from local equity theater and the not-bad St. Petersburg symphony to smoking Camel cigarettes, unfiltered. This was a habit that wasn't an easy one to practice, since smoking wasn't allowed most places and unfiltered Camels were hard to find. But find them they did, father and son. Well, hell, I remember thinking one time when the two of them, engrossed in a ferocious chess match back behind Mom when she was vid-chatting with me, were sending up clouds of that smoke that I could see on the screen.

"Really?" I asked her once. "How do you stand it?" And she shrugged and said, "Two peas in a pod, Peter. And they both seem happy. And I'm tired of arguing."

Kait and I stayed in touch separately, but not often by video. She was leading a rough life at the time and I'm sure she didn't want me to see how she looked or where she was living or who she was living with.

That was all right. Kait was my one remaining tie to altruism: I'd made a decision, right smack in the middle of a very selfish career, to do what I could for her. Easy enough from five thousand miles away, sure; but I'd like to think my heart was in the right place, and several times I had the chance to spend some money on her and did and helped her out. Twice she was in a bad way with things as basic as rent and groceries, and I was well-off by comparison. I sent her a few thousand euros, which was double that amount in dollars. And once she needed ten grand for a rehab stint that would be, she swore, the one that worked, the one that got her clean and committed to staying that way. I didn't really believe, given her history, but that was in my fifth and final year and I was making two hundred thousand euros and had the money to send her, so I paid for the rehab in sunny California and got her started in life afterward with another twenty and I felt stupidly good about myself, as if I'd done something real, something like actually visiting her and being there for her.

But I couldn't, you know. Basketball called to me. Basketball needed me and I needed it. So I bought off my conscience and helped her through that tough time. Hey, I told myself later, after the help I gave that did finally get her off the terrible horse she was riding, at least it worked.

And then, in May of my fifth year with the Rovers, it all came to an end. Suddenly I wasn't a professional basketball player with years of experience behind him and more years of playing in front; instead, I was done and at age twenty-eight I had to grow up and become an adult and get a real job.

It happened in a few seconds: a move I made that was too ambitious, a defender whose own career was on the line, another defender coming across to help out on defense. Fourth quarter, first-round playoff game, down by two with ten seconds on the clock and I decided to take it down the middle and get the bucket or the foul or, maybe, both.

Instead, I lost control, banging into one guy and then landing funny when the next guy, even bigger, came down on my left knee, already bent the wrong way. I knew in that long, long fraction of a second in the air that this was bad, and there seemed to be nothing I could do about it.

There wasn't. Multi-ligament injuries, torn cartilage, dislocation. Worst of all, the second, worse, injury; when the big guy fell on me, it tore the popliteal artery. The dislocation of the kneecap couldn't be repaired and I was on my way to the emergency room in Barcelona. The surgeon there was thinking he'd be relocating the kneecap and repairing the torn ligaments and cartilage and suddenly found himself with vascular surgery on his hands. He did his best. He did what he could do. But that was it for me. The start of a new life, or time for a new chapter, or finally growing up and getting a real job. Take your pick.

The attack on us had failed. No surprise there, given what I'd seen the night before of the damage that S'hudonni ships could do, melting a limousine and tearing apart a being with a beam of light that scattered the resulting tiny particles to the winds.

Of course, that had been Heather, the same Heather I now walked with up the hill behind Malone's Pub, so clearly I knew nothing about what was really going on. She wanted to see where the shots had been fired from and so we walked, the two of us and two armed guards, up the hill to where a circle of seven large stones stood, most of them tipped over but three upright in the soil.

My comm was working fine. "How old is this site?" I asked Heather.

"Four thousand years, give or take. These are pre-Celtic, Middle Bronze Age, around 2000 BCE."

"Religious, I suppose?"

"Yes," she said, "but astronomical as well, letting those people know the equinox and the solstice."

"Like Newgrange, then. I've been to Newgrange."

"Yes," she said, "close enough." She walked over to one stone, on its side, a huge thing maybe five or six meters long and a couple of meters wide. "Look, Peter, see this," and she pointed.

I saw nothing but mashed-down grass. I wondered for a second why that mattered. Then, no Sherlock but not too stupid, either, it came to me. "A shooter was sitting here? Using the stone as cover?"

"Yes." She came up to the stone, looked down to see it closely. "And the stone took some hits, too, from the looks of it. See this?"

I did, and it was clearly fresh. I reached out to feel it but she stopped me. Below us a pair of vehicles roared up, lights flashing, both of them garda, and, behind them, no lights flashing, came a van. "That will be forensics, Peter, and they'll want us off this hill so they can secure it and look for clues. We shouldn't touch anything, and we should go."

"Couldn't you—or one of those ships—do your own forensics? Don't you have techniques that would tell us something? Tell us a lot?"

She looked at me. "Others of the group from S'hudon now here on Earth might choose to do their own investigation, Peter, and then take their own action. But Twoclicks is hoping to leave incidents like these in the hands of the locals." She smiled. "And we're leaving anyway. We have more pressing problems to deal with, you know. Come on."

She started walking downhill, me hobbling along behind her. My left knee didn't much like going uphill or upstairs, but I could do it smoothly. Downhill was another matter. Each bend of the knee, each jarring contact when the foot hit the downward slope, sent knife blades of pain through the knee. It hurt so much I had to alter my gait so the left knee didn't bend too much and the foot came down at more of an angle.

It made for slow going and I had to stop a couple of times and give the knee a rest. On the second of those stops I saw, down at the bottom of the hill, on the far side of a stream that wound its way toward the Shannon, a glimmer of something. That slight shimmer I'd seen back in Ballina? Heather had explained that to me, but hadn't mentioned this so perhaps she hadn't seen it. I thought I should tell her.

But when I turned to wave her over, thinking I'd ask her if she was expecting more trouble, I saw she had her mind on other things. She stood quietly, listening. I thought at first she was waiting for me to catch up, but then she tilted her head the way she did when a message was coming in.

She put her hand up to stop me. "Did you hear that, Peter?" she asked.

"No. Nothing."

"Listen. Listen closely—it's in your range."

And I did, focusing my attention, trying to forget the little knives tormenting my knee and my curiosity about that shimmer.

There was, perhaps, a small whimper, someone in pain somewhere. "Crying?" I asked. "But distant, very hard to hear."

Heather was moving purposefully back up the hill, waving at me, saying, "Quickly, Peter, follow me. It's coming from the top there somewhere."

I turned around and headed back up, grateful, really, to be moving in the direction that didn't hurt my knee. I couldn't keep up with Heather, though, and by the time I reached the flat top of the hill she was off on the other side, a hundred meters or more away.

I started heading that way, moving as quickly as I could, when myBob pinged me.

"myBob," I said, "this better be important."

"It is," he said, "very. It's a family emergency and you need to hear it, even if you can't answer."

I stopped climbing. "Sure. Let me hear it, please."

There was some unusual buzzing and clicking instead of the usual clean connect, and then this: "Peter? Are you there? Can you hear me? I'm leaving this message for you." It was Sarah, Kait's spouse. "Peter, I'm really worried about Kait! Yesterday, when I got home from work, Kait wasn't here, Peter, and we always have a nice dinner together on Tuesdays, just the two of us."

Up ahead, at the far edge of the plateau on the hilltop, I could see Heather looking down, searching for something, someone. She turned and waved to me, telling me to get to her, quickly. I was limping and sore, but an order's an order and I headed that way as quickly as I could, still listening to Sarah. "I've been up all night, and nothing," she was saying. "I'm so worried."

Me, too, I thought, thinking it was a bender. Booze, we could hope; or heroin, we could fear. "God," she was saying, "I've told the police here but you know how that goes. They're not going to do anything, not for days, they say. Anyway, Peter, I need your help, please. I don't know what else to do. Message me back, please. Soon." And she ended it.

There wasn't anything I could do about that at the moment. Instead, I worked on getting over the last twenty meters to Heather. There was a very slight downhill and even that set the knee off again. It hurt like hell. I hate going downhill.

But I got there. Heather was standing next to a flat stone on the ground. It covered most of a hole. "Here, Peter. Help me lift this."

This was no time to be asking questions and telling her I didn't know how much help I'd be. Instead I walked over to the far side and got my hands into the soft dirt, underneath the stone.

"We'll lift it this way," she said, showing me what she had in mind, raising one side of the long, thin slab of stone and then letting it fall on its backside. Great. No problem.

I started lifting, and it was impossible. How much did even a thin slab of limestone or whatever this was weigh? I didn't want to know.

Heather was lifting her side, slowly, inch by inch, and then as she did that I was able to get down lower and find some leverage— my knee was screaming at me—and at least pitch in. Together, long seconds later, we managed to get it up on its side and then let it fall.

There was an entrance into the ground that had been hidden by the stone. "A souterrain," Heather said. "Built for defense, maybe, or for food storage." She tilted her head, getting information. "There are thousands of these around Ireland. Apparently they were all the rage a thousand years ago."

A groan? Did I just hear a groan from down in that hole?

"You heard that?" Heather wanted to know. I nodded yes and she put her feet into the hole and started slipping in. I watched and then seconds after she'd gone out of sight she yelled up to me. "Get down here, Peter. It has stone walls and it's quite an achievement. I can hear someone in the far corner, a few rooms away. I'll head that way."

Shit. All right, then. Mr. Action Hero. I put my legs in and started sliding down and, yes, within a few feet the stone walling began and I found myself sitting in a narrow corridor in a few inches of cold water, stones on both sides, darkness ahead as the sunlight that we'd just opened at the mouth of the souterrain began to give out. I could almost stand up straight and by stooping over I could walk down the corridor. I headed the only way I could, splashing in the muddy water and on into the darkness.

I hadn't gone more than twenty meters and the darkness was already total in the direction I was headed. "Heather?" I yelled out. "Where are you?"

"Straight ahead, Peter," she said back to me, her voice calm and confident. "Keep your right hand on the wall and keep coming this way another thirty meters. Low ceiling, so keep your left hand up to feel the low spots. And keep coming. It's a human, a woman, and she's in bad shape. Very bad shape. Hurry."

I did, and in another minute I was there, Heather reaching out to take me by the hand and then helping me get my hands around the ankles of the person who lay moaning in the darkness.

"Shouldn't we wait for help?" I asked. "They'll be here in a few minutes."

Heather talked as she maneuvered herself to get her hands under the shoulder blades. "No space and not much time, Peter. There's a medic among our security group, and I've called for his help. He'll meet us outside the souterrain. The nearest Irish paramedics are in Glin. They're on their way here but it may take up to twenty minutes. She's naked and cold. I think her problem is hypothermia and dehydration. Let's get her out of this water and out into the fresh air where we can get some fluids into her and start to warm her up."

Heather, I realized, could see just fine, though I saw nothing but black. It finally occurred to me to try my new internals—maybe there was night vision? But myBob told me no when I gave it a try. "Heather has it under control, Peter. Do what she says."

Message received. With Heather leading and me behind holding up the woman's legs, we scuttled along toward the entrance to the souterrain. Eventually—it seemed like a long time but it couldn't really have been more than two or three minutes—I could see the light at the entrance. Another half a minute and we were there. Heather stood in the opening and I could see hands reaching down to help pull the woman up as I came close and let go of the legs. Then Heather had got a lift up and out, and then I got the same.

I got a few pats on the back when I emerged, and a few feet away I could see the medic working on the woman. She'd already been toweled dry and there was a thermal blanket over her. The medic was rigging an IV drip. Heather stood there, watching.

She waved me over and I came, walking toward her, Heather, the hero here who no one had right. None of them, no one here except me, knew that she wasn't what she seemed to be: not a human assistant for Twoclicks at all, but a construction, a made device that could change and morph and be any of several things.

I knew that being with her, loving her, making love to her, was in the same realm as buying a rubber doll. And yet, walking toward her, seeing her smile, hearing her voice, feeling her touch as she reached out to me and asked how my knee was doing, it seemed all right somehow.

And then I forgot all that as I walked over and looked down at the victim, the poor woman we'd found naked in that souterrain, freezing to death in a man-made hole. I looked down and there she was. Kait Holman. My sister Kait. The Lost Soul. Lying there, her eyes open, looking at me. Kait.

17

When I was in the hospital at PlacidWay in Barcelona and then at Mater Private Hospital in Dublin as they worked through several minor and two major surgeries to try and save my leg and, perhaps, my basketball career, I had a lot of visitors. Cecilia, the woman I was dating—tall and too thin and too blond and so a perfect WAG—was there almost every day for those two weeks. That was when the tiny spyeye drones first came out and the journos were using them like mad. The lenses on those spyeyes loved her as she came in and kissed me and told me how she hoped I'd be back a hundred percent and that I just had to work hard on my rehab and on and on and on and on.

I could tell that if the surgeries failed—and they did—she'd be gone in a heartbeat—and she was.

But my teammates were grand and they all came by to see me not for their own promotion but to offer sympathy and wish me well. They knew that the news wasn't good and I'd probably never be back, but they never talked about it that way. It was always next year you'll be back with us and we'll all have a great old time and win the league and all that.

But I had no family that came to wish me well. The parents were gone, and though brother Tom was in Europe I knew he wouldn't come. He was delivering a major paper at the Simposio Internacional de Tortugas Marinas—the International Conference on Sea Turtles—in Helsinki. He said he'd try and stop by after the conference but I doubted that he would. He knew about being selfish now, too, when it came to career and so I expected that he'd get right back to running his new lab and showing grad students how to get tags on turtle scutes. I was right, and that's what he did.

I expected nothing from poor Kait, of course. She'd been wrestling with her personal demons for so long it had about worn her down, I knew. It took all her available energy to get up in the morning and decide to make it through another day sober. She did send me some videos and expressed her worry and said she was sorry this had happened to me and wished me well. But that, I knew, was that.

Eventually, they told me I could go home. I was to make a daily visit with the team's physical therapist and bend and stretch and try to strengthen that knee. And I was to wean myself off the Percocets, which had really helped with the pain, and get myself down to a few ibuprofen a day if I could. It was all pretty damn depressing, and the weather didn't help, a long string of cold, gray, and wet days.

So it was a major pleasant surprise when, lo and behold, on the day I was set to check out, who should show up at my hospital room door but sister Kait, live and in the flesh. It was amazing. For a second I thought I was hallucinating—too many Percocets—or had confused her with someone else.

There she was, my little sister, her hair now a startling blond, and maybe she looked a little too thin and frail. But I was no great physical specimen myself at the moment and at least she had two good legs to walk on. I was at that point in post-op rehab, where walking, normal walking, seemed like a major peak I had to climb. Pain I thought I could handle, but that tricky business of walking across a room to give my sister a hug seemed an impossible feat.

She came halfway and we managed it. She was only able to stay for a couple of days, but I had one family member left who gave a shit, I thought, and that felt good. Very good.

And now, in front of me, eyes open but blank, that empty stare, here she was again. My good sister Kait who'd struggled so and then seemed to be finding herself and now this. What the hell had happened? I had no idea, but I needed to tell Sarah that we'd found Kait. Without thinking about it I told myBob to send a note and was starting to dictate when I realized myBob hadn't responded.

I looked at Heather. She shook her head. "I'm sorry, Peter, but we can't allow any communication out. That message to Sarah will have to wait a few minutes."

"I'd really like to let Sarah know. I can tell her to keep it quiet until you give the all-clear, Heather."

"No. I'm sorry," she said, and turned away.

It had been stupid of me, I suppose, to push it, and there was no real reason to have to tell Sarah immediately. It was an ego thing, and I needed to let go of that. I shook my head to clear it and walked back over to where the medic was working on my sister. No change, but the medic seemed to have done all he could for the moment, and he stood up to stretch.

"I'm her brother," I said, walking over to him. "How's she doing?"

He looked at me, then turned to look at Heather. She smiled and nodded yes. He turned back to me. "Her vitals are depressed, but she'll recover from the hypothermia in due time if she survives the next hour or so." He paused. "But you can see that she's not conscious. I closed the eyelids for her, but I don't know quite what that's about. A drug overdose? Heroin? Was she a user, do you know?"

"In the past," I said, "but she'd been clean for a while now. She seemed to be past all that."

He nodded, sympathetic. "They relapse, you know, addicts. It happens. But perhaps this is something else? A stroke? A head injury? I don't know. She reacts to pinching; there's reflex action. I'm just not sure. They'll have to get her into the hospital before they can give her a workup and find out what's going on." He shrugged. "We've done everything we can do right now, so it's a waiting game."

He was being nice to me, I know. He was convinced it was heroin, and I had to admit that it might be. In the distance I heard a siren, maybe two. The paramedics on their way at last. He heard them, too, said, "That'll be them. They'll take good care of her."

"Sure," I said, "and thanks." And then I thought about what I'd seen the hour before with the older couple who ran Malone's Pub. The miracle cure for the old man. The deal that Twoclicks and Heather had made for a stupid airplane propeller.

I walked over to Heather. "You could cure Kait, this second, if you wanted to. Isn't that right?"

She shook her head. "It's not so simple as that, Peter."

"Heather, just do what you did with the old man."

"Peter, don't ask this of me. Not right now." She shook her head. "There's a lot going on. Kait's a message, you see. Haven't you wondered how she got there? Down in the souterrain, in the cold water, naked, shivering? Who put her there? How? Why?"

"Sure I have. All of that. Every bit of that. But those answers can come later. You can tell me, or I'll help you figure it out. Whatever. Right now. Right. Now. My sister is slipping away up there. Dying. And you can save her, Heather. You can save her. I know it."

She looked at me. Tilted her head a second, listening, talking back sotto voce; to Twoclicks? I hoped so. The guy liked me, right? He wanted me around, right? He even needed me in some sort of PR way, right?

"All right," she said, looking back at me. "But there's a risk, Peter. If I do what I can do for her, there may be trouble. Just my taking a look at her, just the act of scanning, will let whoever set this up know that I'm here, that Twoclicks is here. It gives us away."

"Heather. She'll die." I had to try and save her. I loved her deeply, the little girl who'd gone so horribly, inexplicably wrong for much of her life, dug herself such a hole that it was a terrible struggle crawling out of it. And she'd done it. She'd done it! She'd gotten herself clean, had changed her life, had fallen in love with a spouse and was building something real for herself and her love. God, it was good. Good!

I knew there was risk, but there was even more risk if Heather did nothing. The medic thought she might be gone in minutes. Deep into coma, her systems shutting down. Dead.

"Please," I said to Heather. And she nodded, turned to face Kait, poor Kait.

"This will take a minute or two," she said, tilting her head the way she did sometimes, staring at Kait, reaching out somehow to find and fix whatever damage there was, whatever it was that seemed to be killing Kait.

Heather shook her head. Staggered for a second, turned to look at me with an expression I hadn't seen in her before: worry, maybe even fear. Something had her, something was keeping her from speaking, from breaking free of its grasp. She started to reach toward me and I reached back. Our hands touched, that was all, and she spasmed, once, and then was free of it, whatever it had been.

"Run!" she said to all of us gathered there. "She's a bomb! Run!" And we did, all of us, turning to run away from Kait, little dying Kait. I ran from her, my sister. I ran ten steps, perhaps fifteen, and then, behind me, heard a terrible brief rumble and then the loudest whoomph I'd ever heard, as if it were right next to me, the concussion overwhelming me and throwing me forward, flying through space with someone, something behind me, covering me, lifting me and moving with me in that rush of wind, that terrible concussive wave pushing me down the hill and sending me rolling until I rolled up against a boulder and then was pushed past it and found peace, on the downhill side of that boulder, and came to a stop while heat and flame roared by overhead.

Heather, next to me, had taken the brunt of the heat and concussion and her hair was smoldering, her skin a terrible bright red and black. I raised my right arm to look at how I'd done: not good, nearly the same as Heather.

"Peter?" she asked, looking over at me. "I'm so very sorry."

I didn't feel any pain yet. In fact, there was an amazing clarity to the moment, an awfulness about it that I understood. There would be pain. A lot of it. But I would welcome it, I told myself. My sister was dead in the most vile way I could imagine.

I sat up. All changed, changed utterly, said Mr. Yeats; a terrible beauty is born. "Whistle did this? Whistle killed Kait? Tried to kill us?"

She nodded. "We can heal you, Peter. We *will* heal you."

"But there's nothing you can do for my sister?"

She said, very carefully, "It depends on how she got here, Peter."

"Whistle?" I asked. "He has a transmitter like yours?"

"There are very few of these devices, Peter. It's a remnant technology and only a few remain. I can't promise anything."

"But you'll try? You'll see if she has a copy?"

"It's more likely the original that remains alive."

I was starting to feel the pain in my arm. I heard footsteps behind me and looked as an EMT arrived. "I'll be fine," Heather was saying to her. "Tend to my friend there." She pointed at me, and I had something to ask the EMT but I'd forgotten it. Thoughts swirled. Was myBob sweeping this up? Was there a chance for Kait? Why was it so cold up on this hill? How did Kait get here? Who put her here and then killed her? Why? Hadn't someone told me?

And I had no answers and things were getting hazy anyway. And then darker. And quiet. And then nothing.

When I swam back up from the darkness I found myself in an ambulance with the loud clatter of a helicopter coming to a landing on the open field across from the pub. My arm was wrapped in gauze and there were bandages over my right eye, both of my knees, and the palms of my hand. There wasn't much pain. Heather was lightly shaking my shoulder, and when I was aware enough of my surroundings she helped me stand up and walk out from the back of the ambulance and, together, the two of us walked over to the helicopter. Twoclicks was already aboard. Another helicopter was approaching, a bigger one, and my guess was it would be loaded with the looted artifacts—sorry, gifts—and would meet us wherever we were going.

"Shannon Airport," myBob said when I asked him what the plan was. For a few minutes I was so focused on standing upright and walking, and then climbing into the helicopter, that I forgot my grief. Only when I sat down and slumped back against my seat did it return to me: Kait, heroic Kait who'd battled through so much adversity in her life, was gone. I sat back, dizzy with the pain of that, and closed my eyes.

Heather, again, was waking me up, this time by unwrapping the bandages from around my arm. I dared to take a look at the damage.

And there was none. The skin was pink and new. I flexed the arm, brought it close to look at it. Healed. "What the hell?" I said.

"I've turned off myBob for the moment, Peter," Heather said. "We've repaired the damage, but you cannot talk about this or mention it at all. No sweeps, no conversation with Chloe or anyone. The damage never happened."

"Got it. But how did you do it?"

She smiled, patted me on the head. "Don't worry about it. It's done."

I shook my head. "Poor Kait. Finally turning things around, finally has things figured out. And then this awful thing."

"Peter," Heather said. "myBob and I were going through your memories of the day"—going through my memories; so all that wonderful new hardware in my hard head meant I was now an open book?—"and we found a moment when you thought you saw something, that shimmery effect you'd seen before. Remember?"

"Yes," I said. I knew where this was going, but was afraid to have hope.

"We had to leave very quickly and I wasn't able to walk to the spot near that stream where you perhaps saw it. But if what you saw was a transmitter, then that's how they got Kait to that souterrain so quickly."

There was a chance. "So what died was a copy, you're saying, and the real Kait might still be alive?"

She gave me a slight nod, a strained smile. "Maybe. Just maybe, all right? It means that Kait is a bargaining chip. That there will be negotiations between their side and ours and Kait will be part of those discussions."

"No," I said. "What it means is that Kait, my sister Kait, might still be alive."

"Yes, that's what I'm thinking. That bomb was a message, yes, but what it was saying was that the copy is dead and we have the original."

"I'll do anything, you know that. Go anywhere. Do absolutely anything. Trade myself for her, maybe?"

She smiled. "I doubt that's in the works, Peter," and she patted my head again. Me, her earnest pet. "But I suspect we'll hear from Whistle soon. I have one channel open to receive messages and I believe they'll be sending us something soon."

So there was a chance. Hell, a good chance, that Kait was alive. "They wouldn't be harming her, would they?" I asked.

"No, Peter, she is nothing to them but a small part of some discussions. They have no reason to harm her."

"Why would they do this to her? I don't understand."

"To get at you, Peter. To quiet you. You've done much too good a job for us to suit them. And they know there's potential for more. And to get at me and at Two as well. We've made you an important part of the process, and that's made you a target." She smiled. "I'm sorry. We didn't know how angry Whistle was about how things are going. Now that we do know, we'll see what we can do about that." And she rose, turned, and walked away, up to the front of the helicopter to take a seat and buckle in. We were coming down for a landing on the tarmac at Shannon Airport.

Our plane was a new Boeing 797 outfitted for alien guests and their entourage and flown in for us. It was just finishing its refueling when we arrived. It sat at the far end of the tarmac, surrounded by Defence Forces equipment like those British M-ATVs. We were on the ground, off the helicopter, and onto the 797 in minutes. Fifteen minutes later we were taxiing down the runway and off. The Irish wanted us out of the country as soon as possible, before another screamship showed up—or two of them—and a destructive battle between these immense forces flared in the Irish countryside.

I sat in the main cabin, the huge area holding no more than two dozen very comfortable seats. Across from me was Heather, still in her female-human form. No crackling and tearing changes for the moment.

The door to the front cabin opened and Twoclicks walked through.

"The pain iss gone, friend Peter?"

Amazingly, it was. I raised the arm for one more good look at it and marveled. And, hell, even that deep ache in my left knee was gone. For the first time in years I had no pain there. "Yes," I said. "Yes, the pain is gone."

Twoclicks walked over to pat me on the shoulder. "They wanted to kill you, friend Peter, and used your ssister to do it. But Heather has told you there is hope, yess?"

"Yes," I said. "Thank god for that."

He smiled. To Twoclicks, my "god" was a quaint local custom.

Twoclicks shrugged and looked to Heather. She spoke: "You have control back, Peter. Can you start recording a sweep for us?"

"Sure," I said. "myBob?"

"Done," he said.

"Good. Now look out your window, Peter," Heather said. We had taken off and were banking slowly to head west, so my window was looking down on Ireland in all its shades of green. There, in the Shannon estuary, was a large construction area in the water, a central tower rising from it, already a few hundred meters high with unfinished work above that, so it would be a tall, tall tower, I was guessing, before it was done. It slipped out of view behind us as we finished the banking turn and headed west, toward home.

"That tower? What's it for?"

"Power. Free power for all of Ireland, once it's done. It's Two-clicks' gift to Ireland. Were you recording that?"

"Of course. Can I contact Sarah now and let her know about Kait?"

She smiled, said, "No messaging out, still, sorry. So recording only. In a couple of hours, I think, I'll be able to return live control to you. All right?"

As if I had a choice. About this. About anything.

18

I slept on that long, miserable flight across the Atlantic. No one told me where we were landing and what we'd be doing and I didn't ask. I didn't want to know. I told myBob to shut down, tilted the seat back all the way, and shut my eyes, knowing I was too emotional, too full of grief and guilt and sorrow, to get any sleep; but thinking a quiet hour or two might help me deal with all this. And so, of course, I slept, a deep and dreamless sleep that lasted for hours.

It was Heather who woke me up, touching my shoulder lightly until I felt it and emerged from the deep place I'd been. Slowly I opened my eyes and saw her face there. Human. Concerned. She put her hands on my cheeks, one on each side, and said, "We'll be landing in an hour, Peter, and Twoclicks would like to tell you what's happening before we arrive. Can you manage that?"

"Sure," I said, and brought my seat up, rubbed my eyes, and tried to face the world, or the music. But it wasn't easy. Sleep had changed nothing. I'd watched my sister die horribly and then been told that it was all some short of negotiating ploy and that, maybe, she lived on. And, oh yes, I was working for Earth's conquerors. That was very clear now. Friendly, even jovial, conquerors, as it turned out. And one of them was stunningly beautiful, unless it was a guy. Or a shark. Whatever. Jesus, it was hard to figure it out.

I didn't want to figure it out. I wanted to know for certain that my sister was alive, and then I wanted to find her, get her out of danger, bring her home.

"Can I message out now?" I asked Heather, who had walked over to the galley.

"Yes, Peter, I've removed all constraints. The crisis seems to be over. Twoclicks has heard from Whistle. Apologies have been made. Promises extended."

"Just like that?" I asked. "You say it like it's happened before."

"Just like that," she said. "And yes, it has happened before." She shrugged. "The two of them compete for their father's praise, Peter. That's the best way to think of it."

"Jesus. Wonderful," I said.

"So yes, you're free to take and send messages. We trust you'll be careful, of course."

She came over with a glass of something. "Peter, I'm so sorry. Here's some Gosling's rum," she said. "Try it, it's delicious."

"Rum?"

"In honor of our visit here. We're landing at L. F. Wade International Airport in Bermuda in fifty-five minutes, at about six P.M. local time. Twoclicks is going to do the usual thing with the governor and all that, and you and I can spend the evening relaxing while he's busy. By tomorrow the others should be arriving and we'll begin the discussions."

"Others?"

"A small group of concerned parties is meeting to discuss what's happening, Peter. The violence directed at us, and at you and your sister. You know a few of these people."

"Abigail, right?"

"Yes, and some others. Several S'hudonni will take part as well, by avatar if not in person. Whistle himself may take part."

I nodded. "All right. But now I need to contact Sarah and let her know what's happened, and try and contact my brother, too. And Chloe—I'd like to talk with Chloe."

Heather shook her head. "I wouldn't say anything to Sarah and Tom about the possibility of our finding the truest Kait alive somewhere, Peter. We're not sure about that, you know."

"But I can't let them believe Kait is well and truly dead, can I?"

"I suppose not."

"So what are you saying, Heather? Should I not send a message to them at all?"

She nodded. "There's no reason to. They won't know about Kait's death, Peter, I'm certain. That was just meant for us. Once we meet with all sides in Bermuda, we may know more. In fact, we'll certainly know more."

"All right," I said, and then said again, "All right. But it's OK to tell Chloe that I'm alive and well?"

"No details, though, Peter."

I waved my hand, "Yes, yes, I know."

Heather smiled at my little show of temper and then said this: "Your brother Tom is unreachable in any event, I'm afraid. He's completely off the grid, and seems to want to stay that way."

"Do you know where he is? What he's doing?"

"We do. He's gone deep into the scrub, well into the interior of Florida, near Arcadia. He's living in a campground, in a rented trailer, buying a few supplies at a general store. He's away from the coast, away from everything, unplugged from the cloud or nearly so; so we're keeping an eye on him with a spyeye but can't read much about him. I've watched some footage, Peter. He's unkempt. Very unkempt, in fact," and she had a slight smile, "a bit of a wild man, actually. Very not-Tom."

Oh my god. Tom. My brother Tom, always neat-as-a-pin Dr. Thomas Holman.

Heather reached out to touch my arm. "I think he's gone there to heal from his emotional wounds, Peter. He needs to get away from everything for a while. Assess things, you know?"

I shook my head. "No, that's not Tom, not in some seedy campground. He must be filled with anger, seething. Damn."

She nodded. "Yes, I'm sure he is. I don't think he's ready to hear
from you about anything, Peter."

My turn to nod. "I understand. Too bad."

"There's more," she said. "He's not well. The coughing, the headaches, the behavior. We're worried about him."

"Can't you help? Can't you find out what it is and cure him of
it? You can cure anything, right? I mean, I've seen you do it."

She smiled. "*Almost* anything." And then added, thoughtfully,
"We could, perhaps, do something for him. But not under these circumstances. You need to reach him, Peter. Tell him the truth and
then try to reason with him. Reassure him, somehow. Bring him
in to us. Give us a chance to help."

"I'll try. But when he's like this, you know . . ."

"I know," she said. "But try. We want to help him." And she
walked away, left me to it, sending a sending a message to Chloe, telling her I was OK and I hoped to see her soon and I'd send details
when I could. I didn't say anything about Kait.

In leaving that message, something pleasant about hoping to see
her soon, somehow the whole terrible sequence of events came back
to me in stark relief: the climb up the hill, pushing the stone away
from the entrance to the souterrain, getting down into that dark
man-made cave, finding poor Kaity, and getting her out of there.
The approaching sirens of the paramedics. My begging Heather to
probe, to find out what was happening, to fix Kait somehow. The
certain knowledge that in doing that I'd convinced Heather to
take the one action that guaranteed Kait's death. The explosion.
The terrible explosion.

God, I hoped she was alive—some version, original or copy, of
her. Please let that be so.

Heather came back to my side and sat down. She held the bottle
of rum in her hand. I held up my empty glass. "More of that rum?"

Heather smiled and leaned over to pour. "Of course, Peter. And I'll join you, all right?"

Sure it was all right. Join me. Sit with me and drink rum. Maybe a lot of rum. Maybe destroy some brain cells. That might be a good idea.

I was napping, or half-napping, when we landed. I was awake enough to know I was on a chartered flight with Twoclicks and Heather and, I assumed, a pilot and copilot.

But I was dreaming at the same time, lost in a better past, a time when Kait and Tom and I were having fun at the beach while Mom, sheltered from the sun by an umbrella, was reading a book on her reader: probably a Russian novelist or maybe rereading Dickens.

I was in the water about to go snorkeling. Had my mask up on top of my head, was carrying my fins to put on once I got a little deeper. Tom was behind me looking the same way, following his big brother out into the warm embrace of Mother Ocean. Kait was back at the water's edge, building a sand castle, using the wet sand that you gather up in your hand and then let drip, drip down onto the castle wall, where it accretes like a stalagmite, forming tiny temporary statues on the walls. Kaity loved those little sand sculptures on top of the sand castle walls. It all looked so formidable and beautiful to a seven-year-old girl, protected by her brothers and her mother from any danger. Happy on the beach, while I dived away from her, into deeper water, going my own way with Tom behind me, following me. I was twelve years old and was thinking that maybe this was the day when I would dare to go out past the second sandbar, out to where there were sharks and danger.

But then I didn't go that far, of course. Instead, I got out to the second sandbar and stood up there and took a look to the west, out to the open water of the Gulf. And then I turned around and came back in.

Our wheels hit the tarmac with a good, solid thump and I came out of my hazy half-sleep. Heather sat beside me, watching me.

"Wow," I said, "too much rum, I think."

She smiled. "Plenty more where that came from."

"Are you trying to get me drunk?" I asked, and she chuckled. "I'd say it's 'mission accomplished.' But we have a news conference coming up in about twenty minutes, so we need you to sober up and sweep it live, all right?"

My head was in that strange place where I knew I'd had too much to drink and even felt a little bad about it. I didn't see how I could possibly sober up in ten minutes' time.

"Sure," I said. "Consider me sober."

"Peter," she said to me, and leaned over to put her face close to mine. I leaned her way in response. She had a drink in her hand. Clear liquid in ice. She handed it to me.

"Vodka?" I asked.

"Water," she said, and gave me a little pat on the cheek. "Drink it down now. All of it."

I did as I'd been told. It tasted like water, perhaps with a hint of lemon.

I sat back. I could feel the cold water working its way down my esophagus and spreading then around my stomach, my chest, out into my arms and down into my legs. Amazing what a little water can do. In just a few seconds I felt a lot better. Sharper. Clearer. Amazing, really.

I looked at Heather. "Wow, that's some kind of water."

She laughed. "There may have been a little something in that water, but it's harmless, believe me, and you'll feel much, much better now."

I smiled, nodded. "Yes. My, that worked like a charm. I don't suppose I want to even know what's in it, right?" It was funny: I knew I had to worry about Kait, and worry for Tom and all that. But, really, I didn't care at that moment.

"I'll tell you later," she said, and then, as the plane got to the gate and came to a stop, she stood and reached down to offer me a hand so I could do the same.

"Once more unto the breach, dear friends?" I asked, and she turned to look at me, shook her head. "Shakespeare, Peter?"

"Plenty more where that came from," I said, though in fact that pretty much wasn't true.

"I bet," she said, and started walking forward toward the front of the plane, and Twoclicks, and our little news conference.

"myBob," I said to my helpmate, "turn on the sweep, please, and go live as well as record, all right?"

"Send an announcement, Peter?"

"Sure," I said. "Why the hell not?" And I started following Heather. Up ahead, beyond her, I could see Twoclicks standing at the plane door, waiting for us to get there so we could exit together. I hadn't seen him the whole flight. He waved at me to hurry up and said something to me I didn't quite catch, something with "friend Peter" in it.

I smiled, waved back, and hustled forward. Most of the world knew the news by now, I was sure, and riots and terror and fear and martial law and a terrifying wait for whatever horror was next must be the rule. But I'd had that glass of that very fine water from Heather, and I was smiling as I walked toward Twoclicks. Once more, friend Peter, I thought.

19

We were drinking at the Jasmine Lounge at the Fairmont South-ampton, Heather and I, sticking with the Gosling's rum. I'd had myBob switch off the live sweep feed but I was still recording. I still felt great, somehow a little drunk and fully sober at the same time. Whatever was in that water continued to work wonders.

The evening had gone well, with the news conference at the airport, the drive to Government House for a reception with the governor and his wife, and then some serious chitchat between Twoclicks and the governor and his cabinet. Tomorrow the others would arrive.

For the moment, safely ensconced in the Fairmont with a coterie of British SAS types surrounding the hotel for our safety, Heather and I were free to sit and drink rum concoctions, the best of them a thing called Dark 'n Stormy, made with ginger beer and Gos-ling's Black Seal rum.

Upstairs, Twoclicks was in his suite. He'd call us up there in due course and we'd have another one of those late-night chats that he enjoyed so much. For now, Heather said, he was in the suite's large hot tub with the water hot and the jets bubbling. I had to admit that sounded pretty good.

I realized as I was talking to Heather that she seemed now to be fully recovered from whatever restoration process she'd gone through. Her memory seemed fine. I was still worried about my-Bob, who'd never reacquired that personality he'd had that had made him, in an odd way, my best friend. He wasn't really myBob, at least not yet. He was a helpmate, a machine that did as he was told. I missed the old pal.

I was telling Heather about Kait, about the great kid she'd been, about the problems she'd struggled with in life. It was four Dark 'n Stormies into the conversation before I realized I was feeling good but most definitely wasn't getting drunk. Somehow that didn't seem fair.

Heather read my mind. "It's temporary, Peter, and it will wear off soon. But for the next couple of hours, at least, try as you might you'll still be sober. I'm sorry."

"It's a good thing, I suppose," I said, but I don't think I was convincing even myself of the truth of that. I was kind of hoping for either a glorious celebration of Kait's life or something of an Irish wake for her if she was dead and irretrievable. "When will you find out about her, Heather?" I asked.

"Tomorrow. Until then I'm blocked from the people who would know."

"Whistle?"

She nodded. "And a select few of you Earthies who are working for him. They'd have to know, too."

Then Heather tilted her head, listening, and said "Let's go" to me, and I knew we were heading up to Twoclicks' suite for another one of those long, boozy chats about Earth and humans and sports and arts and history and politics and, no doubt, alcohol. Funny how much Twoclicks liked our alcohol, though it clearly had no effect on him at all. And the more difficult and specialized the production, the better he liked it. Twoclicks was, in other words, a real snob when it came to matters alcohol.

And now rum was on his list. Gosling's rum. When we got to

the suite he was out of the hot tub and dry, sitting on a comfortable couch over by the wide picture window that looked out over the Great Sound. He wore an unlikely-looking hotel robe with a large "F" on it and he held a glass of Gosling's in a brandy snifter, that dark amber color of the rum playing off the soft lighting behind him. Out the window, the lights of distant Hamilton were visible on the far side of the Sound.

"Friend Peter!" he said, his calm, jovial self returned after the chaos of the last couple of days. "Iss nice hotel, yes? Your room is excellent?"

I sat down on a smaller couch, opposite his. "Yes, it's a very nice hotel, and my room is fine."

Twoclicks held up the snifter of rum and said, "Iss especially excellent, this rum."

I had my glass—nothing fancy, just a hotel water glass full of Gosling's—with me, and I'd set it on the end table. I picked it up, stood, and held it aloft. "To Bermuda, and to rum."

Twoclicks was an expert on toasts by this time and held his up as well, and Heather, smiling, did the same with hers. We clinked glasses and each took a nice, long swallow. Twoclicks was right: It was excellent.

I started to walk over to the bar, where the open bottle of Black Seal stood waiting for my attention, when myBob pinged me. "Family priority," he said. "It's a message from your brother."

Tom!

"Let me hear it, myBob," I said, and then, as I saw the look on Heather's face, "and put it on speaker, please." No reason not to share, though I knew she'd hear it either way. But now Twoclicks, too, would get the message.

"Done," myBob said.

And Tom was speaking. "Peter"—his voice was trembling—"I cannot believe you. Fuck you, asshole. Kait is murdered and I have to find out from friends? You were there and you don't even contact me to tell me? You don't even leave me a message? I. Cannot. Fucking. Believe. You." He strung those out, slowly, one by one, that trembling voice barely under control. "I'll get the details. I'll pay my respects to our sister in my own way.

"As for you? I don't know what else to say. Father always said you were a disappointment and never amounted to anything. He was right. Hell, the last time I talked with Mom she was all sad about you, about how you hadn't become the man that Father had hoped you'd be. She died thinking that about you, Petey, did you know that, asshole?"

His voice was calmer. "I'll deal with you later. Don't call. Don't ever attempt to reach me. You know, a week ago I was thinking maybe a little time passes and we could at least talk, you and I. And now look at me. That's what I get. Fuck you. I hope you die."

A message from my loving brother.

I looked at Heather and Twoclicks. "I'm sorry, Peter. I thought no one would know, but Tom has been told," Heather said.

I put two and two together. If Tom knew the details, they had to have come from Whistle's people. Twoclicks and Heather got it right away, too.

"Brothers," Twoclicks said, and shook his head. "Mine iss trouble, too. Much, much trouble."

Yes, I thought, Twoclicks had it right. Brothers. "It's my fault," I said, and then looked at Heather and corrected myself, "Our fault."

She shook her head. "There's a lot more to it than that, Peter, and you know it."

"Sure," I said, but I thought of the moment when she'd knocked on my door and I'd said yes. Selfish, stupid. "Thing is, what should I say to him?"

"There's nothing you can say, Peter. And he won't accept the message anyway," she said.

Twoclicks was still shaking his head over the foolishness of both our brothers. "Heather is right. Perhapss he will calm down later when you are able to tell him the full story, friend Peter?"

I smiled. Not bloody likely, but, hey, one can always hope. I poured myself a half-glass of that nice Bermuda rum. Drank it down. Was it having any effect yet? I hoped so.

In the morning, all our plans changed.

At first I was perversely pleased to have a bit of a hangover. That glass of magic water had worn off at last and I'd gotten drunk, as I'd wanted. Weepingly, pathetically drunk. I hoped that Heather would blame the booze and forgive me for having been maudlin.

But perhaps I hadn't been? Next to me, sitting in a chair and watching me as I woke up, was Heather. "Good morning, sunshine," she said. "Breakfast has been delivered and it's ready for you on the table by the window," and she glanced in that direction.

I smiled, said thanks, then swung my legs over the side. I stood. My head hurt, but my knee felt fine.

I tested it a couple of times, bending it. No pain. What the hell, I thought, and tried a deep knee bend, nice and slow and easy, hanging on to the side of the bed for support. Still no pain. Outstanding.

And then I remembered it all. Yesterday's horror. Kait. Blown all to hell but then somehow still alive, or some version of her alive. Tom. Oh, sweet Jesus. I sat on the bed and put my head in my hands. My god, all of this was immense, overwhelming. What the hell was happening to me? How did I get to be this person? How did I go from making a simple living shooting balls into nets that were 3.048 meters high to being involved in this huge storm? I was right smack in the eye of it, that great wall of anger and fear and unstoppable power circling around me as the winds stirred up by Twoclicks and his brother Whistle looked likely to engulf the whole damn planet.

I was still in that deep knee bend. Heather walked over to the table, got a glass of orange juice, and brought it back. "Drink this, Peter. You need it."

I took it from her, drank it down. It was cold and sweet and good.

"I'm sorry, Peter, but we need to eat and clean up and get ready for a busy day today."

"Sure. Busy day," I said, and managed a slight smile as I looked up at her. "That was a lot of rum last night."

She smiled. "Yes, but you'll feel a lot better in a minute or two, I think."

Oh, no. "The orange juice?"

She smiled. "Yes, the orange juice. We need you in good shape this morning, Peter, and the orange juice will help."

I managed to stand and walk over to the table to pour myself a cup of coffee. There were eggs and muffins and pastries and more orange juice on the table. I wasn't hungry.

I took a sip of the coffee. "What time is it?" I asked. "And how ridiculous was I last night? And what time is the first meeting today? And who's coming? And when do you think you'll find out about Kait?"

I did feel better. More in control of things. I sat in the chair next to the table and had another sip of the coffee. Better. Much better.

"We have a couple of hours, and then it gets very busy. And I'll be surprised if Kait isn't the first thing on the agenda," Heather said.

I felt excellent, and very hungry. Heather walked over to me. She was so beautiful, a nude in a painting. A work of art. And the way she walked barefoot, the motion of it. And all of it a lie.

She got to me, put her hand on top of my head, and gave it a nice rub. Good boy. Being her lover seemed like something from the past, something that had happened years ago.

She was hearing something, stepping back and tilting her head, listening. Then she looked at me and shrugged, resigned. "Sorry, Peter, change of plans. Major change of plans. You need to get busy on that breakfast and get your things packed up. Meetings canceled. Tour over. We're leaving in one hour."

"Leaving? No meetings?"

She walked over to the breakfast table, sat down on the far side, poured herself some orange juice from the carafe. "There's been some trouble: acts of intimidation all over North America, at night for maximum effect and a minimum of casualties. Lots of bright lights and destruction. In Los Angeles, Chicago, New York. A screamship comes in with a lot of noise and lights, hovers for a half hour or so over one public spot or another to draw attention, then destroys it and departs. In L.A. the GigTech Center is a pile of rubble; in Chicago the Navy Pier is gone; in New York there's a large hole smack in the middle of Central Park. There were a dozen of those sorts of things around America.

"Today, as the sun comes up, they're expecting demonstrations, perhaps riots, as people in the cities that haven't been hit yet demand that the government, the military, do something. Silly, of course—there is nothing that can be done. There were very few casualties in all these attacks. The idea was to make a statement, not kill people. The spyeyes? The drone cams? Those were left alone. Whistle—and this must be Whistle's work—wanted all this to be seen by your whole world. It's a statement, showing what he can do with impunity."

"So it's all crumbling, all the apologies and the promises? All that's tumbling down now?" I asked.

"Actually, it's going to be up to you now, Peter, to make sure Earth knows that all this destruction isn't our work."

I nodded. Yes, sure, it was all up to me. Great. But first I had to ask myself, was I a true believer? Was this latest display of power and arrogance the work of Whistle, like Heather said? Was Twoclicks innocent? Was he misunderstood? Did I have to clear that up for all my Earthie friends? I thought so, yes. I believed it to be so, yes.

"What does this mean for Kait?" I asked her. She sighed. "I don't know. But there's nothing to be done right at the moment except get to the airport and make our way home. Twoclicks wants to leave in"—she tilted her head, listening to something—"fifty-five minutes."

"Sure," I said.

"So come on, now, Peter. Sit yourself down. We need to get some food into you, and a couple of cups of coffee."

"Will do," I said, walking over and sitting down and taking the clear cover off the plate. Scrambled eggs, crisp bacon, pan-fried potatoes, cantaloupe slices, rye toast. She knew me, did Heather. She knew me well.

And despite my worry over Kait, despite all the thoughts of her and Tom and even Chloe—was she safe?—I tucked into that food, suddenly ravenous, now that I thought of it. Eggs, bacon, cantaloupe, all down my gaping maw. It tasted excellent and in five minutes or so it was gone. I sat back, sipping on a cup of coffee. Amazing how good I felt, really. Fifty minutes? Plenty of time. A world of time.

As we left the hotel my head was clear, my stomach felt settled and fine, and my left knee still felt like it had in the good old days: which is to say, no pain. Strong. That was odd—the knee hadn't felt this good in years, back before the botched surgeries, back before the very bad day in the paint when I thought too much of myself and wove my way into the middle of the giants and then paid that terrible price for my hubris.

I knew I had problems: poor, dear Kait and the mess with Tom. But they didn't seem all that pressing and I could deal with them once we got into the air and headed wherever we were headed.

I badly wanted to talk with Chloe, too—the real Chloe, not the Hollywood version. I wanted to tell her how I really felt about her. I wanted to make that very, very clear. Surely she felt the same way? Surely. Certainly. So, easy enough, all of this, I thought. The golden glow I was wallowing in had me so full of confidence that I knew that somehow, one way or another, I'd get everything straightened out. Chloe forever after, Kait alive and well, brother Tom with a smile, and an apology for being an ass. That sounded good.

I'd had myBob start recording a sweep as we left the hotel.

Bermuda was dead calm, at least at first glance. It gave me a chance to use my new zoom technology in the eye contacts. Great stuff, very high-quality. No one in the streets, no worried rioters thinking they might be the next target of S'hudon's display of power. Pretty boring sweep.

Then I realized that the traffic had been cleared, that the local police and a lot of imported military from the British naval base on the island were blocking any possible trouble. Bermuda wanted us gone, and as soon as possible and with as little disruption as could be managed.

In the distance, toward Hamilton, smoke was rising in three different spots. Perhaps it all wasn't as calm as I was seeing. I kept my sweep focused on that rising smoke, panned back and forth. I'd zoom in later when I edited. With any luck there'd be some flame once you zoomed in.

We were driving on a long narrow road that ran alongside the water as we approached the airport. Water, water, everywhere. I wondered: If the circumstances were different, would Twoclicks want to stay here for a while? It seemed to have everything he liked in Earthie life: warm water, good alcohol, and creature comforts. But we weren't staying. We were leaving, and right now, thank you.

"Heather," I asked her as we rounded a big curve and approached the small airline terminal, "where are we going?"

Heather was looking out the window and didn't answer, but Twoclicks did. "Home, friend Peter. Back to our landing site. Back to your home."

"Safer there, I suppose?" I asked.

"Yess," Twoclicks said. "Exactly. There is sserious conflict now. Very dangerous. Could get worse. Could get much worse." And then Twoclicks sat back and closed his eyes. Conversation over.

The limo came a stop and armed guards surrounded the car, opening doors, their weapons at the ready. All this protection, once again, for Twoclicks and his entourage.

"Ah," Twoclicks said as he looked with a certain sadness at the armed guards. "I wanted very much to not have it come to thiss."

He waited for Heather and me to get out of the open door and then we turned to help him as he emerged. We walked, slowly for Twoclicks' sake, through the sliding glass doors and into the terminal. No media here, just airport security and a few dozen British military types forming a narrow corridor for us that led deeper into the building, from where, I knew, we'd be walked quickly to our gate and then onto our plane and they'd be glad, the people here, to see us go.

20

Heather came over and sat down beside me. "I have news for you. It's about your brother."

I stared at her. My eyes must have widened. Fear. Worry.

"He's no longer in that campground. The spyeye is watching him and he's headed toward the coast in a car he bought in Arcadia, one so old you have to drive it yourself. Still no electronics so everything is visual."

"Where do you think he's headed?"

She shook her head. "No way to know, but maybe he'll get back onto the grid when he gets closer to a city. He shaved this morning, so that tells us something."

"I should send him a message, something neutral about wanting to talk with him. How's that sound? He can retrieve it once he gets back on the clouds."

Heather nodded. "Yes, that's a good idea, Peter. I've opened your access. Why not do that now while I tell Twoclicks about this?" And she walked away, toward the front of the plane and the private cabin for Twoclicks.

"myBob," I said, "let's send a message to my brother, all right?"

"Yes, Peter," myBob came back. "I'm recording it now for his retrieval."

"Can you put it at the front of his message queue?"

"Of course, and I'll flag it important, too."

"All right. Here it is. Record this."

I opened the vidcam so he could see my face. "Tom, I received that message, brother, and I understand your anger. I was there, Tom. I saw it happen. But I haven't been able to contact you about it until now. I do need to talk with you, Tom, I really do."

I took a breath, stared into the vidcam. "I've asked my AI to ask yours to make this the first thing you see when you get reconnected, Tom. I want to talk to you, man to man. I'll come to wherever you are and sit down with you and talk it through. Anytime, Tom, anywhere. Let me know."

I took a breath, pulled my hand through my hair, nervous. "Please believe me, Tom. Horrible things are happening here and we need to talk about them. We need to get ourselves straightened out, OK? Please, when you get this, give me a shout and I'll be there. You're my brother and we're all we have left for each other. Let's try and fix this. That's it. I love you. Talk to you soon, I hope."

And I clicked it off, said "Send that, myBob," and sat back. Heather came through the cabin door with a mug of coffee. Brought it over to me.

"That was a good message," she said.

"You heard it?" No surprise, I supposed.

"Of course. Let's hope it reaches him. He's important to us as well as to you."

Sure he was. We were important, me and my brother. We mattered for some damn reason. I took a sip of the coffee, stood up from my seat. Why the hell was my knee feeling so good? Hell, why was I feeling so good? It was whatever she'd slipped me in that orange juice, and last night's water. But knowing that and doing anything to come down from all the feel-good were two different things.

Can you be tired of feeling good? For more than an hour now I'd felt great, physically and emotionally. Strong. Despite all the horror: strong.

And it worried me. Part of me wanted my pain back. Let the knee hurt. Let the worry and grief flow and wash over me. Let me feel it.

I wanted to get off the damn plane and go for a long walk, one with sharp pains in the left knee. Hell, maybe go for a run, let those knives of pain slice right through that knee. Let me feel the pain. Please.

But no. I sat back down, put the knee out straight, flexed it and bent it and then straightened it out again. And then again. Very strange and awful, this no-pain thing.

Heather watched me do this and said nothing. She smiled and nodded and sat down next to me.

myBob pinged me. "Your brother's AI refuses to take the message, Peter. No acceptance of the message, no acceptance of anything from you or those associated with you. There's actually a few seconds of Tom in the rejection message. Should I play that?"

What the hell, why not? "Sure," I said, afraid of what I was going to here.

"Here it is," said myBob.

"Fuck you and go away, Peter," said the voice of Tom. There was no video.

Well, I thought, message received. And Heather read my mind, saying, "There's nothing you can do about that, Peter. He won't listen to what you have to say. And then he complains bitterly that you don't tell him."

She sighed. "He's a mess. And now, I have to tell you, we're concerned that he's becoming our mess. The spyeyes say he's heading toward your home."

"And toward your ship that's parked out in the Gulf."

"And toward our ship, yes," she said, and I heard the cabin door open behind me. I turned and there was Twoclicks waddling our way.

"Heather has kept me informed, friend Peter. Is terrible, terrible ssad thing."

"Yes," I said. What could I do but agree?

"But there iss worry that he may cause trouble for uss," Twoclicks added. "His information is hard to read, yess, Heather?"

"Yes," she said, "he's hard to read. The spyeyes have him and several are actually inside the front cabin of the pick-up truck he is driving. He doesn't seem to have noticed them."

"Spyeyes are pretty noisy, Heather. Lots of buzzing, even for the small ones."

She looked at me and rolled her eyes and shook her head. "Peter, Peter . . ."

Oh, yes. Of course. You'd think I'd learn. I was thinking this was human technology in those spyeyes. The latest I'd seen any news on were the size of bumblebees and at least that noisy.

But S'hudonni spyeyes?

Heather knew what I was wondering. "Indefinite flight, Peter," she said, "and we've built them to look like your gnats. Very tiny. And silent."

"And the picture quality?"

She smiled. "I thought you'd want to see. Have myBob take the message from me and feed it into your contact so you'll have a floater of it."

And I did and I did and he opened it and there was my brother, at the wheel of some old pick-up truck. His hands were steady on the wheel and I was reminded that he often had to do his own driving on research trips.

He was thin, but clean-shaven, wearing a clean knit shirt. The detail was amazing. I could easily read the small "USF Marine Biology" beneath the logo of an angry bull over his heart on his shirt. He'd cleaned up for this and wanted to look legitimate, a researcher.

266 • RICK WILBER

He seemed to look right at me and smile as he reached up on the dash, pulled a Camel cigarette from a pack that was out of my vision, and then lit it. The side window was open and he took a long, deep drag on the cigarette, held it for a time in his lungs, then blew a cloud of smoke out the window and into the Florida sunshine.

"He wasn't smoking while he was at the campground. I can't imagine why," said Heather.

I shook my head. No idea. But he was smoking now, taking another long, deep pull. He enjoyed his smoking, did my brother Tom.

"Enough," said Heather, and I told myBob to shut it down. I'd seen what I needed to see. My brother, right there in front of me. In control. Determined. Driving like a man on a mission.

"Exactly," said Heather. "Question is, what *is* that mission?"

I shrugged. I had no answer to that.

While Heather's spyeyes kept an eye on Tom I kept an eye on our escort. Since we'd left Bermudian airspace shortly after takeoff we'd been shepherded by six U.S. Air Force F-35s, the best fighters the Air Force had now that the ghostship fleet had been turned into puddles.

What were they hoping to do? It should be perfectly clear to the Air Force (and to these particular pilots!) that there was nothing they could do except flee if a screamship showed up. Maybe there was some other kind of threat? Something these fighters would be able to deal with?

Heather had a possible answer when she sat down next to me, and leaned over to look out the tiny window. "We still have friends in your military who believe what they've seen from you about us, Peter. They've determined, at least, that Twoclicks is the lesser of two evils. I suppose these fighter planes will keep away any rogue elements of your military; but I'm sure you realize they would be helpless against a screamship or any of its drones."

I shrugged. "It's working, though, right? Nothing's happened, so these guys scared them off?"

She shook her head. "Make sure your sweep is on, Peter, and let's do an interview. I'll be Dr. Heather Newsome. You'll want to record this. A lot is going to happen in the next day or two and you're going to tell your world about it."

I nodded. "myBob, sweep is recording, right?" I asked.

"Always, Peter, unless you say otherwise," said myBob. "And I've been sending out edited work regularly after Heather gives the OK."

I looked at her. She shrugged. Why wasn't I surprised? "All right," I said to Heather. I took a breath, held up three fingers and counted them down for her, then got at it: "So here we are on an Earth-built Boeing jet going from Bermuda to somewhere unnamed back in the States and accompanied by . . ." I looked out the window so my audience would see the F-35s, "a half-dozen of the U.S. Air Force's best remaining fighters. "I'm talking with Dr. Heather Newsome, the top science assistant with Twoclicks and a senior member of the S'hudonni visiting party."

I looked at her. She'd morphed a bit while I'd been peering out the window and now looked all-business, no make-up, attractive, mid-thirties in age, dark hair pulled back into a bun. Dr. Newsome, for sure.

"Dr. Newsome, there have been some aggressive acts by scream-ships over the past few days and it all seems to be some kind of internal struggle going on with the S'hudonni, one attacking the other. Is that what's happening?"

Heather was perfect. "Yes, it looks that way, Peter. Twoclicks, who we're traveling with, seems to be on one side of this conflict and a S'hudonni named . . ." and she whistled his name . . . "seems to be on the other."

She smiled for me. "There is no real translation of his name, so we call him 'Whistle,' just as the edited media on Earth do."

"And Whistle is the one doing the attacking?"

"Well, at least from what we can see from where we sit." She smiled, added, "On this Earth-built passenger jet, with Twoclicks himself on the other side of that cabin door," and she pointed at the door so I looked there. Closed, but I was guessing Twoclicks was hearing every bit of this.

"Are these Air Force fighters we see out the window really going to help us if we're attacked by one of Whistle's screamships?"

"No," she said, "that technology is well ahead of anything we have, Peter. You saw what those screamships did to our ghostships. No, I think our hope is that Twoclicks has his own ships protecting us from Whistle's ships."

I hesitated a few seconds, then drew my finger across my neck and said "End it for now, myBob."

"Done," he said. "I'll have it ready for preview in a few minutes."

Heather nodded, said "Great," and undid the bun on her hair and shook it all loose.

"Whistle seems intent on causing trouble, Peter, she said. "They had an agreement, Whistle and Twoclicks, about which one would control what part of your world. I was there, on S'hudon, when that agreement was reached and the two brothers kissed on it, sealing the pact."

This was all new to me, but it didn't sound surprising in any way. I was on the fringes of all this, but close enough to see the tension and able to recognize the threat.

"And now Whistle has changed his mind?"

"Apparently. Understand that to you it's the fate of your world. But to Two and Whistle it's just another spat. They had a similar blowup over Downtone not that long ago."

"Downtone?"

"The last world they fought over. Inhospitable place for S'hudonni, with the water too cold and the summer's too short. But they each wanted it and so they fought over it."

She looked away.

"A whole world?"

She turned back to face me. "Yes. A whole world. Like Earth is a whole world. And Earth is a nicer one, too; which probably makes the competition all the more mean-spirited."

"You know that boggles the mind, right? That I am here, now, listening to you tell me these things. That Twoclicks is twenty meters away on the other side of that cabin door. That there are screamships and other worlds and, Jesus, all of it. It boggles the mind."

She leaned over to kiss me on the forehead. "It's a very large cosmos out there, Peter. You should come see it sometime."

I laughed. "Right. I'll buy a ticket and take a tour."

Heather shrugged. "You're with us," she said, "so you won't need a ticket." And then she rose and walked away, up toward the front and Twoclick's cabin. I wondered what it was like in there. I hadn't been asked to even take a look at it. Back of the bus for me, though it was the back of a very, very nice bus.

About a half-hour later myBob had that brief interview ready to go and I was thinking how I might pad it out a bit, watching out the window as six new fighters showed up. This worried me for a moment, but the six that had been with us banked and turned and disappeared into the distance and I realized the new fighters were taking over the shepherd duty. There must be carriers involved, I supposed, with planes landing and others taking off. It was all out of sight and all I could do was imagine it: and that, it occurred to me, summed up my entire adventure with Heather and Twoclicks.

myBob pinged. "I thought you'd want to know that your brother has reconnected and he's accepted your recent message. No reply as yet."

Well, well. "Thank you, myBob," I said, and got up to walk around a bit. There was a work station at the back of the cabin and I headed that way, thinking about brother Tom and his anger and wishing it hadn't gone down the way it did with Heather.

No, that wasn't true. I'd been involved with Heather—god, I'd probably loved her despite everything I'd seen—and while I felt differently about it now I still found myself constantly proving myself to her. The dynamic had changed but the goal was the same. So what I was wishing was that Tom could find a way to forgive me for that, to get past the sorrow and pain of that. But his losses—Heather, his science, his future—had so colored his thinking that he couldn't accept the truth about anything. Denial and anger were the only responses he could find, I supposed.

I sighed. Time to get a few shots out the window of our escort and then maybe a shot of Twoclicks and then send that story out, thin as it was.

I wondered if I could find a way to fit my personal crises into that sweep. Dare I mention my brother? My sister? My parents? No, that was too much, too personal, and didn't, in the end, have anything to do with Twoclicks and Whistle and S'hudon's arrival on Earth. I'd keep the family stuff out of the sweep and save it, perhaps, for some future time, a memoir or something. That would be safer. And saner.

So what did that leave me with to post tonight? Not much. A brief interview with Heather in her Earthie guise. Some shots of the fighters out the window. Lots of threatening talk but nothing tangible, nothing like the drama of the death and destruction in Ireland.

I felt the plane's engines throttling back. We were starting our descent. I leaned over to look out the window and could see the F-35s staying with us.

The door to the cabin opened. Heather in her S'hudonni form and Twoclicks walked in.

"Friend, Peter!" Twoclicks said in that breathy sibilance that so belied the power that he wielded. "We have important matters to discuss."

"Your brother has managed to give us the slip, Peter," added Heather. "Take a look. myBob will have it ready for you as a floater."

"It's ready," myBob said, without my prompting. Great, he now did what Heather told him to do and without asking my permission first.

I looked straight ahead as the floatscreen opened up and there was Tom, driving along in that pick-up truck, hands on the wheel, moving along at a pretty good clip on some bridge, open water to his left on the far side of the bridge. He could be anywhere along the coast. It didn't look like there was any other traffic on the bridge, nobody going the other way, at least.

"You know, the quality of the picture is amazing," I said.

Heather put her finger to lips. "Just watch," she said. And then Tom leaned forward and looked right into the camera somehow. He couldn't have seen the gnat-size spyeye, so what was he looking at?

Me, as it turned out. "Peter. I'll see you soon," he said. "Tell Heather and that pompous Twoclicks that I said hi." He took his eyes away from the screen for a second to look at the road and turn slightly left, then turned back and looked right at me again. "And I got your message. Sure, asshole, we'll talk. Soon." He paused. "Oh, and fuck you. And fuck Heather. And don't ever fuck Twoclicks." And he laughed; a deep, rumbling smoker's laugh that got so hard he wound up coughing and then spit some sputum out the window.

Then he reached up to the spyeye lens, reached past it and came back with a cigarette. Lit it, took a drag, and said, "Bye, bye, ass-hole" and the screen went blank.

I looked at Heather, then at Twoclicks. "He knew about the spy-eyes all along. And he knew how to turn them off whenever he wanted. How can he do that?"

"Cannot," said Twoclicks. "Is proscribed technology. Can. Not." And he was so definite I thought he might fold those two spindly arms together to emphasize his point.

Heather was sighing. "It's not possible with Earth technology, Peter, that's for sure. So he must have help from somewhere, and that's almost certainly Whistle. But when Twoclicks got this video he immediately contacted Whistle, who denies having shared any-thing like that with your brother."

"You're talking with Whistle?" I asked Twoclicks in disbelief.

"I thought there was a war or something going on. And you're talking?"

Heather smiled at me. "I've tried to explain. To Twoclicks and Whistle this is almost fun, all this violence and fury. It's competition, and one of them will win more of the prime territory than the other. That means more profit, yes, but, more importantly, it means more stature at home, on S'hudon, with the family." She sighed. "It's all very complex."

"Incredible," I said.

We continued to slowly descend, getting ourselves lined up for a landing. The pilot came on the intercom to tell us to take a seat and buckle up, and Heather and I did that while Twoclicks headed back up to his private cabin at the front.

I looked out the window at the city spread out below some ten- or fifteen-thousand feet below. We were over Tampa and I could see, in the far distance, the new Spire of St. Petersburg, built out over the bay and then rising sixty stories to bring in tourist dollars for the view. Below me there was nothing but lots and lots of housing tracts, walled-in villages of the haves protecting themselves from the rough behavior of the have-nots. In one of those there was a fire, gray smoke billowing from a home. And then another. I could see a lot of flashing emergency lights. The roads were jam-packed, all the cars heading in one direction, east, toward the center of the peninsula and the highways heading north.

"Riots," Heather said, listening to her feed while she leaned over to look with me out the window. "Whistle's actions have most of the world thinking it's an invasion by S'hudon. We can keep ourselves out of the clouds, but Whistle's plan is to stir up visible trouble in front of as many people as possible and it's working, and spreading. Looting of stores in the cities, people stocking up for a long haul. Lots of people heading for the hills, away from the population centers."

The alien invader herself then added, "I'm going to change for the landing, Peter," and I watched this time as that happened. Lots of terrible tearing and breaking and shrinking and then expansion and from the terrible mess right before my eyes a human—human Heather—emerged, kneeling until she was solid and then rising to stand. And I had made love with her, I thought.

"And we both enjoyed it," she said, smiling. Then she sat down in her seat as I sat in mine. She reached over to put her hand on my arm. "You know, it's not going quite the way that Twoclicks hoped it would."

I was still looking out the window as we dropped lower and started to bank to make a big circle over the south part of the city and line up for our approach to the airport. Our F-35 escorts stayed above us, protecting us until we landed and then, I supposed, they'd circle around once and land at MacDill Air Force Base, five miles south of Tampa International.

I looked down. More fires, and people in the streets. The major roads covered in cars, all of it at a standstill, car doors open as people gave up and started walking. Craziness. Insanity. They were terrified and I suppose from what they knew they had good reason to panic.

So here I was in comfort in a splashy plane all kitted out for the convenience of our alien invaders, while down there they were scared to death, and looting stores and trying to get the hell out of Dodge.

I moved in my seat, crossing my legs. There was a twinge of pain from my left knee. Thank god.

I turned to Heather. "Should we be trying to land in the middle of this mess? And what the hell are we going to do once we land? How do we get from the airport over to our island?"

Heather patted my arm. "We have to land somewhere, Peter, and the airport authorities say it's calm there at the moment."

At the moment. I didn't much like the sound of that.

We were in our final approach, coming in over the bay bridges and descending steadily. I watched out the window at what was going on below. It didn't look good and I felt sorry as hell for those people. I felt our landing gear go down. Almost home. Such as it was.

myBob pinged. "Your brother would like to chat with you, Peter."

I looked at Heather. She nodded. I said, "Yes, myBob. Live, please. You can reply."

And there was Tom. He looked tired, staring at the spyeye again. Quiet. Calm. He'd stopped the pick-up and behind him, out the window, I could see some scrub brush and beyond that the big interstate bridge over the bay. He was near the airport, then, right down below us somewhere.

"Peter. You listening?"

"I'm listening, Tom. Listen, I'm so sorry. . . ."

"Shut up. Shut the fuck up," he said. "Look, I'm, I'm having second thoughts, all right? There's a big thing planned for you when you land. Big. I mean, nasty big. They're going to blow your plane all to hell."

"They?"

Angry. "I said shut the fuck up and listen, Peter. Goddamnit. Jesus, you were always like this. Always. Asshole." He paused, looked out his window and looked up. "That's probably your goddamn plane right there. Jesus."

He took a breath. "You *are* an asshole, god knows. But that's no reason to kill you, to watch you be killed. And here I drove like a bat outa hell for three fucking hours to watch this all happen."

He brushed his hair back out of his eyes. "Don't land at Tampa International, Peter. That's all I'm going to tell you. Land somewhere else. Fly the hell far and away. But Do. Not. Land. Got it? Stay the fuck away from Tampa." And he cut the connection. Gone.

I looked at Heather. She was connected to someone and talking fast. I looked out the window and could see the runway ahead of us, the big wide band of the approach apron and then the runway. We were no more than fifty feet up, just about down.

I felt and heard our plane's engines getting more power, but by now we were just a few feet up and then I felt the jolt of the wheels hitting the tarmac.

But the engines were surging now and while we touched down we didn't stay there. Instead we slowly started to rise and then, as we did that, I felt a major shove from below and then the whole plane seemed to rise suddenly in the air. Out the window I could see a great sheet of flame that came and went in an instant and then we were up and rising, rising back into the blue Florida sky.

Heather's grip on my arm had tightened through all this, but now she relaxed. "A bomb," she said, "A large one, on the runway, probably buried. That was meant for us."

Meant for us. People. Human people, were trying to kill us. Trying to kill me. It was a very sobering thought.

I turned away from the window for a moment to look at her. "Tom," I said. "Without Tom. . . ." And I let that thought hang there.

She nodded.

The door to the front cabin opened and Twoclicks waddled toward us. "Friend, Peter. Your brother Tom has saved us. We are in his debt."

"Close thing there, Twoclicks," I managed to say. But I had to wonder, given what I'd seen back in Ireland, was death any more real for Twoclicks than it was for Heather? He said Tom saved us, but I got the feeling that of the three of us, the only life here that was really saved was mine. And I'd take it.

There was a ding and the seat belt light came on. Twoclicks shook his head at these silly Earthies and their silly rules, but then turned around to head back to his cabin.

Heather was listening again. "Buckle up," she said to me, "we're landing immediately at MacDill, the Air Force base. There's some trouble with our landing gear. Damage from that bomb. They're foaming the runway for us and they'll have the crash trucks ready."

Crash trucks. Foam. God almighty.

I felt the engines throttle back and we started dropping fast and banking left, out over the water of Tampa Bay. I looked out the window and could see only water at first, and then a building, huge, great smokestacks with nothing coming out of them. Tampa Bay then, and that was the big power plant at the east end of the bay, shut down now for years.

Heather, sitting beside me, reached out to touch my face. "There is so much to talk about, Peter. We'll do all that later tonight, I think, perhaps at your house?"

"Taking my mind off this crash landing are you?"

She smiled. "Why not go live with your sweep, Peter? And send a hot signal for breaking news. I think this might be pretty exciting."

"myBob?" I asked.

"I heard and you'll be live in ten seconds, Peter." He paused. "Five. Four."

Heather was crackling and morphing beside me. I watched out the window for a few more seconds and then, when the crackling stopped, I turned to look at her. She was the formal science adviser again as she undid her seat belt, stood, and leaned over to look out the window. She was listening again.

"You're hearing the pilot?" I asked.

She looked at me. Smiled. Nodded. "Our landing gear are badly mangled and won't retract. We've been flying this whole time with the gear down. Our friends are back and looking at them now. See?" And she pointed out the window.

I turned to look. An F-35 was right next to us, so close I could clearly see the pilot. He was looking at the undercarriage of the plane and, I was guessing, was talking to our pilot.

"Yes," said Heather, and I turned to look at her again. "I'm listening in. Gear look OK, he says, but he can't be sure. Two of the tires are destroyed but there are twenty tires and the plane is flying light so we may be all right."

I looked back out the window and there was the runway, off to our right as we made the final turn on our approach. Rows of vehicles lined both sides. Lots of flashing lights in reds and yellows. Two huge tanker trunks were laying down foam for us to wade through on our landing." Would that help if the landing gear collapsed? I hoped so.

"See that violet color in the foam, Peter? That's Purple-K, a fire suppressant. They must be worried about a fire when all this bent metal on the landing gear hits the runway."

I looked at Heather. "Thanks for the information, Heather." And she smiled back.

I turned back to the window and started talking to myself, narrating for the sweep audience. "We're a few hundred feet up and coming in for our second landing attempt in the last twenty minutes. But this time we aren't trying to land fast and solid like over at Tampa International. Here, we're trying to ease it on in. Our landing gear suffered some damage during the attempt in Tampa when an explosive device went off beneath us. We managed to get back in the air, but will the landing gear hold up for this landing? If it doesn't, will we slide in safely on that foam and walk off this plane in one piece? We'll know soon. "

We were coming in over shallow water and I could see, down in the water, the long cigar shapes of some sea-grass-browsing manatees. "Down below, where I'm looking now, you can see the slow cumbersome sea cows, the West Indian manatee, that frequent this bay. There aren't many of them left. Victims of technology, those manatees. Let's hope they survive. Let's hope *we* survive."

I should have been speechless with fear, but wasn't. Instead, lost in my reporting, I kept talking. "We're just one hundred feet up now," I said, watching out the window. Heather reached over and took my hand and I squeezed her's hard.

Fifty feet up. "We'll just watch now. Stay with us," I said.

Heather leaned over and hugged me. I kept looking out the window but didn't try to speak anymore. "Brace yourselves," said the pilot on the intercom and I wondered how Twoclicks was braced up front. A special seat, surely, with special bracing. Funny that I hadn't been in that front cabin. I wondered what was in there. There suddenly seemed to be plenty of time for me to muse on how that cabin looked.

"Going to be a little rough," said the pilot, a woman I'd never met despite all these hours of flying and danger. I wanted to meet her and say thank you. Better yet, I wanted to be alive after this and be able to meet her and say thank you.

"Brace" she said again and I decided that rather than put my head down into my lap I'd keep looking out the window. I wanted to see this. I wanted my audience to see and hear and feel this. Heather leaned over to watch, too.

A feather touch of a landing. Soft. A sudden spray of violet foam past the window. Nice, very smooth, gliding along on what was left of our landing gear, wheels just keep on turnin', Proud Mary keep on burnin' and all that. Easy as pie.

And then not. A sudden collapse and we dropped a meter or two, then another meter or two, then again, and then again. We were lucky, I was thinking as we found bottom and a great scraping and screeching noise erupted from below, that the collapse had been slow rather than a drop of ten meters or more all at once.

Funny how at moments of extreme stress the internal clock slows and seconds take their leisurely time to pass by even as the terrible sound of torn metal against pavement roars up from below and the plane slowly starts to turn left in its skid so I can watch out the window as the view changes from the runway lined by vehicles to the foamed runway itself and then to more vehicles and then the runway again and then back again to emergency vehicles and all those flashing lights and I realize we've gone three hundred and sixty degrees but are still on the runway and the screeching and groaning of metal is starting to ease and we're slowing and we're slowing more and then, almost gracefully and with a certain gentle certitude we come to a stop, aimed forward again so I'm looking out to those blessed vehicles and beyond them some low buildings and a golf course and beyond that the blue and inviting waters of Tampa Bay and we are down, and alive, and the only sounds for long seconds are the series of random clicks and scrapes and groans from the torn metal below and around us as we settle into place. We were alive.

PART THREE

WHAT'S NEXT

Forever alive, forever forward.

—Walt Whitman, "Song of the Open Road"

21

Chloe and I sat on the back deck of my house and watched the sun set into the Gulf of Mexico. In the guest room downstairs Sarah Chu napped after the long, miserable flight from Los Angeles to St. Pete. Chloe had used the studio's corporate jet (which is what you get when you're signed for a recurring role on *The Family Madderz*) and she'd stopped on the way to pick up Sarah. The plane, I was sure, was luxurious, but Sarah could barely function, torn still from what she thought was the death of the love of her life, my poor sister Kait. She felt better now that she knew the truth, but was exhausted.

On a cloudless December evening the sun had gone from a strangely mean and vindictive white heat to a nearly pleasant hue of oranges and reds in the space of about a half hour. Now, a few minutes from disappearing, it was easing into that UFO shape it took most evenings, the central bulb of the sun's disk hovering over the wide, flat red disk atop the azure Gulf of Mexico. I was hoping for the green flash, the singular emerald flash that happens now and again; some optical illusion, surely, but a great one, the sky lighting up green for a fraction of a second as the final dot of setting sun sinks below the horizon.

In front of me on the small, round wooden table was my old smarty, with its back brace set up so I could sit with a Lester's Lager in hand and watch the world's turmoil from this pleasant, quiet place. My internals were disabled and eventually, Heather told me, they'd be removed. I wouldn't need them where I was going. All that money wasted.

Things were quieting down and the world was moving on, calmer, unsure if the violence was done or worse was yet to come. The S'hudonni were promising it was over, that it was all an internal matter and the two sides were talking and Earth was safe. Sure.

The cold Lester's was my third of the evening with more yet to come. Lester, who ran The Wharf bar about a half-klick down the beach toward the pass, had been brewing Lester's for as long as I'd known him, more than ten years now. I had my first of his lagers when I was eighteen and I pitched a no-hitter and went to tell my father about my success. Silly idea, but it made sense to a high-school kid who'd just thrown the best game of his life.

That was back when I saw what I saw with Father and Tracy and I'd left in a hurry. After deciding to drive around on the mainland for an hour or so I'd taken the ferry home to our island, parked my car under the basketball standard in the wide paved slot to the left of the driveway, got out, and walked straight to The Wharf. There were no police on the island in those days—they didn't come unless called—and so no problem with my sitting down on a bar stool and asking Lester for a beer.

He tilted his head and raised an eyebrow, but grabbed a cold mug and headed over to the tap. "How'd the game go?" he asked as he put the beer in front of me.

An hour before I'd been watching Father fuck Tracy in the back room of the clinic. It wasn't lovemaking, it was fucking. From the window I could see her legs up in the air in those heels, and his pants down at his ankles, and his hips in and back and in and back as he put it to her. The great hero. And his receptionist.

"We won," I said. "I threw a no-no."

"Wow, man. Hey, the beer's on me. How come you're not out with your pals? How come you're here?"

Lester was an Egypt vet, fought for the Brits in the Second Sand War for two tours and then moved to St. Pete and the Florida sunshine and had the money to open a bar on an island with a washed-out bridge to the mainland and keep it going despite the fact that, like the day I had my first beer, there weren't often a lot of people in there.

I liked Lester. He was a sports fan—a big fan of English soccer, but he loved our sports, too—and he followed my successes and failures on the court and the pitcher's mound. "I don't know, Lester. Just some shit going on. You know. Some shit," and I took a sip of the beer.

Lester had a rag he was wiping the bar with. "Let me guess: something to do with a girl, right?"

I nodded, then gave him my best bitter laugh. "Yeah, in a way it *is* about a girl."

"Well, mate," he said, "she picked a bad day to dump you. Here you are a big star and winning ball games and throwing no-hitters and all. She must be pretty damned stupid."

I took another sip of the beer. "Thing is, she's a little older than me, and that complicates things."

"Yeah, it does. She's in college?"

I shook my head.

"Out of college? She's, like, in her twenties?"

I shrugged. "I don't know. Yeah, I guess, in her twenties. Late twenties."

"Wow, pal. Good for you."

Another sip of the beer. Not too bad. "Yep, good for me. But I just saw her with another guy. An older guy. A *lot* older guy." Another sip. "They were doing it, Lester. Right there in the storeroom on top of some boxes." I shook my head. "Jesus, there she was, the love of my life, getting boinked. And by"—and I almost came out and said it, but caught myself—"this older guy. Nothing special to look at, this guy. Just a guy. And old."

Lester had stopped wiping off the bar. "You walk over here, Petey?"

I nodded.

"OK, then, beers are on the house, kid. You can use a few to maybe drown those sorrows. I'll make sure you get home nice and safe, OK?"

"Thanks, Lester," I said, and took a good, long pull on the beer. Not too bad.

Lester smiled, started talking about sports, something to do with Fulham and avoiding relegation yet again. That, and some more beer, were meant to take my mind off things. Damn near worked, too.

I was thinking of all that as I held hands with Chloe, who'd come all the way across the country to spend a few days with me, holding hands and whatever. Personal and private, me and Chloe, and we liked it. We watched, hard, for the green flash. You have to be a hawk those last thirty seconds to see it. Watch for it. Watch for it. Watch for it.

But nothing. Instead, looking out at the horizon, we saw nothing except water, a darkening evening sky, and that huge S'hudonni ship on its oil-derrick legs. A great round thing, the size of a football stadium, the usual sort of slight shimmer to the off-white color, the ship resting on three of those legs. Master of all it surveyed.

I took a long drink from the Lester's and finished off the bottle. No problem—plenty more where that came from. I grabbed a longneck out of the cooler, used the opener to pop off the cap—very old-school, Lester's Lager—and took a good long pull on the cold, golden beer.

Chloe squeezed my hand, said, "I'll have a sip of that."

I handed it to her and she took a long slug of it. "Really not too bad," she said. "Tastes English."

"Got it in one," I said. "It's Lester's own handcrafted, and he's from Yorkshire, I think. Somewhere like that."

"You know," she said, "I've never been to England. Isn't that strange? I've been all over the world, but never to England."

"We'll fix that someday, Chloe, me and you," I said. "I promise."

"Sure," she said, knowing it might not work out that way, but it was nice to dream.

It was good having her with me. It had been a rough couple of days. The Irish had found all the pieces of my sister that they could and done the forensics they could do and then, at my request, had her remains cremated. There wasn't much, but a U.S. Air Force courier had arrived a couple of hours with the box and handed it to me. I'd said thanks. It was passing strange knowing these remains were of my sweet sister Kait and that I had a job to do. And yet. And yet.

Heather had come by earlier with the news: Kait was alive. That version of Kait that I knew, the real Kait as far as I was concerned, was alive, and, I could hope, well. But she was a long, long way from home.

I had the box out on the deck with me so that this Kait, the one who'd suffered so, could be here for that sunset, too. I reached out to touch the box. Let my fingers linger there. "She loved it here, you know. When we were little kids, me and her and Tom, we'd spend all day at the beach, running around, snorkeling, finding crabs, building sand castles."

"I know," Chloe said. "You've told me about it a few times now." And she reached over to put her comforting hand on my arm.

"Me and Tom, we were the brave ones, going out to the second sandbar, looking at the fish and the shells and the jellyfish."

"I know," Chloe said, "but never past that second sandbar, right? Too dangerous out there, you said."

"It *was* too dangerous. One time, me and Tom, we saw a big bull shark go by just out past the drop-off on the far side." I waved out toward the beach and the sandbars. "It was right out there, and I mean it was huge. We thought that was it for us, and then it turned and swam past us again, and then headed out into deeper water. We swam in to shore, all excited, I mean here we'd had this big adventure and all Kait wanted to do was make the spires higher and higher on her sand castle."

"She didn't believe you?"

"She didn't care." I laughed. "And neither did Mom. 'Boys,' she said with that tut-tut sound she used on us all the time and that shake of her head."

"Probably a dolphin," Chloe said. "That's what you told me, remember?"

"I do. Sure, that's what it was, a dolphin," I said. It occurred to me, looking back, that the form in the water must have been Heather, already on Earth, sussing us out.

We were waiting for the moon to rise and then, toward midnight, we'd be waking up Sarah and taking Kait's remains for a last walk together. The three of us would give Kait's ashes to the water.

She took another long pull on the beer and handed it back to me. "You'll be OK, Peter," she said. "And you know I'll wait for you, right?"

I turned to her and smiled. Chloe, wonderful Chloe.

After that harrowing crash landing at MacDill, Heather and I sat there, stunned, for a few moments. A long spin in the foam and here we were, the fuselage and those within it all in one good piece.

The door to the front cabin opened and Twoclicks came waddling through, closing it behind himself and wearing a huge smile on that odd face. That was an expression he'd learned recently, just for me and his other new Earthie pals. The S'hudonni, I'd learned, didn't smile like that naturally.

"Friend Peter! What fun! What incredible excitement!"

I was finally unbuckling my belt and standing up. "Yes, Two-clicks, it was exciting." "Fun" wasn't a word I was ready to use just yet.

I looked out the window and the emergency vehicles were there and spraying us down to suppress any chance of fire; but it had occurred to me we'd been flying for long hours and it wasn't like the plane was full of fuel.

I assumed we'd jump out on the emergency slide and was mentally preparing myself for that when the door to Twoclicks' cabin opened again and a firefighter was there, dressed in a silver fire suit.

He waved to the three of us. "Let's go, please. We don't want to waste any time getting out of here, all right?"

Hell, yes, that was all right, and Heather and I helped Twoclicks trundle back through his room and to the exit door on the far side. The last look I had out my trusty window showed more fighters running up to the wheeled boarding stairs that had been readied for us. So we'd get to walk down. That was in deference to Twoclicks, I imagined.

We walked through that front cabin and it was Ali Baba's cave: rare bottles of wine, the Ardagh Chalice, a Picasso, a signed soccer ball, a full suit of armor, three or four ancient written documents under glass. Was that the Magna Carta? My god, he liked to travel with his acquisitions right on the plane with him. I was glad it had all been saved.

And then we were through and walking down the stairs and I could smell, at last, the acrid bite of scorched and melted metal and composites and hear the hisses and pops and clangs of debris and bent metal cooling under the spray of water and chemicals. There was no smoke, but a lot of steam.

We had an escort, but before I could get close I heard a sharp command from behind me. "Mr. Holman!" I turned, and a woman dressed in an Air Force uniform but wearing sweep-receiving gear on her head was shouting at me. "Turn off that live feed, sir. Now!"

"myBob?" I asked. And "Done," he said. I hoped he was still recording, but that wasn't something I wanted to mention. I didn't know it, but a lot of people—many millions of them—moaned or cursed in disappointment when the live feed abruptly ended.

And then we started walking down a paved sidewalk that curved through the scrub brush and sand dunes to reach a wide strand of beach with half a dozen boats pulled up on the shore, all of them with weapons poking up and out in various directions.

"Patrol boats," the lieutenant who was in charge said. "SURCs: Small Unit Riverine Craft. Believe me, we'll get you there safe and sound."

How nice—our own little flotilla to take us across the bay and over to my little island and, at least for tonight, some peace and quiet.

We struggled a bit to get Twoclicks into the largest of the SURCs and then Heather and I together got into another and we all shoved off the beach and headed across the bay, four of the SURCs in a loose box and the two boats with the three of us in the middle.

As we headed south and west I could see, off to the right, a bridge packed with traffic, all of it at a standstill. Smoke was still rising from Tampa, behind us, and St. Petersburg, in front. Buildings and cars were burning. But for us, the water was smooth, the sun was shining, the SURCs were armored and fast; and for me, home lay ahead.

22

When you grow up on the Gulf of Mexico you learn to enjoy the bathtub heat of the Gulf water in the summertime. During my years in Ireland the temperature of the place had taken some getting used to, and the water temperature most of all. There was a never a warm summer rain, never a swim in the Gulf with the water temp at 30 Celsius, never that feeling of being sticky with sweat just from stepping outside for a few minutes to walk out to the beach and enjoy the sunset.

But in Ireland the cool, wet damp of the summer showers was a kind of soft blessing and the lashing cold rains of winter were done after a day or two and the sun came out, even in winter, to remind one of the essential gentility of the climate and, for the most part, of the people.

I was thinking of these things as Sarah, Chloe, and I walked the beach at midnight. It was an odd moment. With Heather's permission I'd told them yesterday that Kait, some version of Kait, was alive and that we were going to find her. Sarah had cried and hugged me and then cried some more and then Chloe and I had gotten her comfortable in her room for that nap. They realized they had to keep quiet about what they now knew about that version of Kait.

But this was this Kait, and I was carrying her remains in my left hand, the moon nearly full out to the west in the night sky, bright enough to light a path across the water toward me; bright enough that I could see that S'hudonni ship way out there, shimmering slightly in the pale light from that moon; sitting there, waiting.

In front of me was a wide path of broken shells and soft sand, a Gulf beach at its calmest after what had been a day of offshore thunderstorms. Now that was all done and there was nothing more than the gentle rumble of the remnant shore-break to my side, giving me some background music while it gave the sandpipers something to do as they ran along looking for coquina.

There was a sand dollar half buried in the sand. I reached down with my right hand to pick it up, careful not to break it, and it was about perfect. White, long dead, and this its skeleton, really. A big one, almost the size of a coffee saucer, it picked up the light from the moon nicely. I thought maybe I'd try to take it along with me when I went to find Kait.

I opened the lid on the box with Kait's ashes and waited for the others to come over and help me pour those few remnants of who she'd been into the Gulf, into her childhood playground, back into those better days.

I heard a cough behind, a deep rattle. I turned to see Tom walking toward us between two of the taller sand dunes. I'd sent him a message saying that we were putting her ashes into the Gulf at midnight. Apparently he'd listened to that one message. Maybe, in fact, he'd listened to them all.

"I'm here in time?" he asked, and I nodded yes.

"Well, I'm glad I got here for this," he said. "Poor Kait." He looked out over the water. "It was good here, wasn't it, Petey? Me and you and Kaity on this beach. Damn, that was nice."

Chloe and Sarah stood together, watching as Tom came over to stand in front of me. No hugs between these brothers.

I wondered if he knew that was Chloe Cary over there. She looked plain and sad and ordinary. A friend here to help a friend share his sister's ashes with the sea. There he was, Dr. Thomas Holman, PhD. He of the brilliant mind. He the apple of his father's eye. He the one who'd had the bright future in research, running his lab and keeping the grad students busy.

He was rubbing his forehead. "Fucking headaches," he said. He dropped his hand, reached out to shake mine. "But it's good to see you, brother. Have to admit, it's good to see you."

I introduced Sarah and Chloe to him and he gave them both a hug, not saying much but acting perfectly calm and friendly.

Chloe's eyes were wide after what she'd heard from me about Tom, and Sarah looked wary, too. She'd heard too much from Kait, I was sure. But shake his hand they both did, saying it was a pleasure to meet him. And then Chloe stepped back and Sarah joined Tom and me in holding the box with Kait's ashes upside down, and without any ceremony we shook the ashes into the water, the three of us each holding a side of the box. There was a small shore-break and the water pulled and tugged the ashes out into deeper water as we watched for a minute or two.

"Goodbye, Kaity," Tom said, finally. Sarah's crying was done and she knew the truth about Kait; but these ashes, too, had been Kait, the look on Sarah's face tore at me as she said, "Goodbye, Kait." I said the same and Chloe echoed that and then it was over.

I opened my arms to all of them and we came together and hugged, then we pulled apart and Tom stood there in front of me. My little brother Tom. "You look tired," I said. "You need to take better care of yourself."

He laughed, and the laughter rattled some in those smoker's lungs. He turned to Chloe and Sarah. "Could I have a few minutes in private with Peter? Could you maybe walk down the beach? Give us some space?"

Sarah turned to walk away, but Chloe looked at me, questioning. I could see her wondering if this might go south on us, given our history. Chloe and I had opened up with each other over the past couple of days. The good news and the bad news about ourselves, our families, all of that. She knew to be worried about this moment. But I nodded OK and she turned to walk away, too.

"Always the fucking big brother, Peter, right?" Tom shook his head. "OK, I have some things to say, but first, you have to turn off that fucking sweep, all right? No live, no recording, none of that. This is between you and me and that's it. All right?"

"I've been disconnected for the past couple of days, Tom," I said. "Some kind of hardware replacement coming, they tell me."

There were some big meetings ahead for me and I'd need a lot of new wiring for them, Heather had said. Twoclicks wanted me along, she'd said, for the Big Meet. A S'hudonni royal father was meeting with two fractious sons to settle a dispute. Earth had calmed down a little in the past two days and the father, apparently, wanted it to keep it that way. For purposes of profit, you know. And Kait was there, I'd been told. Part of the negotiations, just like Heather had said. So, OK, I'd be there. Wherever that took place.

I knew all of this and said nothing. I couldn't trust Tom. I couldn't tell him much of anything. I'd been worried for a second that Sarah or Chloe might have blurted out the truth that Kait might still be alive, but they'd both been much too smart for that. Now, from a distance, they walked and talked with each other, keeping a wary eye on us all the while.

Tom was talking: "OK, then. Look, thank you for sending me the news on poor Kait. I'm shattered by what happened. And Petey, I want you to know that I had nothing to do with that. I hope you'll believe me. As soon as you told me she was dead I knew what must have happened. I knew they were going to kidnap her, but they promised me they'd treat her well and that they'd let her go as soon as they got what they wanted. And that was you and Heather and Twoclicks getting blown all to hell. That was the plan."

"You were part of that, Tom? Jesus, she was your sister."

He rubbed his eyes, shook his head. "Petey, I only learned today what they did to her, I swear. Jesus, man, I've been crying all night. I loved her. She was a major fuckup, Petey, she ruined her life and made life miserable for Mom and for Father. But she was our sister, and when we were young . . ." He pointed out so sea. "Right out there, the three of us, in the water, that warm water. Jesus, man, I miss those days."

"You know who killed her, Tom? Tell me. Tell me right now."

"No. Christ, no. I don't know who did it. I never knew. It wasn't like that. I know a guy who knows a woman who knows the right people. It's all up the line, you know? I don't know shit, really."

"She was our sister, Tom. She struggled with her demons, god knows, but she was our sister."

"I'm here, aren't I? I get it. I do. It's tragic and I'm sorry, Petey. I'll miss her. I'll miss the little girl she was when we were kids on this very beach. I'll miss that every day."

I didn't believe him. I hoped to Christ he *was* as shattered by the news as he said he was, but he was too cold about it. My brother, I thought, had sold his soul.

And then I thought, well, hell, we'd both done that. "Why'd you leave, Tom? Why'd you get involved with these people?"

"I took some time off, that's all, Petey. I got off into the woods and scrub over by Arcadia. It was a good thing to do. Helped me make some decisions. I thought I had to do something. They're killing us, these friends of yours. They're ruining the whole country, the whole fucking world."

"Yeah, well, there's not much we can do about that, Tom. I'm trying, that's all I can say. I'm trying."

He nodded. He looked at me, hard. "Me, too, big brother. I'm trying."

I got that message. "I was worried about you, Tom. I'm sorry. I'm so sorry for all that's happened. For how it happened. Me. You. Heather. These fucking aliens. Father. Mom. Kait. Shit, the list goes on, pal. We're a mess. All of us. One real mess."

He looked at me. "I know, Petey."

He reached down into a pants pocket, pulled out a mostly empty pack of cigarettes. He rubbed his forehead again, then reached down and pulled out a Camel. Lit it. Blew out the smoke. "Look, I've given this a lot of thought. I've tried to be fair about it."

He took another drag, then reached down and stubbed the Camel out in the sand, carefully peeled it apart, scattered the tobacco, and shoved the remnant paper into his pocket. "You know I hated you there for a while. Maybe I still do. And the people I've been talking to me, these people connected me to one of those S'hudonni. Not your guy, another one."

"Whistle," I said.

Tom smiled. "Yes, Whistle. These people, they knew that you were traveling with your Twoclicks and that Heather was there, too, and that you and Heather . . ." He let that dangle, tried it again, "That you and Heather were together. Were having an affair."

"Tom," I said. "Look . . ." I was going to tell him that that Heather was gone, and while I liked the new version just fine, I was thinking the past was the past. Things seemed to have changed, and that was fine with me.

He raised his hand. "They knew that Heather had been mine, that we'd been in love, and that you stole her from me, Peter. They knew that."

"Christ almighty, Tom. Listen . . ."

But I couldn't stop him. "No, it's all right. They knew all this shit. And they had a plan. They were going to blow the fuck out of all of you."

"Tom, it's not that simple."

"Sure it is. After you survived the bombing with Kait, they knew you'd be coming back to Tampa International. They knew you'd have to land there to come here to your place and for your fucking Twoclicks to get you to his ship. That untouchable ship. You know how many of them died trying to approach that ship that landed out there? On the water, underwater, drones, ultralights: They tried all that shit and everyone died. Every fucking one of them who tried something died."

He reached into his pocket for another Camel. Pulled out the pack, hesitated, spit out some phlegm, and angrily shoved the pack back into his pocket.

"They have a lot of people on their side. A lot of people who say we'd be better off with Whistle. He's the one who says he'll leave us alone. We'll be a tourist spot, he says, for visitors from other planets in The Six. Other than that, he'll leave us be."

I raised my hand. "Tom. Please."

His voice got louder. "Look, it doesn't matter how true that is. Thing is, you lied to me, man. Again and again. And there was stuff I'd been holding on to my whole life toward you. Resentment, yeah. And anger. You kept trying to make up, but why should I have believed anything you had to say? How could I trust anything?"

He had a point.

"I was so mad at you, so fucking angry after all this that I wanted to believe them. I needed to. "

He took a deep breath.

"I wanted to see the explosion. I wanted to see you and Heather and that fat-ass Twoclicks thing die. So I drove like hell to be there for it."

He took another breath. Looked at me. Smiled. "And while I was driving I really had time to think. About you and all that shit. About poor Kaity. About who we were back then and what we each became."

He reached out and put his hand on my shoulder. "You're my brother. Remember playing catch on the beach? Remember all the snorkeling? Remember the kayaks in the mangroves and catching crabs? Remember all that?"

"Yeah, Tom, I do," I said. "I remember it all."

"So the more I thought about that, the more I drove along toward the airport and thought about us as kids, the three of us, the more I realized I couldn't do it. I had to tell you. And so, finally, I did."

My brother stared at me. "You know what's especially good? They're giving me another chance. You'll love this. There's a Plan B, and that's me. They knew that I could get close to you and that if I was close to you I might be close to Heather and Twoclicks. So," he said, giggling, "get this. They wired me up like Kait. I'm a bomb, and I'm ready to go, Peter. All I have to do is say the word. Literally say the word. And I'll be in tiny pieces and you and Chloe and Sarah over there will be in pieces, too."

Oh, my god. Of course. My brother Tom, the one who knew everything except the truth.

"Ready? Listen." And he paused, took a breath, and said, "Disarm."

And then he raised his arms up high, said, "Voila! Now I'm not a bomb. And you're a lucky bastard that I figured all this out. And I'm a lucky bastard, too."

Should I tell him the truth about Kait, that I knew she was probably still alive? Did he know and was he keeping it a secret? I had no idea. I couldn't trust him. He might tell the whole world the real story and, Heather had said to me, we couldn't have that.

"Tom," I said. "I'm out here for a reason."

"I know," he said. "I watched your message, man. I'll take care of everything: the house, all the business crap. A few months on S'hudon for you. The big fucking star. Well, hell, you do what you have to do."

I would.

I waved at Chloe and Sarah, who were keeping an eye on Tom

and me. They started walking back toward us. I'd told Chloe this moment was coming, I was into truth-telling after all I'd seen and done. I'd told Chloe and we'd made the usual promises to each other. A couple of months apart, that was all.

Tom stood there as I sat down next to the empty box that had held Kait's ashes and started stripping off my clothes. Shoes first, then pants and underwear, then T-shirt. I didn't need a thing, not a single thing. I let the sand dollar drop and it broke when it fell, tiny angels popping out.

So this was it: me and the warm elements of Florida, of Earth.

Chloe and Sarah were back. Naked, I walked over to Sarah and gave her a hug. Then I turned to Chloe and embraced her. She whispered in my ear, "We won't tell him anything, Peter." Good Chloe, superspy. I almost grinned at her and then, instead, I leaned down to kiss her, a warm and loving final kiss. Then I whispered "I love you" to her and she whispered something back. I turned to Tom. "I have to do this. It's the greatest adventure ever, for anyone. I have to go."

"I know. I know you do."

I walked over to him, gave him a hug. He stood there stiffly, but I said, "Good luck, Tom."

"Sure," he said. "Good luck to you, too." And he pushed me away, playfully, toward the water. "Get going. They're out there, waiting for you. And that ship, it's going, man, and you'll be on it." He seemed glad to see me go. I couldn't blame him for that.

I smiled. I reached out to shake his hand. Then I raised my hand for a quick wave to Chloe, who was shaking her head and smiling at the same time. I waved to Sarah, who smiled. And then I turned away to wade into the water, calf-deep, then waist-deep, then onto the first sandbar, where I stood up to wade across it. Then a drop-off and water chest-deep before I reached the second sandbar. I stood and waded across that, too, and then took a quick look back at Chloe and Sarah and Tom. Then I turned around to see the open

Gulf before me and that ship in the distance. I dove in and there I was, finally swimming out past the second sandbar, out where it was dangerous. Out where there might be a shark.

Beside me, in fact. And another, more like a porpoise, in front. Heading out to the ship. Heading to the homeworld. With me.